GW00456625

A PUSH TOO FAR

FIONA CANE

First published in the UK in 2013 as *The Gate* by Caracol Books.

First published in the UK 2021
Test copyright © 2021 Fiona Cane
All rights reserved.

Fiona Cane has asserted her right under the Copyright, Designs and Patents Act 1988 to be identified as the author of this work.

This book is a work of fiction and, except in the case of historical fact, any resemblance to actual persons, living or dead, is purely coincidental.

This book is copyright material and must not be copied, reproduced, transferred, distributed, leased, licensed, or publicly performed, or used in any way except as specifically permitted in writing by the publishers, as allowed under the terms and conditions under which it was purchased, or as strictly permitted by applicable copyright law. Any unauthorised distribution or use of the text may be a direct infringement of the author's rights and those responsible may be liable in law accordingly.

ISBN
Cover design by Adrian Newton
Cover image: Needpix.com

For Simon

BOOK ONE: THE HOMECOMING

Children begin by loving their parents; as they grow older they judge them; sometimes they forgive them.

~ Oscar Wilde, *The Picture of Dorian Gray*

1

The heat rises off the sun-baked ground in shimmering waves. We travel in a line, our eyes glued to the man in front, careful to step in his footprints, keeping pace with the bleep of the metal detector. My hair is matted to my scalp, my khaki shirt stained white from the rivulets of sweat meandering down my back. I smell like a rugby club's locker room. We all do. We haven't had a shower in over a week.

A youth in a black dish-dash and turban watches us from a field outside the village. It's too late for a farmer to be working, and he looks a lot like the dicker who blew our cover barely a week ago. He speaks into his mobile and my pulse quickens. The soldier in front of me raises his rifle. He's itching to shoot, but the man is unarmed. All he can do is watch him right the motorbike hidden behind a mulberry tree, fire it up and speed away.

Our boots kicking up the dust, we enter the mud-walled village through a gate. The place is deserted apart from a young man with a long beard, leaning against a Toyota, chewing on a wheat stem. Farmer? Dicker? Taliban?

"Where the fuck is everyone?" mutters Captain Peterson.

Cut into the walls of the houses, murder holes are clearly visible. The soldiers tense, rifles ready. An ambush, surely? I glance at Glen, my cameraman, who smiles encouragingly.

"Where are the villagers?" Peterson asks.

The man shrugs and gesticulates to the east. "Mosque."

"When will they be back?"

Another shrug. "Later!" Smiling, he points to a bridge. "That way."

The captain scans the surrounding area warily. "Like hell."

There's a hollow crack from a Taliban rifle from the tree line to our left.

"Contact left. Retreat," orders the captain.

My heart speeds up. But I don't move. I can't.

"Run!" Glen says. "I'm right behind you."

It's the nudge I need. Adrenaline spurts down my veins and I sprint ahead, wreathed in smoke.

"Over that ridge!" a soldier yells, running backwards as he fires a volley from his M16 rifle.

Arms pumping like pistons, I take the fifty metres at pace. A bullet scorches the earth beside me. Soil erupts in my face, blinding me. I trip and fall. Cursing, I clench every muscle and brace myself for the inevitable pain but all I feel is a firm grip on my arm. I scramble to my feet and allow myself to be dragged to the relative safety of an irrigation ditch beyond the higher ground.

I crouch on all fours, chin-deep in brackish water. This is not how it was supposed to pan out. The idea that sprang from the hyperactive mind of Eric Lyons, my foreign editor, sitting comfortably behind his desk in New Broadcasting House, was to show how the world's most feared fighting unit, the US Marines, was boosting the efforts of the British troops in Helmand. Glen Chambers, my cameraman, would film them on patrol and, with a bit of luck, I would do a piece to camera while the marines blew up the Taliban in the background.

"Just remember, Megan," Eric said, as I picked up my bag that contained my faded blue flak jacket, medical kit, satellite phone, and laptop, "a real-life battle makes compelling television. The British public relish them, and there hasn't been much out of Afghanistan recently."

"You don't say," I muttered, as I grabbed my press helmet and headed out the door.

But war isn't like that. There's nothing glamorous about this or any other. Never mind the marines' zeal, there simply aren't enough of them. The Taliban keep on coming, bolstered by the recruits from the training camps and madrassas of neighbouring Pakistan. They're a ferocious army, born to kill. And the farmers fight alongside them, partly out of fear but mostly because they make ten times more for a hectare of opium than a hectare of wheat. Drugs and insurgency feed off each other. I've seen it before in Colombia, where the Revolutionary Armed Forces funded their guerrilla warfare by trading in cocaine.

Bullets fizz and crack and dance in the soil above me. A rocket-propelled grenade whooshes through the air and explodes on impact. Shards of metal slice into the earth, and curls of smoke drift upwards into the cloudless sky. My teeth chatter uncontrollably. I clench my jaw and make a silent promise this will be the last time I leave behind my brilliant husband and twelve-year-old twins to report on a war.

"Rapid fire!" yells a disembodied voice in front of me.

My order to run.

I clamber up the bank but lose my footing and slip back into a tangle of reeds. I scrabble free, clawing at the mud until

I reach the top. I stagger to my feet and sprint ahead, following in the footsteps of the marine in front of me. He disappears into the white cloud of a phosphorous grenade. It's our cover, I know, but because I can't see him, I freeze. I'm about to call out when I catch sight of his camouflaged legs vaulting another irrigation ditch. I take a deep breath and leap after him but land awkwardly on a hard-as-concrete rut in the ploughed field. Pain shoots up my leg, razor-sharp. I grit my teeth and run as fast as I can. Knife-like stalks rip the skin from my shins. The burn in my lungs is unbearable. I contemplate sitting down to catch my breath, but this is not where I want to die. This is not the last memory I want for Daisy and Josh, their intrepid mother shot to pieces by Taliban bullets in a field of harvested opium poppies. Another casualty of a crazy war.

The marine I'm following, GI Freddie Parker, I think, jumps into another ditch. I hurl myself after him but trip and end up rolling down the steep-sided bank, landing on my back with a splash. The *duff-duff-duff* of heavy machine-gun fire, hair-raisingly close, and another rapid burst of bullets from the enemy's AK-47 rifles, rain down in a deadly shower. I stagger to my feet but am knocked off balance by the thunder of mortar fire. My ears ringing, I peer at the cloud of cordite blotting out the sky. I can't see them but I'm pretty sure the Taliban have us now from three sides.

The marine yells. His mouth works but I can't hear him. He grabs the scruff of my jacket, yanks me to my feet, and jettisons me free a split second before a mortar shell explodes on the spot precisely where I'd been standing. I urge my jelly legs to run for my life; the life I've always thought charmed. I've dodged bullets in China, Sarajevo, Colombia, Kosovo, and Iraq, but twenty years of reporting from the world's trouble spots hasn't prepared me for this deadly game of cat and mouse. There are fifteen heavily armed soldiers in our group, pushing south of the old front line, but sucked into unfamiliar terrain by the fierce, hidden enemy, the odds are stacked against us. For the first time in my life I am certain I'm going to die.

My heart pummels my flak jacket. My clothes, face, and hands are covered with mud. Blood leeches from the scratches to my limbs. But all I care about is the deep draughts of air I swallow greedily. I think of Josh, of the serious expression he wears, curled on a beanbag with a book after I've said my goodbyes, yet again. I've given up trying to fathom what he thinks about his mother, here one minute, gone the next. He's old enough to know there's a big, bad world out there, whose conflicts have a tremendous pull on his mother. I'm looking forward to the day he's old enough for me to explain the force that drives me.

If I'm still alive, that is.

The thought is enough to inject some vigour into my exhausted limbs. Breathing heavily, I wipe the dirt from my eyes and charge after the soldiers tapering a path through the wheat. Don't give up, I tell myself. Not now. Not after all you've put them through.

I slide down another bank and thank God I'm not responsible for the camera. My heart almost judders to a halt. Preoccupied with saving my skin, I'd forgotten all about Glen. I scrutinise the faces of the six men around me, but Glen's isn't among them. Where on this God-forsaken piece of earth is he? The last time I remember seeing him was in the village when he told me to run. My gut twists. Glen means the world to me, our friendship forged from a hundred hairy situations. Right from the start, when we were thrown together twenty-three years ago, Glen's looked out for me. A rough, tough Aussie, and a fresh-faced graduate on her first assignment as a foreign reporter, we were sent from our base in Hong Kong to cover the student protests in Beijing. We watched help-lessly from a side road while the Chinese army, standing ramrod straight in trucks, indiscriminately shot dead their fellow citizens. We both knew we weren't safe, but a sensa-tional story was unfurling in front of our eyes, and we couldn't tear ourselves away. All of a sudden a great weight had knocked me to the ground. Glen's six-foot-two muscular frame, it transpired. There was blood on my shirt. I'd patted my abdomen. But I was unhurt. I'd looked at Glen, clutching his left arm, blood seeping through his fingers from the bullet he'd taken for me.

"Just a scratch," he'd said, wincing. "But I figure now's the time to leave this shitshow."

Has he taken another bullet trying to film the fight? No. He'd have more sense than to risk his life for pictures today.

The smoke from another shell clears. A marine chewing tobacco calmly aims his M16 assault rifle at the enemy. Earlier, I'd watched the same soldier clean his bullets with baby wipes.

"To get rid of the sand so my rifle don't jam," he'd explained when I'd asked why.

Bruce Davies, another GI who I can barely make out beneath the filthy patina of battle, loads his AT-4 bazooka. Tattooed on his right forearm is a ring of bullets, each one bearing the name of a friend killed in combat in Iraq and Afghanistan.

The mortar explodes on impact. "We're gonna win this goddamn firefight," he mutters.

"The Taliban don't give up. They're hell-bent on taking control of this country, even if they have to die to do it," says Captain Peterson.

I don't like the sound of that. Not one little bit.

"But we have an ace up our sleeve. They'll break contact when we bring in the air support."

Sure enough, the *wok-wok-wok* of helicopter rotor blades thwap in the distance. My heart lifts but immediately sinks when I remember Glen. I bury my head in my hands and pray to a God I don't believe in to keep him safe.

The deafening noise of gunfire subsides, and the Taliban retreat. A swirling blast of dust and gravel, whipped up by the helicopter blades, surrounds us. I shield my burning eyes and allow myself to be led towards the Chinook. Someone taps me on the shoulder. Instantly, I know who it is. I recognise his smell.

"Megan Moreau. I was wondering when you were going to show up. What kept yer?"

"I thought you'd been killed," I yell.

Glen's face is blackened with smoke. His bird's-nest, sandy hair is dirt-grey and strewn with dry grass. There's blood trickling down his trouser leg, but he laughs. "Don't be daft. How many times do I have to tell you? I'm indestructible, me." He puffs out his chest and drums it with his fists.

I know he's joking to lighten the tension, but the last hour has taken its toll, and a lone tear dribbles down my cheek.

He pats me on the back. "Hey there, Megs, my little beauty. It's over."

He might be all Australian brawn and bluster but he has a heart of gold. I clasp his freckled hand and shake my head. For us maybe, but not for these brave guys. "How many dead?"

"Not a single marine."

It's something, I suppose and I'm thankful, but I can't help wondering, what about next time? And what about the hundreds of soldiers and Afghans killed already? What about the mothers they left behind, the girlfriends, fathers, children?

The death toll rises daily. Is this war against the Taliban really worth the bloodshed?

"I'm beginning to lose sight of why we're still here," I bellow.

"You know why. So the Great British public can shop on Oxford Street without risk of a terrorist strike. And your job is to show them what's going on in this hellhole. And you're bloody good at it, so that's quite enough naval-gazing for today, okay?"

I want to protest that it isn't right for the army to suffer such horrendous losses for the sake of some retail therapy in a country where most people have never heard the sound of gunfire. But it's pandemonium out here, and anyway, Glen doesn't do sentimental.

"Loud and clear, Glen. Loud and clear."

"That's more like it. Now let's get the fuck out of Hell-land." He climbs into the helicopter, links his arm through mine, and pulls me after him.

2

———

I'm not sure how many bottles of cheap, in-flight wine Glen and I have drunk by the time our plane touches down at Heathrow. The flame-haired stewardess attending us kept a tidy cabin, which made it impossible to keep a tally. However, I do know that, since leaving Dubai, Glen has ordered two reds to each of my white. Add to that a couple of whiskies, and he really should be flying out of arrivals. But his gait is steady and controlled. Hollow legs is how he explains his apparent sobriety, although I'm sure his liver would provide a different story.

I shuffle after him. The glass doors slide open, and a burst of fresh, spring English air washes over us. But it's a grey day, entirely lacking in sky and, even though I am desperately looking forward to seeing my family, the familiar drag of disappointment settles on my shoulders. I tell myself it's the weather, but deep down I know it has everything to do with the phone call I made to my husband from Camp Bastion a couple of nights ago. After telling him I loved him and having tried but failed to persuade the twins to talk to me (it's how they cope when I'm away, he's convinced me), I told him I'd be accepting the newsreader's job after all.

"Bad, was it?" he'd asked.

"No worse than usual," I'd lied. "I miss you and the kids, that's all. I always do."

"And we miss you, too, terribly. But, Megan, a gob on a stick! Isn't that what you call them? I thought you'd rather give up work than get dolled up every day to sit in front of a camera and read an autocue."

"I've changed my mind. It's a woman's prerogative. Besides, the pay's fantastic."

"Honey, we don't need the money."

"Okay, but I'm almost forty-six. I'm getting too old for this."

"Now I know you're talking nonsense."

Trust Guy to be so damned reasonable. He's my rock, and I love him to bits. There's no way I could have done this job if he wasn't so supportive and understanding. Never mind that his job as a novelist enables him to double as a house-husband, a lot of men would have just said no.

"And I want to see more of the kids. I feel I'm missing out."

"Now that I understand but, Megan, you're tired. Wait a few days, that's all I ask."

"Don't you want me around?" It's possible, after all. He's doing a brilliant job bringing up Josh and Daisy on his own. Maybe I'd be in the way. Cramp his style, that sort of thing.

"I can think of nothing better than—"

"Well, that's settled then."

My mobile phone beeps rapidly as it always does when I return from a war. The novelty value, I assume. My friends are impressed by my courage and daring, even though I'm always explaining I'm a storyteller not an adrenaline junkie.

The blood and explosions are one aspect of war, but my angle is the lives of the ordinary people trying to survive behind enemy lines. It's a privilege having a ringside seat to history, and the thought I might make a difference bolsters me.

"Hop in." Glen wrests my bag from my hand, hurls it into the boot of the taxi, slips in beside me, and sniffs the air. "Mmm. Eau de Bastion. Bonza."

I cuff him around the head. "At least I tried to take a bath."

"Yeah, and those Afghan soldiers got some top-class pictures of you."

I frown. "They didn't see anything. I was wearing a swimsuit."

"Where to?" asks the driver, suppressing a smile.

"Holiday Inn," replies Glen. "I'm assuming you want to scoff, shower, and sleep as usual?"

"Breakfast yes, shower yes, but after that I'm going home."

Glen cocks an eyebrow. "What about your rules?"

"What rules? I can't abide rules."

"Could've fooled me."

"I have rituals. There's a subtle difference."

"You'll be grumpy later."

"No, I won't."

"Yeah, you will. You're tired."

"I'm not tired."

"Ha! My dear Megs, you're not only tired, you're emotional, too."

My frown deepens. "I just want to get home."

Glen's right, of course. These past few days we've thrived on adrenaline. The comedown will be massive. But he has no one to take it out on. Unlike me, he lives alone.

. . .

According to our friends, our Victorian three-bedroom terraced house, a stone's throw from Wandsworth Common, is far too modest for a prize-winning, best-selling author. But Guy Truman is a modest man. He's also married to a woman who spends most of the year sleeping in a tent. Home is where the heart is. As long as we're together, healthy and happy, it doesn't matter where we live.

My stomach flutters as I slot my key in the lock. Returning from Afghanistan's dusty killing fields, I feel like a stranger. No, worse: an alien. I should be used to slipping between two worlds by now, but it's not easy shedding one skin and replacing it with another. I pause in the hallway next to a huge fishing net (has Guy taken up fishing?) and a haphazard bundle of tennis racquets, cricket bats, and hockey sticks. The house beats like a living thing, music blaring from its heart. Daisy is singing along to a song I don't recognise. She's giving it her all. I imagine her twirling barefoot round the oak floorboards of the kitchen and irritating her brother in the process.

"Shut up!" yells Josh, bang on cue. "Dad, tell her to stop."

If Guy responds I can't hear, but I guess he's ignored Josh because Daisy continues. I drop my bag, lean my battered body against the cool white wall, and listen. She sings well, in tune and with confidence. I'm surprised. It's unusual to hear Daisy at all. She's such a quiet child, hiding in the background, happy for her brother to dominate. Guy tells me she's a great little actor and, right now, I'm inclined to believe him. He's been ferrying her to drama club on Mondays after dropping Josh off at cricket nets. I haven't seen her perform yet, although I'm always meaning to. But the inevitable phone call from my editor just as the production is about to open means that, within hours, I'm on a plane heading off to God knows where, to cover a war or some other global catastrophe, for God knows how long. That's how it is.

Guy never lets her down, though.

"I'm your number one fan," he tells her.

I hate to admit it, but I'm the teeniest bit jealous of the attention he lavishes on her. I know it's ridiculous. What father doesn't love his daughter? Besides, it bolsters what little confidence she has. Her wide-spaced, baby-blue eyes are too large for her face, her teeth too big for her mouth, and her long legs too gangly. Latent beauty. But it won't be long before she grows into her body.

The air is redolent with the smell of frying onions. I close my eyes and soak up the warm, homely atmosphere, not wanting to break the spell, trying to quash the nagging feeling that I exist outside of it all. I love this family that Guy and I have created. I am part of it but also a stranger to it. Any minute now, when I walk into the room, I'll disrupt the steady tempo Guy has created this past month. No matter how hard I try, I can't avoid it. A psychologist would no doubt label it my guilt. I love my job. I regularly leave behind my kids, my husband, but I always come back. Recently I've sensed my children's resentment when I return. Their lives run so smoothly when I'm not there. It takes some readjusting. I understand. I feel it, too.

My shoulders are heavy, and the beginning of a headache is bothering the base of my skull. I kick myself for not heeding Glen's advice. I should have waited until tomorrow when the children were at school. Reunions are always much easier between just Guy and me.

I hear the soft pad of bare feet and open my eyes. Guy is watching me, mouth open, hands on hips, a look that says: *why are you standing out here like a lemon?* I reach out and lightly touch his cheek. His tanned, smooth skin feels hot and slightly clammy, and I wonder if he's ill. But the electricity that races through my body as he wraps his arms around me, distracts me. I sometimes think there's a magnetic field around Guy that pulls me to him. Eighteen years we've been together. He's my soul mate. My one true love. I run my hand over his receding hair and gaze into his russet eyes and shudder with lust. It takes all my willpower not to rip the clothes from his body and make love to him, right here in the hall.

"Oh-my-God, that's gross."

Josh's bald statement quashes my raging libido. Embarrassed, I let go of Guy.

"It's perfectly natural," he tells our son.

"But you're *so* old."

He ruffles his hair. "We're not that old."

But Josh isn't listening. Or if he is he's ignoring his father because his arms are around my waist and he's hanging on to me, as if scared I might turn around and leave. He's grown since I've been away, and thinned out, his arms more muscular, and I pray he never grows out of this need to hug his mum.

"Did the marines blow the Taliban to hundreds of pieces?" he asks.

An image of fragmented body parts and sizzling skin springs to mind, and I shiver. "No."

"Oh!" The disappointment is glaring. "Did you see any dead bodies?"

I recall the injured marine, blood spurting from his leg, his severed foot, six feet away, still encased in its boot and yet who'd clutched his undamaged crotch and grinned. "Not this time. No."

"Sounds a bit boring." Blissfully unaware of the mortal danger his mother has faced, he lets go. "Dad and I have cooked an amazing lunch." Spinning on the ball of his foot, he heads back to the kitchen.

Daisy is hovering in the doorway, shifting her weight awkwardly. Her face betrays no emotion, neither happy nor sad, and yet I can't help thinking she is scowling at me.

I envelope her, breathing in her familiar, candy-sweet smell. "I've missed you so much."

She stands still as a statue, as if enduring my affection. Guy tells me I imagine it. That she misses me as much, if not more than Josh, but hasn't learnt to express herself emotion-ally yet.

I bend down and whisper in her ear, "I heard you singing. You've got a beautiful voice."

Her body relaxes and, when I break the embrace, she smiles. My heart swells. I am complete. This is where I belong.

The sun breaks through the blanket of cloud, filling the kitchen with a buttery light. We pull out chairs and sit at the table while Guy carves the beef and Josh loads the plates with vegetables.

"Did the children like the My Little Ponies and the bags of Haribo?" Daisy asks.

"They loved them. It was thoughtful of you."

"Dad and I've been playing lots of tennis. He's given me a secret weapon."

"A secret weapon, eh?" I wink at Guy.

"Yes. But I'm not going to tell you what it is because I might try it on you."

A feel a familiar stab of guilt. I can't remember when I last played tennis, let alone with Daisy. But there's no time to respond. She's already on to the next subject.

"Did Dad tell you I've got the part of the narrator in *Joseph* this summer?"

Has he? I wonder.

"I thought I'd leave that to you," says Guy.

She looks at me anxiously. "You will come, won't you?"

I'll put a line through my diary and tell Eric I'm unavailable, I decide. "I wouldn't miss it for the world."

"So you'll come and watch me play cricket, too?" says Josh. "You love cricket, don't you?"

I recall the games of beach cricket I played with my brothers as a child. "Yes, I do. And yes, I will."

Guy is shaking his head, an amused smile on his face. I know exactly what he's thinking. The more promises I make, the more I'll have to break.

"Let's play cricket now," says Josh.

"You'll have to catch Groucho and Marx first," says Guy.

I groan and pull a face. Groucho and Marx, our frighteningly huge rabbits, have long claws and sharp teeth, and we're all terrified of them. But then I notice Josh is grinning.

He dashes out of the room and returns clutching the fishing net. "It's all right, Mum. We finally figured out a way to catch them."

3

———————

I wake up in our expensive divan. Sunlight streaks through the crack in the curtains, and dust motes dance and, immediately, I know I'm back in England. Hit by a burst of optimism, I realise Guy's right. I'd be crazy to give up my job. It's part of me. Defines me. And if it has an adverse effect on my children, it isn't obvious. Yesterday's homecoming turned out to be a breeze.

I glance lovingly at my husband asleep beside me. He lies on his back, face to the right, left arm hooked over his head, body tangled in the duvet, one leg in, one out. It's unusual for me to stir before him when back from an assignment. Emotionally and physically exhausted, I've been known to crash out for sixteen hours at a stretch. We haven't spoken about Afghanistan yet. We'll do that tonight over supper when the kids are in bed. After that we'll make love.

I scrutinise his body. He's fit for a man of fifty, his muscles toned from his daily jog around the common. But there's a beading of sweat on his top lip, and grey, hollow patches beneath his eyes. I touch his arm lightly. His skin is hot to the touch. He is unwell.

I turn off the alarm clock before it begins its infuriating bleating. It's seven. Time to wake the twins. Guy normally likes to indulge me on my first day back, bringing my breakfast on a tray, running a hot bath. But not today. Today I intend to surprise him and the twins.

I slip out of bed, splash water over my face, brush my teeth, and run a comb through my hair. My aching body is stiff, so I pull on my comfortable faded black joggers and an old sweatshirt and knock, first on Josh's and then Daisy's door.

"Time to get up," I say cheerfully.

My aches and pains forgotten, I bound down the stairs with a spring in my step. I open the well-stocked fridge, pull out eggs, bacon, and the vast plastic ketchup bottle which accompanies every meal in the Truman household.

The twins wander in and smile. Their mother preparing breakfast has real novelty value.

"Are you taking us to school?" Daisy completes her plait, securing it with a purple elastic hair-tie.

"Yes, I am."

She flicks it over her shoulder and beams.

How easy it is for me to please them, I muse, as they pull out chairs and tuck into their breakfasts, smothering their eggs in tomato sauce. I smile and go back upstairs to check on Guy.

"What time is it?" he asks, groggy with sleep.

"Almost eight. But don't worry. Everything's under control."

He groans and tries to sit up, but the effort is too much and he sinks back.

"You're not well." I sit beside him and feel his forehead. He's burning up. "You're running a temperature. I'll drop the twins at school then come home and call the doctor."

He manages a faint smile. "No need. It's just a touch of flu."

"Might be the dreaded Swine. I'll call the doctor to check you over."

"Don't be so dramatic. Eric will be expecting you." His breathing is ragged. He looks completely washed out.

"Eric can wait." I mean it. I still haven't forgiven him for throwing me and Glen into the lion pit. I'm a mother, for God's sake. What was he thinking? And instead of the battle footage he wanted, all we've come back with is an interview with some Afghan women who, along with their children, are addicted to opium. It's a moving piece, heart-wrenching in places. If Eric doesn't like it, I'll write it up for *The Times*. I bend down to kiss Guy. His lips are hot and dry, his breath sour. I fill his glass from the decanter by the bed and hand it to him.

"Stop worrying, Megan. It doesn't suit you." But he props himself up and takes a few sips.

"I'll be back in half an hour. Don't move."

But of course, I'm not. I pass Fran Atwood as I'm leaving the twins' comprehensive.

She winds down the window of her Fiesta. "I'm glad you're back in one piece. Come for coffee and tell me all about it."

The line of cars behind us honk their horns. I think of Guy, ill in bed. Half an hour won't hurt, I reason. "Okay, but I can't stay long."

Propped against the melamine worktop in the tatty, but scrupulously clean, kitchen of Fran's two-bed flat, I fiddle with one of her paintbrushes. A portrait artist, commissioned mainly, she rents a studio down the road.

"Guy told me you were almost killed."

"Yes, but I wasn't, which just goes to show my life is charmed."

She shovels instant granules into chipped white mugs. "I wish you'd stop saying that. It's nonsense and you know it. You take so many risks. I'm just grateful every time you come home unscathed."

I'm not unscathed, not really. Scratch the surface and you'll find emotional scars. But I can't afford to think that way so I laugh, and Fran groans.

My mobile rings while we're drinking coffee. Eric Lyons. I roll my eyes and hold up the screen. Fran pulls a sympathetic face.

"Where are you?" he barks.

"I'm fine. Thanks for asking."

"We've got an interview with Putin, and he insists on talking to you."

I don't believe him. It's just his way of reeling me in. "You don't say."

"I do say, and I don't want to miss this chance."

"Guy's ill. I'll be in tomorrow."

"Come on, Megan. I need you here. Vlad loves a pretty face, and you're the most presentable female reporter we've got."

"Goodness, Eric, you're going to have to do a hell of a lot better than that."

"You're beautiful, brilliant, and accomplished. Now please come to work."

"I'll be in tomorrow."

He responds with a huge sigh. "In time for the meeting at nine."

There's a click, and the line goes dead. That's how Eric

operates. Push, push, push until he gets his way. There's no time in his life for pleasantries.

It's eleven by the time I'm home. I stroll into the hallway but pull up sharp. Guy is lying in a heap at the bottom of the stairs. Blinking rapidly, I stare at his inert body. What's he doing there? Has he fallen? Is he unconscious?

My brain screams at me to do something. Anything. I kneel beside him and lift his arm. His skin is grey, the limb a dead weight in my hands. I feel for his pulse, my fingers grappling with the flesh on his wrist. Where is it?

I dig and dig but I can't find it?

Trembling, I place my ear to his chest.

But there is no sound. No movement. No vibration. Nothing.

I rummage around my bag for the small mirror I take on assignments, hold it under his nose, and wait for the surface to mist over.

I wait and wait, but the glass remains clear.

I grab the handset off the table in the hall and press my finger on the nine.

Once, twice, three times.

But even as I beg the ambulance to hurry, I know it's useless. Guy's body is still. His heart has stopped beating. There's no breath in his lungs.

The man I love with every ounce of my being is dead.

And all I can think of as I cradle my husband's gorgeous head in my lap, is that I never got the chance to say goodbye.

4

E ric Lyons is a tall, big-boned (his words, not mine), bear of a man. On the wall of his glass box, at the far end of the open-plan office, is a map of the world dotted with coloured pins, displaying the exact locations of his overseas staff. His fifty-three-year-old, razor-sharp mind is alert to what his overseas correspondents are doing, as well as those of us kicking our heels at home. For the past two days, since I returned to work, I've felt his eagle eyes trained on me. Hunched over my desk, I stare blindly at the TV monitor, occasionally scribbling some words on the pad in front of me. A big brooding presence, he's worrying about me. He hasn't told me as much, but I can sense it. It's an emotion he's never projected before. Not around me anyway. If I weren't in so much pain I'd be touched. He doesn't know what to do. He just tiptoes around me. He knows my heart is broken. Not in the literal sense. Not like Guy's. After all, *I'm* still alive, if you can call this depleted existence living. It's been four months. The tears have dried up, my anger has faded, but I'm totally lacking motivation.

The office is buzzing with sound, most of which emanates

from the TV monitors the twenty-odd correspondents are glued to, but I'm thinking about Guy.

We met in Florence. I'd fled there to recover from the horrors of the Rwandan genocide, where I'd reported on the indiscriminate and horrific rapes by the Hutu men of the Tutsi women. Guy's first book, *The Devil's Kiss*, was selling like hotcakes having scooped the Booker Prize the previous autumn. Sitting at a table in the quaint little *enoteca*, *Le Volpi e l'Uva*, in a shaded square on the wrong side of the Ponte Vecchio, he was writing and sipping from a glass of Chianti. I was nursing a glass of Verdicchio, and was struck by how hard he was working. His eyes caught mine. But then I was staring right at him. He winked. I blushed and turned away. But he came over, and we got chatting.

"Are you French?" he asked when I told him my name.

"My grandfather was. He came over during the war, married an English girl and never went back."

Three hours later, he walked me back to my hotel. "I think we'll probably get married," he said.

I laughed at his audacity. But in the two weeks that followed, we explored the Tuscan villages of Il Chianti and fell in love. Nine months later, on a red-hot afternoon in a run-down church in Puerto Rica, we exchanged vows.

From the moment Guy held me in his arms, I knew I'd struck gold. And that feeling never left me, not once in eighteen years. We rarely argued, we often laughed, we always supported one another. When the twins were four months old and Eric offered me the opportunity to fly to Colombia to report on the guerrilla strikes against the government, Guy sent me with his blessing. He accepted what I did and loved me for it. He was kind, loving, capable, and calm. He lived up to his name. *You're a true man, Guy Truman*, I used to tell him. And he was. True to me. True to the twins. True to himself.

I lean my elbows on my desk and cradle my head in my hands. I can't believe he's gone. These last sixteen weeks I've barely been able to put one foot in front of the other. For the first forty-eight hours Daisy, Josh, and I clung to one another like limpets to a rock, hardly daring to move. But life had to go on. We had to face the world. The cardiologist at the hospital, where the paramedics took his body, told me he'd died of dilated cardiomyopathy brought about by a viral infection of his heart muscle, leading to cardiac arrest. My mood changed. I was angry with Guy for being wrong. He hadn't had the flu. And I was angry with myself. I was the girl with the sixth sense. Everyone said so.

Glen: *I reckon you sense the story before it happens.*

Guy: *You've got a rare gift there, Megan. Use it wisely.*

But I hadn't known he was going to die. If I had I would have stayed at home. What had I been thinking of having coffee with Fran? I knew Guy never made a fuss. I should have known he felt worse than he was letting on. I should have gone straight home and called the doctor.

"It wouldn't have made any difference," my heart-surgeon brother, Felix, told me at the funeral. "The severe arrhythmia developed suddenly. He collapsed and probably died soon after."

Felix hasn't changed. He's still the capable and daring brother of my youth. He just looks a bit older. It's been five years since Guy and I visited him and Joanne, his Australian wife, in their to-die-for home in Sydney. This was his first trip back to England in a decade. Dad died the year before he left, and with my other brother, Ralph, working as a zoologist in Nairobi, and me stationed in Hong Kong, there was nothing to keep him here. It was good to see both my brothers again. But the awful truth wasn't lost on me. With the Moreau seed scattered across the globe and Guy dead, I was well and truly on my own. And as the nation railed against the death of one of its best-loved novelists, the media wailed, and the public gnashed their teeth, my anger turned to emptiness.

"Megs!" Glen's voice is loud and cheery. He pulls out the chair next to my desk and sits down with a thud.

"Hi."

"No need to ask how you're doing then."

I glance at him. He's unrecognisable from the man I said goodbye to a month ago. His lined, freckled face is cleanly shaven, and he smells fresh as a spring meadow. I manage a wan smile. "No."

"But you're back at work, so that's good."

"Yeah."

But is it, I wonder? I've only come in because I've nowhere else to go. I'm no use to anybody here. I can't seem to summon up the energy to do my job. The thought of writing a piece, let alone recording it, is beyond me. What I'd like more than anything is to fly off to some trouble spot, Syria say, and immerse myself in other people's problems. But it's not as if I can jump on a plane. Not anymore. Not now I'm a single parent. For the first time in Daisy's and Josh's lives, they need me around. Panic is my constant companion. I have no idea what to do.

"I'm going to be a newsreader," I say, interrupting the steady flow of Glen's reassurance, although I haven't heard a word he's said.

He laughs. "Don't be daft. You love your job."

"I did. But things change. There's a job going at BBC News."

"Oh, really?"

"They approached me about it before our last trip."

He sees I'm serious and bites his lip. "Don't do it, Megs. You'll regret it."

"What else can I do?"

"What most working mums do: hire a nanny."

It's the obvious solution but impossible. "Guy wouldn't hear of it."

"Tiger, it's not up to Guy anymore." His voice is kind, gentle.

I narrow my eyes. "We agreed. No nannies."

He sighs. "Yes, but the twins have just turned thirteen. They'll be fine."

I think of the change in Daisy these past four months, after she ran out of tears. Since the twins' birthday a week ago, she's morphed into another being entirely. This new version of Daisy has backcombed hair, eyes so heavy with kohl and mascara she looks like a panda, and skirts that barely cover her knickers. Guy's death has kick-started her hormones. She's hit adolescence head-on. All she wants to do is hang out with her friends on the street. Fran tells me not to worry, that it's her way of coping. But I am worried. She doesn't want to go to drama club. She doesn't want to play tennis.

"They need me." Spoken out loud, the words sound nonsensical. What use am I to them? A mother with no idea what to do.

"I know. But you shouldn't rush into anything."

My phone rings, and an unfamiliar number rolls across the screen. I want to ignore it like the phone at home. But I realise I can't. I am, after all, at work, and part of my job is to answer calls.

One step ahead of me, Glen picks up the handset. "Megan Moreau's phone." His measured expression flickers. "I'll hand you over." He cups his hand over the mouthpiece. "It's

26

Niall Jefferson."

My heart flips. The twins' headmaster. He may look like an overgrown student, but there's something about head teachers that sets off spasms of anxiety in me. Glen flashes me an encouraging look and hands me the phone.

"Mr Jefferson?"

"Please. Call me Niall. I realise this is a difficult time for you, Daisy, and Josh."

Call-me-Niall pauses. Is it affirmation he's after? If it is, I can't find the words.

"And I really hate being the bearer of bad news but … Ms Moreau? Are you there?"

"Please. Call me Megan."

"Yes, of course. I'm sorry, Megan, but Daisy has been skipping school." His rush to the point leaves me breathless. I imagine Daisy with a rope, twisting and turning it as she jumps down the streets.

"I expect this is as big a shock to you as it is to us. She has always been such an exemplary pupil."

The sentence seems loaded, heavy with accusation. "She's upset. Guy … Her father meant the world to her. She misses him."

"I understand, I really do."

Do you, I wonder? You hardly know us.

"Which is why I'd like to arrange a meeting with you, me, and Daisy to talk things through." His voice is kind but authoritative.

"Right. I see."

"Good. When would be a convenient time?"

"I could be there in an hour."

Glen slaps his forehead.

"Er … great. That would be great."

"See you then, then."

I put down the phone, vaguely aware I've somehow managed to rattle the headmaster. Perhaps he's not used to prompt responses. But that's the way I've always operated.

"So you're off to school?" Glen says.

Eric wanders over and arches an eyebrow. "Megan!"

I bat the air with my hand. "I'm sorry, Eric. I'm needed elsewhere."

Those eyes again, in my back, this time, as I rush from the room.

I don't go back to work after the meeting. I can't. I have to deal with Daisy. I'm a single parent. I'm solely responsible.

Daisy, sweet child turned wild-eyed rebel. I still haven't got over the shock of seeing her outside Call-me-Niall's office, her ears pierced, three times in her left, one in her right, traces of blood still visible beneath the studs.

Call-me-Niall is sympathetic. He has to be. Her dad died.

"The teenage years aren't easy. And this is Daisy's way of reacting to the loss of her father. But I'm concerned that, if we don't take a firm hand, she may go over to the dark side."

The dark side? Really?

"With a bit of steady guidance, I think we can save her."

It's as though I've stumbled into a Harry Potter novel. Has she got any tattoos? I wonder as I usher her and her brother into the car. Do I dare ask? I'm drowning in grief, spiralling down the vortex into a big black hole. And now this. What is going on in her mixed-up teenage mind? I can't get cross with her. It doesn't seem right. She's grieving, too.

"You're an idiot, Daisy," says Josh. It may be true, but it doesn't help.

"And you're a geek." She sticks out her tongue.

"You think you're so cool but you're not. You're pathetic."

"Ugh! You're so gay!"

"Loser!"

"Emo!"

"God, Daisy, you're such a plastic!"

"Douche!"

"ENOUGH!" I've no idea what this strange language is they're speaking but I just can't take it anymore.

But I do because I have to.

Five weeks later, at seven o'clock on Saturday night, Daisy goes missing.

5

I t's midnight on Saturday. The radio is playing another dead man's song. Michael Jackson's 'You Are Not Alone'. Bullshit.

I'm exhausted, wrung out. The police have just left, satisfied with Daisy's description of the leader of the hooded street gang who mugged her at knife-point for her mobile phone. A state-of-the-art iPhone. A bribe. We chose it together last week after school on one of her better days because, no matter how hard I come down on her, whether I ground her, deprive her of pocket money, or send her early to bed, she keeps bunking off and staying out late. I've tried talking to her. I've explained I'm here for her, that I can help her through the pain. She listens, eyes glazed, bored out of her brain. But she will not let me in. I have no control over her, and that worries me.

Daisy is unfazed by her ordeal, but I'm horrified. I want to scream at her, sitting there cool as you like, an icepack on her eye, a pile of bloodied tissues on the kitchen table. I'm sure her nose is broken, but she insists it doesn't hurt. I've given up trying to persuade her to let me take her to hospital.

Josh, reliable and dependable as ever, thank goodness, tried, too, but he gave up half an hour ago and went to bed.

I march over to the radio and turn it off. It's distracting, and I need to focus. "You promised me you'd stop seeing Austin and Jake."

All summer she's been hanging out with their gang. Some days she comes back reeking of cigarette smoke. I haven't had the courage to ask her if they drink or do drugs. I'm scared she'll say yes. Then what will I do?

"I told you. I wasn't with them."

I spin round, spraying anger. "So who were you with, Daisy. Hmm?"

She shifts and turns her back on me. Furious, I grab her chair and pull it round so that my daughter has no option but to face me. "Answer me!"

She folds her arms and scowls, magnificently. Where has she learnt to do that?

"Kyle and Trent, if you must know."

Trent? What kind of a name is that? "You're thirteen. You shouldn't be hanging out with boys."

"They're not boys. They're seventeen actually. And what do you want me to do? Stay at home and play with Barbie dolls while you prance around playing the hero?"

Is that what she thinks of me? Even now I've given up the job I love? I've been reading the news for the past three weeks, sitting in front of an autocue dressed in a posh suit, my hair coiffed, my face made up. I don't recognise this strange new version of myself. Eric didn't want to let me go. I didn't want to leave. But what choice did I have?

"I hate you," Daisy adds for good measure.

"You miss your dad. We all do," I whisper. Her words have punctured me. I feel like a slowly deflating balloon. She doesn't say it, but I can guess what she's thinking.

31

I wish it had been you.

But I'm not finished yet. No matter how bad things have become, I must tame this new wild version of my daughter before she ends up stabbed and bleeding in a gutter.

But how I go about it is totally beyond me.

BOOK TWO: THE GATE

If there is anything that we wish to change in the child, we should first examine it and see whether it is not something that could better be changed in ourselves.

~ C.G. Jung, *Integration of the Personality*

6

The house is decrepit. Cracked plaster hangs from the walls in jagged shards and light fittings dangle from the mildewed ceilings, the cables limp and inelastic like overcooked spaghetti. Upstairs the faded carpets have worn to fine corduroy and, in a spare room, one has rotted to threads, exposing splintered floorboards, riddled with woodworm. Even the backbone of the house, the scuffed, winding staircase, creaks arthritically underfoot. I'm not sure why I bought it. It was the first house the estate agent showed me, but somehow it struck a chord. The secret staircase behind a door in a back corridor, perhaps. Or the unkempt lawn with the rickety gate leading to a park.

This is it, I thought. This is where we're going to live.

"It's huge and needs a complete overhaul," I tell Glen over the phone the day I sign the contract. He's at home, waiting for his next job, and I imagine him pacing the kitchen of his flat, itching for something to do. "But that's okay. I can afford the repairs."

Guy's books made him rich. He left me a small fortune. I'm not interested in money but I concede it gives me options.

Glen sighs. "Are you're sure you know what you're doing?"

"Does it matter if I don't?"

His fingers drum on wood. The kitchen table? He's sitting down, I think, surprised.

"Well now, let me see. Oh yes. Daisy. I'm assuming she doesn't know she's leaving London."

"No, she doesn't, but I'm doing this for her so she'll be fine."

Glen falls silent.

"You think I've lost the plot?"

"I didn't say that."

Maybe not out loud.

"It hasn't been long is all I'm saying. But, Megs, it sounds terrific. I can't wait to see it."

"You'll love it. Honestly you will."

The children, however, do not. They haven't said as much. There's no need. Their shocked expressions when I force open the creaking front door to reveal a shabby hallway full of packing boxes, says it all. They gawp at the dirt-smeared windows and wince at the silvery strands of cobwebs, clinging to the walls and ceiling. Stunned into silence, Daisy can't even summon up the energy to insult me.

"It has a secret staircase," I say.

Josh shakes his head. "It's a mess, Mum."

I forge a pathway through the detritus. "But it's going to be great. It just needs a lot of work."

Saturday 10th November. Guy has been gone six months, and we, the remaining Trumans, are moving into No. 17 Primrose Road in the Sussex coastal town of Easthaven, sixty miles south of London. To appease the twins, I've surprised them (and myself) with a forty-inch plasma TV complete with a Sky Plus package. Bribery at its most shameless.

"Sick!" says Daisy on sight of this electrical wonder, her anger temporarily forgotten.

The Indian takeaway arrives in a cardboard box, as if we need any more. I dig out some plates and cutlery from a case in the kitchen, and unpack the foil containers on our coffee table. Our plates heaped with curry, we sit on our old familiar couch in the damp living room and turn on our brand-new TV to watch *The X Factor*.

"You're sure you don't want to watch *Strictly*?" It's what I'd prefer. I love the athleticism and the sequins. Simon Cowell's smug manner and boxy haircut doesn't quite match up to the old-fashioned charm of dear old Brucie.

"I'll record it and you can watch it later." Josh points the remote at the screen and expertly presses buttons.

It's thoughtful of him. I expect watching TV and doing up the house will be it from now on, unless I stick to my guns and write the book I promised Glen I would.

"There's a gap in the market for tell-it-how-it-is tales from the front line. You've seen a lot of action. Why not get it down on paper?" Glen suggested when he realised the life-altering move was a reality.

But writing books was Guy's job. "I dunno. Maybe. When I'm settled."

"I'm not talking fiction, Megs. You're a rare breed. A not-too-bad-looking, female foreign correspondent."

"Gee, thanks."

"Women are going to be interested in what you have to say. Trust me. I'm a red-blooded male. I know what I'm talking about."

I push the conversation to the back of my mind and try to concentrate on the television. A rake-thin metrosexual with peroxide hair and orange skin takes centre stage and attempts to sing through a lip-glossed pout, grinding his narrow hips provocatively.

"Awesome!" says Daisy, her eyes sparkling with happiness. "Simon will *hate* that!"

Monday is here. It's cold. The sky is bruised and heavy with rain, and the leaves, still clinging to the trees, rattle in the salty wind. The weather paints an entirely different picture to the place I visited a fortnight ago when the autumn sun hung low in the sky and I'd breathed in the carbon-monoxide-free sea air full of optimism. High above us, seagulls swoop and dive, their mewling cries drowned out by the howling gale. Cars crash through puddles, sending up sheets of spray that we dodge to avoid getting soaked. It's only a mile to school, and as it isn't raining, it seemed a good idea to walk. I clench my teeth and stare straight ahead, determined to front it out. I can't bring myself to look at Daisy. Neither she nor Josh have set a foot inside their new school. There didn't seem much point. The move was non-negotiable.

Daisy's fury, radiating from her body in waves, began to bubble last night when she stormed off to her bedroom, which was when, I presume, she took the scissors to her uniform.

"What have you done?" I asked as she headed towards the bathroom this morning in her customised grey kilt, not quite a mini but not far off.

"I wouldn't be seen dead in that thing you gave me."

"It's regulation—"

But Daisy slammed the door.

Josh is happy enough having leafed through the prospectus. He likes the idea of a school with its own playing fields and an indoor sports hall.

St Peter's, an ivory tower, a fee-paying, non-selective school like the one I was sent to after my mother walked out. It's smaller than their London comprehensive, with a longer day. Less time at home will, I hope, keep Daisy off the streets and out of trouble. Besides, it's only for a year before they start at the College.

"You've ruined my life," Daisy said when I told her last week, a split second before she slammed her bedroom door in my face. But I already know that. Just as I know slamming doors will punctuate my life for the foreseeable future.

My self-possession wavers as we walk down the hill. What was I thinking, uprooting my children from their old life? It's never easy being the new kid on the block, never mind the Common Entrance exam they'll sit in June. Is it fair of me to expect them to embrace such a cataclysmic change? Glen's right. I don't have a clue what I'm doing.

At the gate, the mothers cluster in groups. The majority are dressed to impress, their hair impeccably groomed, makeup freshly applied. It's the school run, for heaven's sake, not a fashion show, I think uncharitably. But then it occurs to me they're probably dressed for work, and I shrivel inside my stained puffa jacket. Pulling my shapeless beanie hat a little lower, I accidentally bump into another woman. Nose in the air, she glides past me trailing two neat children and a Persil-white fluffy Bichon Frise.

A couple of shiny-faced teenagers hop out of a gleaming black Range Rover, immaculate in blue blazers and striped ties. I steal a peek at Daisy. Hair fashionably tangled, ears perforated with piercings, a bundle of leather bracelets on her wrists, top button of her shirt undone, too-short skirt, blazer sleeves rolled up, she looks sassy and out of place. An eyesore in this Tory heaven.

"Oh my God. Freak alert." Daisy sticks two fingers down her throat, bends over and pretends to vomit.

"Daisy!"

"Any one in particular?" asks Josh. His shoes are polished to a soldier's finish, his top button fastened, hair neatly parted. Of the three of us he seems the most relaxed. Perhaps he feels more at home here than at his scruffy comprehensive.

"Duh! Over there." Daisy jerks her head. "Three grannies in the same coat. Have they no self-respect?"

Josh's eyes bulge. "No way."

In front of us, to the right of an erect strawberry-blonde, stands a stout woman in an eye-catching Jacquard print coat. Behind her in the playground, two other mothers, identically dressed, are engrossed in conversation.

The woman nearest spins around.

"We were just admiring your lovely coat," I say hurriedly.

The woman frowns. Is that because I'm dressed like a tramp? Or because she heard?

"It's Boden." Flashing the briefest of insincere smiles, she turns her back.

"It's *Boden*," mimics Daisy. "Freak!"

Josh giggles. The woman's shoulders stiffen.

"Do you have to use that word?" I hiss.

But Daisy isn't listening. "Honestly, I'd, like, die if you went out dressed like that. Promise me you won't."

I'm chuffed, nervous, and angry, all at the same time, and nod like an idiot.

"I bet their houses are, like, stuffed full of Cath Kidston crap." Daisy screws up her nose. "Seriously, I'm not joking. These people are freaks. This town is a dump. I want to go home."

I put a tentative arm around her slender shoulders and

tuck a few strands of straggly hair behind her ear. "Give it a chance. I'm sure it won't be as bad as you think."

Daisy shrugs me off. "Spare me. You don't have a clue."

I press my lips together. I'm used to tiptoeing round this minefield. Anything I say will be shot down in the flames of her accusations.

"Give Mum a break," says Josh.

"Why should I? She's a total control freak. That's why she's brought us to this shit-hole."

"Daisy, language!"

She glares at me. "What do you know about this school anyway? It's, like, seriously gay and full of losers."

It's an unrelenting whine, this unintelligible diatribe of Daisy's. I want to scream at her to shut up and get on with it like kids without fathers the world over. But I can't because it wouldn't be fair. And I really don't want to draw attention to myself any more than I already have.

Out of the corner of my eye I notice a tall, rangy man bounding towards us in a dark suit, one size too big for him. Anthony Swann, the head. My heart sinks. Two weeks earlier when I met with him to discuss the possibility of the twins joining the school mid-term, I was impressed by his forthright and competent manner.

"No problem is insurmountable," he'd said, lacing his long pianist-like fingers together. "It's unusual to accept new pupils at this stage of the term, particularly in their Common Entrance year, but then so are your circumstances. I am proud to say that my staff are skilful, resourceful, and have shown themselves to be more than capable of adapting to unexpected situations." His narrow mouth had curved into a smile. "That being the case, I'd be delighted if both your children were to join St Peter's."

I beamed, we shook hands, and the deal was done. Just like that.

I smile at him, awkwardly, because my teeth are gritted, and brace myself for this, his first encounter with my daughter, repeating the words *competent, resourceful, adaptable,* silently to myself.

He draws to a halt in front of us and opens his arms expansively. "Ms Moreau. How lovely to see you again. And this must be Daisy and Josh."

Josh extends his hand. "Pleased to meet you."

The headmaster shakes it vigorously. "Welcome to St Peter's." He turns to Daisy, who scowls. I hold my breath as he casts a critical eye over her uniform. Apart from an almost imperceptible flickering of his nostrils, his expression does not falter. "And you, young lady?"

"Meh," she says in her infuriating way

"It's – it's a big change for them," I stutter.

He gives my arm a reassuring pat. "Don't worry, we'll take good care of them. Come on, you two. I'll show you where to hang your blazers and then I'll take you to your classrooms." He smiles at me before striding towards the school, Josh following in his wake.

Daisy doesn't budge.

I nudge her gently. "Go on."

"I hate you." She glares at me, eyes sparking, and stomps after them. At the entrance, she spins round and sticks out her tongue. Throwing me one last daggered look, she steps inside.

My eyes brim with tears. I should be relieved I've managed to deliver them into the safe care of Anthony Swann and his staff. But I'm not because I'm thinking of my first day at school and the headmistress's chilly, straight-backed welcome, the sparse dormitory with its steel-framed beds, the rows of tubs in the bathroom partially separated by a plastic curtain.

You survived, I tell myself. And Daisy isn't boarding.

It doesn't help. Giving up the job I loved and moving to Easthaven for the good of my children was meant to be a new beginning, but standing amongst these well-heeled people, jobless and alone, it feels like the beginning of the end.

Give it a chance, I tell myself. You've only been here a couple of days. Time will tell.

Eyes down, I weave my way apologetically through the knot of mothers clogging the pavement. I don't want to go home. Home should conjure up a wealth of cosy images; flaming logs crackling on an open fire, the comforting smell of freshly baked bread, a contented dog curled on a rug. Chilly, dusty, dilapidated No. 17 Primrose Road with the two megalithic rabbits stuffed in a hutch in the jungle of a garden is about as far removed from homely as is possible to imagine. The tent I used to share with Glen was less of a hovel.

I decide to take a walk along the seafront to clear my head. A healthy lungful of salty air might help me summon up the energy to start unpacking. Then I can begin to renovate the place.

Renovate? Oh my God, who am I kidding? DIY was Guy's thing. I can't navigate my way round a screwdriver let alone a toolbox. To whip the house into any sort of shape, I'll need an army of builders, plumbers, electricians, curtain-makers, decorators. I place a hand to my throbbing temple. It's like I've lost the ability for rational thought. Maybe Guy's death has pushed me to the brink.

"Excuse me. Are you okay?"

I turn to see the straight-backed blonde.

"I'm sorry, I was miles away."

"Megan Truman?"

"Megan Moreau."

The woman looks perplexed, but she manages to smile, revealing a set of large, protruding teeth. "Samantha Young. Pleased to meet you." She holds out a manicured hand, and I offer her my less-than-perfect mitt. "Anthony warned us you were coming."

It strikes me she hasn't meant to use that word, but all the same I'm knocked off balance. "Oh! Right."

She laughs, covering her mouth with her hand. "He's awfully sweet. Always terribly concerned the new mums fit in. My daughter, you see, is in her last year, too." She pauses and blinks rapidly. "We were surprised your two were joining the school so late."

I'm wondering who *we* are when she moves forward and lowers her head conspiratorially.

"But don't worry. He has explained." She steps back and inspects her polished nails. "It must be difficult."

"It is," I reply truthfully, catching sight of the stout woman in the green-and-white Jacquard coat behind her, watching intently.

"Come to dinner," continues Samantha.

My cheeks flush pink. "Really, there's no—"

"I insist. Next Saturday at eight." She hands me a stiff white card with her name embossed in black glossy letters. "Give me yours and I'll email directions. We don't live in Easthaven."

I stick my hand inside my jacket pocket and find a dog-eared offering.

Samantha holds it between her thumb and forefinger as if it's contaminated. "BBC Foreign Affairs Correspondent."

"Another life," I joke. Clearly, Anthony Swann hasn't told her everything.

She raises her eyebrows. "How interesting."

43

"I like your coat," I reply helplessly.

"It's Boden," she says in a way that suggests I should have known.

The sea is wild and deafening, its huge waves whipped into frothy peaks. I battle down the paved promenade towards the pier, leaning into the gale like a front-row prop. The thunderous waves pound the beach, the shingle hissing and clattering in the water's drag. An elderly couple, hunched with arthritis, smile at me as they scuttle towards the café near the beach huts at the foot of the chalk cliffs. Two joggers in black sweat pants and luminous green headbands swoosh by with the wind behind them. It'll be a different matter when they come back, I think meanly.

My mobile vibrates. I pull it out of my pocket and glance at the screen. "Glen!" I say, holding it to my ear.

"Blimey, Megs. What's kicking off down there? It sounds like bombs! Have the Taliban invaded?"

Glen has a loud voice, but I have to cover my other ear to hear him. "The Boden army wouldn't allow it. It's the sea, you idiot."

"Boden army? What are you talking about? Boden? What's that?"

"Clothes. The women down here are particularly fond of them."

"Ha! Gotcha. Bit out of your depth, eh, Megs?"

"Hardly!"

"So it's going well then?"

"Of course."

"Pleased to hear it."

"Where are you? It sounds pretty noisy your end, too."

"Gaza City."

"Is it safe?"

"Nope. Nobody's too sure who started this latest exchange of fire, but Israel has just announced they're launching an attack on Hamas by Tweet. A real-live Twitter war. Mad."

A pang of homesickness grips me. "Be careful, Glen."

"Course. Still, it beats hanging around an empty flat. I gotta fly, but listen, Megs, when you're ready to get back on the road, I'll be waiting. Eric, too. We miss you."

"Don't hold your breath," I say, but the line is dead.

Pleased as I am to hear from him, the conversation has touched a nerve. There's so much missing in my life – Guy, my job, Glen, Fran, Eric even.

A trendy-looking café with a raised wooden deck comes into view. A coffee will while away another hour, I think, and hurry up the steps.

It's warm inside, steamy with bodies. All the tables are full, so I head to one in the corner where a slight young woman with dyed-blonde hair is engrossed in a book, an old military overcoat slung over the back of her chair.

"Do you mind if I share?"

She looks up and smiles. "Please."

"Thank you."

A waitress hurries over and takes my order. I peel off my puffa and stare out of the windows, misty with condensation, and wonder how on earth I'm going to fill the endless days ahead.

"I will miss this view when I go home," the girl says, fiddling with a large metal strawberry hanging from a heavy chain around her neck.

I detect an accent but can't place it. "Where's home?"

"Warsaw. I leave in fifty days."

I laugh. "Not that you're counting."

"I am here three years, one of thousands taking coach to Southampton. I wave goodbye to my country when I am twenty-one, but now I leave because I have saved enough money for deposit on apartment back home. This time I travel by plane. I buy ticket for twenty-seven pounds, cheaper than train fare to London. Incredible, I think."

"Good for you. I'm Megan, by the way."

"Natalia Topolska. Very pleased to meet you, but now I say goodbye. I must go to work."

She slips on a Nepalese hat, complete with earflaps, and heaves on the heavy overcoat.

"That looks like it keeps you warm."

"I buy it for five pounds in Oxfam. A bargain? No?"

"Absolutely. Good luck, Natalia."

She smiles, pulls up the collar of her coat, and hurries out of the café.

7

"As you can see, the architecture is Lombardo-Byzantine in its simple basilica form with this large rectangular hall, central nave, double colonnade of pillars, and arched apse. The Italians adapted the style by adding a belfry tower and a porch. This church is actually a copy of one that was built in Lombardy during the late sixth century."

Gabriel has delivered the spiel a million times. It trips off his tongue like an over-recited poem.

The American tourist whistles appreciatively. "Incredible. Do you mind if I take a snap?"

He's already clocked the expensive-looking camera hanging from the man's neck, but he's pleased to be asked permission. It's amazing how many visitors don't bother. Perhaps that's the American way. He doesn't know. This is the first American to cross the threshold. He smiles. "Not at all."

The tourist turns a swift three-sixty and points at the window above the west door. "I dig that."

Gabriel follows the line of his finger. "Ah, yes. The rose

wheel. Another original feature. You're seeing it at its best with the evening sun behind it."

"And the quote?"

The man's curiosity is heartening. Plenty of his congregation have no idea what it says. *"The Souls of the righteous are in the hand of God and there shall no torment touch them*. It's from the book of *Wisdom* in the *Apocrypha*. The coffin is carried through there after the funeral service."

"I get that." The camera clicks. "The place is in great shape."

Gabriel nods. "We recently spent two hundred thousand pounds on the roof."

The American whistles again. "That's a whole lot of bucks. How d'ya manage it?"

"A lot of very British fund-raising, coffee mornings, summer fetes, you know the type of thing. And we were lucky enough to be awarded a grant from English Heritage."

"Good on you." He slaps Gabriel on the back, hard enough to knock him slightly off balance. "I'd never have guessed you were the priest. You sure as hell don't look like one."

He smiles. He's heard it a hundred times and has given up wondering what a priest is supposed to look like. Still, he's grateful the American hasn't asked him his name. He'd have a field day with that.

"Jeans, corduroy shirt, moleskin jacket. It's a good look," the American continues. "Country and Western if I was to getcha a pair of cowboy boots and a Stetson."

Now that's a new one. He glances at his watch. Four-fifteen. There's a church council meeting in just over an hour. If the American leaves now he'll have enough time to dash home and see Ella. The chat he's promised himself he'll have with his daughter is long overdue. He's worried about her.

She's always been shy but recently she's withdrawn further into herself. Margaret Brown, his indomitable housekeeper, is adamant it's all down to hormones. At thirteen everything comes down to hormones, apparently.

He makes a point of clearing his throat. "I'm terribly sorry, Mr er—"

"Conrad. I can't be doing with any of this mister baloney."

"I'm terribly sorry … Conrad, but I'm going to have to lock up. I'm due at a meeting."

"Jeez, I'm sorry, Vicar. No problem at all. But could I just snap ya over by the altar."

"Holy Table."

"Eh?"

"That's what we call it in the Evangelical church."

"Hell, I didn't know that!"

Smiling wryly, Gabriel does as he's asked. The flashbulb explodes into light.

"Done!"

"Brilliant. Now if I may show you out." He leads the way through the swing doors to the porch, flicking off the lights before he steps outside.

Conrad clasps Gabriel's hand, bends over almost double, and kisses it. "Thank you, Vicar," he says, and backs away, bowing, as if in the company of the Pope.

Gabriel chuckles, waving to the man as he walks away. He peers at the darkening sky. After the balmy late-autumnal days, the weather has turned hostile. Dusk is falling fast as it always does this time of year, blown in on another storm. Shivering, he digs into his jacket pocket and pulls out the hefty bunch of keys.

A car speeds into the drive. It stops with a crunch, spraying gravel. The door swings open, and Jemma Webster, her face almost entirely obscured by large, black sunglasses, clambers out. Her chestnut hair swirling in the breeze, she grabs a handful and hurries over.

He glances nervously at his watch. He tends to be over-protective when it comes to this particular parishioner. She looks agitated, but time is ticking on and he really should get back for Ella.

"Oh! You're not leaving, are you?" Her face falls. "I was hoping to sit in the church."

He sighs. "Well, if I give you the keys you can lock up when you're done." He pushes open the heavy oak door and switches the lights back on.

"Thanks. I'll drop them into the vicarage on my way home."

Gabriel pauses at the entrance while Jemma, her back to him, removes her cream trench coat and sunglasses, and settles in a pew. It's good to see her this together. Six months ago, she'd slunk into the back of his church during his Sunday morning sermon, red-eyed and trembling, and was still there well after the last members of the congregation had left. He'd asked her if she was okay, which she clearly wasn't. He didn't press her for information, that wasn't his style, but Jemma needed to talk, and it wasn't long before her heart-breaking tale spilled out in short angry spurts.

"I don't feel as though I can go on anymore ... My husband's a bully. He's always putting me down ... He says I indulge my son, but I don't ... Maybe he's jealous. I don't know ... I love him but I can't deal with his passive-aggres-sion. I want to talk, but he blanks me ... He's been through a lot, I know. He lost his job, his BMW, the house. It hurt his pride. But he blames me. No. Worse. He hates me."

Gabriel sat and listened. There are two sides to every story, but the picture Jemma painted of her husband that morning was not a pretty one. It was not Gabriel's place to judge a man. That duty fell to God. But try as he might, as the conversations developed over the next few months, Gabriel could not suppress the opinion that Robert Webster was a complete and utter bastard.

Judge not, lest you be judged.

"Forgive me, Father," he mutters.

Jemma swivels around.

He gasps. "Oh my God!"

She reaches for her sunglasses. "I thought you'd gone."

"Do you want to talk?"

"What about?" Her voice is irritated, sharp.

He takes a tentative step towards her. "Your eye. The bruise. Did you fall?"

She shakes her head and folds her arms, exposing a circle of bruises on her bare upper arm. It reminds him of those his mother used to wear when his father took to shaking her after his hardware business went bust. She bore it stoically for years until one night, shortly after Gabriel was ordained, his dinner five minutes late, his father hit her about the head with such ferocity she was deafened in one ear. The following day she told him she was leaving.

He shivers. "Did Robert—?"

Jemma lowers her arms and frowns.

"Why? Why would he do a thing like that?"

"Did I say he had?"

"You didn't have to."

She sighs and removes her sunglasses. "It was my fault."

"No, Jemma. Whatever you said or did, Robert had no right to hit you."

"It's not what you think."

He slides into the pew. "Tell me then, please. I'm worried about you."

She shifts her position, away from him. He's torn. He wants to put his arm around her but he can't. Imagine if someone walked in? Not very likely at this hour, but all the same.

For goodness sake, Gabriel, get a grip. He takes a deep breath and sits on his hands. "You know you can talk to me. Anything you tell me will be in strictest confidence."

Jemma rocks. "I shouldn't have done it. I couldn't help myself."

Her defencelessness is more than he can bear. He frees his hands and draws her trembling frame towards him. She leans against his chest, tiny and warm, her hair, spilling in waves across his shirt, inches from his face. "It's okay. You're safe now. He can't hurt you here."

Jemma Webster is a beautiful woman. Her skin is china-smooth, and she smells of lemons. Six months ago, she'd aroused his protective instincts. Only now, unwittingly, she's awakened something else entirely. Desire, a long-lost ghost he thought he'd buried alongside his wife. A tingling at the tip of his spine oscillates down each vertebra.

What am I doing? She's a married woman.

She reaches for his hand and holds it to her face. "It felt like rape, but it wasn't. Not really. I consented. Well, sort of. But I didn't want to do it. Not like that."

"You don't have to tell me." His voice croaks. He can't control it. He thought she was going to tell him Robert was having an affair. Isn't that what men like him do? Have affairs.

"It's degrading, you know, being treated like that. And it hurt."

"Jemma—"

"No, listen. Please. You have to understand it's easier to give in. Life is better when he's happy. For the past four months he's hardly been at home. I don't know where he goes, but he stays out late. When he comes back, he reeks of whisky. I'm too scared to confront him so I pretend to be asleep, and that worked for a while. But the other night he was drunk and angry. He yelled at me, called me all manner of names, and grabbed my arm. I pulled myself free but collided with the bedpost, and he hauled me back and flipped me facedown on the bed, pinning me with his body and …" She shivers.

He imagines the scene. He can't help himself. It's there, right in front of his eyes. Robert: spitting on his hand, grunting like an animal until, satiated, he slides off her back. She: lying on her belly, hurting and choking on her resentment as he zips up his fly.

His heart is pounding. "Why? Why would he do that?"

"I'm still being punished."

"For what?"

"His job. The house. Don't you see?"

No, I don't see. I don't see at all. "He shouldn't have done that."

Jemma shrugs.

He can't bear that she accepts her husband's behaviour. Him, a man of God. The same God whom he believes in and loves, even though He stood back and allowed His only son to be taunted, beaten, and crucified to death. For years he's thought of himself as a logical man. But right now, reason has deserted him.

"Why don't you just walk away?"

"Believe me, I've thought about it, but life without him simply doesn't bear thinking about. I can't support myself and Dylan without financial help from him."

"But he hasn't got a job."

"He has. He starts on Monday at a marketing company in

Brighton. It's a good job. Good money. Things should improve. In fact, I'm sure they will."

He's doubtful. "There are other ways. Other alternatives. You could find work."

"I'm a thirty-seven-year-old woman who hasn't been employed for twelve years, but I suppose I could find some dreary, low-paid work. Fourteen years ago, I was PA to the editor of one of the top London fashion magazines. I'd never get a job like that around here. It's ironic. I gave it up to go travelling around Australia because my relationship with Robert was going nowhere. But he was devastated and insisted on following me. He proposed to me on an island on the Great Barrier Reef. It was romantic. A year later we had Dylan. Life was different back then."

"You don't have to be a martyr."

She smiles and nudges him with her elbow. It's an intimate gesture not lost on him. "I thought part of your job was to conserve the great institution of marriage?"

He shakes his head. "There are always exceptions."

"At least I have Dylan. Dylan makes it all worthwhile."

It's crazy to put such faith in a child, but he knows what she means. They're the glue that keeps body and soul together. He feels the same about Ella.

It's after six. He's late for the council meeting. He dashes around the corner to the church hall, agonising over how to help Jemma. To confront Robert would be madness, especially as she begged him not to. And when he mentioned taking the matter to the police, Jemma became hysterical. He's powerless. That's the awful truth. All he can do is be there for her, do his job – man of the cloth, willing listener.

All twelve members of the Parochial Church Council are

seated on canvas stacking chairs around the rectangular table. Gabriel hurries in and takes his place at the far end.

"I'm sorry, I was held up."

The chairman throws him a disapproving look, and so do one or two of the others. Elected members of the church, they're an odd and disparate group who think they own him. His wants, he realised early in his curacy, are incidental. He accepts this because he understands he exists as a vessel for their faith. But not today. Today he can't accept the banality of it all. The conversation with Jemma has unsettled him. He wishes he were anywhere but here, discussing the plan for next month's nativity.

He should be at home, talking to Ella.

The meeting stutters to an inconclusive end, arguments still raging about how many angels should be allowed in the tableau.

"As many as want to be," Gabriel keeps saying.

But no one agrees with his liberal view.

Outside, he glances at the blue clock face in the bell tower high above him. Nine-twenty. If he hurries, Ella might still be awake. She'll be angry because he promised he'd be home before the meeting. More than anything he wants to be a good dad, but he never manages to keep to his word.

He unlocks the front door of the vicarage. Over a hundred years old with three floors and six bedrooms, it's far too big for two people. When Steffi was alive, they'd adapted the ground floor so she could run a small nursery, but after her death, he'd closed it down. The yellowing walls are in desperate need of a lick of paint, but that means going cap in hand to the Parochial Church Council. Even so, there's a cosy feel to the place, which is almost entirely due to Margaret Brown. Fresh flowers sit in a chipped china vase on the mantelpiece in the dark wood-panelled hall, the fire in the sitting room is lit, and the heart-warming aroma of baking filters through from the kitchen.

"Oh, Gabriel, I'm so glad you're home." Margaret's face is flushed, and she is wringing her hands.

"What's the matter?"

"I'm terribly worried about Ella."

"Yes. I know—"

"No, Gabriel, I don't think you do. She's very thin, and I know for a fact she isn't eating. I made her favourite fish fingers and chips for supper but she didn't touch a crumb. I tried talking to her but I couldn't get a word out of her. Then she was really quite rude to me before running off to her bedroom and locking the door. I've baked brownies, but she isn't interested. And it isn't like her. It really isn't."

He sighs. "I'm sorry, Margaret. It's my fault. I promised I'd be home when she got back from school."

"I'm not sure it's down to one broken promise."

He holds up his hands. "I know, I know, I'm always breaking my word."

She shakes her head rapidly. "I didn't mean that. I think something is really wrong. She's lost a lot of weight. Surely you've noticed."

He casts his mind back to this morning's breakfast. He was scratching notes for Sunday's sermon on a scrap of paper while Ella toyed with her Rice Krispies, heaping them on her spoon before letting them spill into her bowl, again and again.

"She might be having problems eating because of the braces she's had fitted," he says. "She's the only child in her year with them. It's never easy being the first. I've tried to convince her she'll be having hers removed by the time the others start wearing theirs. But she won't listen. They've made her more self-conscious than she was already. Maybe they've affected her appetite, too."

Margaret exhales. "I really don't think it's the braces. She's spending far too much time locked away in her room on her own. It's not right for a girl of her age."

"She's not on her own. She's chatting to friends out there in cyberspace. Life has changed since we were young. It's the electronic age now."

She frowns. "I'm sorry, Gabriel, but you're deluding yourself."

He recoils, her words like a slap to the face.

"She's mad about Kate Moss and hooked on magazines," continues Margaret.

"Kate Moss?"

"Nothing tastes so good as skinny feels, that's her mantra."

"Kate said that?"

"Yes, Gabriel, she did."

"And she's only thirteen?"

"No, she's thirty-nine." Margaret shakes her head. "She's a model. You must have heard of her. Honestly, Gabriel. What planet are you on?"

His cheeks burn. "I thought you meant … I've been meaning to talk to her for ages, but something always comes up."

Margaret reaches for her coat. "I really don't think you should wait any longer. Something isn't right."

He sees Margaret out and makes for the stairs, but when he pokes his head into Ella's room, the light is off. He strains his eyes. Her duvet is tucked under the pointed chin of her heart-shaped face, her wavy raven hair spread over her pillow like a fan.

She looks so beautiful, just like her mother. I won't wake her, I'll speak to her tomorrow, he thinks and, quietly, closes the door.

8

I drive to school to collect the twins, having achieved nothing all day. And even though I've spent the entire afternoon watching the minute hand of my wristwatch limp through the hours, I'm late because I couldn't find the car keys amongst the mess.

Josh and Daisy are the only children waiting at the gate. I pull up beside them and steel myself for the inevitable fireworks. They yank open the rear doors and jump in, but instead of the grouchy faces and snide remarks I'm expecting, they chatter away excitedly.

"We played rugby. Can you believe? During school hours," Josh says as he fastens his seat belt. "Mr Saunders reckons I'll definitely be in the 1st XV. There's a match on Saturday against Vinehall. It's forty minutes away, so we're going in the mini bus."

"That is so gay! Our hockey match is in Surrey," sneers Daisy.

I can't believe what I'm hearing. Daisy, playing hockey? I want to whoop with delight but don't for fear of how she'll react.

"I thought you said you were too cool for sport," Josh says.

My thoughts exactly.

"My social life is everything," he adds, mimicking his sister.

I brace myself.

"God, you're such a geek," she says.

"Yeah? Well, at least I'm not a troublemaker."

My inflating heart sinks. "Oh, Daisy. Already?"

Daisy ignores me and glares at Josh.

"What happened?" I ask.

"I'm not in trouble. Swanny just gave me some advice."

I frown. "Advice?"

"Don't stress! About my uniform, that's all."

"Right. He gave you some *advice* about your uniform then sent you to the shop." Josh snatches a St Peter's plastic bag from Daisy.

"Geroff!" screeches Daisy, piling into her brother.

"Her new *longer* skirt is in here." He holds the bag above his head like a trophy, fending of Daisy's fists with his other hand.

"Josh! That's enough," I say.

"Yeah, Josh. Butt out."

"Apart from that she had a great time," continues Josh. "She beat everyone at tennis and then auditioned for the school play."

Tennis and hockey. A play. The information is beyond my wildest dreams. "Daisy, that's brilliant."

"Duh. It's not like I have a choice." She rolls her eyes and crosses her arms.

Josh grins. "Everyone's talking about Daisy Truman."

I glance nervously in the rearview mirror and, to my amazement, see Daisy suppress a smile.

But Josh isn't finished. "Especially Dylan Webster. I don't think Dylan has met anyone like Daisy."

It's a step too far. The inevitable fight breaks out, and I have to stop the car to sort it out.

I meet my new neighbour for the first time during a rare break in the rain while I'm sweeping the leaves off the front porch and she is putting out her rubbish. A trim woman in her early sixties with a steel bob, neatly dressed in a lime-green cashmere jumper and tailored charcoal trousers, she introduces herself as Margaret Brown and asks if I am settling in. She tells me she works as a housekeeper for a widower and his thirteen-year-old daughter, a pupil at St Peter's, but today, Tuesday, is her day off. Her friendly manner sets me at ease and, when the clouds open and the rain returns, I invite her inside for a cup of coffee.

"Be warned, though. It's a bomb site."

The kitchen is no better than any of the other rooms. Blisters of paint are peeling off the walls, cupboard doors hang from their hinges, and the tiled worktop is chipped and uneven. I grab the kettle, wander over to the cracked ceramic sink, and turn on the tap. The pipes chunter, and a spurt of rusty water shoots out. I wait for it to run clear, fill the kettle, and switch it on.

Margaret takes in her surroundings and smiles. "The couple who owned this place before you were very old."

I unhook a couple of mugs off the tree by the antiquated cooker and spoon in instant coffee. "The man I met can only have been in his sixties. I wouldn't call that old. Not these days anyway."

Margaret's eyes crinkle with amusement. "No, sixty isn't

old, but Bertha and Albert are well into their nineties. You must have dealt with Jim or Derek, their sons. They've been trying to persuade their parents to move for years. In the end the stairs got too much for them. Albert had a fall. They're in assisted accommodation now, much to their boys' relief."

I rest my hands on the tiles. "How wonderful to have been married that long."

Margaret tilts her head questioningly. "You're on your own?"

"Yes, since Guy, my husband that is … I mean, was." Flustered, I wave my hand and frown. "He died in May. It was sudden. I … I miss him terribly."

She walks over and presses her hand on mine. "If it's any comfort, I miss my Bill, too. He died ten years, five months, and nineteen days ago. Not that I'm counting." She raises her eyebrows and gives a rueful smile. "It seems like only yesterday we were strolling hand in hand along the seafront."

I look into her watery blue eyes still scarred with pain. "I'm so sorry."

She gives me a knowing smile. "Thank you, and don't worry. It gets easier."

I place the mugs of steaming coffee on the table and gesture to Margaret to sit down. "And this widower you work for. His wife?"

Margaret pulls out a chair and sighs. "She was killed in a car crash on a rainy night in October just over two years ago."

"How awful."

"Yes, it was. The driver of the other car was drunk. He lost control and crashed head-on into Stephanie's Micra. Fortunately, Ella wasn't in the car."

"That's terrible. Poor man. Poor child."

"It's affected Ella quite badly. She's a sweet girl but very quiet, very withdrawn."

"The polar opposite of my daughter then. Daisy has way too much attitude for a thirteen-year-old. In her mind, she's already sixteen."

Margaret laughs. "Sounds like she keeps you on your toes. But what about you? Have you met any of the other mothers?"

I nod. "One has invited me for dinner on Saturday, but I don't want to leave the twins on their own quite yet."

"If it's a sitter you're after, I could do it. I don't work Saturday nights."

The winding country road narrows, and I turn into a long driveway, bordered by mature rhododendron bushes. Round a sharp bend, a vast seventeenth-century twin-gabled house, illuminated by a row of sunken spotlights, comes into view.

"Samantha's forty-four and worth a bob or two," Margaret explained when I told her where I was going. "Her father is Gordon French, of French and Co. He moved here from London in the early eighties and was *the* local magnate up until five years ago when he sold the estate agency for millions. Charlie, her husband, works for Goldman Sachs."

I wasn't impressed, although I realise I should've been, and made the appropriate noises.

I park my Golf between a black Range Rover and a sleek silver Jaguar – Sussex society clearly isn't concerned with the size of their carbon footprints – and cross the drive, trying to ignore the butterflies in my belly.

When no one answers the front door, I head to the back and step into a vast kitchen with salt-and-pepper granite worktops, green handcrafted cabinets, and a pristine cream Aga. A woman in a black dress, who I assume is the maid, takes the flowers I've brought and ushers me through the cavernous hall to a taupe drawing room. Heavy curtains hang from wrought-iron poles, *objets d'art* dot the antique walnut cabinets, and silver-framed photographs crowd a round mahogany table. Half a dozen or so guests huddle in front of the open fire, all of them dressed to the nines, and I find myself wishing I'd given my outfit, a black dinner jacket, white shirt and jeans, more thought.

A good-looking teenage boy with a light fluff of facial hair breezes past and hands me a flute of champagne. Samantha's son perhaps?

"Megan, how lovely to see you." Samantha hurries over in a green satin shift and killer heels, a string of swollen pearls around her neck. She leans forward and brushes her cheek against mine, once, twice.

"Come with me. I want to introduce you to Leonora Carter. She's lived in Easthaven all her forty-one years and is dying to meet you."

She takes my arm and leads me to the other side of the room where a pear-shaped woman with mousy hair is talking animatedly to the young man.

"My son, James, and my very good friend, Leo Carter," Samantha says before flitting off towards another group of guests.

James says hello and immediately excuses himself.

"Megan Moreau," I say, offering my hand to Leo, taking in her enormous grey-blue eyes, framed by eyelashes, flared into sea urchin-like spikes. I recognise her immediately; the woman in the Jacquard coat with the Cheshire cat grin.

Her too-big eyes widen. "Oh! The mother from the state school. Are you part of the Government's great experiment? Did Anthony Swann have his miserly arm twisted and offer you free spaces? We've three children but, even though my husband's the school doctor, we only get a tiny bit off the bill. Scholarships at St Peter's are as rare as hen's teeth."

"No, I—"

"You're a war journalist with the BBC, aren't you? I've seen you on TV. Gun blasts and battles." She shivers. "Terrifying."

"Actually, I found looking after two newborn babies far more frightening. Nothing can compare to that."

Leo arches an eyebrow. "Not even a state school education?"

I stiffen involuntarily.

"I have a son the same age as your twins. We'll have to get them together. It would be awful if they got in with the wrong crowd."

I check Leo's expression, but it isn't a joke.

"You look fit. Do you play tennis? Everyone plays tennis around here. My daughter Coco's only nine, but she's already backed by the LTA."

Somebody clinks a spoon against a glass. The room falls silent.

"Dinner is served," announces Samantha.

In the red-flocked dining room, I peer at the names written in neat black italics on folded cards at each elegantly laid place; silver cutlery, crystal goblets, starched white napkins, white bone china. I glance at the name to my right. Richard Drummond-Stone.

"Call me Dickie," he says. "Everyone does."

Samantha's husband, Charlie, appears at my other side, trim and balding, in a striped shirt, blue tie, and jacket. He fills my glass, and I gulp it down, silently berating Guy for daring to leave me alone.

. . .

The meal is well under way, and although I'd like to have drunk copious amounts of the expensive red wine on offer, I can't because I'm driving. Seated to my left, Charlie is engrossed in conversation with a highlighted blonde in a low-cut dress, so I chat to Dickie. A chinless divorcee with an impressive head of greying blond hair, a haw-haw laugh, and a noticeable overbite, Dickie tells me all about his Labradors (three in all), his country estate (enormous), the pheasant shoot he runs, and an unspecific marketing job he has in town. He makes no mention of his ex-wife, nor refers to any children. Is it a set-up, I wonder, our hostess's attempt at joining two singletons?

"Samantha has told me all about you," Charlie says breezily, suddenly turning his attention to me.

It's a ridiculous opening line. His wife knows nothing about me, but I smile anyway. It would be rude not to. "Whereas I know nothing at all about you."

He eyes me quizzically, fiddling with a heavy-looking signet ring on the little finger of his left hand.

"But I'm guessing you work in the city."

He pokes his cheek with his tongue.

I hold up my hand. "Don't tell me. Venture capitalist. Goldman Sachs."

"Otherwise known as the bank that does God's work."

I smother my laugh with a cough, covering my mouth.

Charlie frowns and stabs the table with his forefinger. "We raise capital for companies to help them grow. Growth creates wealth, which creates jobs. It's a virtuous circle."

I want to point out that it was the reckless trading of bankers that recently brought the world to the brink of bank-ruptcy, but that would be graceless. "I imagine you make more money than some countries."

He snorts derisively. "You're a war journalist, aren't you? What do you know about banking?"

I was a foreign correspondent, but I don't bother correcting him. "That certain bankers behaved a bit like war-time profiteers, taking advantage of a global crisis."

"You mean we didn't fuck up like the other guys."

I don't but I drop the subject anyway and toy with the stem of my empty wine glass.

"You haven't turned to drink then? I thought that's what your sort did when you swap the adrenaline hit of war for real life."

I smile sweetly. "Not yet."

"But you do feel guilty."

I squint at him. "Guilty? No. Why?"

"For spending all that time away from your children."

I bristle. "Guilt is part of life for all working mums. Besides, there are a lot of fathers who do what I did and who really miss their families, too. But we love our jobs, and that's what drives us."

"Other working mums aren't quite so selfish, though, are they?"

My cheeks burn. "I'm not sure I understand."

He leans back in his chair. "I mean, they don't doge bullets and they go home at night. What if something happened to you? As a mother you're irreplaceable."

I'm shocked. "Surely a father is irreplaceable, too."

"A father doesn't have the same choices."

He's getting his own back, I know, but I'm angry now. "The twins were not quite one when I did a story on the Bentalha massacre during the Algerian Civil war. Soldiers from the Armed Islamic Group hacked children to pieces and dashed them against the walls. They raped and pillaged and sliced open pregnant women then called the killings an offering to God. A couple of the very few survivors spoke to me simply because I was a woman."

I'm on a rant. Charlie has got the rise out of me he was after. I am not a war bore. It's not what I do. And to make matters worse, Charlie is grinning at me. Fortunately, the woman with the pneumatic cleavage touches him on the arm and leans forward to whisper something, almost spilling out of her dress. His attention diverted, I nurse my mental wounds and watch Charlie's hand disappear under the table. A second later, the woman blushes.

That'll amuse Glen, I think.

If they chuck the car keys on the table, make your excuses and leave. Unless, of course, you're a secret swinger, he said when I told him about my invitation to dinner in the country.

I glance at Samantha. The epitome of refinement, she is chatting away to her guests, oblivious. What did I expect? This is a capitalist's home. Charlie Young's wealth defines him. He can afford to be ruthless. But as much as I dislike what he stands for, I'm in no doubt he feels the same about me.

This is not a war, I think miserably. I'm a guest at a party.

Dickie is talking to me again. He's not bad-looking for a man in his late forties, if you discount the ski-slope chin. Good skin and a full head of hair and what the media call pillow lips. Can a man have pillow lips? I imagine puckering up to them. Too soft, I think. Squidgy. Horrible.

"I gather you're a war correspondent for the BBC?"

Only after Dickie has been blinking at me for some time do I realise he's asked me a question. "Sorry, I was miles away."

"Like that ghastly woman, Kate Adie."

Oh God, a Daily Mail reader.

"Are you a lesbian?"

Here we go. "No!"

"So why the short hair and trousers? Can't understand all this fuss about the deaths in Afghanistan. It's disgraceful the way the media manipulate politics. I'll bet you haven't heard any complaints from the soldiers."

"Er, no."

"Bloody impressed with your work." He thumps the table, spilling claret, and dabs at it with his white linen napkin, staining that as well.

Somehow, I make it through the rest of the evening. I meet Leo's husband, Mark, a local GP, who, unlike his wife, is self-deprecating and friendly. I warm to him immediately.

"Where did you train?" I ask, taking coffee from the maid (Mark confirmed my suspicion) as we took our seats in the drawing room.

"The Middlesex, and after that a couple of years in Nairobi."

"My brother's based in Kenya."

"Lucky man. What does he do?"

"He's following a family of elephants. A young calf was kidnapped last week by another herd. The females in his family worked together to retrieve him. Ralph hadn't seen behaviour like it before."

He smiles wistfully. "Ah. A dream job."

I nod. Like mine used to be.

"Africa gets under your skin. It's hard to leave, not that you ever really do." He pats his chest. "It stays with you, here."

My African memories are of the atrocities of Rwanda and Algeria, not of wild animals and wide-open plains. But I smile. "But now here you are in Easthaven."

He grins. "It's not as bad as all that. There's the sea, the South Downs, the glorious English countryside."

I steal a glance at Leo, the Easthaven mainstay, sandwiched on a couch between Charlie Young and a man whose name I've forgotten, both laughing uproariously at something she's said.

"So how did you two meet?"

"At a colleagues' party not long after I moved down from London. She was the life and soul, and I was captivated."

"Does she have a medical background?"

"Leo? God, no. She faints at the sight of blood." He laughs. "Don't worry, we're not all like Dickie and Charlie. And some of the mothers actually have jobs."

9

argaret Brown is a noisy cook. The sound of clashing saucepans, rattling cutlery, and the screech of the food processor drifts up the stairs to Ella's bedroom. Sitting at her desk, Gabriel glances at the pink walls plastered in posters of tousled-haired pop stars. A string of heart-shaped fairy lights is draped over her dressing table mirror. Fluffy cerise and purple cushions are scattered over her bed and, on the bedside table, the little pewter pot with the Tooth Fairy sitting cross-legged on top, which Steffi gave her when she lost her first tooth. He picks up his favourite photograph perched in pride of place beside the screen. The evening sunlight gives Steffi's skin a rosy tinge, a moment in time he remembers as if it were yesterday. If he concentrates hard enough, he can hear her infectious giggle.

Ella took the photo with her brand-new digital camera during Steffi's last summer, not that they knew it then. His meagre stipend meant he was always struggling to make ends meet but, with a little help from Steffi's parents, he managed to scrape together enough money for a fortnight's holiday on the Greek island of Cephalonia to celebrate her fortieth birthday. The Ionian Sea turning an inky blue, Steffi clambered onto the smooth slab of rock to pose for her daughter. Then Ella said something that made her laugh. Of all the pictures of Steffi this one shows her as he recalls her, carefree and heart-breakingly beautiful. He holds her face to his lips and returns the frame to its rightful place.

Closing his eyes, he clasps his hands and tries to pray as he has done a million times before. He wants to thank God for allowing him fifteen years with his wife, but his entreaty doesn't ring true. How could it when not a day has passed since the crash that he hasn't wished for her back? Neither time nor his faith has relieved him of the crippling pain.

It was shortly before Gabriel met Steffi that he became aware of God's presence. He was just about to enter his third year at Bristol University. All summer, his father had been lashing out at him, criticising his appearance and finding fault with everything he said and did. After one particularly emas-culating earbashing, he fled the house, ran into the nearest church, and prayed to a God he barely believed in. His mood improved dramatically, so he went back the next day and every day after that until he returned to university. Aware of God's grace, determined to follow Christ, he grew calmer and stronger. Three weeks into term, his confidence restored, he met and fell in love with Steffi and, two years after graduat-ing, enrolled at theological college. He took a year out to teach, but it only confirmed his desire. His vocation was the church and, with Steffi's backing, he became a priest.

And then Steffi died. No, that's not true. She was killed. Murdered by a drunk as she drove home from a rare night out with girlfriends.

He thought his grief might kill him. When his emotional wounds failed to heal, doubt reared its ugly head. How could he thank God for allowing him the few years he had with his beautiful Stephanie when he's angry with Him for taking her away?

Still, at least he has Ella. Eight years younger than Steffi was when he met her, she's the spit of her mother with hazel eyes and wavy raven hair. Her smile is enough to brighten his day. Not that she's smiled much lately. Not since the train tracks have been fitted to her teeth.

He sighs and catches sight of a magazine lying open on the floor beneath her desk. Curious as to his daughter's choice of reading matter, and mindful of Margaret's words, he picks it up and stares at a glossy-haired singer with impossibly white teeth. She reminds him of someone. He scrutinises the picture until it comes to him. Jemma Webster. The woman he recently fantasised carrying to the safety of his metaphorical castle.

Clenching his jaw, he flicks through pages dominated with pictures of celebrities, punctuated with articles on the latest fashion and beauty tips, and ludicrous features crying out to be taken seriously: *How to get a Man Plan. Do men prefer girls without makeup? I thought my boob had exploded.*

Ella is thirteen. Far too young to be reading stuff like this. Isn't she?

He folds the magazine and stares at the cover. Beneath the picture of a glammed-up WAG is an advert for the accompanying thirty-two-page booklet, scarily titled *When Sex Goes Bad.* He drops the magazine on the desk, stands, and stomps out of the room.

"Gabriel, is that you?" Margaret says as he thunders down the stairs.

He flinches. If he stops, she'll start nagging him about Ella. It's all she seems to do these days. He's told her he's talked to Ella and that she's assured him there's nothing wrong but, no matter how many times he reiterates this, Margaret won't let it drop.

"She's second top of the class. Her teachers can't praise her enough," he told her last week. "Anthony Swann says she's in with a chance of winning the top scholarship to East-haven College, and God Himself knows how much that would help fund her education."

"She's becoming a recluse, and it's not normal," Margaret replied.

"That'll be her hormones. You said so yourself."

And she's right. He's seen the magazine. But he doesn't want to discuss his daughter's sexual awakening with his housekeeper. Those conversations are way out of his comfort zone.

"I'm just on my way out," he says briskly, before Margaret can stop him.

The rain is falling, cold and sharp as needles. He pulls up the collar of his jacket and marches, head down, into the weather. He hasn't far to go. Twenty metres tops. He reaches in his pocket for the keys but pauses at the entrance.

This is where I belong, he reminds himself. He unlocks the church, and goes inside, glancing briefly at the notice board as he makes his way into the main hall. I'll sit down and work out how best to approach the subject with Ella.

Of what, exactly? Sex? Menstruation? Contraception? "Dear Lord, I'm not up to it," he murmurs and, shuddering, leans against a pew.

"Gabriel!"

He starts at the sound of Jemma's voice.

"Are you okay?"

He feels her warm hand on his arm, and covers it with his. "Sorry, I'm a million miles away."

"It's good to see you. I hoped I would." Her face is pale, the bruise beneath her eye turning yellow at the edges.

"Is everything all right?"

She sighs. "It's Robert, that's all. We had another fight."

"Did he hurt you?"

"No. He hit me with words this time, not his fists, although I sometimes find that's worse. He's very clever with words."

He gesticulates to the pew. "Tell me."

But Jemma remains standing, staring at the cross on the Holy Table. "I find it hard to believe God sent His only son to die for our sins. Isn't that a bit crazy? What parent in their right mind would make such a sacrifice for a bunch of miserable sinners?"

He hears the truth in what she says. "Put like that, it does sound mad."

She turns and fixes him with her cobalt eyes. "Everything I do is wrong. The way I dress. My conversation. The house. My lifestyle. He keeps telling me to get a job. *Can't you see that's what you need? It isn't healthy devoting all your time to Dylan. It's harmful. Dangerous*. He actually used that word. Can you believe it?" Jemma sighs again and lowers her head.

He glances at the stepped cross. "Is it possible to spend too much time with your child?" He says the words out loud, although he's not addressing Jemma.

"Well, *I* don't think so. And yet whenever Robert goes on about it, I do feel guilty. And that's not all. He says I'm an idiot for coming here and keeps asking me why I insist on going to church when I'm not religious."

Gabriel knows Jemma married Robert in a registry office. He knows her belief and love of God has come about through him, that it has sustained her through this dark period in her life. But he sees no point in suggesting she explains this to her husband. It might provoke another attack.

"I'm sorry," he says.

"It's okay. Really it is. I was drawn to the church through fear. I hoped I might find God and that he would help me. But I didn't find God. I found you." She reaches out and touches him lightly on the cheek.

Up until that moment, Jemma is who she always has been, a beautiful woman seeking solace in the company of a priest. Now he stares at her, aware that this has changed. Her flawless face moves towards his, her lips slightly parted. He knows what she is about to do just as he knows he should stop her. She cups his face in her hands and presses her soft, warm lips on his. But it's only after he's tasted her sweetness that he pulls away.

He steps back, horrified. "No. This is wrong."

He means it. And it's not because she belongs to Robert Webster but because he is a father to Ella. What would it do to her if she saw them now? He backs away, wringing his hands.

"Gabriel, I—"

"Don't."

"It'll be all right. We'll work it out."

"No, Jemma. I can't."

"Because I'm married?"

His head is throbbing. "Yes. No. I don't know."

"I'll leave Robert. I'll get a divorce."

His pulse is racing. A vision of loveliness, she stands before him, offering her body to him on a plate. He's hard and aroused and aching with desire. But that is all. And that's not what she's after.

Just say it. Tell her you don't want her.

But he can't. The words would rip her to shreds. He's led

her on. He didn't mean to. And now he's got to let her down. His body is rigid with tension. "You're gorgeous, Jemma."

Misty-eyed, she moves towards him, flings her arms around his neck, and kisses him again. He stands there, impassive, like the idiot he's become, and kisses her back.

No. No. No. That's not what I meant.

Her hand wanders to his thigh. She runs her fingers over his groin. He shudders, and she gasps.

His body has betrayed him.

Her mobile rings. Moaning, she breaks away. "It's Dylan," she says, diving into her handbag on the floor of the aisle.

He stands there while she chats to her son but doesn't hear a word. Weak-kneed and light-headed, he breathes deeply, desperate to regain control.

"Gabriel, I'm really sorry. Dylan needs a book for his Latin test this afternoon. I have to go."

He's all over the place, surprised, relieved, terrified, culpable.

"I'll call you. I promise." She kisses him on the lips and dashes out of the church, leaving Gabriel alone to face his God.

10

The day after Daisy was mugged, I woke up full of energy. There was so much to do and so little time, I ran around as if I was trying to outstrip the invisible gremlin chasing me. This past week, my mind, which had calmed since I made the decision to move out of London, is back in overdrive. I've spent hours obsessing over why I reacted to Charlie Young's needling, and worrying whether the other guests noticed. It's not like me. *Take me as I am* is my motto. I'm not the sensitive type. How could I be after all I've seen and done? Adapting to new places has never been a problem either. I've had enough practice. Since boarding school, I've been to university, travelled the world, survived, and witnessed all manner of atrocities. I've learnt that to thrive in a new community you must accept its habits and rituals. But Guy's death has dented the self-confidence I took for granted. I was a free spirit, but my love for him kept me grounded and secure. I'd grown so used to him being there I hadn't realised how much I'd come to rely on him. But Easthaven is my home now, and I need to fit in. I want to make a good impression.

To divert my mind, I spent the week blitzing boxes (how did I manage to accumulate so much stuff?), unpacking and tidying the contents away. I even scraped some of the peeling paint off the walls.

And then, last night, Samantha rang and invited me for coffee, putting an end to my fretting. I'm to meet her and Leo at The Singing Kettle tearoom after the school drop off today.

It's just gone eight o'clock, and I'm preparing breakfast with the radio tuned to Heart. The news is on, but I'm only half listening. Rashers of bacon sizzle and spit in the frying pan on the antiquated stove. I pick up the kettle, pour the boiling water into my mug, and reach for the bread just as the newscaster starts talking about missing Polish woman, Natalia Topolska. Wasn't that the name of the girl I met in the café? I wonder, reaching for the volume.

"Sussex police are growing increasingly concerned as to the twenty-three-year-old immigrant's whereabouts. She was last seen leaving the Langridge Hotel on Easthaven seafront, where she works as a cleaner, at six-thirty p.m. on Saturday. A colleague at A. L Bright's alerted police after Natalia, an economics graduate renowned for her reliability, failed to show up for work yesterday morning. Subsequent attempts to contact her have proved fruitless. She isn't answering her mobile and hasn't returned to her rented flat. Although there is no evidence to suggest Natalia has been the victim of a crime, the police are anxious to find her. She is five foot two, pale, slight, with shoulder-length, dyed-blonde hair and is wearing a hooded sweatshirt, jeans, and trainers."

I should contact the police, I think, as the twins rush into the room. Daisy plonks herself at the table and pours Frosties into a bowl. I place the milk in front of her, bend down, and plant a kiss on the top of her head.

"Geroff! You'll ruin it."

78

It is Daisy's hair, backcombed today to a mass of knots. "Impossible."

Daisy scowls and sloshes milk over her cereal. "What do you know? You've absolutely no style whatsoever."

"Better get my hands on a Boden catalogue then."

She rolls her eyes. "Ugh!"

"What are you doing today, Mum?" asks Josh as I hand him a bacon sandwich.

"I'm having coffee with Leo Carter and Samantha Young."

Daisy's eyebrows knit together. "Why?"

"Because they asked me."

"Duh. Yeah. But why?"

I toss some carrots in a bowl for the rabbits. "I thought it would be fun to get to know some of your friends' mothers."

"Why? You don't *normally* bother."

The barb hurts, but I steel myself. "Things are different now."

She drops her spoon into her bowl. "No shit!"

"Daisy, please."

"Well, I think it's neat," says Josh. "I don't know Georgia Young, but Oli Carter's cool."

"Georgia thinks she's sick, but she's, like, really fake," adds Daisy.

I panic. "You haven't had a fight?"

She bangs the table, eyes sparking. "Why must you always think the worst of me?" She pushes back her chair with such force it hits the floor with a thud.

Ten minutes later, she stomps back downstairs, her face as black as her mood. It darkens further when she realises I'm intending to walk them to school.

"Do you have to?" She rolls the waistband of her skirt over a couple of times, but I keep quiet. "It's so embarrassing."

"Yes, I do."

The sky is a dreary, elephant-grey, but at least it's dry. I reach for Guy's golf umbrella and spot a leaflet on the floor tucked behind it.

Take the stress out of decorating with Fine Design.
No job too big or too small.
For further information contact Jasper Baker.

I glance at the picture of a very modern living room, fold it in half, and put it in my pocket. It could be just what I need.

"Did you give Groucho and Marx the carrots?" I ask Josh.

"Yup. I swear they've grown. If we don't make them a run soon, I reckon they'll break out of their hutch."

I sigh and lock the door. "I'll buy some chicken wire and posts and try and cobble something together."

"It's okay, Mum. I'll help."

I smile at my son and we head off down the street, Daisy shuffling along some distance behind us, her eyes fixed on the pavement. At the gate, I stop and wait for her to catch up.

"I've got a rehearsal tonight," she mumbles

My heart sinks. I'd forgotten all about the musical. I haven't even asked what they're performing. Or have I? I'm not sure. "Did you get the part?"

She shrugs but avoids eye contact. "Hmm."

"Well done, Daisy. That's brilliant."

"Whatever!" Having suffered the walk with me, she slips into her cool persona and swaggers into school, chin in the air. Heads turn. Boys call out. Parents frown.

"She hasn't got the main part," says Josh.

"Oh, what a pity." When Guy died, she pulled out of her drama club's production. She had the lead in … in … What was the musical? I can't remember. "But there'll be other opportunities, I'm sure."

"No, I mean she got it but she turned it down."

"Really? Why?"

"Because she's too cool to play a goody-goody!"

I've no idea which role she went for, but I don't want to admit it. "So what did she get instead?"

"Rizzo, obviously."

Grease! Of course. Daisy wouldn't want to play the part of Sandy. Bad girl Betty Rizzo is far more up her street. A wave of apprehension washes over me, but I dismiss it. I'm becoming paranoid. Why look for problems where there aren't any? They're thirteen. They'll cut the bit about the unwanted pregnancy. Be grateful Daisy's involved.

A few mothers linger at the gate. Samantha is there, but she's engaged in conversation, and I don't want to intrude. I wait under the branches of a large cherry tree and look over the flint wall at the lush green playing fields, nestled in the curved bowl of downland, whose tapering foot comes to rest on the beach a quarter of a mile away. In front of the white-washed school, pristine beds of aggressively pruned roses run parallel to the long grey asphalt that leads to the tennis courts. At the far end of the rugby pitches, some three hundred yards away, is the chocolate-box-pretty, thatched cricket pavilion. Life is on the up, I think with a smile.

A car pulls up abruptly alongside me with a squeak of its brakes. A tall man, with mud-brown hair tied in a greasy ponytail, jumps out, followed by two startled-looking children, clutching school bags. The man chivvies them through the gate and is rushing back to his car when a stout, balding, bulldog of a man appears out of nowhere and steps in front of him, blocking his path.

"You've got a nerve showing up 'ere," Bulldog says in a loud, angry voice. "Go on, sling your 'ook."

The mothers stop chatting and turn towards the men. Bulldog's face is puce, the muscles in his neck strained, but Ponytail stands his ground. Bulldog slams his palms into Ponytail's shoulders, shoves hard, and Ponytail sprawls backwards into a group of mothers, Samantha among them. One of them screams and topples to the ground beneath him. Another woman tries to wrest her free, but Bulldog marches over, grabs Ponytail by his lapels, and hauls him to his feet. Holding him with one hand, Bulldog balls his fist, draws back his arm, and swings. There's a loud crack as his knuckles connect with Ponytail's jaw, whose head jerks back at a violent angle, and a thread of blood flies in a perfect parabola and splatters on a green-and-white Jacquard coat. The occupant shrieks and scurries backwards. Bulldog releases his hold, and Ponytail's head hits the pavement with a thud. He lays stock-still, staring at the sky.

Nobody speaks. Nobody moves.

The image of Guy's inert body flashes in front of my eyes and I hurry over. Nostrils flaring, Bulldog steps towards me. I put a preventative hand on his chest and his muscles twitch beneath my fingers. He snarls and bares his teeth, but I will not let him pass.

"That's enough," I say with as much authority as I can muster.

"I'm done." He grunts and, massaging his hand, walks away.

I crouch beside the injured man. "Are you okay?"

"Fine!" Puffing with pain, he clambers to his feet, wiping

his bleeding nose.

"Are you sure? Your nose might be broken. I could run you to A&E."

The mothers have formed a semi-circle around us but none of them offer any assistance.

The man waves his bloodied hand and shakes his head. "I'm fine."

I glance at the other mothers. "We should call the police. I'd be happy to provide a statement."

The man shakes his head and limps off down the hill.

A gentle murmur breaks out, rapidly increasing in volume.

"Megan! Are you all right?"

Over my shoulder I see the tall, angular figure of Anthony Swann approaching, his face taut and pinched.

"Perfectly. Just a little surprised to see parents fighting."

His face tightens. "Quite. It was brave of you to help."

"A knee-jerk reaction but, heck, there wasn't a Kalashnikov in sight."

He arches an eyebrow. "Well, that's one way of looking at it."

Samantha approaches, wide-eyed and visibly shaken. "Are you okay?"

"Yes, I am. You?"

But Samantha, her forehead concertinaed in a frown, has turned to Anthony. "We should have been warned he was back."

"Back? From where?" I ask.

The headmaster clears his throat. "Prison."

"Prison?" A St Peter's parent. Really? "What on earth was his crime?"

Anthony Swann opens his mouth, but Samantha beats him to it. "Murder."

11

_____

The Singing Kettle, a three-minute walk from school, is situated on a quaint street with flint-walled houses on one side, shops, a restaurant, post office, and the tearoom on the other. We arrive there shortly after Anthony Swann explained that Ben Styne, the victim of the fight, was the drink driver who'd killed Stephanie Jones – mother of Ella, the child Margaret Brown looks after – and that he was, in fact, convicted of manslaughter. Ben's wife, who divorced him while he was in prison, has custody of their two children, Tilly and Jack.

"He must have been granted visiting rights," Samantha says, opening the door and heading for a table by the window. "Unbelievable."

I deposit my umbrella in the stand, hang up my puffa, and sit down beside her. "How awful for Ella."

"Precisely, which is why no one rushed to his aid."

"How does Ella's father cope?"

Samantha shakes her head. "He's the forgiving sort."

I'm about to ask her what she means when the brass bell above the door clangs and Leo charges in, a large

84

handbag slung over her shoulder, and followed by a blast of cold air.

"Miranda just called and told me what happened. Can you believe the arrogance of the man?"

Which man? I wonder.

"Miranda's going to have to get her coat dry-cleaned," continues Leo.

Samantha tuts. "Disgraceful. It's Ella I feel sorry for. Georgia tells me she's been behaving oddly."

"Well, she would. She's a geek." Leo sheds her Jacquard coat and plants her bum on a chair.

Samantha frowns. "Don't be mean. There's nothing wrong with being bright. She's not eating. The girls think she's anorexic."

The doorbell clangs again, and a slim, brown-haired woman in a cream trench coat and sunglasses sweeps into the room. She hangs her coat on the stand and sashays over in a figure-hugging red skirt and black silk blouse. Feeling large and ungainly in jeans and baggy jumper, I shift awkwardly in my seat.

Samantha beams. "Megan, this is Jemma Webster, Dylan's mum."

"Pleased to meet you," she says.

Leo rolls her eyes. "For God's sake, take off those glasses. It's only a black eye, and it's almost gone."

"I bumped into a wall," she explains, but the sunglasses remain firmly in place.

"Anyway, it's hardly surprising she has problems with a father like that!" says Leo.

Jemma frowns. "Who?"

"Ella Jones." Leo grimaces. "Gabriel is a religious nut."

"Al-Qaeda?" I ask.

Leo snorts. "Don't be ridiculous."

"Gabriel's a vicar," says Samantha. "And Leo's never spoken to the man."

"Did you know his wife?"

"Different social scene. But I never heard a bad word spoken against her.

"Ali Styne's no better," continues Leo. "Honestly, the insensitivity of that woman. She should have moved her children to another school. It's bad enough for poor Jack and Tilly that their father's a murderer without him causing a scene."

"He didn't actually start the fight," I say.

The waitress appears at our table to take our order.

"Cappuccinos all round and a plate of your toasted teacakes," says Leo, and the waitress smiles and hurries away. "And I reckon Ella Jones is behaving oddly because Dylan thrashed her in the scholarship exams."

I pull a face. Academia a competition? Surely not.

"You must be so proud of him," says Samantha.

Jemma blushes. "Yes, of course."

"Who was the man who hit Ben Styne?" I ask.

"Roland Meadows. His wife was best friends with Ella's mum," says Leo. "Dreadful nouveau types. Made a fortune from fish and chips. Their children were in the state system until three years ago." She clicks her tongue. "I wish Anthony was a bit more choosy. His sort really lowers the tone."

I cringe. Has she forgotten my roots?

Samantha sighs. "He can't afford to be."

The last time I sat down with a group of women for a chat over coffee was with some young Colombian mothers who'd been terrified into acting as mules by drug barons who'd kidnapped their children. Their stories had chilled me to the bone. With so many atrocities happening in the world, it really is amazing what the English can find to gripe about.

Our coffees arrive and a dish of teacakes dripping butter. I move the African Violet out of the way, and the waitress places them on the green-and-white gingham tablecloth.

Leo loads her plate. "We need to get a move on. Jemma has to leave early."

"Really? Why?" asks Samantha.

Everyone turns to Jemma, who's hardly said a word. Perhaps bitching about unfortunate people isn't her style either. Or maybe she's shy. Are beautiful people ever shy?

She flicks her hair over her shoulder. "Doctor's appointment."

Samantha touches her hand. "Nothing serious, I hope?"

"Just a smear."

"Samantha has a proposition for you, Megan," pipes up Leo.

Samantha smiles. "You're just what this school needs, which is why I want to persuade you to join The Friends of St Peter's."

"Samantha's the chairman," explains Jemma. "And Leo and I are committee members, too."

So that's why I'm here. "Oh. Gosh. Well …"

Samantha blinks rapidly. "Is that a yes?"

The weight of their expectation fills me with dread. I loathe committees. The word itself makes me want to scream.

Samantha's eyes widen expectantly. "Well?"

Other than it being a slight to my autonomy, I can't think of a plausible reason why I should refuse. It's not as if I've got anything else to do. "Why not?"

Samantha smiles her toothy smile. "I knew you'd say yes."

Perhaps you know me better than I know myself.

"It'll be great," she adds, as if aware I need convincing.

"You'll be far more involved, which can only be good for Josh and Daisy."

But I'm thinking along different lines. I'll become an Easthaven mum. Daisy and Josh will be the focus of my life. *It's what you wanted*, my conscience nags.

Leo grins. "Talking of school, Oliver got the lead in *Grease!*"

"Good old Oliver," says Samantha. "Did you offer to make the costumes?"

Leo folds her arms and glares at her. "I'm no Sally Rogers."

"Sally Rogers?"

"She offered to make the costumes last year the day before the auditions, and bingo, Johnny ends up in the lead role," explains Samantha.

"That's wonderful, Leo," says Jemma warmly.

Samantha sighs. "Georgia was really upset not to get Sandy."

Leo wrinkles her nose. "I don't see why. She can't sing."

"Yes, she can."

Leo shakes her head. "Trust me, she really can't."

"And of course Daisy is Rizzo," says Jemma. "And therefore has upset nobody."

I laugh with relief. "When's the opening night?"

"Not until the end of March," says Samantha. "Grace Potter demands perfection."

Leo laces her pudgy pink fingers together. "Which should fit perfectly with you, Megan."

This flies over my head.

"I don't want to use the *P* word but …"

Samantha groans.

"*P* word?"

Leo folds her arms. "Pushy."

I laugh before I can stop myself. "Oh. Is that what you think?"

"Well, your children are incredibly talented. Coco tells me Daisy is a brilliant little tennis player," she adds on the back of another of her Cheshire cat grins.

"I wouldn't go that far. My husband taught her in the park."

Samantha laughs. "You're very funny, Megan."

"So you keep saying."

Jemma removes her sunglasses. There's a yellowing bruise beneath her breathtakingly blue eyes. She looks far too young to be a mother of a thirteen-year-old, and I find myself wondering if she was a child bride.

"It must be tough for you, giving up work, your loss, moving down here." She reaches over to press my hand.

Leo rubs her chin. "Modest or arrogant? I can't work it out."

"You're jealous, Leo. Admit it. If Daisy is selected, Coco will be demoted to number two," says Samantha.

Leo raises an eyebrow. "And Georgia will be dropped."

"It's only right. Daisy has beaten her twice already." If Samantha is disappointed, she doesn't show it. "No need to be modest, Megan. Daisy is a very good player."

I'm all at sea. This is not the type of conversation I'm used to. These women have never met my children, and yet they seem to know more about them than I do. Having been an absent parent for most of the twins' lives, I was lucky enough to be at home when they took their first steps, Josh first with Daisy in pursuit. My career was all about sacrifices. I learnt to deal with the heartbreak of every missed milestone. What would these women say if they knew I'd never made it to an open day let alone a play, or a game of tennis? But to come clean seems a very bad idea.

Leo leans back in her chair. "Perhaps she thinks our children have no talent."

"I hope that doesn't mean you're going to retract your invitation." Samantha turns to me and winks.

My heart sinks. Oh God. What now?

"Of course not." Leo dives under the table, pulls an envelope of her handbag, and hands it to me.

I open it.

Megan, plus one.
Leonora Carter at home
on
Saturday 15ᵗʰ December.

Did the others put her up to this? I wonder as my mobile rings. "Excuse me."

"Megs!" Glen's voice almost blows my ear off. "How are yer, mate? Having any more trouble with that army? Er … what was it called?"

"No, Glen," I say hurriedly. "I'm having tea with friends, and you're shouting." I roll my eyes at the others who are listening, riveted.

"Gotcha! Have I blown your cover?" he whispers.

Leo tugs at my arm and mouths, "Who is *he*?"

How do I describe Glen and do him justice? "Er … Glen. A good friend."

"HER CAMERAMAN," he yells, and I wince in pain.

Leo claps her hands. "An Australian! Megan, invite him to the party."

I'm astonished. A minute ago, I could have sworn she hated me. I shake my head and press the mobile to my ear again.

"I heard that, Megs my little darling. And the answer is YES. I'D LOVE TO."

"Great! That's settled. He's on the list," says Leo.

"When is this little gathering?" he asks. "And will I meet the army?"

"We'll talk later."

"Can't wait."

The last thing I hear before the line goes dead is his distinctive throaty chuckle.

He can't come, I decide, as I rub my ringing ear. I'll talk him out of it. Easthaven isn't ready for his rowdy banter. Or his drinking for that matter. He'll ruin my reputation. But then I remember it's not exactly flying all that high.

Leo presses my arm. "He sounds a real character."

"Oh he is."

What the heck, I think. It might be fun.

12

I t's Friday morning and Gabriel is in his study staring blindly into space. He's told Margaret he's working on a sermon but he doubts she's fooled. She's thrown him some very searching looks this week as he's mooned around the house. She knows something is wrong but, ever tactful, leaves him in peace. Ironic really, because his conscience is driving him to distraction. He is possessed by guilt, his thoughts on a loop replaying *that* kiss. In his darkest moments he's convinced he has the Devil on his shoulder.

Why didn't he stop her? Anyone could have wandered in. His curate, for one. He'd have had some serious explaining to do if Ashley King had caught him with a married woman and member of his congregation. Ash would've had to report it to the Dean. Martin Shepherd would have been furious. He'd have ended up in front of the bishop and defrocked. And then what would he have done? It's not as if he's geared to a life outside the church.

You're searching for problems where there are none, the Devil nags. *Ash saw nothing, so forget it.*

But that line of thinking doesn't help. The problem still

exists. He knows he should talk to Jemma, that he's delaying the inevitable, but he hasn't the strength to face her. His weakness is crippling him. Really, he's no better than Robert.

I need to pray. I need to beg for God's forgiveness. And I need to do it in church.

He glances at the clock. Nine o'clock at last. The moment he's been waiting for. No chance of bumping into Jemma. It's Friday, which means she'll be drinking coffee with friends. He cringes. He shouldn't know that. When did they become so close?

He prises his jacket off the chair, puts it on, and double-checks the time. Tense to the point of rigid, he lets out a pained sigh and opens the study door. In the hall, Margaret is polishing the ancient brass doorknobs. She sees him and smiles indulgently. He knows she thinks he's worrying about Ella, and his mood darkens still further.

"Going out?"

He nods.

"To church?"

He makes for the door. "Yes."

"Gabriel?"

He pauses, one hand on the latch.

"Have you spoken to Ella?"

"Yes, Margaret, I have."

Staggering under the weight of his lie, he walks out into the rain. St Matthew's looms, dark and imposing, in the poor light. The car park is empty, though, and his spirits lift. Ash is late, but at least he'll be alone. The heavy door opens with its familiar creak. Shivering, he turns on the lights and the heating and checks the noticeboard. A cream-coloured enve-lope is pinned between an announcement about the new creche times, and a reminder about Thursday evening's youth night. He takes a closer look. It's addressed to him. Nothing odd about that. He often receives letters from his parishioners in this way.

The neat handwriting is unfamiliar, and yet a sense of dread creeps over him. He unpins the envelope, trudges into the main hall, sits in a pew, and opens it.

Dearest Gabriel,

So now you know I love you.

I've wanted to kiss you for a very long time. Probably since the first time we met, if I'm honest. You were very kind to me that day, even though I was a total stranger. You made me feel safe, and I hadn't felt that way for the longest time.

After I got to know you, all I wanted, each time we met, was for you to reach out and touch me. Two weeks ago, it happened. You held me in your arms, and when you returned my kisses, I knew you felt the same.

Darling Gabriel, gorgeous you, I'm floating on air. You're all I think about, every second of every day. I'm bursting with happiness and aching to see you again.

Your Jemma xxx

By the time he reaches the end, he's breathing heavily. He scrunches the letter, rams it into his jacket pocket, and buries his head in his hands. He has to do something. The way he sees it he has two options. Tell Jemma it was a mistake. A terrible, foolish mistake. Or he can risk everything, his reputation, his job, his daughter's sanity, and his religion, and run away with her.

Put like that, it's a no-brainer. Unless, of course, he's lying to himself and is in love with her. And if he is, what about Robert? Could he run off with another man's wife? He rubs his eyes with the heels of his hands. Call yourself a man of God? You're a joke, Gabriel, and a pathetic one at that.

And then it hits him. Another option. He straightens up and stares at the stepped cross. He'll move away. It's the perfect solution. Ella isn't happy here. That much is obvious. How can she be when she's surrounded by memories of her mother? She'd be far better off starting from scratch somewhere new. Yes. That's what he'll do. He'll ask Martin Shepherd to move him to another parish. He kneels, clasps his hands together, and closes his eyes, determined to make his peace with God. Certain that he can.

He's deep in prayer when the church door opens. He doesn't look up. Ash wouldn't expect him to.

"Gabriel!"

At the sound of her voice, he freezes.

"Darling, I'm so glad you're here." Her voice is breathless, eager.

Before she can reach him, he's on his feet and in the aisle.

"I've missed you so much," she says.

Her sudden presence knocks him off balance, and he holds up his palm like a policeman controlling traffic. She pulls up abruptly. Her smile flickers and dies. He lowers his hand, but she steps closer. He raises it again. "No!"

"Gabriel, what on earth's the matter?"

He can tell by the way her eyes scrutinise every cell of his skin, every twitch of his facial muscles, that she's confused. But what can he say? That he's failed as a Christian, a human being, a father? Because that's how it feels. His guilt is crushing him. He cannot bear the strain. It's God he needs to talk to, not Jemma.

In an effort to assert himself, he rolls back his shoulders. "I'm fine."

She sits in a pew and cocks her head to one side. "I'm not sure I believe you."

"Truly I am." Suddenly and inexorably tired, he perches

on the edge of the pew in front, so he's facing her but not too close, and hangs on to the end.

She reaches out and touches him. "It's good to see you. I hoped I would."

He stares at her hand, aware of its warmth, its softness. She shouldn't be here. She should be drinking coffee with her friends. "And you? Are you okay?"

She frowns. "You seem upset. I'm not sure it's me who should be spilling my woes."

"Please do." He wishes he meant it. But he doesn't. All he wants is to be alone. Alone with God.

She leans over and strokes his cheek. He winces and pushes her hand away.

"What's wrong?" There's an audible tremor to her voice.

"I can't do this." His mouth is bone dry. He wants to get it over with, but he can't seem to find the words. "I want to explain—"

"That you're a vicar and I'm a married woman."

Her smile lights up her face. It's as if he's seeing her for the first time; cornflower irises, rosebud mouth, chestnut hair, dainty nose. Beneath her raincoat, the top three buttons of her black silk blouse are undone, the swell of her breasts visible above the black lace of her bra. He drinks her in. Every last millimetre of her. She is the most beautiful woman he's ever seen.

A minute passes, maybe more, before she speaks again, not that Gabriel is aware of time. He's lost in his subconscious.

"You once explained that had we not sinned we would never have understood what God had done for us."

He comes to with a jolt.

"In sending His son to die for us, it was clear He loved us. *It's important to remember it was the sinners who flocked to*

Jesus, not the religious nuts, you said, and then you reminded me about the story of the Pharisee and the Tax Collector. The Pharisee thought his stack of good deeds was enough to save the world. At least they would have been if everyone else had been more like him. But it was the Tax Collector who sought forgiveness. Guilt brought him to repentance, and God forgave him."

"Let guilt do the work intended and then file it away forever," he says in a flat voice. How easy it sounds. He jerks to his feet. "But what if I was wrong?"

"Don't be silly." She rises shakily to her feet. "Talk to me, Gabriel. Tell me what's bothering you. You don't look well. You're very pale. Are you ill? Is that it?" She moves closer.

"Don't. Please!" His voice is louder than he intended.

Wobbling slightly, she clings to the pew. "But we kissed."

He shakes his head. "I didn't mean to."

"Well, you did, and it was wonderful."

"You said."

"You've read my letter."

"Yes, and I'm flattered. I really am. But I can't do this anymore."

"But we haven't done anything. Not yet."

Gabriel would challenge this if he could find the words, but he can't. Instead, he wrings his hands.

"What's the matter? Tell me."

"I'll regret it if I do."

"We've all done things we regret."

But he isn't hearing her. "I would lose everything."

"No, you wouldn't. You'd have me."

He lowers his gaze.

"So you're saying I'm not worth it? Is that it?"

There's desperation to her voice. He stares at his shoes, but still he doesn't speak.

"Speak to me, Goddamn you."

Her anger startles him. He lifts his head and forces himself to look into her eyes. "I'm sorry. I can't pretend to be something I'm not."

Her face crumples, and a tear trickles down her cheek. "You're not making any sense. If you're saying you can't give up being a vicar then I'll wait for you until the divorce comes through. That's what you want, isn't it? You as good as told me I should leave Robert."

His shoulders droop. Dear God, what have I done?

"What is it? I need to know."

Say it, Gabriel, he tells himself. She *will* get over it. Say it! He opens his eyes and looks at her directly. "I don't love you, Jemma."

He watches her face twitch and fall as she absorbs his words. His heart beats violently. And all the time she doesn't speak, he hates himself.

"Is that all?" she asks eventually.

He can't believe his ears. Isn't that enough?

She's smiling now. "It doesn't matter. You wouldn't have kissed me if you didn't have feelings for me." Her expression is triumphant, as though she's finished the crossword in record time.

"Of course I have feelings for you. You're gorgeous. What man wouldn't?"

Her eyes widen. "But you're not just any man. You're the man I love."

He shakes his head. She's not making any sense. "Listen to me. You've got it wrong. I don't … I won't ever … love you." There. He's said it. There's no taking it back.

She grabs her hair, tugging at it. "You can't know that."

"I never meant to hurt you. I never meant to kiss you."

Her beautiful face is contorted with pain. He wants to put his arm around her to comfort her, but he knows he cannot.

Instead, he delivers his final blow. "It ends now."

He's barely finished speaking when the door to the vestry opens and closes. Footsteps *clip-clop* over the tiles.

"Hello, Gabriel." Ashley King, cheery as ever, comes into view. "I thought I heard you."

Gabriel's turns his bloodless face to the curate.

"Oh, hello again," Ash says cheerfully, on sight of Jemma. But then he takes in her tear-drenched cheeks and, frowning, runs his hand through his shoulder-length hair. "I'm sorry. This is a bad time. I'll wait in the vestry."

"Actually, no, it's perfect timing, isn't it, Gabriel?" Jemma's brittle voice is bitter.

His insides shrivel. She thinks I planned this.

"I know when I'm not wanted." She turns and hurries down the aisle and out of the church.

"Something's upset that one," jokes Ash. "I often see her here. She comes to pray," he adds when Gabriel doesn't respond.

"Yeah."

"Something you said?"

"You could say that."

Ash pats him on the back "Ah. I see. Like that, is it?"

Gabriel nods exhaustedly. "Yes, Ash. It is." He can't see the point in denying it.

"Do you want to talk about it?"

"No. I'm due somewhere."

"Catch you later then."

It's unnaturally dark outside. Gabriel bows his head and walks rapidly away from the church. He can't go home. Not while Margaret is there. He needs space to clear his head.

The roads are lined with cars, the pavements clogged with Friday morning shoppers. He meanders through them, past KFC and Tesco Express, and on past the Winter Gardens, turning left into a street of shops that cater for the summer tourist market. He crosses the main road at the zebra crossing and walks past the Lifeboat Museum onto the promenade. The tide is high and the flat sea a ghostly white. Seagulls glide on the wing, black dashes on the distant horizon. But Gabriel's eyes are blind to his surroundings. All he can see is Jemma's sad, depleted face. Try as he might, he cannot shift her image.

How did it come to this? I only ever meant to help her.

On and on he walks, past the beach café at the foot of the downs, up the steep hill on to the cliff road, turning right as he reaches St Peter's.

Always so weak, the Devil says.

No, not the Devil. His father this time, and he's a child again. An insecure, unhappy child, cowering under a bully's gaze.

You need to toughen up. Stop hiding behind your mother. Be more like your brothers.

Time and time again he'd needled him. It wasn't until his mother told his father she was leaving that Gabriel finally found the strength to stand up to him, ordering him to leave the house before he called the police. But it was too little too late. His brute of a father had died of a stroke barely a week later.

The rain starts all of a sudden, falling from the pewter clouds in sheets. Within seconds he's soaked. He pulls up his jacket collar and scurries up the steps of the Grand Hotel, through the revolving doors, into the elaborate Victorian foyer.

The uniformed concierge is quick to pounce. "Can I help you, sir?"

At the end of the high-ceilinged hall, beyond the stylishly dressed Christmas tree, a welcoming fire burns in a grate. He strides towards it, checking his watch. It's just gone eleven a.m.

"A drink." He prises the crumpled note out of his pocket and tosses it in the flames. "Whisky, please. On the rocks."

After his third whisky, Jemma's image blurs. After the fifth it fades away.

It's over, he tells himself. You don't have to worry anymore.

Margaret leaps up from the bottom stair where she's been sitting, waiting for him. Her hair is dishevelled, her face pale. "Where have you been?"

"I went to the cinema," he replies with a carefree wave of his hand.

Her mouth drops open. "You're drunk."

"I am not."

She steps closer and sniffs. "I can smell alcohol on your breath."

"I had a couple of whiskies. It's hardly a crime." He backs off and removes his damp, creased jacket and drapes it over the banisters.

"I've been out of my mind with worry. I was about to call the police." She brandishes the phone she's clutching in his face.

"Well, I'm here now."

Margaret glares at him, her face blotched with anger. "Don't you dare use that tone with me. Not today. Not when you've been gone over twelve hours."

This information comes as a shock. Somewhere along the

line he's lost track of time. "I er … I had something I needed to sort out. It took longer than expected."

She folds her arms and taps her foot on the parquet floor. "Something more important than your daughter?" Her voice is acid sharp.

Gabriel has never seen her like this. "It was important."

"And yet you went to the cinema?"

"Yes, that's right, I did."

His head aches. He touches his temple, but Margaret grabs him by the arm and half steers, half drags him into the kitchen. "What are you doing?"

She lets go and shuts the door behind her. "Ella was sent home from school."

His stomach churns. "Why? What did she do?"

"She fainted."

"Fainted?"

"You told me you'd spoken to her. Why did you lie to me?"

"I can't get a word out of her other than she's fine."

"And you believed her, even though she's starving herself to death."

He shrugs.

"There was a fight at school. Matron thinks that's the reason she fainted. That and her weight, of course."

The shock of what she's saying has a sobering effect, and he sits down with a thud. "Ella?"

"Not Ella, no. She wouldn't hurt a fly. And she wouldn't talk about it, so I rang my neighbour, Megan Moreau. She's a new mother at the school and strikes me as very sensible. She told me Ben Styne turned up this morning and was attacked by Roland Meadows." Her voice is gentle now she's got his attention.

Nauseous, he clasps his throat. "Styne was at the school?"

"Yes, and Ella was in a terrible state when she got home. She wanted to know where you were, but of course, you haven't got a mobile so we couldn't call you."

He notes the accusation. "I'll get one. I promise."

"She needs *friends*, Gabriel."

He bats the air dismissively. "She's got loads of friends. She's always chatting to them on Facebook."

Margaret bangs the table with her fist. "Who? Who does she chat to on Facebook? Not her school friends, that's for sure. She told me she doesn't have any, not since she fell out with Georgia. It's not healthy. It really isn't. You need to do something. You need to help her. And if you can't, then you need to send her to someone who can. I think she should see a doctor." Margaret sighs and sinks, deflated, into a chair.

His stomach roils. "Yes, yes. I'll speak to Mark Carter first thing in the morning."

"After you've spoken to Ella."

"Yes. And, Margaret, thank you."

She frowns. "Where were you, Gabriel? I know it's none of my business, but it's not like you to disappear." When no answer is forthcoming, she turns to go. She's got as far as the door when she wheels round. "Oh, and Martin Shepherd rang. He wants to see you."

The Dean? Gabriel's guts twist into a knot. Ash must have spoken to him.

"He wasn't all that surprised to hear you'd gone AWOL."

"You told him?"

"Yes, I did. I'm hoping he'll knock some sense into you, seeing no one else can. But Gabriel …"

He's sweating now. "Yes?"

"Promise me you'll talk to Ella first."

13

———

I t's happening. I'm moving on, I think, as I hurry back from the shops. I've met Samantha and Leo for coffee on three consecutive Fridays, survived my first St Peter's committee meeting, during which we discussed plans for the sponsored walk and summer barbecue, and enlisted the help of Jasper Baker to transform my house.

"Think of me as your fairy godmother," he said, when he pitched up with his assistant, Sebastian. "I am here to weave my magic and transform this … this …" he screwed up his nose and looked searchingly at Sebastian who shook his head despairingly, "this *hovel* into something unrecognisable. By the time I'm done, you won't know yourself."

"Really?" I cast a worried look over the colour board he'd prepared for the living room.

"Oh dear, Sebastian," he said, shifting his whippet-thin body to roll his eyes at his equally slender assistant. "I fear we have a non-believer in our midst."

"It's very bold, not really what I'm used to."

He flicked his limp-wristed hand. "You don't have to tell

me, love. If you have any self-respect whatsoever, you're going to have to trust my magic."

I shouldn't have doubted him, because together with his consort of builders, Jasper has transformed the living room, one of the bathrooms, and the children's bedrooms into 'fabulous bright, modern spaces'.

The house renovations underway, I unpacked my old laptop, retreated to a small box room at the front of the house, and started on my book. I'm only two chapters in, but revisiting the stories that define my past is great therapy, and the intense concentration it requires completely occupies my mind. There's no time for dwelling on Guy.

And then in early December, Guy's mother rang to invite us to spend Christmas at the Truman home in Hampshire. I was grateful. All his immediate family will be there; father, brother James and his two boys, and sister Nicky and her three children. Josh and Daisy were ecstatic when they heard they'd be spending Christmas with their cousins. Guy's mother, Sylvia, I know, is suffering as much as I am. I'm hoping we'll support each other through the emotional turmoil the celebrations will evoke. The Trumans are a close family. Guy not being there will be tough on all of us. He meant so much to them, as they did to him.

I trudge up the path, laden with shopping bags, wondering what to cook the twins for tea. Something I can heat up for Daisy after her rehearsal, perhaps.

Margaret's door swings open with a rush. Her face is pale and taut with worry. Clearly, she's been waiting for me.

"Have you got a minute?"

"Sure. Fancy a cuppa?"

.   .   .

The builders bashing away upstairs, I carry the tray with the two mugs of tea and a plate of Margaret's homemade shortbread into the newly refurbished living room and place it on the low oak table.

"I love what you've done with the place," she says, closing the door.

The tiny white lights on the heavily laden Christmas tree we bought last week are on, and the silver tinsel, draped over the branches, and the mismatched baubles from our old house in London, sparkle brightly. It gives the brand-new room a homely feel.

"Not me. Jasper, my brilliant interior designer. He shows me endless fabric and wallpaper books, asks me what I like, then comes back with swatches that bear no resemblance, and we plump for them instead. Ingenious. He's upstairs at the moment, transforming my bedroom."

As if on cue an almighty thud is followed by a man swearing in a high-pitched voice.

Margaret laughs. "It's stunning. I love that aubergine wall."

"A feature wall, apparently."

I flop onto the burgundy velvet couch, unwind my scarf, wriggle out of my puffa, and stretch my legs on the thick mushroom carpet. On the opposite couch, in her sensible skirt and brogues, Margaret perches, ramrod straight, legs bent and slightly to the left. The model of the perfect housewife. Something I will never be, however hard I strive.

"You've been a great help to me since I moved down," I say. "I honestly don't know what I'd have done without you."

"I enjoy spending time here. It's such a lively house."

I imagine her at home, a proud woman preparing a meal she eats alone at the kitchen table because, no matter how lonely she is, she will not let her standards slip.

"It's something I've missed out on, not having had children. My husband, Bill, was infertile, you see. We always thought I couldn't get pregnant because I'd been on the revolutionary new pill. Bill was devastated to discover his low sperm count was to blame. Back in the sixties, nothing much could be done for couples like us. Hard to imagine now."

"You didn't want to adopt?"

"We thought about it, but Bill wasn't keen."

"But you're so good with children."

"I was a primary school teacher for forty years. And I had two nieces who spent a lot of time with me. Sadly, they both live in Canada now." She places her coffee on the table and dabs at her nose with an embroidered white cotton hanky.

I lean forward and pat her on the leg. "You know you're welcome here anytime. Us widows should stick together."

She tucks the handkerchief up her sleeve and smiles wistfully. "You're far too young to be a widow. Gabriel, too."

I have an atheist's morbid fascination for priests. Having acquired the soubriquet *Sexy Vicar*, Gabriel sounds more interesting than most. "Tell me about him."

"I wouldn't know where to start," she says wearily.

I sense all is not well in this particular house of God. "The church must be a constant pull on his resources. How does he cope being a single parent?"

Margaret shakes her head. "If I'm completely honest, he doesn't."

"It's not easy. Look at me. I tried doing both."

"Yes, I know, but unlike you, Gabriel doesn't have a clue about the real world."

I recall Samantha's worried comments about Ella over coffee at The Singing Kettle. "There've been some rumours flying around about his daughter."

Margaret frowns. "What kind of rumours?"

"That she's anorexic," I say, treading carefully.

"I'm not surprised."

"Is it true?"

She lets out an exhausted sigh. "I really don't know, but actually it's Ella I wanted to talk to you about."

"Fire away," I say, in an unnaturally upbeat voice.

She fiddles nervously with a strand of hair. "She's not very sociable, and I was wondering whether Daisy would come for tea at the vicarage one day?"

I hesitate, not convinced she's thought the invitation through. Daisy isn't the automatic choice of playmate for a shy, retiring child. Margaret must know that. She's seen enough of Daisy these past few weeks. But Margaret's been so kind to me. Like a mother, in fact. Something my life has lacked these past thirty-five years.

"Wouldn't it be better if she came here?" It's a safer alternative, on so many levels. "How about you give me Gabriel's number and I'll ring and arrange a date."

She clasps her hands to her chest. "You'd do that?"

I slap the arm of my chair. "Consider it done!"

Clearly, I must be deemed to be a person of my word, because Margaret's tight, dejected expression gives way to a quivering smile.

14

W hen it comes to rehearsals, Miss Potter is a woman possessed. Dylan heard she was, but this is the first school play he's been in, or *first time treading the boards* in Miss Potter's language, so he's never seen her in action before.

Oliver Carter is singing. He's been at it for ages. It's hilarious. He can't sing in tune and he can't sing in time. Everyone is sniggering, which is killing him. His freckled cheeks are crimson, and his eyes are scrunched like he's in pain or something. It's hard to keep a straight face.

"Okay, let's take it from the top again." Miss Potter, bats away a fly that's bothering her with her clipboard. "And no laughing, anyone, please."

She nods at scrawny Mr Simpson. He smiles creepily and plonks his hands on the piano keys. Oli gets off to a decent start, hitting nearly all the right notes. Tilly joins in, and for once they're in sync.

Miss Potter points her finger. "Cue chorus."

Dylan sings and falls in line behind Oli for the dance. The girls follow. And then it's Oli again. This time he's got the notes and the moves, his legs and arms travelling in the same direction as everyone else's. Daisy saunters centre stage, hand on hip, and sings her line in a throaty drawl.

Awesome.

They're into the second verse. Nobody has fluffed their lines. Oli's face has relaxed. Only the big note at the end, and we're through. You can do it, Oli.

Oli sucks up a lungful of air, opens his mouth wide. But his voice cracks into a piercing shriek.

Tilly squeals and covers her ears. "Seriously, Oli, you're tone deaf. I'm not actually joking."

Oli glares at her. "I am not. It's this stink. It's well dodgy."

Miss Potter swipes at the fly. "It's not affecting anyone else."

"You sound like a strangled cat," says Georgia Young.

Bruno Richards rubs his ear. "No, I think you'll find that's you."

Dylan laughs. He can't help it. Everyone else is laughing, too.

"Enough!" Miss Potter slaps her clipboard against her thigh. She struts onto the stage and sighs. "It's not working, Oliver. You're going to have to speak that last line."

"No way."

"It's perfectly okay. Rex Harrison won an Oscar doing precisely that in *My Fair Lady.*"

"Rex who?"

"Maybe we should try it one more time," suggests Tilly.

Miss Potter shakes her head. "I think we'll leave it there for today."

"Oh, Mi-*iss*," choruses the chorus, Dylan included. He's having a blast, unlike poor Oli, who didn't even want to be Danny.

"You're the best singer," Miss Potter explained when she cast him.

"Mum was well chuffed," Oli told him after. "So it's not all bad."

You have to hand it to Oli, thinks Dylan, as his friend flings himself to the floor and writhes about, clutching his throat. It hasn't been easy for him. A redheaded nerd who can't play sport, he has more nicknames than is funny – Carrot Top, Ginge, Ginga, Ginger Nob, Copper Knob, Dura-cell – it's incredible he's made it into year eight without dying it.

"I wouldn't mind, but it isn't even red," he told Dylan.

"You sure?"

"Course I'm sure. It's my hair, isn't it?"

"So if it's not red …?"

"Auburn. Duh! I thought you're supposed to be smart."

No, Oli can make as many mistakes as he likes. Rehearsals are where it's at. Two hours eyeing up Daisy Truman. And it gets better. She's Rizzo and he's Kenickie.

Sick.

Cool word, *sick*. Like *sweet* and *class*. Daisy taught him. She's speaks like that all the time.

Not everyone's pleased about his role, though. Take his Mum for instance.

Dylan: "I've got a part in the school play."

Mum: "I didn't know you liked acting. Is it a big part?"

Dylan: "No."

Mum. "I suppose that's okay. It'll look great on your CV."

Dad: "His what? Oh God, did you really just say that?"

Mum: "You'll just have to work harder at weekends."

Typical. Work, work, work. That was all she thought about these days. He'd wanted to swear at her. Bad idea. His parents would start arguing. They were always arguing. Usually about him. Something he'd done. No. Something he hadn't done. Not enough work, not enough piano practice, not enough time in the cricket nets. So he bit his lip and walked away.

Miss Potter claps her hands. "Come on, kids, time to go."

"Pants," says Tilly. "I didn't get to sing my bit."

"What *is* that smell?" Bruno asks. "It's minging."

"Probably a dead mouse. I'll ask Mr Swain to check it out," Miss Potter says, dabbing her nose with a tissue.

Daisy skims past. "Meet me in the dressing room in five," she whispers.

The back of Dylan's neck tingles like it always does when she speaks to him.

"And don't get caught!"

"Okay. I won't." His voice is croaky. Another effect she has on him. That and the hard-on that's busting out of his boxers. He rushes to the toilets before anyone notices.

Five minutes later, all parts of his body under control, he creeps back into the theatre. He scans the area. It's empty. He sprints through the stalls, up the stairs onto the stage, and into the wings. The smell is stronger here, well rank. He stops and listens, pinching his nose to block out the stench. A couple of flies buzz past his face, close enough for him to see their blue, hairy bellies. He swipes them away and listens again.

Silence.

He glances over his shoulder in case Miss Potter is lurking somewhere, and scuttles through the wings, thudding into a dilapidated trunk of fusty costumes dumped by one of the backstage crew. He freezes and holds his breath. Nothing. Whistling quietly, he straddles the trunk and tiptoes towards the dressing room. He takes a minute to compose himself, raps on the door, and waits, heart drumming. He's not sure if he's excited now or scared.

"Daisy?"

No one answers, but he thrusts down the handle and sticks his head into the room anyway. His mouth drops open at the sight of Daisy, cross-legged on the makeup bench, a cerise feather boa draped around her shoulders, her lips painted red.

"Fancy a smoke, babe?"

"Shit!"

She raises one eyebrow – how'd she manage that? – and waggles a finger. "Language!"

He finds his voice. "Like you care, potty mouth." That croak again.

She picks up the packet of cigarettes, flicks one out, and catches it between her scarlet lips. Reaching for the plastic lighter on the bench beside her, she strikes the flint. He watches, transfixed, as she lights up, fixing him with her baby-blue eyes. She takes a long hard drag, tips back her head, and exhales. A plume of smoke spirals up to the ceiling.

Dylan blinks rapidly.

Her eyes ping open. "Want one? Or are you going to stand there catching flies?"

Dylan is not like Daisy. He's not cool. He's never hung out in London with older boys.

"You're more Charlie Brown than Robert Pattinson," she said when he'd finally summoned up the courage to speak to her.

He'd spent ages in front of the bathroom mirror that night, studying his features. Big brown eyes. Small button nose. Freckles, way too many. Stupid kid's haircut. Not quite Charlie Brown but not far off.

He started waxing his hair into a quiff, dressing differently.

"I'm glad you're growing your hair," Mum said. "But I'm not sure about the gel. And do you have to wear your trousers quite so low? I can see your boxers."

Duh!

The cone of ash at the tip of Daisy's cigarette outgrows its strength and falls to the floor in a silver shower. "Well, do you want one or not?"

It must be obvious he's never smoked. He focuses on the fine smattering of freckles on the bridge of her nose. Even her freckles are cool. He puts his hands on his hips. "Bet you've never snogged anyone."

No, Dylan. Wrong! Very wrong, he thinks, because she rolls her eyes, has another drag, and looks down her nose.

"You're such a baby."

His cheeks burn, and he turns away.

She prods him with her foot. "So who'd you snog?"

He shrugs.

She sucks on the cigarette, leans forward, and blows the smoke in his face. He coughs and waves the air frantically.

She laughs. "Baby."

He bites his lip and frowns.

"Do you want me to show you how?" she asks in a throaty whisper.

He nods.

Daisy uncrosses her legs, slides off the bench, drops the cigarette butt, and grinds it into the floor with the toe of her Ugg boot. "We have to get close," she whispers, placing her hand behind his head and drawing him towards her.

Their noses touch briefly. They're the same height. She inclines her head and presses her mouth on his. Every single one of the hairs on his skin and his dick stand to attention as the tip of her tongue slides between his lips. He closes his eyes.

But then the tongue is gone.

"God, you're dumb."

Heart somersaulting, he opens his eyes. "What? Why?"

"Duh! You're meant to open your mouth, idiot."

Suddenly it all makes sense. Quick as a flash, he places his hand behind her head, fixes his lips on hers, and thrusts his tongue inside her warm, wet mouth. Their tongues collide and dance, Dylan falling into the rhythm Daisy sets, slowly, softly. She tastes of strawberry ice cream and smoke. His heart speeds up. His breathing deepens. He's not even bothered by the fly buzzing by his ear. He doesn't want it to end. She's blown his mind.

Eventually, Daisy pulls away and wipes her mouth with the back of her hand. "Pretty sweet, for a *ba-by*."

He copies her. His hand, he notices, is covered with lipstick.

"Now, let's see you smoke." She picks up the packet, pulls out two cigarettes, and lights them both. She hands one to him, her half-closed eye watering.

He rushes a drag and gags.

"You're too pumped. You need to chill. Watch," she says when she's stopped laughing and he's stopped retching. She sucks in her cheeks, tips her head, and blows a smoke ring, followed by a second, a third.

"Awesome. How d'you learn to do that?"

"Yes, Daisy. How *did* you learn to do that?"

Dylan's head snaps round. Miss Potter is standing in the doorway, arms folded, her eyebrows knitted in an angry frown.

15

Ella Jones is a coy, skinny waif with twiglet legs and dark, wavy hair, painfully self-conscious of the train tracks on her teeth, and worryingly pale. It's easy to see why the other girls think she's anorexic. What she needs is a substantial meal.

"Do you like lasagne and garlic bread?" I ask as I open the door.

She nods.

"Great, then that's what I'll make for supper. It's the twins' favourite."

"It's really good," confirms Josh.

It's kind of him. Although I make a mean lasagne, which I serve at least twice a week, I'm not a good cook, most of my meals bordering on the inedible. Ella smiles bashfully, and I catch a glimpse of the pretty girl she is. "You have very beautiful hair," I say. "I'm so envious."

She fiddles with a strand as if noticing it for the first time. "Thank you."

Daisy would frighten her half to death. No wonder

Margaret said Ella wouldn't mind her being at a play rehearsal. "I should warn you, the house is a pigsty."

Josh groans. "You promised you'd tidy it."

"I meant to but I lost track of time. Why don't you go to your room? That way you won't notice the mess."

Josh throws me a filthy look.

I throw out a suggestion. "You could listen to some music. I'll call you when supper is ready."

"Daisy's got my iPod."

"Well, borrow hers."

"She lost it."

I groan. Another black mark for Daisy and another argument I don't want to have. "Well, play on the computer then."

Josh groans. "O-*kay*."

His lack of enthusiasm is obvious. But he turns to Ella anyway. "Do you like *Call of Duty*?"

"Er … I think so."

"Josh can't get enough of it," I say and head for the kitchen where 'My Sweet Lord' is blaring out of the radio. I stall, not because of the song, but because my foot gets stuck to something sticky on the floor. I glance at the carnage and groan. The dishwasher is full, and this morning's breakfast dishes litter the work surfaces. The fat-encrusted frying pan, upended in the sink, has given the water it's soaking in a brown, greasy film. Books of wallpaper and fabric samples stand in towers beside the kitchen table which is itself covered in a layer of paperwork I'd been intending to file. Dirty laundry lies on the mud-streaked floor, while the washing machine spews clean, wet clothes into a plastic laundry basket.

I slap my forehead. Without Guy to keep things in order, mess tends to creep up on me, lurking around the house in the guise of Coke cans, newspapers, household bills, shoes, odd socks, bowls, and plates. And, before we know it, we're living in a dump. Not so Josh. His red-and-white bedroom is immaculate, the Arsenal duvet cover on his bed perfectly straight. Neat piles of books are stacked on his desk, a few clothes draped over the arm of the squat blue armchair. He craves a tidy life. He's organised. Has an ordered mind. Just like his father. It's probably why he's always questioned things.

How do birds fly? Why is the sea salty? What did Nelson have for breakfast before the Battle of Trafalgar? Is it possible to prove the existence of God? "How does the heart pump blood?" he asked his Uncle Felix, four days after his father died.

"Well, it's basically a muscle with four chambers. During every heartbeat, the top two chambers, the atria, contract to pump blood into the lower chambers, the ventricles. Then they contract to pump blood out of the heart into the arteries and around the body."

"So what happened to Dad's?"

"His left ventricle became stretched, which weakened his heart muscle so it couldn't pump blood efficiently. That led to an arrhythmia, a disturbance of the normal electrical rhythm of the heart, which eventually caused it to stop."

Josh knows everything about the heart now. He understands dilated cardiomyopathy, having researched the condition on the internet. He knows his dad was unlucky. Severe arrhythmia developed suddenly.

Forty-five minutes later, the kitchen tidier, I'm pouring the béchamel sauce over the top of the lasagne when the news comes on; the lead story, the latest report on the missing girl.

"*It's been two weeks since Natalia Topolska went missing. Since finding a one-way ticket for a flight to Warsaw in her flat, the police have stepped up their search. According to her best friend, Ania Nowak, Natalia, who has lived and worked in Easthaven these past three years, was looking forward to returning home. The police have found nothing to indicate that she has been a victim of crime but—"*

A loud thud in the room above distracts me. Somebody screams.

"Mum! Mu-um!"

I rush into the hall. "What is it?"

Josh's worried face appears over the banisters. "Quick! It's Ella!"

I bound up the stairs two at a time and dash into his room.

My trembling son is kneeling beside the prostrate girl. "We were going to play on the computer, and I was getting her a chair when she just fell over. Like a tree. Is she dead?"

I feel for a pulse in Ella's tiny wrist. "It's okay. She's fainted, that's all."

Josh's shoulders, which are up around his ears, retract. I slide my hands under Ella's armpits and hoist her into a seated position. Her head lolls forward, and I put a steadying arm around her shoulders.

"Will she be okay?" Josh asks.

"The worst she'll be is embarrassed. Run downstairs and get her a glass of orange juice and some biscuits. She'll come round in a minute."

Josh hesitates, his face almost as white as hers. "Mum—"

"Go on. Get a move on."

Ella moans and lifts her head as if it weighs a ton, her eyes wide and enormous in her ashen face. "Where am I?"

"At Josh's house. You fainted. You'll be fine in a bit." I nod at Josh, who scuttles off.

Ella tenses and grabs at the cuffs of her shirt. "You won't tell my dad, will you?"

"Sweetheart, I must."

"He'll be angry."

"No, he won't."

Two minutes later, Josh appears in the doorway with the orange juice and a handful of biscuits.

"What was it you wanted to tell me?" I ask.

He looks at me pleadingly for a moment then shakes his head. "Doesn't matter."

16

D ylan can't meet the headmaster's eyes. He feels them, though, drilling into him as he stares at his shoes – same tactic he uses when his Mum lays into him. Mr Swann isn't yelling, though, but somehow that makes it worse.

"Please do me the courtesy of looking at me when I'm speaking to you."

His toes curling, Dylan raises his head. The headmaster is eyeing him sternly from behind his desk, fingers steepled.

"Thank you. Smoking is not allowed at St Peter's."

Dylan nods.

Anthony Swann uncrosses his legs and leans on his desk. "Have you lost your voice?"

"No, sir."

"And are you familiar with the rules?"

"Yes, sir."

"I should hope so. As head boy you're expected to uphold them not break them. I'm very disappointed in you, Dylan."

He winces. "Yes, sir. Sorry, sir."

Anthony Swann gets up and prowls around the room.

"You did brilliantly in the mock scholarship papers. You outshone all your classmates."

You don't have to tell me, thinks Dylan. He'd been astonished all the subjects he'd revised had come up.

"However, since then your grades have fallen. Dramatically, I might add."

Dylan squirms. "Yes, sir."

Anthony Swann pauses by his desk. "You've been distracted. Am I right?"

Dylan shakes his head.

The headmaster smacks the desk. "Speak up! I can't hear you."

Dylan jumps. "No, sir."

"Oh, come on, Dylan. You were on track for the top scholarship and yet in one month you've fallen so far behind that any award looks out of the question. Unless, of course, you knuckle down to some really hard work. It would be a pity to throw it all away. So I'll ask you again. Have you been distracted?"

"Yes, sir."

The headmaster returns to his chair. "Good. That's a start. Now let's move forward. Keep your eyes on the ball, Dylan, not on the girls. Don't let yourself down. You've got a great future ahead of you if you focus on what's important right now."

Relief washes over him. Mr Swann is done.

"You'll be pleased to hear I'm not going to suspend you."

His spirits lift. "Thank you, sir."

"But I'm afraid you cannot remain head boy."

He takes a step back as if struck. His face crumples. "Couldn't you suspend me instead?"

"It's not that simple." His voice is gentle now. "I pinned my hopes on you, Dylan, but you let me down."

"I won't do it again. I promise"

"You should have thought about that before you broke the rules. You've left me with no option. The head boy is a role model. He should lead by example."

A tear spills over his eyelid. Dylan wipes it away angrily.

"You'll learn from this, Dylan." Anthony Swann's hand is on his shoulder. "You're a good boy."

Dylan stiffens, suddenly confused. Angry one minute, kind the next.

"I want you to think about this conversation. Don't let the bitterness you feel now cloud your future judgment."

Dylan pulls back his shoulders and stares straight ahead.

The headmaster sighs. "Could you send Daisy Truman in and then wait in the hall. Your parents should be here any minute."

Dylan's eyes are glued to the clock above the bursar's office. Twenty-two minutes and thirty seconds he's been waiting. The second hand is ticking slowly. Too slowly. He thinks there must be something wrong with it. He feels sick, and his palms are sweating. He rubs them on his trousers and turns to look at the photograph on the wall of him playing rugby. Head down, eyes on the ball, his right leg dead straight, his arms stretched out for balance. Just the way Owen Farrell kicks at goal. He'd been a hero that day. He'd converted the kick and they'd won the tournament. Most of the school had been watching. They'd gone wild. He'd felt about nine feet tall.

He used to be proud of that photo. Not anymore.

He glances at the clock again. Another minute gone. He wishes he could unscrew the glass and turn back the time to this afternoon's rehearsal. It was bad with the headmaster, but it'll be far, far worse with his parents. His mother will go ballistic. He rubs his palms together, drums his feet, and tries to figure a way out of this mess. But there's no escape.

He groans and shakes his head. He needs to think tactically, as if it's a game of rugby. Take it on the chin. Don't answer back. What's the worst that can happen? They'll be fine once they get over the shock.

Yeah, right!

The door of the headmaster's office swings opens, and Daisy struts out, confident as you like, and winks at him. No kidding.

"Aren't you in trouble?"

She shrugs and flops down in the chair beside him. "Meh."

"Won't your par—" No dad, he remembers, and stops himself. "Won't your mum be mad at you?"

"She'll go apeshit."

"Don't you mind?"

Her jaw drops open. "Er … no. She's, like, such a fun sponge."

"But didn't Swanny punish you?"

"Not really. I got a lecture, though." She lowers her voice and looks down her nose. "*How do you feel about corrupting a straight-A student with an impeccable school record?*"

"Swanny said that?"

"I know, like really weird or what?"

"What did you say?"

"Pretty damn good actually."

"No way."

"Duh! I told him I had no idea. He didn't believe me, though, and tried again. *Do you feel guilty?*"

"And?"

"I wanted to say it was a laugh, because it was. A really

good laugh. But judging by his expression, I decided the time had come to, like, stray slightly from the truth. So I compromised and said, not really."

She's fearless, he thinks. Or reckless. Or both.

"It *was* fun, wasn't it?" she asks.

He slumps forward and rests his chin on his hands. At the time he thought so. He'd got one hell of a rush from the smoky strawberry kiss. But is the fallout worth the crime? "Oh yeah. Sure."

"God, Dylan. You can't be a nerd all your life."

"Thanks a bunch. I'm in a whole heap of trouble. My parents are going to go nuts."

"Forget the fricking 'rents." She crosses her legs and leans back. "Dad told me you only get one go. Make the most of it, he said."

"I'll bet he didn't mean get caught smoking."

"God, Dylan. Chill. I was beginning to think you had more guts. But hey, I guess my first impression was right after all."

"Oh really? And what was that?"

She swivels in her chair, turning her back to him. "Never mind."

He grabs her arm and pulls her round to face him. "I do mind. I mind a lot."

She tries to shake him off.

"So who's being brave now?" he jeers.

She leaps to her feet, eyes flashing. "Okay. Fine. You want the truth. You're a loser. That's what I thought when I first saw you." She holds her forefinger and thumb to her forehead in an L shape.

He frowns and clenches his teeth, the muscle in his jaw working overtime. She doesn't know what she's talking about. She's got him wrong. He wants to scream at her, but he can't find the words. Can't think what to say. How can he when a part of him thinks what she says is true?

He's huddled in the corner of the Panda, out of the direct line of fire, listening to his mother's rant. Not for the first time he wishes he had a younger brother or sister, or better still, three or four of each to share the load, because no matter what he does, good or bad, he's always the centre of his mother's attention. It was great when he was young, but he hates it now. He hates the expectation. It's tough having to be brilliant at everything. Unrealistic. But she's determined he'll be one of life's achievers and will stop at nothing until he is. Nothing. She's even arranged for him to take elocution lessons after school. She says they'll give him the edge over his tongue-tied contemporaries when he's interviewed at Oxford or for a job in the city. Those were her exact words. It's, like, totally nuts! He hasn't even passed Common Entrance yet.

"I blame you."

It's the first time his dad has spoken. The words directed at his mother. It's not what Dylan is expecting. His mother neither.

"Me. Why?"

"You know why." The raised blue vein on his dad's neck throbs angrily.

"It might have escaped your notice, but I wasn't the one caught smoking."

"For fuck's sake, woman, shut up."

His mother gasps. "Don't speak to me like that."

Dylan cringes and slides further down in the seat.

"When will you get it into your pretty little head that the reason this happened is because you push him too hard." His dad takes his eyes off the road for a moment to glare at his mother. When he looks back, he has to turn the wheel aggressively to avoid crashing into a car.

Dylan's heart leaps into his throat.

His mother slaps the dashboard. "I do not."

"Yes, you do. All this extra coaching you're making him have after school – maths, Latin, English. You even had the cheek to challenge Anthony Swann about the punishment. He's the headmaster, for heaven's sake. He makes the rules. The children adhere to them. That's life. But not you. Oh no."

"He was caught smoking," she says, her voice cracking. "He's no longer head boy."

"Fuck knows it's not a competition. Why, Jemma? Is it for him? Or is it for you? For the envied looks and praise you get from the other parents? And now it's backfired. Frankly, I'm not surprised. It was only a matter of time before Dylan rebelled."

Dylan holds up his hand. "I *am* here, you know."

"You haven't got a clue, have you?"

Her voice is ugly and shrill. Dylan wants to cover his ears with his hands, but he doesn't dare. He's in far too much trouble already.

"After everything we've been through, I thought you of all people would understand how tough it is out there, even for the straight-A students. You've read about the graduates with 2:1s struggling to find jobs. But then why would you? You're never around."

His father bangs the steering wheel with the heels of his hands. "Oh, here we go. The blame game."

Dylan hates it when they fight. Really loathes it. But these days they seem to be fighting all the time, tearing strips off each other like demented dogs.

"We've been through this a hundred times. You wanted to

educate Dylan privately, and to do that I have to work fu … really hard to fund our lifestyle."

"You lost your job."

"Yes, I lost my job. So did hundreds of other people. But now I have a new one."

"We lost our house, our cars."

"Shit happens."

Dylan can't bear it anymore. "SHUT UP. PLEASE SHUT UP."

His parents stop shouting but the silence that greets him is deafening.

"You really screwed up, Dylan," his dad says eventually.

Dylan stares at his knees. "Yeah, I know, and I'm sorry."

"I don't want you to have anything more to do with that Truman girl," his mother says. "She didn't even look sorry."

"Oh, for goodness sake, stop blaming other people. Dylan's trying to take responsibility here."

Dylan leans forward and puts his hand on his mother's shoulder. "Dad's right, Mum. It was my fault. I could have said no."

He's not entirely sure why he's leapt to Daisy's defence other than, now he's thinking about it, she was right. It had been kind of fun. He's never experienced that kind of buzz before. There's more to life than winning prizes.

His dad cranes his neck and smiles. "Well done, son. It's not easy admitting you made a mistake. I'm proud of you. And so is Mum."

His mother stretches her arm through the gap between the seats and pats his knee. "Yes, I am. I'm sorry, Dylan. I didn't mean to upset you. You've been punished enough already."

"Did you like it?" asks his dad.

Dylan starts.

"God, Robert. What kind of a question is that?"

"Just curious. We wouldn't want him getting a habit, now would we?"

The cigarette. He means the cigarette. "No. I didn't. It made me gag."

"Right. That's good," he says, with just a hint of disappointment.

17

I'm mulling over my brief encounter with Gabriel as I drive to school. Apologetic, but clearly agitated, he'd stood in my cluttered kitchen and tried to explain his daughter.

"She probably hasn't eaten all day."

All day? All week more like. "She's very thin."

He frowned and ran his hand through his dark-blond hair. "Since Stephanie – my wife – died, I've been preoccupied with work. I should have realised how much harder it was for Ella. No matter what happens, she'll be without a mother for the rest of her life."

I felt the familiar iron grip on my heart. "I know how difficult it is bringing up children on your own."

His eyes settled on mine. Almost-black irises, fringed by long feminine lashes, totally at odds with the macho cleft in his chin. Blond hair, brown eyes – the true definition of beauty, according to my biology teacher I seem to remember.

The phone rang. Anthony Swann wanted to see me. It was clear from the tone of his voice he was angry.

"Trouble?" Gabriel asked when I put down the phone.

"Daisy," I said by way of explanation. "I'm sorry but I've got to go."

I'm annoyed for two reasons. First of all, this is the second time in three months I've been summoned to a head-master's office for a consultation about my daughter's behaviour. Secondly, Daisy, the offender, gets to sit outside while I take the rap. Now that is grossly unfair.

Anthony Swann is on the phone and has his back to me when I enter his office. The airy room is flawlessly tidy, not a paperclip out of place. A couple of distressed brown leather sofas and two chairs are artfully arranged around a low glass coffee table in front of the towering, sash windows. On the black leather surface of the antique walnut desk to the left, is a pad of lined paper and a pen. With journalistic dexterity, I make out the inverted headline: *The Adverse Effects of Competitive Parenting.*

I'll look forward to reading that.

"Much appreciated, Tom." He puts down the phone and turns around. "Thank you for coming, Ms Moreau. Please, sit down."

He motions to the stiff-backed chair opposite his desk, not the armchairs where we sat in October. I perch stiffly on its edge, a throwback to my boarding school days and too many hours spent explaining my behaviour to the puritanical Miss Barclay. The atmosphere is very different from our first meeting, before Daisy had made her presence felt: not strained exactly, but formal.

Well, I did warn you, Anthony, I think defensively.

"I haven't suspended Daisy because I believe such drastic action could prove counter-productive in the long run. Instead, she'll have to report to me at one-thirty every afternoon for three weeks. Daisy must learn to take responsibility for her actions."

I breathe a silent sigh of relief. "Thank you. I appreciate it."

"It's a shame. She was doing so well."

If Daisy is relieved by the leniency of her punishment, she doesn't show it. She's too busy, during the short car ride home, stealing furtive glances to gauge my reaction. I thought about yelling at her. I certainly screamed the air out of my lungs on the way over. She's far too young to be smoking, but to do it at school, and with Dylan Webster, wasn't very clever. She's expecting fireworks. Perhaps she even hopes for some. But I don't deliver. My mood is one of total calm. It's not that I can't be bothered to be angry. I just can't see the point in having an all-out row.

"Is Dylan upset he's no longer head boy?" I ask.

Daisy's shocked expression says it all.

"You didn't know?"

She jerks sideways to face me, eyes wide. "Why? It wasn't his fault."

"A head boy should set a good example. But, Daisy, he could have said no. Should have said no."

She eyes me suspiciously. "I shouldn't have made him do it. It wasn't fair."

"Life isn't fair. You know that."

"Why are you being so nice?"

"If I told you, you'd probably think I was crazy."

She smiles, for the first time in God knows how long. My heart swells.

"You are crazy. Like, totally bonkers."

"Like mother, like daughter, eh?" I pull up outside the house, cut the engine, and unclip my seat belt.

"Do you think he'll be mad at me?"

She really likes this boy, I realise, as I resist the urge to stroke her hair. "Not if you tell him you're sorry."

Because she is. That much is obvious.

18

Tom's new boots are pinching him, but that's not why he's annoyed. It's Tuesday night, which means he's missing valuable drinking time with his mates down his local. But Anthony Swann needed him for a job. And he never says no to Anthony Swann.

"Tom, I want you to change the light bulb in the room under the stage. It's blown, and Grace needs to dig out some props. Oh, and while you're at it, can you see what's attracting all those flies. It smells like a sewer down there."

"Okay!" No point in arguing with a man like Anthony Swann. Once his mind is set, that's it. He doesn't mess about. That way he gets things done.

Tom sighs and shakes his head. He wouldn't mind, he likes Anthony Swann, but Tuesdays are sacred, the highlight of his banal life since his wife of thirty-seven years passed away. Tuesday means Quiz Night at the Sloop Inn. There'd be a pint of Harvey's waiting on the bar with his name on it but, after this, he still has to stop by his place and let Lady out.

Tom taps in the code, unlocks the theatre door, and is hit

by a blast of putrid air. He flicks on the light. Half a dozen flies buzz around him. He bats them away and marches down the centre aisle, the smell worsening the nearer he gets to the stage.

I'll bet my warm beer there's some quarry rotting away. It'll be that arrogant ginger moggy what's brought it in, I shouldn't wonder.

He climbs the steps and scuttles crab-like through the narrow wings backstage, taking care to avoid a fusty old trunk, a rickety desk, and some chairs. He thinks about opening the trap door but decides it'll be a whole lot easier to take the stairs. He pulls the large bunch of keys out of his pocket and works his way through the labels until he finds the right one, a laborious process which does little to improve his mood. Lady will be hungry, not to mention desperate for a piss.

He turns the key, opens the door, and a swarm of flies engulf him. He swipes at them, gagging at the overpowering stench of rotting meat. It must be something pretty big. A rabbit, possibly, or a rat.

He covers his nose with his handkerchief, bounds down the stairs, ducking to avoid the low ceiling in the dark, damp cavity. "Where's the sodding light switch," he grumbles, turning on the torch. His resentment growing as the seconds tick by, he finds it and tries it, just in case.

Nothing.

"I'm not going to change the bloody bulb until I've got rid of this God-awful smell." Breathing heavily into his handkerchief, he swings the beam, scything an arc through the darkness across a large, tartan bundle beneath the trapdoor. A heap of rugs perhaps? He shines the torch into the corners, looking for the carcass.

Nothing.

An eerie sense of foreboding prickles his spine but, desperate to be shot of the place, he trains his light on the mound and inches towards it. Still clasping his handkerchief over his nostrils, he places the torch on the floor, crouches beside it, and peels back the rug.

A sightless blue eye stares out of a fleshless face pulsating with maggots, its lipless smile locked in a toothy grin. Tom gasps, springs up, and backs out of the room, retching into his handkerchief.

But it isn't until he's outside on the asphalt that he doubles over and throws up over his brand-new boots.

19

T he news that a body has been found in a local prep school broke yesterday. A crime scene swarming with SOCO, guarded by police and door-stepped by the national media, St Peter's has closed for Christmas a week early. The twins are not only delighted but appear remarkably unaffected by it all.

Michael Parton, an old friend of mine from the BBC, has been sent to Easthaven to cover the story and has stopped by to say hello.

"Eric gave me your phone number," he explains when I answer the door.

I laugh. "I bet he did."

I lead him into the messy kitchen and am impressed when he doesn't bat an eyelid.

"The police reckon the woman's body had been there at least three weeks. It couldn't be formally identified because it was badly decomposed, black, bloated, and stinking to high heaven," he says, clearing a space at the table. "But forensics has matched the DNA of a strand of her hair to one taken from her hairbrush."

What he's telling me is horrific, but his enthusiasm for his job is infectious, and I can't help but smile. "I see you've got your finger well and truly on the pulse."

He grins. "Thank you, Megan. Where are the twins? I was hoping to meet them."

"It's eight o'clock in the morning and there's no school, Michael. They're asleep."

"Right!"

I hand him a cup of coffee. "So is it the missing Polish girl, Natalia Topolska?"

"'Fraid so. DCI Marshall, the SIO, is going to make an announcement on the one o'clock news."

I shudder. I couldn't claim to know Natalia, but from the brief chat we'd had it was obvious she'd embraced life. Dead at twenty-three. What a waste. "Have they any idea of the motive?"

"Not yet. They know she was killed in the staffroom, strangled with a heavy-duty piece of costume jewellery, apparently, after being hit on the head with a chair. The killer moved her body to the theatre in the X-cart she used," he says, at once answering the question on every parent's lips.

"Really? How on earth do you know all this?"

He taps his nose. "Friends in high places. The bodily fluid forensics Identified inside the cart matched the DNA of the remnants of a urine stain found in the staffroom."

"So an inside job?"

"Not necessarily, but it looks like it. The staffroom wasn't broken into, so either the killer had access to a swipe card and Natalia disturbed him, or she'd propped the door open and he ambushed her while she was cleaning. The killer clearly knew the layout of the school and the code to unlock the theatre, because that door hadn't been forced either. Word has it DCI Marshall is keen to talk to Fernanda Pinto and Lana

Rodrigues, two other employees of A. L Bright's, who failed to show up for work the Monday Natalia was reported missing because they'd flown to Spain. They're either guilty as hell or were running scared. Marshall's considered to be a bit of a stickler for detail. He wants the entire staff, teaching, maintenance, catering, fingerprinted."

"Wow! It's not what you expect in a town like Easthaven."

"Actually, a couple of years ago there were a spate of murders in Adlington, a sleepy little downland village about eight miles inland. Danny Marshall was the SIO on that case, too."

"I vaguely remember reading about it. Could there be a connection?"

"Definitely not. The Adlington killer was shot by armed police. How are you settling in? Do you like it here?"

It's freezing outside. Proper Christmas cold. Nothing like the mild winter the meteorological office predicted back in sunny October. The snow that fell on Wednesday has frozen solid and, because the council was unprepared, the lack of grit means the waterlogged roads have an icy veneer. Driving is lethal. A smattering of cars and lorries lie upturned and abandoned on the roadsides. The buses aren't running, the railway network has staggered to a halt, and yet the supermarket has never been so full. I wrestle my way through the jam-packed aisles, lugging my wire basket, heavy with cans of Fosters and two bottles of Jack Daniels. Christmas is ten days away, and Glen is on his sleigh.

"Santa wouldn't turn his nose up at my Landy. It can get through anything. I'll be there," he assured me.

"Are you sure you can be bothered?"

He chuckles. "I haven't been this excited since the Wallabies beat the Poms at Twickenham last month."

I can't understand Glen's enthusiasm for Leo's party. A rugged, straight-talking Aussie, he'll stick out like a dog's balls, to coin one of his favourite sayings. That is if we actually make it. Leo lives in the country. Not as far out as Samantha but far enough off the beaten track to make driving there tricky.

She called me this morning to check if me and Glen were still planning on coming.

"Of course."

"But he's travelling down from London."

"He's Australian."

"I know," she replied huskily.

God help her if she's expecting Hugh Jackman, I think, and take my place in the checkout queue behind a large woman with two screaming kids and the biggest trolley of shopping I've ever seen. I place my basket on the floor and resign myself to a long wait. Not that I'm in any hurry. Margaret is keeping a watchful eye over the twins.

I drive home tuned in to Radio Four. It's been ten days since the school was closed and nine days since the body was formally identified as Natalia Topolska. As has been the case every day this week, the Easthaven murder is the lead story.

"DCI Danny Marshall of Sussex CID has confirmed the case is now a murder enquiry. He is keen to talk to anyone who saw Natalia arrive at St Peter's on Saturday evening at 7p.m. She was working out of hours having taken on an extra job, so was not expected to be in the school at that time.

"The heinous crime has stunned the community of this

pretty coastal town. Leonora Carter, mother of three St Peter's pupils, told me how horrified she'd been that her eldest child was rehearsing for next term's musical on a stage that concealed a rotting corpse."

I shudder, not at Michael's words but at the danger our children might have been in.

"If anybody has any information as to their whereabouts, please call Sussex Police."

The sumptuous smell of cinnamon and nutmeg greets me as I walk into the hallway, decked out with holly and mistletoe and bows of fir. Since school broke up, Daisy and Josh have turned hyper with festive anticipation. Despite my reservations about a Guy-less Christmas, their euphoria, though exhausting, has kept his ghost at bay. I hurry into the kitchen where the twins are marvelling at the dark square of Christmas cake they've just taken out of the oven. Josh is prodding it with a skewer, while Daisy issues orders. Her cheeks are pink, her striped apron covered in flour. It's like an image from a lovely dream, and I want to pinch myself. But when Daisy sees me and scowls, there's no need.

"We're going to feed it with brandy and, in a couple of days, cover it in marzipan and icing," Josh tells me proudly. "Margaret has given us three snowmen to put on top. Do you think Granny will like it?"

"She'll love it." I put down the bags and give him a hug.

When I release him, Daisy is holding up her hands. "Whoa. Chillax."

After a thousand rejections, I've learnt not to force things. Instead, I turn to Margaret. "Do you fancy a coffee and a quick chat? It was madness in Tesco, and I need some time to recover before Glen arrives."

Her eyebrows flex. "Glen?"

"Her cameraman," chorus the twins.

She smiles. "I'd love one."

Glen hasn't seen my children since they were babies, not in the flesh anyway. He's seen them grow from tiny babies to the teenagers they are now in photographic form. Daisy and Josh are looking forward to meeting him. He's played the hero in most of the stories I've recounted over the years. An Indiana Jones character, unshaven and dishevelled, he doesn't disappoint: ancient mildewed holdall, ripped waterproof jacket, scuffed boots, and a weathered Akubra on his head. He looks like he's trekked across the Nullarbor not driven down from London.

"Great place you got here." He drops the holdall, wraps his arms around me, and lifts me off the floor. "Tatty chic."

"I think you'll find it's shabby."

"Oh, I wouldn't go that far." He puts me down and eyes up the twins. "Hello, Buttercup."

Daisy frowns and backs away.

Undeterred, Glen holds out his hand. "And you must be Josh."

"Have you just got back from Afghanistan?" my son asks politely, shaking his hand.

"The Congo, actually."

Daisy screws up her nose. "You should have had a bath."

"Daisy!"

"Well, he called me Buttercup!"

Glen throws back his head and laughs loudly, which startles Daisy.

"How about a cup of tea and a bacon sandwich?" I say quickly and usher them all into the kitchen.

It's been ages since I've seen a familiar face, let alone a friend as old and reliable as Glen. I reckon I know every line and freckle on his ugly mug. I've been looking forward to his visit, but seeing him again has resurrected painful memories. Down here there are no tangible memories of Guy and our old life, just a few photographs. My eyes prickle, and for an awful moment I'm certain I'm going to cry.

If Glen notices, he doesn't let on. His attention for the time being is focused on Daisy and Josh who are telling him about the murder at their school.

"The smell really grossed me out," Daisy says once we're gathered around the table. "And there were, like, loads of flies."

I'm not surprised. I've seen enough corpses to understand the process. Natalia had been dead so long the bacteria in her gut had started breaking down her body, creating the gaseous smell and causing her body to bloat, her organs to swell.

A born entertainer, Glen's lavatorial humour is completely in tune with the mind of the average teenager, and it isn't long before he's recounting the time he set fire to one of his farts while camping in the Outback.

"I ended up burning the hairs off my arse."

The twins laugh uproariously, much to Glen's satisfaction.

He has a child of his own back in Australia, the product of a seven-year relationship with a woman I know only as Dawn. She walked out on Glen six years ago when Jacamo was two, a subject Glen has always been reluctant to discuss. I flip the crispy bacon from the pan onto thick slices of white buttered bread, and imagine how much he must miss his son, living half a world away.

While we tuck in, Glen steers the conversation onto the weird food he's eaten over the years. He has a hundred anecdotes, all of them revolting, and most of which I've heard. The twins, of course, are riveted.

"I'll never forget the time I got lost in the Bush and was so hungry I had to roast a rat on a stick over a fire."

Daisy screws up her nose. "You got lost in a bush?"

"Not *a* bush *the* Bush, and the rats were the biggest rotten bastards you've ever seen. But they tasted bloody good straight off the barbie."

The kids snigger behind their hands at Glen's colourful vocabulary.

"What's the weirdest food you've ever eaten?" asks Daisy, squeezing a huge dollop of ketchup on her bacon.

"Fish eyes, snakes, and kangaroo and bull's bollocks."

"Enough, Glen! We're eating," I say.

"Have you been to China?" asks Josh.

"Sure. Plenty of times. It's where I met your ma." He winks at me, and I smile.

Josh's eyes widen. "What about dog then?"

"Listen, mate, if it's got four legs and isn't a table, the Chinese will eat it. Or a pulse for that matter. Monkey brains are a great delicacy. I was served the whole bloody head on a plate once, the skull sliced open like a boiled egg so I could scoop the brains out with a spoon."

At six, Glen disappears into the bathroom. The clean-shaven, sweet-smelling figure that emerges, forty-five minutes later, is barely recognisable. His sandy hair is slicked back, his black jeans pristine, his green checked shirt meticulously ironed. I've witnessed this transformation he refers to as regeneration many times, but it never ceases to surprise me.

He holds out his arms and gives me a twirl. "Are the East-haven beauties ready for me?"

"I really hope so," I say, trying to ignore the sudden fluttering of butterflies in my belly. Don't worry, I tell myself. Tonight's conversation will be about Natalia's murder.

He points at my smart jeans/tuxedo jacket combination and pulls a face. "You're going like that?"

I glance down at my clothes. "What's wrong with it?"

"There's nothing wrong with it. It's a perfectly decent jacket, and the jeans are a great fit but, Megs, it doesn't do you justice."

I put my hands on my hips. "Excuse me, Gok Wan?"

But Glen isn't listening. "Do you still have that slinky red number you wore to the Royal Television Society Awards?"

"The year you were nominated for best camera operator?"

"Which I didn't win because I hadn't been shot unlike Alan Jameson, who did. Well? Do you?"

"Er … yes. Probably."

He grins. "Great."

"You can't be serious. That was years ago. I've piled on the pounds since then."

"Try it on," he says, pushing me towards my bedroom.

"I tell you, it won't fit."

"Humour me."

The strapless dress fits like a sheath. I must have lost weight, I think, as I admire my slender self in the mirror. Inspired, I sit at my dressing table and rummage around for some makeup. I find an old tube of tinted moisture and apply it to my face. When I peer at my reflection, the wrinkles and crows' feet that have crept up on me these last few years have almost disappeared. Encouraged, I add a touch of blusher, mascara, eyeliner, and a dab of grey eyeshadow. The effect is dramatic. I look years younger. Carried away now, I trot down the landing into the bathroom and run some of Josh's wax through my hair until it stands out in fluffy peaks.

"Wow," says Glen when I join him in the hall. "You look hot."

Daisy is in the living room, bouncing excitedly on the couch as she waits for *The X-Factor* final to start, and Margaret and Josh are heating up pizzas in the kitchen, so our shouts of goodbye go unheard. A big Jim Carey fan, Josh insisted I rent the *Yes Man* DVD for them to watch after-wards. It seemed a fair deal.

"How old is Margaret?" Glen asks, catching sight of the case on our way out.

"Early sixties at a guess. Why?"

He holds open the door of the ancient Land Rover. "There's a geriatric sex scene in that film which sent my skin crawling off my bones."

I slap my forehead. "Oh God."

Glen laughs. "Jeez, it's good to see you, Megs." He gives my bottom a friendly pat. "Great arse, girl."

I aim a kick at his chest. "Get off."

Chuckling, he dodges my foot, shuts the door, jumps in beside me, and fires the ignition. "Second thoughts, you'd better lock that door. It rattled so much on the way down I'm amazed it didn't fall off."

I throw him a meaningful look. "Should we go in my car?"

He grins. "Nah. The roads are shocking. And this is way more fun."

I laugh. "It's good to see you, too, Glen.

"Seems I was wrong about Easthaven. Thought it would be a bit dull, but what with the body under the stage, seems you've got plenty to occupy you."

"Don't be flippant. It doesn't suit you."

"Doesn't seem to have affected the twins. They're on great form."

The antiquated Land Rover is freezing, and I draw my wool coat tight around me. "Daisy was caught smoking the same night the body was found. It sounds awful, but the holidays couldn't have come at a better time. I wouldn't have minded quite as much if she hadn't persuaded Dylan Webster to join her. He *was* the head boy, before they were caught."

"Nice one, Daisy. So what will you do with the kids next term?"

"St Peter's will be open by then."

"You think?"

I haven't thought that far ahead but I don't want to admit that to Glen. "Shut up and drive."

Without a satnav or a GPS, we do things the old-fashioned way. I'm pretty good at reading maps, but it's dark and there's no light in the Land Rover, and we miss the drive at least three times. By the time we arrive, ice has formed on the inside of the windscreen, my feet are glacial, and my sense of humour is fading fast.

Glen pulls up beside a pale blue Panda, one in a long line of cars parked outside the quaint little cottage. "From the way you've been describing these people, I was expecting a fucking great mansion."

I prise open the door, and get out awkwardly. "Leo's husband is a doctor."

"So?"

"She doesn't work, and they educate three children at private schools."

"Ah. I get it. Posh but poor."

I blow on my hands and totter across the gravel in my high heels. Nobody answers the front door, so we follow the path round to the side and enter the house via the utility room. The black Labrador, asleep in its basket, lifts its head and wags its tail, unleashing a powerful doggy smell. I notice a pile of wellies, waxed jackets hanging from large iron hooks, and a chest freezer whirring contentedly at the far end. We shed our coats and make our way through another door into the kitchen. It's heaving with bodies and condensation dribbles down the leaded windows. Having frozen half to death on the way over, I'm soon uncomfortably hot.

We inch our way through to the narrow, low-ceilinged hallway in search of our hostess, and into the living room – a sea of beige, black, and brown dresses. I squirm self-consciously, but fortunately, Mark Carter spies us. He gesticulates to the bottle he's holding and mouths something that looks like *glasses*.

Glen grabs my arm. "Look. It's Pablo Pino Ortiz! Thought he was banged up in a Colombian jail."

I start. "What? Where?"

He jerks his head and speaks through clenched teeth. "Over there."

I glance surreptitiously at a man with almost-black hair, dark eyes, and a jutting jaw, and gasp. Glen's right. He's a dead ringer for the leader of a drugs cartel we had the misfortune to meet in a Colombian jail.

"Sadistic bastard," mutters Glen. "You remember the state of Lucia's body?"

I'll never forget the butchered corpse of the teenage girl the police showed us after they'd arrested Ortiz and twenty-eight members of one of Colombia's largest drug rings. Like all the other girls he enticed with vast quantities of cash, Lucia was educated and pretty and carrying half a kilo of cocaine in her stomach stuffed in condoms she'd swallowed. She was met by a trafficker and taken to a hotel to wait until she'd passed the drugs. But one of the condoms burst, and she died an agonising death. Cut-throat pig that he was, Ortiz sliced open her corpse, removed the remaining drugs, and left.

"That's Robert Webster, Dylan's father," says Mark, approaching from behind. "Champagne." He hands me a glass.

"He looks like someone we once knew," I explain sheepishly. "Meet Glen, an old friend of mine."

"Ah yes." He offers Glen the other glass. "The Australian."

"Thanks, mate, but I'm not a fan of the foaming cleanser."

"Champagne," I say.

Mark smiles. "I'll get you a beer."

"Thanks, mate, I'm as dry as a fuck with no foreplay."

I roll my eyes, but Mark laughs. "No problem. Oli's in charge of the beer. I'll go and stir him into action."

"Your language is a little fruity for this gathering," I whisper as Mark heads off in the direction of the kitchen.

Glen clicks his tongue. "Gotcha!"

"Megan Moreau?"

I look into the obsidian eyes of Pablo Pino Ortiz and jump.

"Robert Webster." He holds out his hand. "Bit of a fan, actually. Love what you do."

"Did," I correct him, ignoring the amused noises emanating from Glen. "I've retired."

"Can you give something like that up? I imagine it's in the blood."

Glen thrusts out his hand. "Time will tell. Glen Chambers. Please to meet you."

Robert flashes a set of white teeth then turns back to me. "Your daughter has made quite an impression on my son."

At the mention of my daughter, my palms turn hot and clammy.

"Easthaven must be a real culture shock," he continues, oblivious to my discomfort. "Suffers from small-town syndrome. Everyone knows what everyone else is doing. And if they don't, they make it up."

Glen winks. "Speaking from experience, eh, Bob?"

"It's a completely child-centric society," he adds, ignoring Glen. "A St Peter's mother's world revolves around her children."

Glen tuts. "Sounds like a man wanting to pack up and move out."

"Your beer, sir," says Mark.

"Thanks, mate."

Leo trots over, dressed in a revealing, low-cut black dress, her hair curled, her cheeks flushed. Miss Piggy, I think ungraciously as Mark plants a kiss on her lips.

"Pablo fancies the pants off you," Glen whispers in my ear.

"I doubt that," I reply behind my hand. "He's married to a phenomenally beautiful woman."

He grins lasciviously and scans the room. "Really?"

"Behave!"

"Hi, Megan," says Leo, staring wide-eyed at Glen. "I'm so glad you could make it."

Mark slaps Glen good-humouredly on the back. "My wife's got this thing about Australians."

Glen lowers his head in a reverential bow, reaches for Leo's porcine hand, and kisses it.

Mark laughs uproariously, and I smile. Despite my reservations, I have to hand it to Glen. I'm proud of him and feel far more at ease than when I went it alone at Samantha's last month.

"Has Megan told you about the murder?" Leo asks. "We're all terribly shocked—"

But I don't hear the rest because Robert has leaned worryingly close and is resting his hand on my bare arm. "Mmm. You look fantastic and you smell terrific. Dance with me later."

He melts into the crowd and an unpleasant shiver runs down my spine.

"Is Jemma here tonight?" I ask Leo, interrupting the animated conversation she's having with Glen. I haven't seen her since the Friday morning she left early to visit the doctor.

She turns to me, eyes sparkling. "Nope."

"Oh dear, is she ill?"

"She's stressed."

My heart sinks.

"I mean, we all are, aren't we? Any one of our children could have been killed, but here we all are, putting a brave face on things."

She hasn't told Leo it was Daisy who got Dylan into trouble, I realise, relieved.

"Hello, Megan. You look fantastic. I absolutely love your dress."

I turn to see Samantha, smiling toothily. "Thank you. So do you."

"We've got the tits and the teeth, now all we need is the hair," mutters Glen in my ear.

"You must be Glen." Samantha performs her ritual brushing of the cheeks, which Glen doesn't quite get the hang of and he's left kissing thin air.

Samantha reverts her attention to me. "Where did you get that dress? It really is stunning."

"Vintage designer?" asks Leo.

I open my mouth, but Glen beats me to it. "Dolce and Gabbana."

Samantha's eyes widen. "Really?"

Glen nods. "Oh yes! Yours is lovely, too, Sam. Designer?"

She's wearing a mink jersey dress with a ring of sequins at the neck. It's unusually simple and low-key for Samantha, and although I know nothing about fashion, it's clearly *not* designer. I throw him a disapproving look.

"Gosh, no." She laughs and covers her mouth with her hand. "It's Boden."

Glen cocks an eyebrow. "Boden. Really?"

"You're both gorgeous, as always," I say hurriedly before he lands his size tens in it.

"Fancy a dance, Glen?" Without waiting for an answer, Leo puts her hands on his back and pushes him towards the music.

I follow them into an empty room, lit by fairy lights, and stand in the corner while Glen spins Leo around the wooden floor, her arms aloft, head thrown back. Guests join them, but none of them dance quite as hectically, and I'm not surprised when, after ten minutes, Leo staggers over to me. Beads of sweat are visible just below her hairline, and she is puffing heavily.

She fans her face. "Wow!"

The next song on the iPod has me shaking. It's *our* song, I say out loud as if it's Guy beside me, not Glen. Glen takes my wrist and gently eases me towards him. The pain of loss engulfs me and I lean into his chest and listen to Elvis singing 'Love me Tender'.

My nerves are still zinging when, searching out a forti-fying drink, we bump into Charlie Young emerging from the cloakroom followed by the well-endowed blonde. He smiles without a hint of embarrassment. The blonde, however, blushes and drifts away.

"Well, if it isn't our very own Martha Gellhorn." He nods at Glen. "Are you going to introduce me?"

His patronising tone grates. "Glen Chambers."

Glen grabs his hand and gives it an earthy shake. "G'day, mate."

Charlie emits a short, sharp laugh. "Marvellous. Your very own Crocodile Dundee. I'm surprised to see you here. I thought a newshound of your calibre would be staking out the school, trying to solve the crime."

I'm seething but I refuse to rise to the bait. "This is Charlie Young. You just met his wife, Samantha. He's a banker."

Charlie smiles his smug, city smile.

Glen clears his throat. A touch pompously, I think. "Tell me something, Chas. If you're in the bath and you wanna take a piss, do you get out?"

Shocked, I steal a glance at Glen, but he's not smiling.

Charlie's narrowed left eye flickers. "What kind of a question is that?"

"Trying to figure out if you're a gentleman, but seeing how you aren't prepared to answer, I take it you're not. Happy Christmas, mate."

Charlie Young's face as we walk away is a picture.

I reach for Glen's hand and give it a squeeze. "Oh boy. You're good."

Glen and I laugh all the way home, which helps keep us warm in the freezing Land Rover. Once we're done trashing Charlie and his mistress, we move on to the silken charm of Robert 'Pablo Pino Ortiz' Webster.

"A short man with a politician's arrogance. Bet he's hung like a bell tower," says Glen. "Cocky in more ways than one."

I'm still giggling as we walk through the door into the warm house.

"Sounds like you had a good time," says Margaret.

"Yeah, we did. Did the children behave?"

She feigns surprise. "Of course."

Glen, the committed drinker, is a *little thirsty* having consumed a paltry three bottles of beer all evening. I direct him to the living room, say goodbye to Margaret, then dig out the Jack Daniels and a couple of tumblers from the kitchen. By the time I come back he's removed his boots and has stretched out his muscular frame on the burgundy couch.

"Posh room, Megs."

I half fill the glasses and hand him one.

He gulps it down and holds out his tumbler. "Let's make a night of it."

I fill it and groan. "I'm not young anymore and I'm already pissed."

"Stop writing yourself off. You're doing fine."

I sink down beside him, wrap my arms around his leg, and rest my chin on his knee. "Yeah, right."

"After tonight, men'll be queuing up."

I poke him in the ribs. "They're all married. And the only one who isn't thinks I dress like a man."

"The Colombian drugs dealer was salivating over you."

I pick up a cushion and thwack him in the chest.

Glen grabs it and puts it behind his head. "Ah ha. You noticed."

"He was probably drunk."

"A little tip for you, Megs. He might have been drunk but he meant whatever it was he said."

"He said he wanted a dance."

"I'll bet he did. That's a euphemism for f—"

I press a finger to his lips, reach for the bottle, and top up our drinks. "Thanks for getting me through tonight. I'd have made a prize idiot of myself if you hadn't been there."

He ruffles up my hair. "You'd have done fine, my tough little Megs."

"I don't feel all that tough."

"That's because you've got a soft centre. Best way to be."

I let out an exhausted sigh and, a little drunk now, snuggle up to him. "I wish Daisy could see that."

"She seems fairly chilled."

"Oh yes, cool as a cucumber, my daughter. To me anyway. She hates me."

"It may seem like that, but deep down she loves you. You know that."

"She and Guy were close. She adored him. No matter how hard I try, I can't fill the void."

"Maybe you're trying too hard. Give her time. She's hurting, too."

It's been ages since I've been this close to a man and, now I am, I realise how much I've missed the physical contact. I undo a couple of buttons of Glen's shirt, slip my hand inside, and run it over his coarse chest hair. Sighing, I rest my head on his ribcage and breathe in his comforting masculine smell. Nothing like Guy's but almost as familiar.

The sound of the sitting room door slamming shut has me leaping to my feet, and Glen sits up with a start. I sprint past the empty bottle of Jack Daniels, lying on its side on the floor, open the door and rush into the hall. Daisy is already halfway up the stairs. I'm horribly hungover. My mouth is lined with fur, and my head is throbbing violently, but I chase her onto the landing and grab hold of her. She wriggles, fighting like a fish to free herself.

"Get off. Let go of me."

"Listen to me. It's not what you think."

"LET GO OF ME. YOU'RE DISGUSTING."

"We fell asleep. That's all."

"Don't lie to me."

"It's the truth." Glen is at the foot of the stairs. The top four buttons of his shirt are undone, his hairy chest on full display.

"GO AWAY. I DON'T WANT YOU HERE."

Her shrill voice sends a terrifying shiver down my spine. She kicks out at me, connecting with my shins, but still I cling to her. "Listen to me!"

"Let go of me. I hate you." Tears stream down her face as she yanks her slender limbs in all directions.

Josh appears, bleary-eyed and pale, and stares at me beseechingly. "What's going on?"

My heart lurches. I let go of Daisy who shoots past Josh into her room.

"Ask them!" yells Daisy, slamming the door.

I go to hug him, but he steps back.

"You haven't been to bed," he says in a quiet voice

I shake my head. "We were talking late into the night and fell asleep."

He glances from me to Glen and back. "But what about Dad? I thought you loved *him*."

"I did. I do. You know that."

"Course she does, mate."

"But …" Josh gesticulates at Glen, at the undone buttons and hairy chest.

He doesn't need to say anything. I know what he's thinking but I can't seem to find the words to explain.

20

The midnight service is over. Ashley King, the curate, Mary Strong, the organist, and most of the two hundred-strong congregation have gone. Only the St Matthew's stalwarts, Morris and Janice Greening, remain.

"I've never seen the church so full, Gabriel," Janice says. "You've been a rock these past few days, keeping the community's body and soul together."

"Poor girl had been there three weeks. Terrible business. Nothing like that ever happened during the Blitz," says Morris.

Janice sighs. "I won't sleep easy until they catch the man who did it."

"Try not to worry, Mrs Greening,' Gabriel says as he snuffs the candles. "The police are convinced it's an isolated incident."

"Let's hope so." Morris shakes Gabriel's hand, and they step out into the cold. "Merry Christmas to you, Vicar. See you bright and early."

The smile Gabriel has worn all evening like a mask,

doesn't waver until he closes the door behind them. He shuts his eyes and lets out a weary sigh. It could have been worse. *She* could have been there.

He pulls himself together and glances around. Other than locking up the church, there's nothing left to do apart from switching off the heating and the Christmas tree lights. He wanders into the vestry, reaches for his jacket, and heads out the side door. Shoulders hunched, he walks down the path to the vicarage, dragging his guilt behind him. It's been over a month, but he can't seem to shake off the memory of the kiss and the pain he witnessed when he turned Jemma down.

How could I stand there tonight and preach when I've rejected God?

You're human, not a robot, whispers the Devil on his shoulder. *Isn't that what you tell the miserable sinners in your congregation? If you weren't susceptible to temptation, you wouldn't be able to respond to God. Sin is a disease which infects all humans. It binds the lot of you as one.*

I'm a priest. I should know better.

You're as human as the next man. How could you hope to understand the essence of God's goodness if you've never sinned? But don't worry. God is in charge, not you. If *you repent, He* will *forgive you.*

He draws to a halt outside the vicarage, screws up his face, and clutches his hair. "Shut up. Shut the fuck up!"

He shakes his head vigorously, desperate to escape the sneering cynicism. But his belief, the code he's lived by for most of his life, doesn't make sense anymore. It's too trite. Too convenient. Too simple.

I should be punished, he thinks, and unlocks the door.

It's almost one, but the house is still warm from the fire he lit for Margaret. All the same, he wishes Ella had taken up Steffi's parents' offer and spent Christmas with them. She's gone downhill these past couple of weeks. Pale as death, she barely speaks and is worryingly thin. He'd taken her to the doctor but, apart from her dramatic weight loss, Mark couldn't find anything wrong.

He finds Margaret asleep in an armchair by the dying embers of the fire. Her chin is resting on her chest, and she is snoring softly. He appreciates her support, but he's also infuriated by it. Tomorrow she's promised to prepare a wonderful turkey lunch with all the trimmings, although he doubts either he or Ella will have the stomach for it. Sighing, he bends down and gently rouses her.

She jerks awake. Embarrassed, she fusses with her hair. "Oh, you're back. Happy Christmas, Gabriel." She rises slowly and kisses him on the cheek.

He's far from happy, but he nods and wishes her the same. "How was Ella?"

"Better tonight. She ate some supper and chatted a bit before she went to bed. She seems pleased to be at home, which is something."

Her words comfort him. One less thing to worry about.

He walks her to her car and is turning out the lights downstairs when he hears the gurgle of water draining from the bath. Ella must still be awake. He bounds upstairs but, on the landing, all is quiet. He wanders to the bathroom anyway and is reaching for the doorknob when he hears Ella talking in a low monotone.

He remembers the magazines, and his pulse quickens. Has she got someone in there? No. Impossible. Nobody could get past Margaret.

But he presses his ear to the door. Just to make sure.

"And blessed is the fruit of thy womb, Jesus."

He starts in surprise.

"Holy Mary, Mother of God, pray for us sinners now and at the hour of our death."

Frowning, he knocks lightly.

But there's no answer.

His chest pounding, he hammers the door with his fist. "Ella! What are you doing in there?"

Nothing.

He grabs the doorknob, expecting it to be locked, but it swings opens with such force it crashes into the wall.

And then he sees her. Sheathed in a beige towel, she is cowering on the tiles, her wide eyes too large in her pale, gaunt face. Blood trickles down her forearms from a plexus of jagged cuts on her wrists.

His hand flies to his mouth.

There's a clink as something metal falls on the tiles. Like a weapon offered in surrender, the scissors she has used.

21

It's Christmas morning, but Gabriel will take no further part in St Matthew's celebrations this year.

"Take as long as you need," the dean said when he called him at dawn. "Ashley will cover for you. He's more than capable. Ella is your priority now."

Ella finally fell asleep three hours ago. He's still with her, sitting at her desk while he waits for Mark Carter, listening to the quiet rhythm of her breathing. In blissful ignorance of his soul-wrenching pain, Stephanie smiles at him from the safety of her photo frame.

"Why, Steff?" he whispers. "Why harm herself like that?"

He grips his trembling hands tightly until the knuckles shine white. He wants to pray, or rather, thinks he should, but he can't summon up the energy. Instead, he replays the conversation he had with Ella after he cleaned her wounds. He wants to make sense of it, wants to understand the reason behind her actions.

He'd carried her to bed, limp as a rag doll. "Are you unhappy?" he asked as he tucked her in.

He buries his head in his hands. Of course she's unhappy.

You don't slice open your wrists with a pair of scissors if you're full of the joys.

Tears had poured down her cheeks. "What do you care?"

He'd flinched. "I'm your father. I love you."

"No, you don't."

He leant across and rested his hand on her leg, fatherly, comforting. "Popsy, you know I do."

But Ella rolled over and curled herself into a tight little ball. "Yeah, right. That's why you never come home. Why you have time for everyone else but never have time for me. Not even at Christmas. It's not me you love it's your *congregation*!"

She uttered the word with such hatred that even now, as he recalls it, Gabriel shudders. It's true. He has neglected her but not through choice.

"I want to take you to a doctor."

Ella's eyes flashed angrily. "You don't have time."

"That's not fair."

She pulled the duvet over her head. "Go away! Leave me alone."

"Popsy, please, I'm worried about you, but I can't help unless you let me in."

"Go away. And don't call me Popsy. I'm not a baby."

He knew he'd handled it badly, which was why he'd rung Mark. He had to. He wasn't getting anywhere on his own. In fact, he seemed to be making matters worse. Thinking about it now, he realises he's scared. Scared out of his wits as to what she might do next.

The doorbell rings, and he scoots downstairs. "I'm so sorry. I didn't know what else to do."

Mark dismisses the apology with a smile. "It's just another day to me. You of all people should understand that. Where is she?"

. . .

Ella lies on her back, her bandaged arms folded across her chest. The meekness she's showing in surrender surprises Gabriel. But then that's very much part of her character, he reminds himself, unlike the self-harm, which is not.

"There's nothing wrong with feeling upset and isolated. A lot of children feel the same," Mark says, gently. "You mustn't feel ashamed, Ella. When something's troubling you, it's okay to share it. We all do that. We all share our problems."

"Like Dad talks to God, you mean?"

Her voice, heavy with sarcasm, is like a knife to his heart.

"What did God ever do for us apart from take Mum away?"

Gabriel pounces. He can't help himself. "Is that what this is about? Are you angry with God?"

Mark holds a cautionary finger to his lips. "I know you miss your mother. I can only imagine how awful these last two years have been without her, but your dad is here for you. He's been very busy lately and he realises he should have spent more time with you. And that's what he intends to do now. He needs you, too, Ella."

There's a long silence.

"Okay." Her voice is little more than a whisper, but Gabriel's heart lifts.

"Good girl," says Mark. "I'm going to give you some advice on what to do if there's no one around to talk to when you next feel the urge to self-harm. Okay with you?"

She nods.

"You could try counting backwards from ten. It helps bring the mind to attention and should give you time to think if it's what you really want to do. Or you could mark your arm with a red pen or rub ice on your wrist. But the best thing you can do is talk. To your dad, a friend, your teachers."

Ella nods again.

"Good. Right, I'll call in tomorrow to see how you are."

Gabriel is impressed. Mark has handled the situation with ease. "I don't understand it. She's such a sensible child," he says when they're out of earshot.

"It makes no difference. Roughly twenty-four thousand teenagers in this country are treated in hospital for self-harm, but thousands more go untreated."

"But why? Why would you hurt yourself like that?" Gabriel winces, recalling the dripping blood. She could have bled to death.

"It's their way of coping, relieving the tension of whatever it is that's worrying them when things get too much. Screaming without words, if you like. The physical pain makes them forget the mental pain for a while. It's the only thing they can control in a life that feels out of control. An addiction."

Gabriel shakes his head and tries to assimilate the information. Mark is talking about the child he loves. The child whose pain he's been ignorant of.

"It's best to keep her life as normal as possible. I'll drop by tomorrow and again next week, to keep an eye on things. I was surprised at how clean the wounds were. She's been looking after them. Some girls contract horrible infections because they don't wash their wounds, or because they use the same razor again and again. It's a contradiction, I know, but she's a bright girl."

Gabriel raises his eyebrows. The irony isn't lost on him.

"I suggest you go to your local chemist and buy some vitamin E cream. It can help reduce the appearance of scars."

Gabriel rubs the back of his neck with his hand. "She'll be scarred for life?"

"Not necessarily. The wounds aren't particularly deep. She's young, and the skin heals quicker, but this isn't the first time she's cut herself. Some of the scars are about five, maybe six weeks old."

"I had no idea."

"You wouldn't. I didn't spot them either. That's the point. She's gone out of her way to keep them covered."

He shivers. "Tell me she won't try and kill herself."

Mark shakes his head. "I can't. Although self-harm is a bizarre form of self-preservation, a recent study found there's a thirty-fold increase in suicide risk."

Gabriel clasps his head and leans against the wall.

"But while she's self-harming, she is, in a strange way, coping."

"Really?"

"The good news is we now know and can, therefore, try and manage it. The problem could have become far more serious if you hadn't found out."

"That doesn't bear thinking about."

"You must inform her teachers. And Margaret. That way we can all protect her. And try and find the cause. We need to know why she's doing it. Once we do, we can address the problem."

"What if she doesn't stop?"

"Then I'll refer her to a psychotherapist."

He stares out the kitchen window at the clouded sky. Oh God. What are you doing to us? First you take Stephanie and now Ella.

Outwardly, Ella seems to have recovered. Her cuts have healed, and she is talking again. Margaret tells him she's pleased to have her father to herself. Is that all it was? No matter how much he wishes it, deep down he doubts it's true.

His nights are sleepless, his mind overrun with worry – Ella, God, Jemma – his days busy, filled with activity to keep Ella occupied. They spend the days between Christmas and New Year eating out, watching films, shopping in the asphyxiating crush of the Primark sale. He shadows Ella round the store, galled by the child labour involved in producing such cheap clothes. Someone should put a stop to it, he thinks. But watching her study each garment with such obvious excitement, he shoves the issue to the back of his mind.

The days wear on. Ella's cheeks regain their healthy glow, and her smile returns. Yesterday she even laughed when he told her one of Ash's jokes. He's enjoying her company, feels as though he's making up for lost time. He's proud of himself. But then he remembers how long it's taken him, and his body buckles with shame.

You asked to be punished, the Devil goads. *Be careful what you wish for*.

And so he shies away from God.

Margaret supports him. She's pleased with everything he does. It keeps him buoyed and spurs him on.

"And you're talking to her?" she asks.

"All the time. She's really opening up."

Margaret's eyes light up. "That's great. So why did she do it?"

"I think you're right. It was a cry for help."

Margaret's face falls. "You think? Gabriel, you must ask her."

There's half an hour until New Year, and he still hasn't broached the subject. Jules Holland's *Hootenanny* is on the television, but he can't focus on the acts. He's wondering how he'll explain himself to Margaret on Wednesday.

"I've really enjoyed this Christmas," Ella says suddenly, reaching for his hand.

Gabriel squeezes it and smiles. "Me, too. It's a shame you have to go back to school."

Her face falls. "Do I?"

He kisses the top of her head. "It's okay. The police wouldn't have opened it again if it wasn't safe."

She looks away and sighs. "I don't fit in. They call me a geek. I hate it."

He puts his arm round her and is relieved she doesn't shrug it off. "There's nothing wrong with being clever. They're jealous, that's all."

"Why when I haven't got a mum?"

A lump lodges in his throat. "I didn't mean—"

"I miss her, Dad."

"I know. I miss her, too."

"She was beautiful, wasn't she? Not like me. And these braces make me even uglier."

He grips her tighter. "That's not true. You grow more and more like her every day."

"You would say that," she says but snuggles closer, her head on his chest.

"It's true. You mean the world to me."

"More than God?"

"More than God." Big Ben chimes midnight, but he ignores it. "And is that all?"

She shrinks from him. "What do you mean?"

He reaches for her hand, but she slides away, frowning furiously.

"I'm worried you're keeping something back."

Nothing.

"Talk to me, Ella."

Red-faced, Ella leaps to her feet and rushes out of the room. He follows her upstairs, explaining, apologising. But Ella barricades herself behind her door and refuses to speak. Defeated, Gabriel goes to bed but, try as he might, he cannot sleep. He hasn't exposed the root of her problem, and unless he does, like a tumour, it will keep on growing.

22

Somehow, we make it through Christmas. Guy's parents do their best to jolly me along but, from the moment we arrive to the minute we pack up the car to leave, I'm utterly and inconsolably miserable.

Daisy is in a foul mood the entire time and doesn't speak to me. Not one word. Sylvia can't fail to notice.

"A misunderstanding," I say, when she asks why.

"About what?"

I don't elaborate. What would I say?

I explain my relationship with Glen to Josh, who seems fine. On the surface, at least. "Close friends who've known each other a long time, like a brother, that's all."

"Yeah, I know."

The conversation is awkward, and I'm not sure he believes me, a fear compounded during lunch when I catch him looking at me with an *is she?* or *isn't she?* expression on his face.

Glen phones on Boxing Day to apologise again for his part in the confusion.

"Nothing happened," I remind him.

But that's not strictly true. As he traced his fingers over my bare shoulders there was a moment, no longer than a heartbeat, when I felt the tiniest frisson of excitement. Considering how many times we've shared a tent these past ten years, it was weird. I've seen the bugger naked, for heaven's sake. But I was gloriously drunk and high on the fun we'd had. Glen's phone calls screams guilt, and I can only assume he felt something, too.

The holidays limp to an end. Anthony Swann writes to all the parents informing them that, despite the ongoing police investigation, the school will reopen, with only the staffroom and theatre cordoned off.

Your children's safety is of our utmost concern, which is why we are upping the security. Please find enclosed electronic wristbands and passes for parents which must be shown to the guard at the gate. In addition, the police have installed five CCTV cameras on the interior and exterior of the building, which will be monitored closely. A team of Police Community Support Officers will patrol the surrounding area, providing a visible presence.

I'm not the only one relieved. Daisy can't wait to get back to school and away from me.

The media are out in force at the gate, fishing for quotes from any parents willing to give them. I catch sight of Michael Parton and his cameraman but keep my head down and hurry home.

. . .

The following day, a fresh batch of snow arrives. I haven't seen a cold snap on this scale since nineteen eighty-four. I'm no Thatcherite, but it's a different country now. The double-dip recession, shortage of grit, health and safety and, in my view, a lack of backbone, leaves Anthony Swann with no other option but to close the school.

Jasper and his army of builders are back in force. Dust-sheets cover the furniture and floors, and plastic sheets hang from doorways, but the house is filthy and the noise unbearable. Jasper flits in and out of the open front door, overseeing the chaos with an arched eyebrow and a few choice words. I retreat to the living room, light a fire, set my laptop on my knees, and try to work on my book, the BBC News channel a constant companion in the background. But my mind keeps sweeping back to the ever-widening gap between Daisy and me.

What would Guy do? I wonder. It's a futile question. If Guy were alive, the problem wouldn't exist.

"Daisy's a lot like you," he used to tell me. "Fun-loving, determined, loyal, and brave. She sees the good in people but at the same time isn't afraid to swim against the tide of opinion. A tiger, not a sheep."

If we're so alike I should be able to read her like a book.

I groan and head off to the kitchen to make yet another round of coffee for today's workforce of decorator, plasterer, and electrician. While I'm waiting for the kettle to boil, my gaze strays to the pinboard smothered in photos of Guy and the twins. Josh and Daisy as babies, waving their arms at the camera, their proud father looking on. Daisy wearing a determined expression as she takes her first steps towards Guy, his arms outstretched to catch her if she falls. Josh riding his bike for the first time, Guy watching, clapping. A school photo of a pigtailed Daisy smiling angelically. Josh and Daisy holding hands one Christmas in their brand-new Peter Pan and Tinkerbell outfits, surely the cutest picture ever. Life was uncomplicated back then. Guy was alive and Daisy was a doting daughter.

How quickly things came to be broken.

I'm cracking eggs into a bowl at breakfast a few days later, when a headline on the radio catches my attention. Two explosions have ripped through Aleppo University as the students sit their exams, killing more than eighty people. Syrian state television accuses the rebels of firing rockets at the university. Activists blame the government. It's yet another chilling incident in the two-year conflict. Supported financially, militarily, and diplomatically by Iran and Russia, well over four thousand children and almost three thousand women have been killed by Assad's regime. Diplomacy has failed. The fighting intensifies. Qatar and Saudi Arabia supply weapons to the rebels, but still NATO holds back.

I recall the rocket blast in Homs last February that killed *The Times* journalist, Marie Colvin, and French photographer, Rémi Ochlik. It could have been Glen and me, I think for the millionth time. I stop whisking and glance at the eggs, beaten to a *MasterChef*-like foam. Will it scramble? I reach for a saucepan in the cupboard below, place it on the hob, add a dash of butter, and tip in the eggy froth. The pan's too hot and, although I'm stirring frantically, the mixture catches on the bottom. I remove it from the heat, drop some bread into the toaster, run upstairs, and wake the children.

Josh is first down. I hand him the plate of food which he stares at, mystified.

"Scrambled eggs on toast," I explain.

"Mmm. Thanks."

Daisy, when she finally arrives, refuses the offering with a wave of her hand.

"Think of the orphans in Syria," I say.

She stares at me impassively and takes the plate without speaking, smothering the egg with a thick layer of ketchup. Her lack of emotion is far more potent than anger. With nothing to react to, I'm eviscerated. But I guess that's Daisy's aim. She may not be top of the class like Josh, but she's no fool.

Since Glen's visit, breakfast is conducted in virtual silence, a code of practice I've learned to respect. There's nothing worse than beginning each day with an argument. So I sit there, nursing a mug of tea, watching my children eat, trying to keep a lid on my anger while ruing the loss of my past life. Being a housewife is bad enough, but being an unappreciated mother flies way off the scale.

"Actually, Mr Swann wants to raise some money for Syria," volunteers Josh suddenly, his mouth full.

And it dawns on me then, I know exactly what to do.

Blue skies and sunshine do wonders for a place. After weeks of dreariness, the town sparkles like a polished jewel. The town's elderly residents, in a frivolous nod to the sudden dry spell, abandon their hats and coats and take to the pavements in force. We pass at least a dozen silver-haired strollers, all of whom wish us good morning and comment on the weather.

Under the watchful eye of PC Coleman, the usual mothers loiter at the gate while their children, chattering excitedly, troop into the building. I, too, am in a buoyant mood because, at last, there is a purpose to my day.

Daisy's spirits, however, are far from high. "I totally forbid you to follow me. It's just too embarrassing."

"Okay. I'll wait five minutes."

Her forehead crinkles in a spectacular frown. "Must you?"

"Yes, Daisy, I must. Anthony Swann is expecting me."

"Well, tell Swanny you can't come."

"You know I can't do that."

"You're, like, the worst person ever."

"Whatever!" I say and Josh sniggers.

Her mouth drops open. "I can't believe you actually just said that."

"You'll get over it." To say my patience is wearing thin with my bilious daughter would be an understatement.

"Just don't speak to me," she says and stomps off towards school.

Josh goes to follow, but I catch his arm. "Are you okay with this?"

He shrugs. "S'pose."

"You could try being a bit enthusiastic."

"I think it's a good idea but I kind of hoped you wouldn't have to come to school."

"You won't notice me. I promise."

St Peter's smells of polish and boiled cabbage. The wood floors have an impressive sheen, the white walls are freshly painted, and bright-faced children jostle for space in the narrow corridors. Strange to think such a wholesome place has played host to a murder. The cake and clothes sale over, the pupils are rushing back from the gym to their classrooms, arms brimming with booty. On sight of Anthony Swann, they slow down, pipe down, and greet the headmaster with a cheery, *good morning, sir*. A few are told to do up their top buttons, some are asked to tuck in their shirts , and one is advised to shine his shoes before returning to school the following morning. Unlike the *laissez-faire* approach of Call-me-Niall, Anthony Swann is a stickler for manners and appearance.

We pause outside his office. "Today has been a great success and a welcome break from tradition. Just what St Peter's needed. A job well done."

"Oh … er … good." As an absent parent, I have no knowledge of what constitutes a typical fund-raiser.

"We'll have to get you more involved in future," he adds.

I recall my earlier promise to Josh. "I don't think—"

But Anthony has darted into his office to gather his things.

I glance at the vast canvas print of all the St Peter's pupils and teachers and the eye-catching self-portraits including one resembling a dish of breakfast – egg-like eyes, a sausage nose, and a bacon rasher for the mouth. Rows of still life dominate another wall. My eye is drawn to a sleek purple aubergine flanked by a shiny red pepper drawn by Georgia Young.

"It's impressive, isn't it?" Anthony says, appearing by my side.

"Mm. Very."

"Her mother wants to enter her for an art scholarship."

"I'm not surprised."

"Ah, but the talent is all hers."

I stare at him questioningly. Did he mean to say that?

"Either that or she had it commissioned." His eyes flash mischievously. "Helicopter parenting, I believe it's called."

I tilt my head. "I'm sorry?"

He laughs. "Mothers who hover over their kids. My

parents never set foot in my school. Mind you, I would have been horrified if they had. We should discourage it, really, but it's difficult. With the amount of litigation around, we're nervous of the repercussions." He opens the front door. "After you."

We cross the gravel driveway, passing the theatre, cordoned off with blue-and-white police tape, to the gym where the children from years six to eight have congregated. In a departure from the planned schedule, Anthony Swann has coerced me into speaking to the three oldest year groups about my life as a foreign correspondent, with a Q&A to follow. I'd tried to convince him today wasn't about me, but he wouldn't take no for an answer.

"It's all been organised," he said. "I'd hate to disappoint them."

He opens the door and I take a deep breath. A hundred pairs of eyes swivel in my direction. Freakishly, I catch Josh's. Colour flares his cheeks, but instead of smiling at me, as I had hoped, he lowers his head and stares at the floor.

The Syria Awareness Day, although considered by many to be an unmitigated success, backfires on me, the detractors quick to voice their disapproval.

"Why can't you just be normal?" Daisy asks.

"Normal?"

Josh sighs. "She means like other mothers."

"You think you're *so* clever but you're not. You're just embarrassing."

The criticism is delivered in plain English, which makes a change from her linguistic cool. "I am being like other mothers. Fund-raising is what they do."

"Yes, but a chair-free day. What even is that? We had to sit on the floor for lessons and stand for lunch. Sorry, soup and a roll." Daisy pauses to roll her eyes. "That was your idea, wasn't it?"

"The money saved from lunch was donated to Unicef. It's easy to raise money from sales."

"So what? That's what schools do."

"I know, and yesterday's cake and clothes sale raised a lot of money."

She bounces her fist off her head. "Exactly! So why no chairs?"

"We take them for granted. I thought it would make everyone the tiniest bit aware of what the children in Syria are going through."

She throws up her arms in exasperation. "We are aware! You've been telling us how awful life is for everyone everywhere else in the world all our lives."

"And it hasn't done you any harm, has it? Stop being so theatrical."

Her eyes narrow. "We had the piss taken out of us all day."

"Not *all* day," says Josh. "Only after they found out you're our mother. It was the different surname that did it. They kept shouting out Josh Moron, Daisy Moron, you're SAD. But they're idiots. So I ignored them."

"Why did you have to come into school?" continues Daisy shrilly. "You were so *obvious*."

"Obvious?"

She prods her cheeks with her index fingers. "In our faces!"

"I honestly tried not to be."

"I totally preferred it when you weren't around. I think you made a big mistake giving up work."

I flinch. "That's the most ungrateful thing you've said yet."

She clenches her fists into tight little balls. "Yeah? Well, deal with it."

"And who would look after you? Hmm?"

"We'd board!" Scowling, she storms out of the room.

And it's not just Daisy's nose that's been put out of joint. Samantha, Leo, and Jemma are already seated in The Singing Kettle when I arrive, five minutes late, for our Friday get-together. It's the first time I've seen Jemma since Dylan's demotion. She's lost weight, I notice, and looks drawn. Pleased to see her, I make a move to hug her, but she doesn't get up.

Leo straightens up. "Good of you to show up!"

I smile and take my place. "I'm sorry. Something came up last week, and I completely forgot to cancel."

"You mean, you went to see Anthony Swann to plan the Syria Awareness Day," Leo says.

I shrug. "Can't seem to shake off the shackles of my past."

Leo glowers. "That would be in your previous life as Saviour of the World."

My smile wilts. "I was trying to help."

"It's the sort of thing the Friends usually organise," explains Samantha coolly. "You really should have run it past us first."

"It's not appropriate for one parent to run a campaign," adds Jemma.

Not you as well, I think miserably. "It wasn't a campaign."

"Self-publicity more like." Leo stabs the tablecloth with her finger. "The Friends would never have allowed a 'no chairs' policy. The younger children really struggled. Poor Sid was exhausted when he got home. And Oli was starving. A bowl of soup and a roll is never going to sustain a growing teenage boy."

I shake my head. "I really don't see it like that. The situation in Syria is catastrophic. My objective was to raise funds for the orphans while increasing awareness of what it's like to go without. Let's face it, our children all lead pretty gilded lives."

But I can tell by their expressions they aren't interested. Clearly, I've overstepped the invisible line I hadn't realised they'd drawn.

Leo folds her arms. "Spare us the lecture."

Samantha frowns. "Your methods weren't appropriate,"

"This is a community. Everybody mucks in," adds Jemma.

Thwack. Thwack. Thwack. They whip me with their prejudices. Syrian children are dying daily, but all that matters to these career wives, these professional mothers, these unworldly people with their petty rules and principles, is their position in the social pecking order of this small, provincial town.

What am I doing here? I hold up my hands in a gesture of defeat, my letter of resignation mentally prepared. "I'm sorry. It won't happen again. You have my word."

Margaret Brown is unloading shopping from her car when I arrive home, an hour later. I help her carry the heavy bags into her kitchen.

"You're an angel," she says.

"Hardly."

"You seem upset. Everything okay?"

Grateful for the chance to vent my frustration, I hurriedly explain. "And afterwards, they carried on as if nothing had happened, chatting about the children and some ridiculous theory that Ben Styne killed Natalia Topolska."

"I think it showed imagination. I'm afraid a lot of people here live in a bubble. Take Samantha, for example. She didn't think the St Peter's blazer was a good enough fit for Georgia so she found out where to buy the material and had one tailor made!"

My mouth drops open. "You're kidding?"

"I'm being catty, but it's true."

"They think I did it for the attention."

Margaret places two bags on her spotless linoleum. "And did you?"

I put down my load and groan. "No, of course not. I'm a reporter not a crusader. It's always been about other people. In this case the Syrian children."

"Gabriel was very impressed."

"He was?"

"He thought it was very spiritual of you."

I bat the air with my hand. "I'm not the least bit religious."

"I didn't say you were."

23

I t's Monday morning, and I'm reading the *Easthaven Gazette* when the doorbell sounds, off-key and faltering, like an aging soprano. It's too early for the postman, I'm not expecting Jasper, and Margaret is at work.

My eyes widen at the sight of Gabriel Jones, pale and baggy-eyed, and brandishing a bunch of white and purple stocks.

"They're a belated thank you for having Ella for tea before Christmas." Red-faced, he thrusts the flowers at me. "I'm sorry, I should have called to tell you I was coming."

"No, not at all. They're lovely."

He flashes a brief smile and wrings his hands.

"Coffee?"

"Thank you, but I must get back."

Passing the time of day with a priest is not high on my list of priorities, but I can see the poor man wants to talk, even if he can't admit it. "Oh, go on. I'm having one."

He hesitates.

"Please, I insist."

I put the flowers in a vase, clear some brochures off a

chair and add them to a pile on the worktop. "Sit down and I'll make some coffee." It's more of a command than a suggestion, but it has the desired effect.

"Thank you."

Upstairs, the builder starts up his hammer drill. "Sorry about the noise. I'm having a lot of work done."

His eyes dart round the cluttered kitchen. "That's good."

"Ha! They're starting in here next week." I switch on the kettle, take a couple of mugs out of the dishwasher, and sprinkle some coffee from a jar into them. "How's Ella?"

He rolls back his shoulders. "Much better, thanks."

"Really?"

Mistaking my question for disbelief, Gabriel folds his arms.

"I'm concerned, Gabriel. That's all."

He blinks, as if caught in the headlights of my sympathy.

"I have two children of the same age, remember." I pour boiling water in the mugs, a splash of milk, and take them to the table.

"Sad. Angry. Lonely. Uncommunicative," he mumbles.

"It's not easy for her. She lost her mother." I reach out to touch his hand, but he moves it away. "I'm speaking from experience."

His eyes flicker. "You lost your mother?"

It strikes me then this is exactly what happened. She walked out of my life when I was eleven, running off with Jeff, my father's best friend. *People aren't always what they seem*, my father said the day she left. *Remember that, Megs.* At the time I thought he was talking about Jeff, but when my mother later abandoned him for a pretty Italian called Antonio, and wrote to tell us she wasn't coming back, I realised he'd been talking about my mother. *Couldn't resist another bite of the apple, eh, Eve*, my father said, screwing up the letter and throwing it in the bin. She might be dead for all I care. The point is, for me she no longer exists, dead or alive. I nod.

"How did your father cope?"

"He didn't really. He married Aunty Jill, an old family friend, who had us packed off to boarding school. I wouldn't recommend that."

He sighs. "I've taken time off work. Things improved over Christmas until I asked her one too many questions, and now I can barely get a word out of her."

"You mustn't blame yourself."

"In the absence of anybody else, it seems the obvious thing to do."

"Where's Ella now?"

"At school. The doctor says it's important to keep her life as normal as possible. But it will never be normal, will it? Not without a mother."

I know what he means just as I know how lonely it is dealing with problems on your own. But I also know there's no point wallowing in grief. "It's good she's at school."

Gabriel nods but doesn't elaborate.

"This is it, Gabriel. It's difficult and it's miserable, but you have to be strong, for Ella's sake, if nothing else."

He groans and buries his head in his hands. "Goodness knows what you think of me."

"Well …"

He raises his head and smiles sheepishly. "I sound pathetic, don't I?"

I tilt my head from side to side.

"Sorry." He takes a sip of coffee, winces, and puts the mug down.

"I take it God hasn't been helping much recently."

"Wow! You don't mess around, do you?"

"Nope." I gulp a mouthful of coffee and gag. "Oh, I'm sorry. This is absolutely disgusting. I'll make you another, and use a teaspoon."

It breaks the ice. He smiles, properly this time. Relieved, I empty the contents in the sink and start again.

"And you're right about God. Trust a journalist to hit on the truth."

"I'm an atheist." Why? Why did I say that?

He grins. "But are you sure?"

I narrow an eye and wag a finger at him. "I know your game. Don't you dare try to convert me."

Gabriel holds up his hands.

"Anyway, where's your dog collar? It's pretty devious walking round without one." The kettle boils, and I shovel a teaspoon of coffee into each mug, add the water and milk, and stir.

"Did you used to walk around with a badge saying 'journalist'?"

"I had a blue press helmet and flak jacket, a press card hanging round my neck. But that's not the point. That's completely different. You can say what you like to a journalist."

"You can say what you like to a priest."

I hand him a mug. "So what then? Anonymity? Is that it?"

He grimaces. "Wearing a dog collar sets me apart from the rest of society." He takes a tentative sip of coffee. "Mmm. Much better."

"It's the attention to detail. Using spoons really helps."

He laughs again.

"Or is it that you don't want people to know?" I press.

"It's no secret. Everyone knows what I am, but I found walking around in a uniform, wearing robes, turned me into a caricature. I'm no better than the next man." His shoulders droop, and he sighs, self-pityingly, and stares at his coffee.

"Well, that's true, obviously," I say, but he doesn't react. "A priest called Gabriel. Did your name in any way influence your choice of career?"

"What do you think?"

"Sorry. I bet everybody asks you that."

"As I'm sure everyone asks you why you didn't take your husband's name." He lifts his head and looks me directly in the eye. "I'm a huge fan of Guy Truman."

My jaw drops. "You've heard of him?" The only other person in Easthaven who's associated me with Guy is Anthony Swann. Guy's books were bestsellers, but he was notoriously publicity shy, gave few interviews, and on the rare occasion he did, made it clear his private life was off limits. He wanted to be judged by his words alone.

Gabriel shrugs. "I've read all his books. He was a brilliant writer."

It's a compliment, I know, and anyone can hand out those. But given his matter-of-fact delivery, I believe him. "Yes, he was."

"Is it true he wrote all his manuscripts by hand?"

"On yellow lined paper. He had incredibly neat handwriting and hardly made any mistakes."

"My favourite was *The Kingmaker.* Can't understand why it's never been made into a film."

"The critics didn't like it. They thought he peaked with *The Devil's Kiss.*"

"Because it won the Booker Prize."

I slam the table with my palms. "Okay, stop! This is too weird."

Gabriel pulls a face. "I'm sorry."

"You're surprisingly knowledgeable."

185

"Priests do have brains, you know."

I laugh. "You're not at all how I expected."

"Forgive me if I don't ask you to elaborate."

"Actually, it's pretty wonderful to be talking about Guy. Since he died, I've tended to steer clear of the memories. That way I avoid the pain. And what with the twins and moving down here …" I leave the sentence hanging. "Listen, Gabriel, about Ella. I was wondering, is she eating?"

A cloud passes over his face, and the smile vanishes. "Yes, she is."

"I'm sorry but I had to ask."

"I know."

But it's a question too far. He thanks me again, makes his excuses, and leaves.

It's Friday, which means coffee at The Singing Kettle. Josh is outside feeding Groucho and Marx, Daisy is eating her way through a bowl of Frosties, and I'm busy burning the bacon when my mobile, lying on the table, bleeps.

"Could you read it to me, honey? I've got my hands full."

Daisy groans but picks it up and reads, still munching on her cereal. "It's from Sam." Her eyes dart accusingly in my direction. "Who's Sam?"

"Samantha Young."

"Oh. Well, coffee's cancelled."

"That's it?"

"Yup. Oh no, sorry. She ends the text with an x."

Talk about sugaring the pill. I shake my head and lever the frazzled bacon onto a plate.

. . .

Twenty minutes later, having washed up and chivvied the children into action, I'm still mulling over the short to the point of rude, two-word text. Was she in a rush? Or are they excluding me? Do grown-up women do that? Irritated, I snatch the car keys and open the door.

"Aren't we walking today?" asks Daisy.

"No, we're not."

"But it isn't raining," says Josh. "And you said—"

"Do you want to walk?" mutters Daisy, nudging him.

You're reading far too much into this, I reason, as the children clamber into the car. There's bound to be a perfectly innocent explanation.

"It's an exeat this weekend, so no Saturday school," I remind them at the gate.

"Great, we'll have time to make Groucho and Marx's run," says Josh.

"Good idea."

I wave goodbye, and even though I tell myself not to, I can't resist scanning the area for familiar faces. But there's no sign of Samantha, Leo, or Jemma.

What did you expect? I wonder as I drive away.

24

I t's been two weeks, long enough to believe Samantha, Jemma, and Leo are avoiding me. I've seen them at the school gate, but they either leave as I arrive or are too engrossed in conversation to talk. Samantha has cancelled coffee twice more by text. The second time, *In London all day, coffee cancelled,* was slightly more expansive than the first but still brief enough to convince me I've fallen out of favour. With no friends to hang out with and very little direction to my life, I have no alternative but to knuckle down and write my book. It's not easy. Since the builders started ripping out the kitchen, the dust and decibel level have increased significantly.

I close the door of the recently renovated box room, settle down at Guy's old desk, arrange my pens in a neat line and my notebooks in an orderly pile. I turn on the laptop and am about to start but have this sudden impulse to reorganise the furniture. I'm moving the leather armchair from one side of the room to the other, when my mobile rings. My spirits lift. It's Glen.

"Where are you?"

"HQ. How's things?"

"I'm being completely stonewalled by Samantha, Leo, and Jemma. But otherwise fine."

"Jemma?"

"Dylan's mum, the boy Daisy corrupted."

"Ah! Have you tried talking to them? Apologised?"

"I can't, they're ignoring me."

"Strewth, you sound like a girl."

"I am a—"

"Talk to them, Megs. By the way, I'm off to Syria next week with Jez Dixon."

My heart skips a beat. "Syria?"

"Yeah, and we're going undercover. Anyway, I just wanted to check in. Say goodbye, that kind of thing."

The upbeat tone of his voice doesn't fool me. He's scared. "Be careful, Glen."

But what I actually mean is *please don't die*.

I sit at Guy's desk, mulling over Glen's words. If anyone deserves an apology, it's Jemma. Unlike the others, she has something to be upset about. It's been weeks since Daisy got Dylan into trouble, and I still haven't said sorry.

Her address, hastily jotted on a scrap of paper one Friday morning, is skewered on the spike on the kitchen worktop, between Samantha's swanky card and Leo's Christmas invite. The rod has passed through the second line of the address, making it difficult to decipher the words, but I can just about make out *15 Holbrook Gardens*. I check the location on the internet and discover it's a twenty-minute walk tops. The weather is foul but, feeling sluggish, I decide the exercise will liven me up.

I make the electrician a cup of tea and tell him I'm going out.

"Anywhere nice, love?"

"I'll let you know."

He winks. "Gotcha."

I pull on my recently washed puffa, wrap my scarf around my neck, and venture outside. It's cold, and the leaden sky casts a depressing greyness over everything. Even the sea, merging with the ashen sky on an invisible horizon, is dishwater dull. It's as if I've been condemned to a life without colour. I shouldn't be here. I should be in Syria, with Glen.

The Webster's two-storey Victorian house is located one street back from the seafront. Cars are parked bumper to bumper, and I'm glad I didn't drive. I pause on the pavement, framing my apology. It's important I reassure Jemma, too. Tell her I'm keeping a close eye on Daisy.

I take a deep breath, climb the three stone steps, and ring the bell. The door swings open, and Robert Webster appears, naked to the waist, a white towel draped over one shoulder. Startled, I back down to the street.

"How lovely to see you," he says, zipping up the fly of his stonewashed jeans.

My eyes directly in line with the substantial bulge in his trousers (right again, Glen), I tilt my head until my gaze is level with the defined muscles of his abdomen. Clearly, he works out. Is that because he has a beautiful wife? Or because he's vain?

"Excuse my appearance, but I've just got back from Amsterdam and was in desperate need of a shower. Come in."

I hesitate. "Is Jemma home?"

"'Fraid not, but she should be back any minute. I'll make coffee while you wait." Instead of hanging around for an answer, he heads down the chequer-board-tiled corridor.

I dither, deliberating whether to come back later.

Go inside and get it over with, my conscience nags.

I follow him to the kitchen, where he whips off the towel and rubs his short dark hair, giving me a clear view of the lion's head tattoo on his right arm. Vain. Definitely.

"Grab a seat while I grab a shirt."

I take in my surroundings – gleaming white cupboards, surfaces, walls, floor, even the tablecloth on the round table – impossibly sterile, not a speck of dirt.

After five minutes, Robert reappears, buttoning up his black linen shirt. "It's good to see you again. I've missed you." He laughs loudly.

What at? I wonder. The absurdity of his remark?

"Colombian?"

I do a double-take.

"Great coffee. The best, don't you think?"

Of course, the coffee. "Oh, instant's fine."

"I'm afraid I'm a bit of a coffee snob." He ducks down and emerges seconds later, cafetière in hand. He unscrews one of the white containers and heaps two spoonfuls of ground beans into the jug. "So, what brings you here?"

I glance at the Ikebana flower arrangement on the table, the three solitary stems perfectly in tune with the décor, and clear my throat. "I dropped by to apologise."

"Really? How noble of you. What did you do?"

Wrong-footed, I stare at him, open-mouthed.

He places the coffee, a small white jug of milk and two white cups and saucers on a tray, and sets it on the table. "I'm guessing this is about the kids."

I shift awkwardly. "Got it in one."

He thrusts the plunger down, pours the coffee, and passes me a cup and the jug of milk. "Sugar?"

"Not for me."

"Sweet enough, eh?"

I cringe.

"Sounds like a real firecracker, your daughter."

That's one way to describe Daisy, I suppose. I lean forward and rest my forearms on the table. "Listen, this apology is well overdue, but I'm very sorry my daughter led your son astray. And if it's any consolation, Daisy is sorry, too."

Robert slaps the table and laughs even louder than before.

"It might sound funny, but she really is."

He leans forward conspiratorially and places his hand on my arm. "Between you and me, I think it was good for Dylan. He's a different child."

His honesty is as disarming as his physical proximity. I retract my arm as politely as possible. "There's nothing good about smoking."

"True, but they all have a go sooner or later. I'm not sure Dylan liked it all that much. Daisy – pretty name by the way – may well have done us a favour." He fixes his dark-brown eyes on mine. "It would have been so much better if Jemma had been able to have a second child. She devotes far too much time to Dylan. It's not healthy for either of them. Secondary infertility they call it. We couldn't believe it at first; she fell pregnant with Dylan so easily, you see." He takes a slug and drains his cup. "Apparently, as many as one in five couples suffer from it." He picks up the cafetière. "More coffee?"

"No, thank you. I'll hit the ceiling."

"Can't get enough of the stuff. I suppose I'm addicted. Still, it's got to be better than alcoholism. My name is Robert Webster, and I've got a caffeine habit. England is full of addicts, don't you think? I blame the government. The threat of national bankruptcy drives us to it. We've suffered, but you can probably tell from our modest abode. Crunched, they're calling it."

His openness is unexpected. Sensing an opportunity to find out more about Jemma, I steer the conversation back to babies, or lack of them. "What about hormone injections? Or IVF?"

"She had hormone injections, hundreds of them. Did most of them herself. I couldn't watch." He shivers. "Anyway, they didn't work, and IVF isn't available on the NHS for mothers who've already had a child. And we couldn't afford to go private. Actually, that's not strictly true. We could have if we'd sent Dylan to a state school, but Jemma wouldn't hear of it." He throws me a meaningful look.

"I'm sorry." I leave it at that. Last thing I want is to get into a discussion about the pros and cons of state education.

"Why? We have a wonderful healthy boy. We should be happy. I am happy." He lets out a tortured sigh. "Christ, how did we get on to this subject?" He shakes his head. "As I said, I believe Daisy's had a positive effect on Dylan. He's been a mummy's boy far too long." He claps his hands together, bringing an end to the subject.

I smile. I've got him wrong.

"So tell me, Megan Moreau, how's the BBC's most attractive war reporter enjoying her retirement here in East-haven? Is it everything you dreamed of and more?"

Then again, maybe not. "I'm still finding my feet."

"Which is code for what exactly?"

"I mean we haven't been here long, but I think it was the right decision."

"How's that Aussie friend of yours, Greg?" He winks. "Bet he's missing you?"

I glance at my watch. "Did Jemma say when she'd be back?"

His face falls. "I'm sorry, I'm boring you."

"Not at all," I say truthfully.

"I'm not entirely sure. I've no idea where she is. She could be at Samantha's planning the sponsored walk. Or she could be at Pilates, or is it yoga? Or making costumes for the play with Leo. But I'd hazard a guess she's in church." He rolls his eyes. "St Matthew's in fact. After years of happy atheism, she's found religion. Either that or she fancies the vicar."

"I doubt that." But then I remember Gabriel's liquid brown eyes, his blond hair, and cleft chin. Is he the vicar of St Matthew's? No, he can't be. Jemma would have mentioned it when his name came up in the tearoom on the morning of the fight.

"I was joking," he says, mistaking my thoughtfulness for affront.

The front door opens and closes. Footsteps patter on the tiles. Robert rises to his feet, his body tensing visibly as Jemma enters the room. She sees me, halfway between sitting and standing, and her mouth falls open in surprise.

"Megan's dropped by for a chat." Robert lands a perfunctory kiss on her cheek. "I'll leave you to it." Without a backward glance, he hurries out of the room.

"I should have called."

"Don't be silly. It's lovely to see you." But she stares straight through me, fingering the spot of Robert's kiss.

I tuck my chair away tidily. "I've missed our Friday coffees."

"Yes, it's a shame. We're all so incredibly busy these days."

I've heard her list of hobbies and I don't doubt her life is full, but too busy for coffee? I want to believe her, but there's something about her manner, the way she sweeps away the comment, the strain in her face, that's unconvincing. Is that because she's shocked at finding me at home, drinking coffee with her husband?

"I'm here to apologise about Daisy," I say quickly. "I'm sorry she got Dylan into trouble. She's been a bit of a handful since her father died."

"No need to apologise. We were a bit shocked but we've spoken to Dylan. He won't do it again."

"I'm not so sure about Daisy. She's well on her way to being a difficult teenager."

"I'm very lucky. Dylan's always been such a good boy."

I nod slowly, watching her face, but her expression is unreadable.

"I'd offer you coffee but I see you've already had one." She gathers up the cups and heads over to the sink.

I take my leave, muttering something about a lunch date, acutely aware that I've been dismissed.

25

It's a bitterly cold day, and it's snowing again. The third dump of the season, the novelty has well and truly worn off. Still, I've finally splashed out on a pair of rubber-soled, fur-lined boots and am marvelling at how briskly I can walk on the icy pavements when, rounding a corner at speed, I almost collide with Gabriel Jones. He slides out of the way, grabbing a lamppost to steady himself.

"Apologies." I raise a foot. "New boots."

He holds up an envelope and gesticulates to the post box up the hill behind me.

I laugh and, grateful for some company, walk with him. "You seem happier than when we last met."

"Your optimism rubbed off on me."

"Very funny."

He slots the letter into the box and looks me directly in the eye. "I mean it. I needed a good talking to."

I cock my head, but his expression is set. He isn't joking. "I'm flattered, I think."

"I'm glad I bumped into you as it happens. I wanted to ask you and the twins for lunch one day over half-term."

A list of negatives spring to mind as we continue down the hill towards St Peter's. I don't do religion. He's not my type. But then again, I could do with a friend. I'm pretty low on those. "Why not?"

"Hold back on the enthusiasm, why don't you."

"I'm sorry, I meant to say I'd love to."

The school in view, I catch sight of Jemma Webster approaching from the opposite direction. It's three days since my visit, and I've been hoping to bump into her. I wave enthusiastically, but despite my boots, slip on the ice.

Quick as a flash, Gabriel steadies me. "Are you okay?"

"Fine. But I think it's safe to let go."

"Sorry. Sorry."

I look around for Jemma, but she's been swallowed up in the crowd of mothers. "Dammit!"

"What's the matter?"

"I saw someone I wanted to catch up with. A friend. At least, I hoped she was. To be honest, I'm not sure anymore."

"Intimidating place, the school gate."

A few months ago, I would have laughed, but not anymore. "Honestly? It's one of the most terrifying places on earth."

He laughs. "Surely not as bad as Afghanistan?"

"I tell you, Gabriel, it's not far off."

It's half-term. Last night's forecast predicted snow, but we're out in the garden in shirtsleeves, making the most of the unexpected sunshine. Work on Groucho and Marx's run has begun in earnest. The rabbits, whiskers twitching, are watching Josh methodically unravelling a bundle of chicken wire. I smile, pick up the sledge hammer, and bang away on the wooden fence pole. The ground is soft, but the weight of the hammer makes it hot work.

"Do they actually need to be fenced in? This garden looks pretty rabbit proof to me," says Daisy, who's playing Swingball.

I wipe the sweat off my brow. "This way we won't lose them in the undergrowth."

"And the fox won't get them," says Josh.

Daisy gives the ball an almighty thwack, and it flies around the pole at speed. "As if."

She's got a point. Our rabbits would give General Wound-wort a run for his money. With their long, razor-sharp incisors, a fox would have to be very brave to take them on.

"When are you going to help?" Josh has unrolled the wire and is trying to nail the end to the first pole.

"I am helping. I'm keeping up morale." She takes another swing and sends the ball skywards this time. The pole rocks this way and that.

"Well, I wish you wouldn't," he mutters.

I roll up my sleeves. "Did I tell you, we're having lunch with Ella Jones and her father today?"

Daisy grabs the swinging ball and lets out an anguished groan. "Do we have to? She's, like, such an emo!"

I frown and turn to Josh now hammering away. His cheeks are flushed, and beads of sweat stud his brow. "You don't think so, do you?"

He stops what he's doing and pulls a face. "She's a bit weird."

"Because she fainted?" I ask.

He shrugs.

"She's a schizo. I mean, like, totally spaced, you know, a freak."

"That's unkind, Daisy. She's shy. Painfully shy." I curse

myself inwardly. I should have asked them before accepting.

Daisy sighs, long and loud. "Whatever!"

"I wish you wouldn't say that."

She flings down the plastic racket. "Yeah? Well, I wish you wouldn't try and organise my life, but you can't help yourself, can you?"

I'm about to shout at her but I bite my lip. "I should have asked you and I'm sorry, but her father is worried about her, and I believe it's important to provide support where we can."

Daisy gives me one of her, *oh my god, you've really lost it* looks, before throwing her arms up into the air. "Fine," she says and stomps back into the house.

"I take it you don't want to go either?"

"I'm cool."

I smile. Yes, you are. Thank goodness.

"But, Mum, there's something you should know." Josh drops his hammer, and his hands fly up to the back of his head, his elbows flexed inwards.

I recognise the pose. He's upset about something. "What is it?"

"I tried to tell you when she was here."

"Ella?"

"Yes. Ella. After she fainted. I … I saw something."

I put my arm around his shoulders. He's trembling and he doesn't resist. "What, Josh?"

He lowers his hands and looks at me pleadingly. "On her wrists." He shudders, and I grip a little tighter. "Cuts and scars. Hundreds of them."

I cancel our lunch date over the phone, my guilt increasing with every word I utter. Lying was never my strong point. And I mean that as an out-and-out criticism of myself rather than some weak attempt at self-deprecation. Honesty is not always the best policy, it can backfire terribly in work and social situations. I've lost count of the times I've been accused of being tactless. But how could I not lie? It would be unfair to put Josh in such a difficult situation. Besides, I'm not entirely sure that, even with all my worldly experience, I could feign enjoyment while skirting such an enormous issue.

Gabriel sounds pleased to hear from me until I rush straight to the point. "I'm sorry, I've been a total idiot and double-booked. I'm afraid we can't come for lunch today after all."

"Oh no, what a pity. Ella was really looking forward to it. And Margaret's made one of her famous shepherd's pies." He pauses. "I er … I was looking forward to it, too."

"I've tickets for *Billy Elliot*. Brain like a sieve," I lie, glibly now. "I'm very sorry."

"Sounds great. I've always wanted to see that show."

"Oh well. Some other time," I say hurriedly and put down the phone.

On Friday morning, we're invited to an impromptu thirteenth birthday party for Josh's friend, Bruno Richards-Gonzalez, thrown by his Spanish mother, Madelena Gonzalez.

"I hope you can all come," she enthuses over the phone. "I hear so much about you. Bruno and Josh are bery good friends, no?"

I don't know, but I accept, enthusiastically.

The party is a huge success. Madelena introduces me to her friends, a cosmopolitan gathering of Spanish, English, French, and Greek women. They are friendly and uncomplicated, and I immediately feel at home.

Leo is there, too, with her three children. She throws open her arms as if greeting a long-lost friend. "Where've you been hiding? I've missed you."

It's an odd thing to say – I haven't heard from her for weeks – but seems to be heartfelt, and I'm grateful. "Are Jemma and Samantha here?"

She empties the bottle of wine into her glass. "God, no. Honestly, Megan, for someone so worldly, you can be very naive."

I assume, by that, she means Madelena isn't their kind of person. "How is Jemma?"

She rolls her eyes. "Convinced Robert's having an affair."

I'm in the middle of a sip of wine and almost choke.

"He's a shameless womaniser, but he'd never leave Jemma." Leo drains her glass, picks up another bottle, and checks the level. "He adores her. She's beautiful and a brilliant mother, but that business with Dylan really took it out of her. We didn't see her for weeks, and it wasn't for want of trying. She was devastated."

I wince. Jemma still can't have told them it was Daisy's fault.

"Dylan may not be head boy anymore but, if you ask me, he's still pretty special." She raises her eyebrows and laughs. "Ha! You can't say that anymore, can you? It means something else entirely. Don't get me wrong, I love Jemma, I really do, but she can be a monumental pain in the arse. I don't know about you, but I'm a little thirsty and all the bottles in here appear to be empty." She puts down the bottle she's been scrutinising and heads off in search of more wine.

Madelena is the perfect host. Lunch rolls into tea, and by the time I take my leave, I realise I have fallen a little bit in love with her.

∿

Today, with the twins back at school, I have no option but to continue writing my book. The clamour from the builders as invasive as ever, I retreat to my study, turn on the radio to block out the sound, and dig out old shoeboxes crammed full of photographs for inspiration. Heady with nostalgia, I spend an hour rummaging through them. A picture taken in Afghanistan, days before Guy's death, of a line of helmeted marines, rifles slung over their shoulders, walking through a poppy field under a cloudless evening sky, sets me thinking. It's an incongruous image, the camouflaged helmets of soldiers on foot patrol walking through a field of pink flowers in full bloom. Beauty and destruction. Never mind England, Afghanistan is a country of addicts. I remember the mother and two young daughters lying on the floor of a filthy dwelling, sharing an opium pipe in a village we were passing through.

God help me if Daisy starts experimenting with drugs. If she's smoking at thirteen, I hate to think where she'll be getting her thrills in a couple of years. Not that it's always down to thrills. People turn to drugs if they're unhappy, or damaged. Or they self-harm like Ella. Poor kid. She must be in one hell of a state if she feels the need to cut herself.

I put down the photo and Google self-harm.

Self-harm is a way of dealing with very strong emotions. For some people it gives the relief that crying may provide for the rest of us. It is also a form of addiction. The body releases a natural opiate-like chemical to reduce the pain which induces a rush. Self-harmers cut themselves because they are depressed, have eating disorders, have suffered physical, emotional, or sexual abuse, have low self-esteem, or are bullied or bereaved.

I shiver. Poor Ella and poor Gabriel. How do you deal with something like that on your own? No wonder Gabriel was upset when he came around. And I responded by lying to him. I groan. You had to, I tell myself, for Josh's sake.

I shake my head, unconvinced, and decide there and then to offer my support. It's never too late, a problem shared and all that. Without deliberating further, I grab my coat and Guy's umbrella and set out in the rain.

It's a brisk twenty-minute walk from Primrose Road to the vicarage. Margaret opens the door in a pair of Marigolds, holding a can of polish, and smiles.

"Is Gabriel in?" I ask, after we've exchanged pleasantries.

"He's over at the church. Pop in and say hello. He won't mind."

St Matthew's is a massive building with a bell tower reminiscent of an Italian campanile. An evangelical church, I note, as I prise open the heavy door and make my way inside. Does Gabriel speak in tongues? I rest the umbrella against a wall beneath a crowded noticeboard, push my way through the swing doors into the main hall, and take in the high, pitch-pine ceiling, stained-glass windows, and blue-and-white-chequered arches. On the raised chancel floor, at the far end, a simple altar is covered in a white linen cloth embroidered with a gold cross. And on the south wall, stone tablets commemorating the *Old Contemptibles*, the self-adopted name of the British troops of the First World War, supposedly derived from a comment made by Kaiser Wilhelm II.

Gabriel appears from a side room, behind the pulpit, brandishing a feather duster. His worried expression dissolves on sight of me. "I thought I heard someone. What a pleasant surprise. How are you? How was *Billy Elliot*?"

My toes curling, I clear my throat. "It was wonderful, thank you for asking. Sorry for letting you down."

"Don't be. Are you okay? You look slightly fraught."

"Do I? It must be the builders. They've ripped out my kitchen."

He smiles. "So you're here to escape the noise?"

"No. I …" My confidence deserts me. Why am I here? I've just lied to this man, and now I'm about to stick my nose in. What business is it of mine? He may not even be aware of it himself. I manage a wan smile. "Nice duster."

"I've just been cleaning the organ loft. It's overrun with cobwebs. Like a great deal of this church, it's woefully under-used. I'd like to open it up, incorporate a shop that sells really good coffee."

"A Christian Starbucks! How novel."

He frowns. "Religion wouldn't be the mandatory topic of conversation."

"It's a great idea," I say hurriedly. "What does Ella think?"

His left eye twitches. "Ella? I don't know. I haven't asked her."

"Look, Gabriel. I've been meaning to talk to you about her."

He frowns.

I take a deep breath. "Josh saw some cuts on her arms when she fainted, and it upset him, which is why I've come here today because I wondered if you needed a friend, you know, to talk to, because I know I would if either Josh or Daisy were hurting themselves." I brace myself and rest a hand on the pew.

He rubs the back of his neck for what seems an age. "I walked in on her. There was blood everywhere."

My stomach lurches. "It must have been horrible."

"She was reciting the Hail Mary. A Catholic prayer," he

continues, staring at the floor. "Her way of getting back at me."

"It may seem like she's punishing you, but she isn't. Cutting herself is a physical response to a difficult emotion," I say quietly.

He looks up, eyes clouded with pain. "I've lived most of my life in the dark, walking around with my Christian blinkers on, blind to reality, blind to what's happening right in front of me. Can you understand that?"

"I understand it perfectly."

"Do you? You strike me as someone who wouldn't miss a trick."

"I'm not as savvy as you think. I may have lived in the real world, the big, awful, terrifying world of guns and wars, of drug cartels and mind-blowing disasters, but I haven't lived a *real* life. This is my first bash at parenting. And boy, am I finding it tough."

"You give the impression of being on top of your game."

I smile at his choice of words. Being a mother is hardly a game. "An illusion. Believe me. I'm only just getting to know my children."

"You're just saying that to make me feel better."

"No, I'm not. I had no idea, for example, Daisy was good at tennis until Leo told me."

"You're modest, that's all."

"Hardly. It's the same with Josh and rugby. Cricket, too, for that matter. I've never seen them play."

"Wow! That's quite an admission."

"And last month Daisy was caught smoking."

"Ah."

"Quite, but it's amazing how much talking it through with my friends helped me come to terms with it." I pause. It's not quite a lie. I spoke to Glen. "But maybe you've talked Ella's problem through with someone, in which case I'm making a total fool of myself."

"God, you mean?"

"Well, no, actually I didn't. In my limited experience, He's pretty lousy when it comes to offering advice."

He presses his lips together, and I'm certain I've offended him.

"I'm sorry. I'm not helping. I should go."

"No. Don't go, please. I'm glad you came. And you're right. I haven't talked about it to anyone apart from Margaret. She's very supportive. She listens and nags me to talk to Ella, but we usually end up arguing, which solves nothing."

I suggest we sit down and, not knowing how else to comfort him, take his hand in mine. "How long has it been going on?"

"I don't know, but she's been acting strangely since November."

I recall the fight outside the school gate. "Do you know what triggered it?"

"I assume she misses her mother. I'm not much of a replacement."

"Okay, that's quite enough of that. You've had your moan. Guy was a far better parent than me, but I'm all they've got. Positive thinking, Gabriel, is essential."

He nods and chews his lip.

"Is she being bullied? Girls can be bitchy. I remember that much from my own schooldays."

"Not according to her teachers."

"So go through her things."

"I can't do that."

"Your daughter is cutting herself. Of course you can. Does she keep a diary? Facebook perhaps?"

"She has a computer. She's always on it." He smiles his

heart-stopping smile. "Thanks, Megan."

"For what exactly? I haven't done anything."

"For persevering with me. I must drive you mad."

I hold up my finger. "Uh-huh. Positive thinking, remember?"

The doors at the back of the church swing open with a loud whoosh. I crane my neck and see Robert Webster standing at the back of the church.

His eyes widen on sight of me. "Megan?"

I lever myself out of the pew, into the aisle.

Gabriel follows. "Can I help you?"

"I'm looking for my wife. I wanted to take her out for lunch. I can't find her, but I rather assumed she'd be here. Robert Webster." He thrusts out his hand.

Gabriel shakes it, but avoids eye contact. "Gabriel Jones."

"Well, well, well." Robert grins as he looks him up and down. "Good to finally meet you, Gabriel. What great company you keep. I'm one of Megan's biggest fans."

I cringe. Why must he be so smarmy all the time? "Our kids are friends. We're arranging play dates."

Robert slaps his thigh. "Well, that *is* a relief. Terrific!"

He's clearly joking, but an awkward silence follows. I glance at Gabriel.

His face is pale and he's twitching nervously. "Mrs Webster hasn't been here for weeks."

So Jemma does know Gabriel. Strange she didn't mention it.

Robert frowns. "Oh! Right. Better leave you to it then."

And as quickly as he arrives, he's gone.

I shake my head. "Funny guy. Still, I'm not surprised you haven't met him."

Gabriel rubs his neck again. "What makes you say that?"

"He's an atheist, too."

26

Gabriel is driving Ella to school. She's pale and uncommunicative, which is odd because yesterday evening she'd seemed happier than usual. He imagines it's because her scholarship exams start today. Although he's learnt that when it comes to Ella, he shouldn't assume anything.

"Don't be nervous. You're a clever girl. You shouldn't have any trouble."

She shrugs non-committedly, staring at the KFC on the corner of the street.

There's a question on the tip of his tongue, *has something happened to make you cut yourself again?* But, wary of jeopardising their improved relationship, he doesn't ask. It's important he keeps the line of communication open. He needs her to know she can talk to him, if she wants.

He tries a different tack. "You'd tell me if something was wrong, wouldn't you?"

She nods.

"Good. Call me on my mobile if you need me. I can

answer calls, at least, even if I can't text." He pulls up at the gate, and Ella gets out. "Bye then, darling. Good luck."

But she just walks away, head down.

Gabriel locks the car and marches into the vicarage. He flings his keys on the hall table, wanders into his study, and sits at his desk. It's his turn to deliver Sunday's sermon. He likes this new development, job-sharing with Ashley King. Turns out it's what Martin Shepherd had wanted to talk to him about before Christmas and not, as he'd feared, about his relationship with Jemma.

Not that we had a relationship. It was a misunderstanding that almost got out of hand. She appreciated my kindness and was a bit too effusive in her gratitude. Nothing more. Understandable, considering her husband. Gabriel shivers, recalling the shameless way Robert had flirted with Megan. She'd dealt with it brilliantly, of course. An impressive woman. Competent. Brave. Attractive, too.

He shakes his head and refocuses on his sermon, What is Faith? Hmm. Let's see. What if I start with *seeing is believing* then switch it to *believing without seeing*? Apart from the disciples who witnessed the crucifixion, it's what every Christian does. Blind faith. The corner stone of Christianity.

He picks up his pen, but his mind drifts to Ella. If he hadn't seen her slashing her wrists, would he have believed she was capable of such a thing? If only he knew what had driven her to do it? He bites his lip. Megan's right. It's time I found out.

He springs to his feet and rushes upstairs. Heedless of Steffi's smiling face, he sits at his daughter's desk and clicks the Barbie-pink mouse. The computer whirrs and flares into life but, apart from the Facebook logo in the bottom left-hand corner, the screen is blank. He clicks on the minimised page, drags up a conversation, and glances at the two icons – a thumbnail photo of Ella, and a picture of Mickey Mouse. He tugs his ear and starts to read.

- E: *Why are you being so mean?*
- MM: *You're the talk of the college. I need to protect my reputation.*
- E: *I don't understand?*
- MM: *Cos I hate being lied to.*
- E: *I haven't lied to you.*
- MM: *You have. You said you'd send me photos, but you haven't because you're ugly, a geek, and a loser. Well, I got one anyway, and I'm posting it on my wall. Bet it goes viral.*

Gabriel is trembling. Who is this creep? Where did Ella meet him? He says he's at college. Which college? What pictures? What wall? How dare this … this Mickey Mouse talk to his daughter like that? Has she fallen for this scumbag? Is he the reason she's been cutting herself? He bangs the desk with his fist. Evil little bastard should be taught a lesson. Blood rushing to his head, he hammers the keys.

Who are you? And what are you playing at?

His finger is poised over the carriage return, his breath coming in short rasps. He's a millisecond away from sending the message. But a nagging voice inside his head stops him.

Are you sure you know what you're doing?

He waits, staring at the screen through the red mist. He's never been this angry before. No. That's not true. He was incandescent the night Stephanie died, had wanted to wrap his hands around the throat of that miserable drunk and squeeze every last drop of life out of him.

He clamps his teeth together. The muscle in his cheek working overtime, his mind darts in all directions. Think, Gabriel, think.

This joker is not going to tell you anything. You'll frighten him off. Do not send the message. Not until you've thought this through.

That voice again. The voice of reason.

Sweating now, he deletes his message and storms onto the landing. His head is spinning. He needs to find the boy. He'll ring Easthaven College. All the colleges in the town, in fact – the sixth form college, the community college – and ask if there's a boy there called …

And then it hits him. He's read about perverts like this in the newspapers. He lists backwards, into the wall, and leans against it, breathing raggedly.

Gabriel and Mark Carter are in Ella's room, reading the conversation.

"I'll print it off," Mark says. "Just for the record."

Gabriel sighs and runs his hand through his hair. "Thanks, Mark."

Margaret is waiting for them in the kitchen. He wants her there because he needs her support.

"What does he mean, *bet it goes viral*?" Gabriel asks as they sit at the kitchen table.

Mark sighs. "That his friends will pass the photos on to their friends who'll pass it on to theirs."

"Why would they do that?"

"Because it's funny."

Gabriel clasps his head in his hands. "But that's sick."

Margaret pours Mark a cup of tea. "I don't understand the internet at all."

Mark takes the cup. "The question is, does Ella actually know this Mickey Mouse? Or did she meet him online?"

Margaret's hand flies to her chest. "She must know him. Otherwise, why would she talk to him? She's a bright girl. She doesn't talk to strangers."

"I think she met him online," Gabriel says. "I think he's a paedophile pretending to be a boy to groom her. That's what they do."

Margaret gasps. "Oh my goodness."

"We don't know that for sure," Mark says. "We don't know anything about their relationship other than it's turned sour."

Gabriel thumps the table. "Relationship! It's not a relationship. Mickey is a bully. Anthony was wrong. I should've guessed something was up when she said she didn't want to go to school. All the symptoms were there – quiet, withdrawn, not eating – but I ignored them."

"You haven't ignored them, Gabriel. You've dealt with them as they've happened. But Ella hasn't opened up about what's upsetting her."

"That's the part I don't understand. Why hasn't she?"

Margaret shakes her head. "She's probably scared of the repercussions. That we'll tell her off. Or that Mickey will get in trouble and blame her."

"Margaret's right," says Mark. "Most parents tend to overreact, so children avoid telling them in case it makes things worse. She's also probably terrified you'll ban her from the internet."

Margaret folds her arms. "And so he should."

"Maybe, but right now, Gabriel shouldn't put up any barriers. He needs to show Ella she can trust him, which is why I don't think you should go to the police or Anthony Swann until you've talked to her."

"She'll know I've been snooping. She won't talk to me."

"She left the computer on and the private message open," continues Mark. "Maybe it was a cry for help. Look at it another way, Gabriel. She's been cutting herself. She may be relieved you now know why. She's isolated. Her self-esteem has taken a knock. It's debilitating. She was vulnerable in the first place because her mother died, and now she's withdrawn, socially. Her scars are months old. I wouldn't be surprised if this cyberbullying has been going on for some time."

"Cyberbullying! Whatever next?" Margaret wrings her hands. "But why would anyone do such a thing?"

"Who knows, but bullies are often deeply insecure, jealous characters," says Mark.

Margaret snorts. "Jealous of a thirteen-year-old girl. That's absurd."

"Think about it. The fact that he has a username enables him to do and say things he wouldn't face to face. Classic insecure behaviour. And Ella is clever. Maybe he isn't." Mark clears his throat. "There are websites where children can talk to someone of a similar age who's suffered the same experiences. I'll give you some addresses. Ella may find them useful once she's opened up. But she won't find any respite from this until she does. I urge you to talk to her, hear her side of the story, before you take any further action. If you don't ask her permission to pass on the information, I predict it will only make matters worse."

Ella doesn't speak in the car on the way home, and she doesn't make eye contact either, just stares out the passenger window. Gabriel knows he must broach the subject of Mickey with his daughter, but he doesn't know how. Margaret warned him about launching straight in, suggesting he waited until she was back home and settled.

"She'll make a beeline for her computer," he said. "She always does."

"Yes, well, maybe that's a good thing."

"How can talking to Mickey be a good thing?"

"It isn't, but she'll see she left her computer on, and you can follow her and explain how you came to be in her room reading her messages." She shook her head. "Oh, Gabriel, I don't know. All I know is you mustn't rush into it."

He follows Ella down the path to the front door. Once inside, she makes a dash for the stairs. Gabriel sighs and heads for the kitchen, a plan forming in his head. Five minutes later, carrying two mugs of tea, he reaches his daughter's door. Taking a deep breath, he asks if he can come in.

The silence that greets him is deafening.

Holding both mugs in one hand he barges in, spilling hot tea on his skin. He barely registers the pain because, although the room is dark, it glows blue with the light from the computer screen and he can see his daughter, curled up in a tight little ball under her duvet.

"Ella."

"Go away," she says, her voice muffled.

Gabriel places the mugs on the bedside table with trembling hands, sits on the bed, and gently prises back the covers. Specks of blood are splattered on the sheets. His gaze shoots to her forearms, to the crust of dried blood in a criss-cross pattern. Beside her, a compass.

A wave of nausea hits him. Beads of sweat break out on

his brow. He can't shy away from it. He must speak to her. Now. "Do you want to tell me why you've hurt yourself?"

Nothing.

Gabriel wipes his forehead. "Has someone upset you?"

Ella jolts upright and slams her fists into the mattress. "Georgia Young has been spreading rumours about me. She's supposed to be my best friend." A lone tear trickles down her cheek.

He steels himself. "How do you know?"

She frowns at the computer.

His heart in his mouth, Gabriel walks over to the desk. Celluloid Steffi smiles at him. You'd be so much better at this than me, he thinks, reaching for the mouse. The screen flares to life. He glances over his shoulder, but Ella is flat on her back, staring at the ceiling. Praying silently to God to give him strength, he begins to read.

- E: *I thought you'd finished with me.*
- MM: *Why?*
- E: *You were cross this morning. But I'm made up about that.*
- MM: *Course you are. By the way, it was Georgia Young spreading rumours about you.*
- E: *Georgia? You sure?*
- MM: *Yeah. Do you want to know what she's been saying?*
- E: *…*
- MM: *Hello? Anyone there?*
- E: *…*
- MM: *She says you're boring and anorexic and she puts up with you cos she feels sorry for you. Guess you didn't know how much she hates you. And it's not just her. Everybody does. Everybody but me.*

Gabriel recoils as if Mickey's hand has reached out of the computer and punched him. He wants to scream, shout obscenities, but he mustn't. He must stay calm. "Who is Mickey, Ella?"

She frowns again. "His name is Mikey, and he used to be a friend of mine."

His brain is bursting with questions. How do you know him? Why are you talking to him? But when he speaks, his voice is level. "Have you spoken to Georgia about this?"

"I hate her. She's mean. They're all mean. I never want to go back to St Peter's. Please don't make me."

Gabriel sits beside her and clasps her to him. She is sobbing uncontrollably now, her body heaving. He thinks this might be a good thing. But he's not sure.

"It's possible Mickey … Mikey is lying. Georgia is your friend. You're always telling me about the kind things she does, like saving you a place in science so you didn't have to sit next to smelly Jamie Fenton again. And what about the time she gave you her last Fruit Pastille? Only a true friend would do that."

Ella pulls away. "She hates me. Everyone does."

Gabriel picks up her hands. "Darling, that's not true."

"Yes, it is. He said so."

"Who is he, Ella? Where did you meet him?"

"He goes to Easthaven College."

"But where did you meet him?"

She shakes her head. "I haven't met him."

Gabriel is both relieved and horrified. "Have you … have you seen a picture of him?"

She nods. "He's fit."

Well, of course he would be. "Has he ever told you his real name?"

"Yes. Mikey."

"Mikey who?"

"What difference does it make?"

"Well, he isn't very kind, and perhaps that's why."

"You don't know anything."

"I know he might be lying about Georgia. And even if he isn't, he is bullying you." He braces himself. "Is that why you've been cutting yourself?"

No answer, just a long, sad stare.

"I can help you, Ella, if you let me."

She flings her arms around his neck and cries and cries until she has no more tears to shed.

27

Madelena and I are drinking tea in my newly refurbished kitchen – glossy black cabinets, speckled granite work surfaces and gleaming stainless-steel appliances. Jasper's idea, of course. Josh and Bruno are playing *Call of Duty* in his bedroom, and Dylan is hanging out with Daisy in hers, listening to her iPod, apparently. The door is shut, and I definitely heard music when I excused myself from Madelena to eavesdrop, but short of bursting in, I can't be sure.

"Is it okay they're alone in Daisy's room?" I ask Madelena as I slot the lasagne into the oven.

"Sure. Why not? Dylan is a polite boy. Well brought up."

I can think of several reasons: Jemma's opinion for one thing, the fact that he's cute-looking, not to mention Daisy's track record. But she's been more docile since making up with Dylan and seems happier. So I leave it at that.

Madelena and I have seen a lot of one another lately. A part-time GP, she's a confident woman, easy in her own skin, and married to Ivan, a Scotsman she met in a bar in Madrid. Bruno is the youngest of her four children so, when it comes to schooling, she's seen and done it all. The one thing she doesn't understand is cricket. And that's what we're talking about.

"I try but I do not understand the rules." She picks up the Easthaven Gazette and puts on her clear-framed spectacles, dangling from a cord around her neck.

I take a bottle of white wine out of the vast fridge. "I'm not surprised. A lot of English people don't either but I come from a family obsessed with cricket. We'll watch a match together and I'll explain."

"Have you heard anything more about the Natalia Topolska murder?"

I half-fill two large glasses, which I take to the table. "Last I heard, they'd fingerprinted the staff and swipe card holders. Samantha Young included."

Madelena's eyebrows shoot up. "Samantha has a swipe card?"

"Yeah, in her role as Chairman of the Friends, apparently. None of the prints match the ones they found on the X-cart, though. The police interviewed the two Spanish girls. Turns out one of them had taken out a loan with some shark. They were late with their repayments, and he'd been threatening them, which is why they'd fled the country. DCI Marshall reckons it's a case of mistaken identity. Seems Natalia was in the wrong place at the wrong time."

"Have they found this guy?"

"Not yet. He's vanished."

Madelena sighs. "I worry about the children."

"I know, but we have to trust the police know what they're doing."

When supper is ready, I call up to the children. Josh and Bruno charge in and sit next to one another at the table Madelena has laid. A few minutes later, Daisy and Dylan appear, their cheeks flushed. Panicked, I plonk the bowl of salad down slightly harder than I mean to.

Daisy screws up her nose. "Ew. Salad."

"And lasagne!" says Josh enthusiastically. "Mum's signature dish."

"He means her only dish."

I wince, wishing Daisy would drop her annoying habit of referring to me as *her*.

"I thought a signature dish had to be unique," says Dylan.

"She means trademark," says Bruno. "Mama's is paella."

Josh licks his lips. "Now that is good."

Madelena shakes her head. "Nonsense."

"He's right. You're an excellent cook. Whereas I am not."

"We shall see." Madelena spoons up a forkful, closes her eyes, and chews. Her lids flicker open. "Mmm. Delicious. Wouldn't you say, Daisy?"

To my astonishment, Daisy laughs. "Yeah. It is."

Madelena holds up her glass. "Cheers, then."

The clink of our glasses is drowned out by the strident clamour of the doorbell. Madelena jumps a few inches off her seat, spilling her wine in the process.

"I'm sorry. I keep forgetting to ask the builders to tone it down."

I cross the hall to the porch and heave open the heavy door. Jemma is standing on the doorstep, her face set in a stern expression.

"Oh! Hello. You're early." A minute earlier, and she'd have seen the flushed faces of her son and my daughter. "We've just started supper. Come and join us. There's plenty to go around."

"Is Dylan here?"

"Er, yes." And then I twig. "Oh … oh my goodness. You didn't know."

She blushes. "I thought he was with Oli Carter, but Leo told me she saw him get into your car."

"I'm sorry, I should have rung."

She manages a weak smile. "Don't be silly. He should have told me."

"What you need is a glass of wine."

I take her by the arm and steer her into the kitchen. To her credit, if Jemma is angry with Dylan, which I would have been if Daisy or Josh had pulled a stunt like this, she doesn't show it, but sits at the table, after Madelena has smothered her in kisses, takes the wine I offer, and joins in the conversation and even the laughter. And once the shock of seeing his mother has died down and he realises he isn't in trouble, Dylan, the freckled skin on his face creamy white one more, relaxes, too.

"You must come for lunch in the holidays," I tell Jemma as we say goodbye.

"I'd like that," she says, and gives me a brief but unexpected hug.

The next day, while Daisy is at a rehearsal, I find Josh lying on his bed reading *Lord of The Flies*, something that would have delighted Guy.

"Should I be worried about Daisy and Dylan being alone together?" I ask

He pulls a face. "Mum, that's gross."

"I didn't mean …"

He scowls.

"Great book," I say, backing awkwardly out of the room.

"They snog, if that's what you're asking."

. . .

It's okay, I reassure myself later as I climb into bed, all teenagers snog. I snuggle under the duvet, roll onto my side, and close my eyes. But why did Dylan lie to Jemma? And what if they want to do something more than kiss? I slap the empty side of the bed in frustration. Jesus! It's not Jemma who should be worried, it's me.

"I need you, Guy. I need to talk about this."

I groan and glance at the alarm clock. Twelve past midnight. Too late to phone Fran, or Madelena either, for that matter. Sighing, I slide back down, resigned to a sleepless night.

"Well, sure, if they leave it at kissing," Fran says, when I call her the following morning, after I've dropped the kids at school. "But don't forget, physically, Daisy is fairly developed for her age."

She's referring to my little girl's breasts, already an impressive 32B, and her periods, which started when she was eleven. The date is etched in my memory precisely because I wasn't there. I was in Libya reporting on NATO's air-strikes against Gaddafi's failing regime. It's testament to Guy's parenting skills that I wasn't aware of her emotional landmark until I stumbled across the pads in the bathroom cabinet two months later. I remember feeling I'd missed out again, that my experience of their childhood was like a book with various pages missing. It was your choice, I remind myself for the zillionth time.

"Her hormones will be running rife," Fran says. "You remember what it's like?"

"Do you think Guy talked to her about contraception?"

"Probably. He wasn't one to shy away from difficult issues."

"Maybe I should talk to Daisy anyway. Just to be on the safe side."

"I wouldn't bother. You'll only embarrass yourself."

"What kind of advice is that?"

"Megan, they cover it all in PSHE."

"Are you sure?"

"Positive. Sex lessons start when they're about seven."

I gasp. "Really?"

"If you want my advice, which you clearly do, why not have a casual chat?"

"Casual! We're talking Daisy here."

My head throbbing, I say goodbye to Fran, shuffle wearily into the kitchen, and flick on the kettle. I'll take Fran's advice and have a word with Daisy one evening after school, I decide as I flop onto a chair.

But the next two evenings, Daisy stays late to rehearse so doesn't have the time to invite Dylan home. Inevitably, I let the matter slide.

I'm letting the children walk to school without me because tonight is the opening night of *Grease!* and it seemed fair to cut Daisy some slack. The picture of calm, she has just said goodbye.

"I'm impressed," I tell Josh who has misplaced his maths homework. "It's not easy standing up in front of hundreds of people."

He shrugs. "She's got her play face on. She'll be crapping herself later."

"Josh!"

"Well, she will." He finds the exercise book he's looking for, buried amongst the newspapers that have gathered, like autumn leaves, in a pile in the corner of the kitchen, and hurries after his sister.

I, however, am far from relaxed. I'm excited but I'm also nervous. Tonight will be the first time I see my daughter perform. I'm uneasy, too, about accompanying Gabriel. He called me a couple of nights ago to tell me that, thanks to my advice, he'd discovered the cause of Ella's self-harm.

"She's much happier now, and her wounds are healing."

"That's brilliant news."

"I gather Daisy is performing in *Grease*! Mind if I tag along?"

The first person I see at the pre-performance drinks is Robert Webster. Fortunately, he's engrossed with a leggy blonde and doesn't notice our arrival. Samantha is deep in conversation with Dickie Drummond-Stone, dressed in the same beige cords and maroon jumper he had on when I met him. As Gabriel heads to the bar, I try to catch her eye, but someone taps me on my shoulder. I whirl round and come face to face with Robert. He leans over and kisses me a little too close to my mouth for my liking, and for a fraction longer than is comfortable.

"Can I get you a drink?" he asks.

"I'm okay but thanks." I turn back, but Samantha and Dickie have moved further into the room and are chatting animatedly with Anthony Swann.

Robert follows my gaze. "That's Samantha for you. Never misses an opportunity."

"Don't be mean."

"Incredible, isn't it? Dickie and Sam? God knows what

she sees in him. Although I hear the clue is in the name. Rumour has it he's hung like an elephant."

"You're kidding!"

"Well, okay, perhaps his penis isn't quite as long as an elephant's. They're about six foot, and we're probably only talking six—"

"What about Charlie?"

"I imagine he's busy poking the pussy of some pretty little fund manager in his London flat."

"Robert! We're at school." I catch sight of Gabriel, squeezing through the crowds.

Robert nudges me in the ribs. "Oh, c'mon, don't be a prude. Charlie's a complete bastard. Sam deserves some fun, don't you think? Mind you, she should have set her sights a bit higher than dear old Dickie."

"Here you are." Gabriel hands me a glass of wine.

Robert's eyes widen, and a sly smile creeps over his face. "Well, hello there, Vicar. Good to see you again. We were just talking about the show. Have you seen it?"

Gabriel frowns. "Actually, no."

"Too busy with your holy orders?"

"It's set in the fifties," I explain hurriedly. "Cool guy Danny falls in love with sweet, wholesome Sandy and—"

"Kenickie, played by my son, gets bad girl Rizzo, played by Daisy, pregnant. Imagine that?"

I glare at Robert. "In the film! This is a school production."

Robert holds up his hands. "I was joking."

I glance at Gabriel, whose cheek muscles are working furiously. "Not funny."

"Sorry. Sorry."

Mark Carter rushes over, and Gabriel's face relaxes. "Good to see you all." Mark raises his beer glass. "How are you guys bearing up? Oli was a bag of nerves this morning, and it seems to have rubbed off on me."

I smile. "Nerves are a good thing."

"Hope you're right, Megan. He's adamant he can't sing. Nonsense, of course. Otherwise, why would Grace have chosen him for the part?"

I pat him on the back. "Daisy assures me he's brilliant."

Mark smiles. "With a bit of luck, Leo and Jemma will be calming them all down. They're helping Grace with the costumes and makeup."

Robert winks. "Very public-spirited of them, don't you think?"

"Leo's got herself all worked up about them reopening the theatre," continues Mark, oblivious. "She's convinced they'll find another body under the stage, although the children don't seem to be the least bit bothered."

The bell sounds for the start of the performance. Mark slaps Robert on the back. "Come on then. We're under strict instructions to sit with the girls at the front. See you both later."

Gabriel raises a sardonic eyebrow. "Funny guy, Robert."

"A real hoot," I mutter.

Madelena and Ivan are already in their seats. Relieved, I sit next to her, Gabriel on my other side.

Madelena leans over and whispers in my ear, "He is gorgeous. Such a handsome couple."

"We are not a couple."

She chuckles mischievously. "No, no, of course not."

I groan inwardly. Oh God, what have I done?

The lights go down, the curtain goes up, and the characters take to the stage. Another wave of apprehension rushes over me. I'm a huge fan of the film, the characters ingrained in my psyche. Grace Potter's production – a red-haired

Danny who can almost hold a tune, a dark-haired Sandy who drowns out Danny in all the songs, a baby-faced Kenickie, and Rydell High's pint-sized headmistress, a boy dressed as a woman – for comic effect, I assume because the kids in the audience howl with laughter every time he comes on – takes some adjusting to. I slide lower in my chair and try and suspend my disbelief as my English teacher taught me. But it's not easy, especially when Georgia Young, who's playing Frenchy, trips over Bruno's foot in one of the dance sequences.

And then Daisy takes centre stage. In her makeup she looks at least eighteen. I hold my breath. But she delivers her first line in a perfect American drawl, and I exhale with relief. And when she opens her mouth to sing, in a clear confident voice, every hair on the back of my neck stands on end.

The curtain goes down to deafening applause. Many of the audience are on their feet. I'm not, though. I'm too astonished to move. I've experienced so many emotions in the last two hours I don't know whether to laugh or cry.

Gabriel touches me on the arm. "Daisy was sensational."

"They all were." I beam and turn to Madelena. "Bruno was fantastic."

She reaches over and gives me a hug. "Ah, Megan, so was Daisy."

A hum of excitement fills the foyer as parents greet their children with hugs and kisses. Carried away on the wave of emotion, I scan the area for Daisy. Jemma, Leo, and Samantha are huddled together, but I can't see my daughter.

"Here she is." Josh drags his sister over.

Daisy's arms dangle awkwardly by her sides. She knows this is the first play of hers I've seen but she doesn't know that I'm regretting all those performances I've missed. My emotions bubbling uncontrollably, I throw caution to the wind, open my arms, and envelop her, squeezing her until she yelps in protest.

"You were wonderful. I'm incredibly proud of you."

Instead of the scowl I'm expecting, she stares at me, wide-eyed. "You really mean that?"

"I really do."

Josh embraces his sister "You were awesome."

"Okay, don't overdo it." But from the huge smile on her face, I can tell she's feeling about ten foot tall.

Later, I scan the almost empty room for Gabriel, but he's no longer there. Looks like we're walking home, I think. But any annoyance I feel at his sudden departure dissolves in my Daisy-induced high.

28

It's the last day of the holidays. Bruno, Oli, and Josh are playing *Call of Duty* in Josh's bedroom again. They asked Dylan if he wanted to join in, but he'd much rather hang out with Daisy.

"You're weird," Josh said and closed the door.

He hasn't seen Daisy since before Easter. She went to stay with her granny in Hampshire for a week, and then someone called Fran and her kids came to stay for four days. He missed her. She said she missed him, too, but he's not sure whether to believe her. He thinks she likes him. In fact, ever since she rang him to say sorry for landing him in trouble, he's pretty sure she does. She was properly upset. Kept saying over and over that it stank.

"My bad," she said finally. "Friends?"

"'Course," he said, playing it cool. He had to. He wasn't sure she was serious. Why would someone like Daisy want to be friends with someone like him?

She must be desperate.

He's desperate, too, but in a different way. He's mad about her, totally obsessed. When he sees her, his stomach lurches, and everybody else magically disappears. It's like they're the only two people in the world. He's never felt like this before. He thinks he's in love with her. He's itching to tell her, but he doesn't dare. When he practiced it out loud, it sounded dumb. He can't imagine what it would sound like to Daisy. She'd laugh at him, and he couldn't bear that. It's too big a deal. He wishes he could take time out from thinking about her, but he can't. He wants to be with her all the time. Nothing else matters apart, maybe, from cricket.

They're in Daisy's bedroom listening to music. At least that's what they've told her mum they're doing. She's downstairs in the kitchen with Leo and Madelena.

"They're well into their second bottle of wine, which means they're pissed so they won't care what we're doing." Daisy sits on the bed, plants the iPod in its dock, and turns it on. "Do you like Ed Sheeran? It's the only decent music my brother's got." Without waiting for an answer, she pats the bed beside her.

Dylan does as he's bid. "I like your mum. She isn't stressy like mine."

"Oh my God, I can't believe you just said that. She's, like, the stressiest person on this planet."

No way, he thinks. Megan is laid-back and funny. Not as funny as Leo Carter. She's completely mad. His mother is about as far from laid-back as it's possible to be. His dad's okay, though, apart from when he flirts with his friends' mums and when he's arguing with Mum. It used to drive him nuts, but now he turns the volume up on the television or his iPod so he can't hear.

"She puts it on when we have visitors," continues Daisy. "But she's actually a complete cow. You have no idea what it's like to live with her. Most of the time I wish she was dead."

He gasps. "You don't mean that."

She purses her lips and tilts her chin in the air. "Actually, I do."

Dylan can't imagine wishing either of his parents dead, however annoying they are. It would be unbearable. But it's probably because she misses her dad. Losing a parent must be the worst thing ever. He'd like to ask her about him, but he's scared it'll upset her.

She smiles suddenly. "Do you want to lie down?"

His pulse speeds up, but he's determined to play it cool. "Sure, why not."

They are facing one another, holding hands, their arms bent in front of their chests, their noses touching. He's so close he can see the lemon flecks in her pale-blue irises. They press their lips together and kiss. They've never done it like this before. Lying on the bed.

After what feels like forever, his jaw starts to ache. He tries to ignore it, but now his neck is stiff, and his right foot is cramping. He pulls away, sits up, and wipes his mouth with the back of his hand. Daisy sits up, too. Her cheeks are pink. And her eyelids are drooping.

"Are you okay?" he asks.

"I'm good. Why?"

He shrugs. "No reason."

"I could feel it, if that's what you're worried about."

He smiles. *She means my hard-on, but she's too embarrassed to say. Wow. It's not like her to be shy.*

She rolls onto her back. "I've got a surprise for you."

Dylan's heart thuds.

"Scared?"

"I don't know. Maybe a bit."

She takes his wrist and guides his hand under her T-shirt. Every nerve in his body tingles as his hand brushes over the warmth of her soft belly, the ridges of her ribs, until his fingers rest on her bra. He holds his breath.

"DAIS-EE! DY-LAN!"

Daisy springs up with a start. "Jesus. I wish she wouldn't do that."

"Better than her walking in, I guess." He takes a deep breath. Phew. That was close. Too close.

"True."

Dylan bends down and kisses her on the lips. "I'll see you tomorrow."

Grinning, Daisy takes hold of the bottom of her T-shirt and yanks it up. He stares at her bra, mesmerised.

"DYLAN! DAIS-EE! What are you doing in there?"

The voice is nearer now. Dylan leans over and plants a kiss on the top of Daisy's left breast then rushes to the door, twisting his neck to check she's covered before he opens it. "Sorry. We didn't hear you."

"Of course you didn't."

Megan smells of wine, but all the same he reckons she knows what they've been doing.

His mother is waiting on the doorstep. He's cross they have to leave. He wishes she'd come inside. Have a drink, maybe, like Bruno's mum and Oli's mum who are laughing loudly in the kitchen.

"Couldn't we stay a bit longer?"

His mother frowns. "Have you forgotten your appointment?"

He scowls, remembering his elocution lesson. For God's sake, what's that all about?

His mother prods him, and he turns to Megan. "Thank you for having me."

"A pleasure, Dylan."

He walks down the path, crossing the road to where the

Panda is parked. Before he climbs in, he takes one last look at the house in case Daisy is watching from the window. She isn't, but Ella's dad is walking down the path with a bunch of flowers.

His mother sees him, too. "I don't believe it."

"Neither do I," says Dylan. "Daisy says they *so* don't believe in God."

29

Gabriel hands me the over-the-top bouquet of flowers he's cradling. I force my mouth into something I hope resembles a smile but which, judging by the strain, is probably more of a grimace. Jemma's car is still parked over the road. I hope she can't see. God only knows what conclusions she'd draw.

"Why are you giving me flowers again?"

A burst of laughter explodes from the kitchen. Gabriel backs off slightly, his eyes darting nervously over my shoulder.

"To apologise for disappearing the night of the play."

"Thank you, but you really didn't have to."

"I know, but I wanted to. Megan, there's something I want to—"

"I'd ask you in but I've got company." I nod in the direction of the laughter.

"I'm sorry. I was going to leave them on the step. There's a card." He delivers this clumsy explanation in a hurry and, despite my irritation, I can't help feeling sorry for him. He raises his hand. "Bye then."

He really should get out more, I think, and toss the flowers on the hall table.

"Ooh! An admirer," says Leo from the kitchen doorway. "Who are they from? Anyone we know?"

Madelena giggles. "I can guess."

"No, you can't."

"Glen," says Leo.

Madelena's eyes widen. "Glen?"

"The gorgeous Australian hunk Megan used to work with."

I groan. "You are way off the mark."

Leo points at the flowers. "There's a card, look."

Quick as a flash, I remove the card, but Leo snatches it from me. "Give that back."

But Leo has opened the envelope. "Oh-my-God!"

Madelena's eyes bulge. "What? What?"

Leo waves the card. "The Sexy Vicar! But he's such a prude."

Madelena nudges Leo on the arm. "But gorgeous, no?"

I roll my eyes and shake my head.

"*Dear Megan, so sorry about the other night, Gabriel.*" Leo grins. "What happened the other night, Megan?"

"Nothing."

Madelena winks. "That is not true."

"You went on a date with The Sexy Vicar?" persists Leo.

My face grows hot. "No, I did not."

"They were at the play together," Madelena says.

"But why's he sorry? No, don't tell me, he tried to lure you into his bed." Leo clasps her face. "You didn't, did you?"

I tap my foot and glare at them. "When you two have quite finished."

Leo takes me by the hand. "We need more wine." She leads me back into the kitchen. "I'll pour you another glass, and you can tell us all about it. Who would have thought it? Megan Moreau and the Sexy Vicar."

It's over an hour and another bottle of wine later, and I still haven't managed to persuade them there is nothing going on between Gabriel and me. If I wasn't so drunk I'd be upset. Guy hasn't been dead a year. Romance is way off the cards. "Nothing's going on, so don't go telling anyone there is."

"Issa beautiful thing," slurs Madelena. "You should not be embarrassed."

"Oh my God, Mama, you are *so* drunk," says Bruno, hurtling down the stairs followed by Oli and Josh.

Josh narrows his eyes at me.

"I'm fine," I say.

Oli sighs. "Honestly, Mum, how are we going to get home? I've got an exam paper to finish before tomorrow."

"We were celebrating," says Madelena.

I shake my head and sigh. "I'd better order you both a taxi."

Half an hour later, Josh is making coffee and I'm clearing up. I drop the three empty wine bottles in the recycling box outside the back door and put the half-drunk fourth bottle in the fridge.

"You're pathetic." Arms crossed, Daisy is leaning against the far wall, watching me like a hawk.

"Don't speak to me like that."

"Why not? You'd say the same to me if I got drunk."

"Yes, I would, because you're only thirteen and shouldn't be drinking."

She juts out her chin. "So it's okay for a single parent to get drunk. Great role model."

"It was Leo—"

"Typical. Blame someone else."

Josh thrusts a mug of black coffee at me. "Here. Drink this. You'll feel better."

How does he know? I wonder, flopping into a chair. "Thanks for doing the washing up."

He shrugs. "S'okay. I'm cool."

"Yeah right!" says Daisy. "Course you are."

"Give it a rest," says Josh.

She clenches her fists and stamps her foot. "Why must you always side with *her*?"

"I'm not siding with anyone, I'm just bored of hearing you whine."

"Loser!"

"Idiot."

"Emo!"

I groan and bury my head in my hands.

"Nob!"

"Dickhead!"

I look up. "Daisy!"

"Well, he is."

Josh smirks. "You're so lame, Daisy."

I slap my hands on the kitchen table. "Oh, for God's sake, give it a rest."

"I will if she will," Josh says, scowling.

Daisy smirks. "I will if he apologises."

"What for?" asks Josh.

"ENOUGH ALREADY!"

The twins visibly jump before they fall silent.

I take a calming sip of coffee before setting the mug quietly on the table. "Thank you. That's better."

But the silence doesn't last long.

Josh opens the fridge. "What's for supper?"

I groan. "We just had lunch."

"No. We just cleared lunch away. Lunch was at least four hours ago."

"Can't you stop thinking about food for a minute?"

"Nope."

I rub my throbbing temple. Great, a headache. Just what I need. "I don't know. What's in the fridge?"

"Who are the flowers from?" asks Daisy suddenly, staring at the bouquet that I've dumped in the sink.

Josh shuts the fridge door and exchanges a worried look with his sister.

My heart sinks.

"Is that why you were celebrating?" asks Josh.

Daisy spins round and glares at me.

"We weren't celebrating. That was just Madelena being silly."

Josh bites his lip. "Who are they from?"

I'm madly trying to formulate an answer when the door-bell rings. What now? I wonder. But just as I'm about to ask Daisy to answer it, it occurs to me it might be Gabriel, and I stand up, as quickly as I dare without arousing suspicion, and hurry to the door.

But it isn't Gabriel. It's a flamboyantly dressed woman of indeterminate age. And on second glance, once I've stopped staring at her wild, grey hair and focused on her face, which is attractive but plump, the pale, smooth skin etched with fine lines, I'd put her age as somewhere in her early seventies. She's wearing a floral smocked top, flared jeans, and white clogs, beneath a woolly Afghan coat, and has a familiar smile which she brandishes with an easy, but unsettling, charm.

"Hello, Megan." Her voice is instantly recognisable, unaltered after all these years.

I clutch my neck in shock. "Oh my God! Eve!"

30

Everything I believe to be real – time, place, colour – recedes like a tide, leaving in its place a washed-out shadow. I suck up mouthfuls of air with deep, gasping breaths, but my lungs have shrunk to tight little balls. Spots dance in front of my eyes. I close them and lean against the doorframe to steady myself.

"Oh dear, I've shocked you," Eve says.

"What do you want?" My voice is low, faltering.

"I wanted to know if you're coping. Are you?"

Her voice is honey-sweet. Distant childhood memories spring to mind: the two of us, making daisy chains in the garden; picnics on the beach, the sand soft between my toes. But then reality hits. I despise this woman and everything she stands for.

My eyes flick open. "I haven't seen you for thirty-four years and almost nine months." My rapid-fire delivery surprises me. I hadn't realised I'd been keeping count.

She tilts her head to one side and sniffs. "Have you been drinking, darling?"

I'm too stunned to reply.

"So like your father. He couldn't get through the day without a lunchtime tipple. Drank like a fish. No wonder he died young."

"Is that all you can say?" I glare at her. She looks ridiculous. An aging throwback to another era.

"I'm your mother. I wanted to see you."

"Not good enough."

She blinks in alarm. "I—"

"It's not open to debate. Now go!"

She shudders. "Megan, please." She takes a step towards me, but I back away. "I wasn't sure where you lived. Ralph told me."

"You've seen Ralph? No. I don't believe you. He would have said."

"I bumped into him in Florence in September. We had a drink."

I gasp. Ralph went there on holiday. He told me he was going. I recommended places, the *enoteca* where I met Guy. Why hadn't he told me he'd seen Eve? I stare at her, open-mouthed.

"I've been living there with Paolo these past twenty years." She lets out an exhausted sigh and brushes the air with her hand. "It didn't work out with Antonio. He wanted children and, well … I knew Paolo from way back. He was my tutor at art school. We had a passionate affair, but I left him when I graduated. He was my first … my only true love. He died last year."

I stare at her in disbelief. "What about my father? You had three children by him. Are you telling me you were still in love with Pao … this man, when you married him? That you didn't love Dad? Ever?"

"Ralph told me how angry you all were, and I understand. I really do. But—"

"Why are you here? Do you get some sort of macabre satisfaction from inflicting pain?"

"I wasn't happy married to your father, which is why I wasn't any use as a mother, so I left," continues Eve as if I haven't spoken. "Once Ralph had calmed down, he told me what had happened to all of you. But you see, Megan, I already knew what you'd been through. I'd read about it in the papers. You'd made a name for yourself and, well, Guy Truman was famous. It must have been terrible for you. But, darling, I understand. Paolo meant the world to me. I believe a part of me died with him. I was devastated. Devastated." She pauses to ensure her words sink in. "It's taken me a while, I wasn't sure if I should but, in the end, I knew I had to come."

She steps closer, but I hold up my hands. I'm fuming, about to explode. But when, eventually, I speak, it is with the utmost control.

"Well, that's great, Eve. You came and now you can go. You don't know me. That was your choice. You didn't know Guy. You never met him. And you don't know your grand-children. You are a horrible, selfish, thoughtless woman, and I don't want you in my life."

Eve's face crumbles, but she doesn't let up. "You need your mother."

"I don't have a mother."

"Megan, please." Her eyes are fixed on mine, pleading with me to reconsider. They're a faded, watery blue, the whites shot through with red, spidery capillaries. The eyes of an old woman. A lonely old woman.

"Mu-um, the rabbits have dug a tunnel out of their run." Josh tears through the hall. "Could you help me…" He sees the stranger on the doorstep and falls silent.

Eve smiles. "Your mother used to shoot rabbits."

Josh's mouth drops open, but Eve doesn't notice. Her equanimity restored, she's turned her attention back to me. "Aren't you going to introduce me?"

"No."

"Why ever not, darling?"

"Will you please stop calling me darling."

Josh tugs my sleeve. "Are you okay, Mum?"

I place my hand on his shoulder. "Yes, I'm fine," I lie.

"Who's this?" Daisy strides into the hall, and for once I don't care that she's being rude.

"Your granny, dear," says Eve.

Daisy narrows her eyes and crosses her arms. "My grandmother has short blonde hair and lives in Hampshire."

"Not *that* granny, your other granny."

"We don't have another grandmother. She died." Daisy's eyes glint, defiantly.

"When Mum was eleven," adds Josh.

"Ah. Of course she did," Eve says, not unkindly. "Here. The phone number of the hotel where I'm staying." She thrusts a folded piece of paper in my hand, turns, and walks away.

Daisy pulls a face. "Random."

"Totally," agrees Josh. "Can I have a Coke, Mum?"

I clench my hands into fists. "Sure."

"Cool," says Daisy, and they charge back inside.

My mind is reeling. Did Eve honestly believe I'd be pleased to see her? Was she expecting a reconciliation? A tremor passes through me. Light-headed, I start to sway. My fist unclenches, and the scrap of paper I've absently ground into a ball drops to the ground. It skitters over the paving slabs into the flowerbed where the tulips are coming into bloom.

"Are you okay?" Margaret Brown hurries down the path towards me. "You look like you've seen a ghost."

It occurs to me that's exactly what I've seen. I cover my eyes with my hands.

"Come inside." She takes my arm and leads me into the living room where I collapse onto the sofa. "Do you want to talk about it?" Sitting beside me, she squeezes my hand.

I sigh exhaustedly. "I had an unexpected visitor."

Margaret groans. "I told him he should telephone, but he wouldn't listen."

I tilt my head.

"She's still grieving, I said, leave her alone. Honestly, the man has no idea."

The penny drops. "Oh, Margaret, it would take more than an eager priest and a bunch of flowers to floor me." I lean forward and bury my head in my hands. When I speak, my voice is muffled. "I had a visit from a woman I haven't seen for thirty-five years."

There's a pause while Margaret digests the information. "Goodness. You mean your mother?"

I shake my head and lower my hands. "I mean the woman who gave birth to me who walked out on me when I was eleven years old. No mother would do that."

"Why now?"

"I don't know. I really don't. She wanted to know if I was coping. What kind of an opening question is that? And then she as good as accused me of being a drunk like my father, which he wasn't. But I can tell you, Margaret, if Dad drank, she drove him to it. Apparently, she never loved him. She was unhappy. That's why she left her three children." I'm worked up now, indignant. "Honestly, you've been more of a mother to me these last five months than that selfish, cold-hearted cow ever was."

She puts her arm around me. "I can't imagine how you must feel."

"Angry, Margaret. Very, very angry. How dare she?"

Josh appears, followed by Daisy, worried looks on both their faces. "What's wrong?" he asks.

I jerk upright. "I felt a little faint that's all."

Daisy rolls her eyes at Margaret. "That'll be the wine. She's drunk loads."

"Is it because of that woman?" Josh plonks himself on the other side of me. "Who was she, Mum? She seemed to know you."

Daisy clicks her fingers. *Snap. Snap. Snap.* "It was that woman, wasn't it? You know, Josh? What's-her-name?"

His forehead crinkles, and his eyes dart up to the right. "Oh yeah. The one who sent you away to that school."

"Aunty Jill? How on earth do you know about her?"

"Dad told us. He said she gave you a hard time."

I imagine the scene, the twins playing up, angry their mother has gone away yet again, Guy justifying my career by detailing my difficult childhood. No. Perhaps that's unfair. Perhaps he told them because he knew I never would. My childhood, post Eve, wasn't something I liked to discuss. I kept it firmly where I'd left it. In Devon. In the past.

I was seven months pregnant when Guy broached the subject more determinedly than usual. He couldn't understand why I didn't want to talk about it. It was 27th July 2000. I remember the date because I was exhausted, having just returned from Russia after interviewing Vladimir Putin, the ex-KGB officer who'd been inaugurated for his first term as President in May. Eric was delighted, but the trip had left me with puffy ankles and heartburn. Given the energetic state of my hormones, this was not a good coupling.

"Our pasts shape us," Guy said.

245

"Ah, I get it. You mean I'll be a crap mother, too."

"That's not what I said."

"You implied it. You think I'll make a mess of it like Eve. But I'm different. Unlike *her*, I never wanted to be a mother. My career is what matters. I've never lied to you about that. You can't be a foreign correspondent and have children, I said. But you wouldn't listen? Oh no. You insisted on children. 'You'll regret it if you don't,' you said."

But instead of arguing, he wrapped his arms around me and kissed away my angry tears. "You'll be a great mother," he whispered. "Wait and see."

He was wrong, of course. I wasn't a great mother. I wasn't maternal. I was impatient and I continued to work. But when these precious little beings came screaming and kicking into the world, to my surprise, I fell in love with them. And as Guy and I held each of them tight to our chests that night, sitting side by side on my hospital bed, I remember whispering to him that I could never leave them. Not ever.

"I know you won't," he said.

The past shapes us.

Had Guy meant that I became the person I am because Eve left me? Did she motivate me? Would I have been a completely different person if she'd stayed?

"So was it Aunty Jill?" persists Daisy.

Margaret squeezes my arm. "I should go." Smiling reassuringly, she leaves the room.

I pat the sofa next to me, but Daisy shakes her head. "I haven't seen that woman for a long, long time. For all I know she could have been dead."

Josh whistles. "So it was Aunty Jill. She has some front turning up like that."

I sigh and shake my head.

"That woman," begins Daisy carefully, her eyes fixed on

mine, "is actually your mum, isn't she? That's why she called you darling. She told us she was our granny because she is."

I sigh wearily. "Yeah. That was Eve Moreau. Turns out she's alive after all."

"No wonder you wouldn't let her in."

Her easy acceptance surprises me.

"Not much of a granny, if you ask me," says Josh.

I glance at Daisy who's frowning. What's she thinking? I wonder.

After what seems an age, she speaks. "Why did she leave you and Uncle Ralph and Uncle Felix?"

I take a deep breath. "She ran away with another man."

"Was she in love with him?"

I think about the brief affair she had with Jeff before she left him for Antonio, a man I never met and whom she left for Paolo. "No, she wasn't."

"Why didn't she take you with her?"

Even after all these years the question hurts, a searing pain that cuts right through my core. I used to ask it myself most nights that first term at boarding school, crying myself to sleep, my face turned to the dormitory wall. Was it because she didn't love us? Or me? Was it my fault? My shoulders droop, weighted down by years of not knowing.

"I don't know," I reply honestly.

"Dad says she was selfish," says Josh. "That's why she left."

"And lazy," adds Daisy. "It's hard work bringing up children."

My stomach is twisting into knots, but I laugh. "Really?"

Daisy sniffs. "Well, you're always telling us it is."

"It can be, but only when you have to do it on your own, and she wasn't on her own. She had my father. Maybe she just wasn't cut out for it."

But Daisy isn't listening. "Dad didn't find it difficult."

I wince.

"Yeah, but he wasn't on his own, was he?" says Josh.

Daisy curls her lip. "He was most of the time."

"I always came back," I say in a voice barely above a whisper.

"But Dad won't, will he?" Daisy says, turning on her heel and marching out of the room.

"Yeah, but that's not the point, is it?" Josh's stomach makes a strange gurgling sound. "What's for supper, Mum?"

31

It's eight o'clock on Friday morning, and I'm in the kitchen with Daisy who can't stop sneezing.

"It sounds like hay fever. When did it start?" I ask.

"Yesterday when I was – ah – ah playing tennis – ah-choo. I'd just pulled off – aaah – a near-perfect drop shot–choo."

"Drop shots. Wow!" I reach for the box of tissues and offer them to her.

She takes one, blows her nose, then hurls it into the bin with impressive accuracy. "Dad taught me last summer."

I snap my fingers. "The secret weapon."

"You remember."

"Of course I do. You were going to try it out on me."

She screws up her nose. "Do you actually play tennis?"

"I used to."

She looks at me doubtfully. "Dad said to be a great player you need touch, and the drop shot was, like, the ultimate weapon. Soft hands he said I needed, and backspin. Anyway, it was game point, and I was rallying cross-court with Georgia when she looped up a moon ball. I was going to hit a topspin forehand, but I changed my mind at the last minute and sliced the bottom of the ball. It hit the tarmac and died, like, totally fierce. Georgia was stranded. Epic fail." She pauses to grab a handful of tissues and blows her nose again. "I spent hours trying to do it with Dad last summer, but yesterday was the first time it worked. I was five-one up and I was, like, really pumped, but then I started sneezing and I had to fight like crazy to win six-four." Daisy's eyes are sparkling with passion.

"Would you mind if I came and watched?"

"I can't play with snot streaming down my face." She clamps her nose in a clump of tissues. "My eyes sting. I feel like shit."

I let the swearword go. No sense in starting an argument. Not now things are going so well. By some miracle, Eve's arrival has passed without incident apart from the night Josh came home from school without Daisy. He had no idea where his sister was, and I was worried, certain her disappearance was a reaction to Eve's visit. But a couple of hours later, she appeared.

"Where have you been? I was just about to call the police," I lied. After last summer's shenanigans, it wasn't enough to totally freak me out. But unlike then, she didn't scream at me, or pout, or flounce off to her bedroom, but simply said, *I'm sorry. I didn't mean to worry you.*

I assumed she'd been with Dylan and told her, in no uncertain terms, never to disappear like that again and left it at that.

"It's probably hay fever. There's a lot of pollen in the air and lawns being mown." It wasn't Gabriel's flowers. I shoved them in the dustbin the moment the twins had gone to bed the night of Eve's visit. "I've got some antihistamine tablets upstairs. If you take one now you should be fine by this afternoon."

It's warm and sunny, and the smell of freshly cut grass lingers in the air. I round the bend above St Peter's and walk under the overhanging branches of the ancient cherry tree, bloated with baby-pink blossom. The sound of leather connecting with willow drifts over the school's flint wall, where boys in pristine whites are dotted about the emerald outfield. Josh's cricket match, it seems, is already underway.

The long cold winter is over at last. A spring in my step, I hurry towards the school gate, no longer guarded by PC Coleman. The three CCTV cameras on the walls of the main building, the gym, and the theatre, the only outward sign that the murder investigation continues.

I catch sight of Jemma Webster, a heavy picnic basket in hand, a green folding chair slung over her shoulder. I'm about to rush after her when my mobile rings. My heart leaps. It's Glen. He's alive, thank God.

"Jez and I didn't go to Syria. Eric sent us to Afghanistan instead. Only now we're stuck in the biggest fucking sandpit in the world."

"It could be worse."

"I need to get back. My cat's missing me."

"You don't have a cat."

"Okay. I've run out of shirts."

"You're in Dubai. Buy some."

"I miss you, Megs. Jez Dixon smells like a pig's arse."

"That bad, huh?"

"Yeah. But hey, how's things in the Truman household?"

"On the up, I think. Call me when you get back. We'll arrange lunch."

"I'll hold you to that. Catch yer later. The BBC will roast my balls on a barbie if my phone bill gets any bigger."

I cut the connection, smiling. Someone calls my name. I look over my shoulder and see Leo, weighed down with paraphernalia.

She grins. "This is normally a really close match, but Daisy should seal it for us."

"You think?"

"Coco's playing, but Georgia's been dropped." I must look panicked because Leo continues, "Don't worry, it'll do her and Samantha good not to have their own way for once. Have you seen Jemma?"

"Yes, I—"

"Have you heard? Dylan's been made cricket captain. That should cheer her up. I'm going to watch the game with her later. Oli's playing. Come on. We want to be sure to get the best seats."

The girls are on court warming up. Leo sets down her chair between two benches. Three mothers are already seated, but there's a space at the end of the one next to Leo. My palms are sweaty, but I can only imagine how Daisy's feeling. Her opponent, in a royal-blue dress, hair tied in a long blonde plait, has a professional air about her, and grunts as she powers the ball back over the net. Daisy catches my eye and manages a half-smile. The warm-up over, she jogs to her kit bag and takes a long swig from her silver water bottle.

My fears dissipate the moment Daisy strikes the ball. Her serve is fast and accurate, and she follows it up, hitting the lines with ferocious forehands at least a dozen times. After barely fifteen minutes she's five-love up. Jasmine, her opponent, dramatically flings her racquet to the ground in disgust.

Her mother, a sour-faced woman who's been yelling instructions for the duration of the match, throws her daughter a filthy look. But no amount of shouting, foot-stamping, or face-pulling is going to help Jasmine now. All Daisy has to do is drive the final nail into Jasmine's coffin. This must have been what Guy got such a kick out of, I think, and clench my fists and will my daughter on.

"How's Daisy doing?" asks Leo, whose attention has been focused on Coco's match on the adjacent court.

I rub my hands together. "She's just about to wrap things up. Coco?"

"It's close, but I think she's got the edge."

Daisy bounces lightly on her toes, waiting for Jasmine's serve. The ball arcs towards her, high and loopy, but instead of running to the ball, Daisy opens her mouth into a wide yawn. She inches sideways, swings too late, and hits the ball with the frame of her racquet. The ball shoots off sideways.

"Fifteen-love," calls out Jasmine.

Daisy rubs her eyes and shuffles to the other side of the court. Jasmine serves again, high to the forehand. Daisy watches listlessly as it falls out of the sky. With an audible groan, she swings her racquet. The ball sails past her, bouncing twice before it reaches the back netting.

Jasmine punches the air triumphantly. "Ace! Thirty-love."

But Daisy doesn't react; she just stares at her strings.

"DAISY! WAKE UP!" the coach yells from the sidelines.

"What's going on?" asks Leo.

I frown and shake my head.

"Forty-love," calls out Jasmine.

Daisy is dragging her way back to the deuce court. This time she doesn't even see the ball. She yawns again and staggers over to her bag.

"DAISY! DAISY!" The coach is on her feet. "The game isn't over yet."

But instead of sprinting back into position, Daisy slumps to the tarmac. My scalp prickling, I open the gate and hurry to her side. "Daisy, can you hear me?"

"What's wrong with her?" the coach snaps.

"I don't know. Daisy! Daisy!"

But her head just lolls to one side.

"Is she on any medication?"

"No." But then I remember the antihistamine. "I mean yes. I gave her a tablet for her hay fever."

She puts her hands on her hips. "That'll be it then."

"I'm pretty sure they were the non-drowsy kind."

"Well, she can't go on. She's practically asleep."

Leo rushes to my aid. "I'll help you get her off the court."

We hook Daisy's arms over our shoulders and half carry, half drag her through the gate and lower her onto the grass.

"Could she be drunk?" whispers Leo.

I glare at her. "She's not drunk. She doesn't drink."

"What's happened?"

I look up to see Georgia Young standing over us in her tailored blazer. "Daisy's had a bit of a reaction to her hay fever pills."

A nasty, crowing kind of smile settles on Georgia's lips.

Shocked, I narrow my eyes.

The smile vanishes. "Poor Daisy."

The coach, a young woman with an elfin haircut, crouches beside me. "It's an important game. The first round of the U13 Sussex Cup. Coco's just won her match, but Milly and Becca are down and almost out in both of theirs, and now it seems we're going to have to forfeit Daisy's match."

"What about a replacement?" Leo asks.

"Daisy could have been substituted if she hadn't started her game," the coach says irritably.

I can't believe what I'm hearing. Do they really think this match is more important than my daughter's health?

"That's ridiculous," snaps Leo.

The coach shrugs. "It's the rules. A replacement might be able to play the doubles. Let me just check." She stands up, digs in her pocket, and brings out a folded piece of paper, which she opens and reads.

I frown. "I should get Daisy to Matron."

A smile breaks out on the coach's face. She turns to Georgia. "Go and get changed. You're playing the doubles."

"Okay." Smiling, Georgia skips off towards the changing rooms.

"Thank God for that," says Leo. "Right, Megan, I'll give you a hand."

It's a short walk across the playing fields to Matron's room, but it takes Leo and me a good five minutes to stagger there with Daisy. Leo chatters away, but I'm too angry with her to respond. To make matters worse, when we arrive, Matron isn't in.

"I've got to get back. Coco doesn't play properly if I'm not watching."

"Sorry for holding you up."

"Don't be silly. You could hardly manage Daisy on your own. Will you be okay from here?"

Hind like a rhinoceros, I think, and grit my teeth. "I'll be fine."

Daisy groans but we stagger on. Pausing to catch my breath, I see Gabriel. He waves and scurries down the asphalt towards us. I roll my eyes. That's all I need.

He catches us up, offers his help and, without waiting for

a response, gathers Daisy up in his arms as if she weighs nothing at all. "Where's your car?"

"At home."

"Not to worry, we'll use mine."

I frown. "What about Ella?"

"She's with Margaret. I was on my way to speak to Anthony Swann. You can't manage on your own, and it's really no trouble."

We walk to his car and continue home in silence. Fuming silently, I lead Gabriel up to Daisy's room where he gently lowers her onto her bed.

"I'm really tired," she mumbles.

"I know, sweetheart."

"Don't call me that."

Her protestation comes as a relief. "I'm sorry about the pills.

Daisy manages a weak smile. "Meh."

I want to hug and kiss her, but I feel uncomfortable with Gabriel hanging about, so I tell her I'll get her some water and hurry down the stairs, Gabriel following, as planned. I thank him and tell him how kind he's been.

"Would you mind seeing yourself out?"

"I—"

"Great, and thanks again."

I spin round and march off to the kitchen, silently congratulating myself for getting rid of him. I grab a glass from the draining board, fill it with iced water from the new fridge, but jump at the touch of a hand on my shoulder.

"I'm here to help," he says.

I sigh and head back to the hall, spilling water. "Believe me, Gabriel, the last thing I need is for you to get all religious on me." It's a non sequitur and unfair and, with a bit of luck, rude enough to send him on his way.

"Promise I won't." He leans forward and plants an unexpected kiss on my cheek. "Has anyone ever told you how gorgeous you look when you're angry?"

"Has anyone ever told you about how a priest should behave?" I snap, startled by his newfound confidence.

"Plenty." He walks away but turns back at the door. "There's something I've been meaning to tell you."

I'm angry and put out, and frankly, not in the mood. "Some other time."

"You were right. Ella is being bullied. But on the internet."

My interest piqued – it's the journalist in me – I ask him who the bully is.

'We don't know. He's hiding behind a pseudonym."

"Classic paedophile behaviour."

Gabriel's face falls. "That's what I thought."

"Have you contacted your Internet Service Provider? It can be very difficult tracing the sender if they're using a different ISP, but it is possible."

"Whoa, Megan, slow down. In English, please."

"The Internet Protocol address. It's a unique number given to every device connected to the internet, assigned to ISPs within regions to identify computers, like a street address for a house. You need to find it."

"How do I go about doing that?"

"*You* can't. You get your ISP to do it for you."

His stares at me blankly.

"Your Internet Service Provider."

He puts his hand to his head. "How do you know all this?"

"We did a piece on cyberbullying and cyberstalking when I was reading the news." I sigh, defeated. "Okay. Okay. I'll help. Just let me check on Daisy."

32

It's been an infuriating few days. Gabriel reported the abuse to the Internet Service Provider, but they wouldn't give out Mikey's IP address without a court order. When Gabriel contacted the police, they said the email, in isolation, did not constitute enough evidence that Ella was being groomed or stalked by an adult, and suggested it could be one of many incidences of bullying between children.

"How much more proof do they need?" I asked when Gabriel showed me the printout of Ella and Mikey's conversation. "Mind you, sometimes you have to push a bit harder to get a reaction. Go back and give them hell ... you know what I mean, and get Mark to write a medical report. If they hear from her doctor that she's self-harming, I'm sure they'll change their tune. Is she back at school?"

"No, I'm keeping her at home."

I'm angry on his behalf and would do more to help but I have my own problems to deal with. Daisy recovered overnight and went back to school. Anthony Swann rang and made all the right noises before asking a few pertinent questions. He seemed satisfied the antihistamine had triggered

Daisy's collapse, and I thought that was that, but then the rumours started.

Madelena has taken pity on me, and we are walking Baxter, her miniature Schnauzer, along the seafront promenade from the chalk cliffs to the Victorian pier. It's sunny but cold, and the glassy sea glitters under a washed-out sky.

"I think I've put the worst behind me, that I'm coping, and then something else is thrown at me. I used to be laid-back, rarely suffered from nerves, hardly ever lost my temper, but now I'm jittery, angry, and unable to sleep. It's pathetic."

"Nonsense. You are a strong woman, but you are still grieving for Guy. And you have had a lot to cope with recently. First your mother appearing out of the blue and now this."

"People are blanking me at the school gate. Samantha gave me the cold shoulder again this morning. She still hasn't forgiven me for organising the Syria Awareness Day."

"That is not like her."

"Thanks, Madelena. That makes me feel a whole lot better."

"No, I mean, she is not herself. She is worried about losing the staffroom swipe card. I think she is in trouble with the police."

"She told you that?"

"Leo told me."

I roll my eyes. "Idle gossip. I wouldn't believe a word *she* says. Josh told me Georgia has incited her friends to call Daisy names all because of some silly rumour put about by Leo that Daisy collapsed because she was drunk."

"You do not know it was Leo."

"I'm pretty certain."

Madelena loops her arm in mine. "Rumours are bery

259

common in Easthaven. It is a small town at the end of a train line, so eberybody know what eberybody else is doing."

"I could cope if the rumour was true, but it isn't. Daisy doesn't drink."

"And you know this for sure?"

"Please don't tell me you believe this bullshit."

"The doctor in me thinks you should have had her checked out."

I take a deep breath to get a grip on my temper. The last thing I want to do is fall out with Madelena. "How about we change the subject."

"Good idea. Have you thought any more about going back to work?"

When Glen posed the question four days ago, it had seemed a good idea. As he so rightly pointed out, the twins were settled now. But even though he assured me Eric had been keeping my seat warm, I was worried it would be tempting fate. As a compromise, he suggested I come up for some 'fancy tucker' with him and Eric to let them try to persuade me. But two days later, the rumours about Daisy had kicked off.

I turn to Madelena. "How can I? Daisy's back in bolshy adolescent mood. Her marks are terrible, and she's got a major exam to pass. And all because of some throwaway comment from Easthaven's own motormouth. I'm terrified all hell is going to break loose."

"Okay, so that was a poor change of subject."

My trip to London, two days later, is a wonderful distraction, if not a solution, to my problems. Glen greets me with one of his infamous bear hugs while Eric, on a no-holds-barred charm offensive, showers me with over-the-top compliments. The banter over lunch, more engrossing than the mindless chatter I've grown used to, quickly turns to Afghanistan.

"General Martin Dempsey had just arrived in Zabul, to check out the Afghan forces when a suicide bomber's car, travelling between the governor's vehicle and a US military convoy in Qalat, blew up," says Glen.

I whistle. "Three US soldiers were killed, weren't they, an Afghan doctor and two civilians serving with NATO?"

Eric nods approvingly. "Spot on." He laces his fingers together and smiles at me like an indulgent uncle. "Still keeping tabs. You're missing it, Megan."

I frown. "Yes, but my priorities have changed."

Eric pulls an astonishing face, both hurt and disappointed, his chins wobbling as he shakes his head. "Funny, I never had you down as a martyr. Far too feisty. Seems I was wrong."

"I'll think about it," I say, amused. "Will that do?"

I arrive home in a buoyant mood and bound into the kitchen. Margaret and Josh are sitting at the table, their faces contorted with concern. I don't have to ask. Something is wrong.

"Where's Daisy?"

Margaret stands, smoothing her skirt. "The truth is, I don't know. She wasn't at the school gate."

"She's bunked off again," says Josh. "We waited for her for ages, but I figured she'd forgotten Margaret was picking us up and had walked home."

I'm aware of the familiar rumble of fear in the pit of my stomach I'd become accustomed to last summer. I glance at my watch. Seven thirty-five, which means she's been missing just over two hours. It's not that long, and I probably wouldn't be worried if it wasn't for the rumours and Daisy's black mood. Don't panic, I tell myself. She came back the other day. She's probably with Dylan. We're not in London. There are no knives or guns in Easthaven. She'll be fine.

But then I remember what happened to Natalia, and my pulse races. "Have you spoken to the school? Dylan?"

Margaret rubs her hands together. "I'm sorry, I know I should have, but with all these silly rumours flying around, I didn't like to."

Her eyes are dull, her skin grey. I want to tell her not to worry, but that would be daft. She is worried, should be worried. And so am I.

"We should call the police," she says.

We all jump at the sound of the front door banging. I rush into the hall in time to see a flash of Daisy's white trainer at the top of the stairs.

"Daisy!" I chase after her, but she slams the bedroom door in my face. I barge in anyway and stand there, hands on hips. "Where the hell have you been?"

Daisy flings herself facedown on her bed and covers her head with a pillow.

I yank it from her and clutch it to my heaving chest. "I demand an explanation."

Daisy responds by covering her ears with her hands.

I'm fuming now, at my wit's end. I drop the pillow, grab her arm, and force her to look at me. I'm as close to being out of control as I have ever been. "Margaret has been worried sick. I want you to go downstairs and apologise to her immediately."

"Get off. You're hurting me."

There are tears in her eyes, I notice, as I let go of her. Inching away from me, she presses herself against the wall.

But I don't let up. "Why can't you think about someone

other than yourself for a change? You're thirteen, for goodness sake. You're not a baby anymore."

Daisy clamps her lips together. It's not like her. By now she should be screaming obscenities.

"Have you nothing to say for yourself?"

She frowns and juts out her chin.

The strain of the past eleven months spills over. I grasp my daughter's shoulders and shake her. "You are the most infuriating child."

Daisy's head hits the wall, and she squeals.

I drop her and clasp my cheeks.

"Okay. I'm sorry." The hairdryer force of her breath washes over me.

"Oh my God!"

Daisy shrinks back and covers her mouth with her hands.

"You've been drinking."

She shakes her head, eyes bulging.

"Don't lie to me, Daisy. I can smell the alcohol on your breath."

33

Another sleepless night, another headache brought on by the incomprehensible exploits of my daughter who pointedly refused to tell me where she'd been and why she smelled of alcohol. Margaret, ever the saint, prepared me a cup of tea, her solution to all of life's problems, and sat and listened as I let off steam into the small hours. Try as I might, I couldn't understand why Daisy was keeping schtum. Margaret tried to convince me she needed time.

"And what do I do until then? Hmm? Pat her on the back and say there, there, never mind, you're under a lot of stress. That it's perfectly natural to express your feelings by disappearing off somewhere with God knows who, God knows where, for a drink. She's only thirteen."

"Her father died."

"Do you think I don't know that? I have to face that terrible reality every morning when I wake up in an empty bed. Guy's special bed, for heaven's sake, with the zipped-together mattresses, firm for his bad back, medium for mine.

He was the love of my life, Margaret. My soul mate, and I miss him more than words can do justice."

"Daisy isn't coping as well as you and Josh are. She'll come through this. You know she will. You're an excellent mother, Megan. Hang on to that."

"Hardly."

"Look how much you've done for them already, moving here, giving up your job, getting involved in the school, their lives. It will get better."

"Hell yes. Things could be worse. She could be into drugs. How long before she tries her first spliff, or her first snort of cocaine? What am I saying? Maybe she already has."

"You're right. It could be worse. She could be cutting herself."

I winced and fell silent.

"Be patient. That way she'll have someone to open up to when she feels she's ready."

Finally, I smiled, at her persistence and the wisdom of her words. "How come you know so much about children?"

She shrugged. "I've been around a long time."

Today is another day, a *tabula rasa*. Telling myself to be positive, I haul my weary body into my black-tiled wet room. The most frustrating thing about yesterday, I think, as I stand under the jet of water, is that I was wrong and Leo was right.

When I knock on Daisy's door thirty minutes later, there's no answer, but I open it and walk in anyway. Daisy is curled up under the duvet, a few strands of her blonde hair strewn over the white pillowcase. I'm wondering if she's asleep or just pretending to be, when I spot the dog-eared edge of a photograph sticking out from under the pillow. I inch closer and gently prise it out. It's one I took of her and Guy in our garden last Easter, their arms round one another, beaming from ear to ear. It's creased and covered in fingerprints from being held so often.

"I think he was scared, you know," I say quietly. "That's why he didn't want to see the doctor. Do you remember when you were six and you had your tonsils out? He told me you woke up in the recovery room and yelled for him. The nurse tried to console you, but you just cried even louder. You were still screaming when you returned to the ward where Dad was waiting. I'm not sure he ever told you he couldn't be there when you woke up because he fainted at the sight of blood." I pause, but there's no response from Daisy. "I'm telling you this because—"

"Because you can't bear it that he was perfect and you're not." She tosses back the duvet and sits bolt upright.

"I'm telling you so you know it's okay to be afraid sometimes. And you're right. He was the nearest thing to perfect any human could be."

Daisy folds her arms and fixes me with her intense stare.

If looks could kill, I'd be dead. I sigh, and leave the room.

I'm late when I set off to school to watch Daisy's tennis match. My strategy is to arrive after all the other parents are seated, that way I can select a position furthest from the other mothers. Leo will be there and possibly Samantha, if Georgia's playing. Is she? I'm not sure. I've donned a baseball hat and sunglasses for the occasion, too. A disguise. I'm nervous about the reception I'll get. I'm not up to another verbal pasting.

It's a sunny day, but a cold wind is blowing in from the

north. Overhead, the seagulls screech as if in protest at the return to winter. I shiver, zip up my puffa and toy with the idea of hiding behind a bush and watching the match from there. Dictators, terrorists, and drug dealers I can face. But three provincial housewives have reduced me to a gibbering wreck. If only Josh was playing at home, Madelena would be here. But Josh and Bruno's cricket match is in Brighton, and Madelena and Ivan have trekked over to watch.

School has finished for the weekend, and the gate is empty, but the tennis is already underway, and a group of parents are seated by the courts. Head bowed, I walk along the asphalt but pull up sharply when Samantha and Jemma emerge from the gym. I tug the peak of my hat down, veer off the path onto the grass, and increase my speed. Are they headed to the courts? I dart back across the asphalt to hide behind the gym and wait, not daring to break cover until they've gone. When I peer round the building, I can't see Samantha or Jemma, but Leo is sitting in her blue folding chair beside Mark. I spot a space on a bench on the opposite side, take a deep breath, and prepare to move. But somebody screams, loud and shrill. The spectators gasp and leap to their feet. Somebody shouts. The tennis stops, and Mark Carter sprints from his seat to the tarmac.

My heart flips over. Daisy?

I rush over. Mark is bent over a prostrate child, but with two mothers blocking the gate, I can't tell who it is. Seeing me, however, they move out the way.

I clasp my face. Daisy, my precious child, is lying there unconscious, her body placed, by Mark, in the recovery position.

34

I kneel beside Daisy and try to rouse her, calling her name, over and over. Mark speaks to me in a calm voice, insisting it's okay, that she's unconscious but breathing and an ambulance is on its way. But I can't stop thinking about Guy's body, lying inert at the foot of the stairs. I'm trembling all over, struggling for air.

"Is this what happened before?" Mark asks.

I stare at him blankly.

"On court with Daisy."

I shake my head. "My husband collapsed like this for no apparent reason. It was his heart. I – I can't bear it. I really can't."

Mark clasps my shoulders. "She's going to be fine. It's not her heart."

The A&E at the District General Hospital is uncomfortably hot and bright with artificial light. I follow Daisy's speeding trolley wheeled by two paramedics, an Asian man, and a petite young woman, through the waiting room, heaving with people of all ages, to the curtained-off area of the resuscita-tion unit. Daisy's ashen face is almost entirely obscured by an oxygen mask, and it's all I can do not to scream about the unfairness of it all.

A flame-haired nurse, in a navy tunic, approaches us.

"She's in good hands now." The Asian paramedic smiles reassuringly and applies the brake.

The nurse's alabaster arms are covered with freckles. She cuts open Daisy's white tennis shirt and attaches electrodes to Daisy's legs, arms, and chest with calm efficiency.

A grey-haired doctor in green scrubs, a stethoscope looped around his neck, hurries over and peers at Daisy over tortoiseshell spectacles. "Who do we have here?"

The paramedic hands him the clipboard. "Daisy Truman. Thirteen, unconscious but breathing."

The nurse smiles reassuringly and wires Daisy up to the ECG monitor.

"Are you her mother?" the doctor asks, as the paramedic takes his leave.

I nod.

"Hello, Mrs Truman. I'm Mr Tredwell, the consultant on duty."

I don't correct him. I can't see the point.

"Does Daisy have any allergies?"

"No, apart from a touch of hay fever the other day. At least that's what I thought it was."

"Does she take medication?"

"I gave her a Benadryl tablet, but she hasn't needed one again."

"Did she have a reaction?"

"You see that's the thing, I'm not sure."

He stops writing and looks at me questioningly.

"She became very drowsy when she played tennis."

He sucks his plastic biro. "I see, but she didn't take Benadryl today?"

"No."

The nurse, who has inserted a cannula in Daisy's hand and hooked up a drip, picks up her arm and scrutinises it.

"Does your daughter use recreational drugs? Cannabis, cocaine, ecstasy, ketamine, nicotine?" the doctor asks.

My stomach lurches. "I think she smokes occasionally."

The doctor doesn't react. But why would he? He's not here to judge.

"Has she been unusually irritable or sulky recently?"

I sigh. "Well, yes, but her father died."

The curtains part and Mark Carter bursts in. I'm surprised to see him but relieved. "Has she regained consciousness?"

The doctor frowns. "Sorry. Next of kin only."

"I'm her GP. I was there when she passed out." Mark turns to me. "Have you got her water bottle?"

I slip it out of the pocket of my puffa jacket. "It's almost empty, but it doesn't smell of alcohol. I suppose it could be vodka."

Mr Tredwell eyes me over his spectacles. "Excuse me?"

"I doubt it," replies Mark.

Mr Tredwell clears his throat. "I'm afraid I must ask you to wait outside."

Mark smiles apologetically. "Of course. I'm sorry. I'll be in chairs, but please, get the contents of the bottle to toxicology," he says as the flame-haired nurse ushers him away.

"Mrs Truman," continues the consultant. "Is this a round-about way of telling me your daughter has a drink problem?"

"No. It was just a rumour propagated by a parent. At least I assume it was a parent."

He takes off his spectacles and rubs his eyes. "You've lost me, I'm afraid."

"Last time she collapsed she was accused of being drunk. But it's okay, I have the water bottle. We can prove she wasn't." My cheeks are smarting, my armpits are damp, and I'm aware I sound desperate.

"You say she collapsed. Did she topple over?"

"No. She just sat down, slumped forward, and fell asleep."

Mr Tredwell knits his eyebrows together and studies the bottle. He looks at Daisy thoughtfully for a moment. "I'd like a word with your doctor after all. If you'll excuse me."

The ECG monitor whirrs rhythmically. I reach over the metal sides of the trolley and grip Daisy's hand. It's warm but limp, and I squeeze it reassuringly, something I know she would never let me do if she was awake.

The curtains fly open with a metallic clatter, and another nurse enters our bay. This one is tall and broad-shouldered with baby-blue eyes. "I need to try and rouse her. Name, please?"

I frown, taken aback by her forthright manner. "Daisy."

The nurse grabs Daisy's shoulders and shakes her. "DAISY! DAISY! CAN YOU HEAR ME?"

"Please, don't," I say, horrified.

"Ah. Sister Lawson. Good," says Mr Tredwell, reappearing by my side.

"She just shook my daughter."

"We're just trying to wake her up." He shows me the empty plastic biro case he's holding. "I'm going to rub the base of her fingernails with this."

Daisy groans and moves her head.

"Sister Lawson, bloods, please."

The nurse disengages the drip and attaches a syringe to the cannula, which fills with Daisy's blood.

"Test for pregnancy …"

I flinch.

"… blood sugar, anaemia, Epstein Barr, thyroid, and a white blood cell count. And instruct toxicology to test for these recreational drugs. Here."

The nurse takes the form he hands her, completes her task, draws the curtains, and marches out of our bay.

Pleased to see the back of her, I turn my attention to Mr Tredwell. "Do you think there are drugs in her bottle?"

"At this stage, I'm not ruling anything out."

Why would Daisy do that? I wonder miserably. Unless she did it to spite me. Or attract attention. And she certainly managed to do that.

"I'm going to run an EEG to check out the electrical activity in her brain before we let her go." He smiles again, warmly this time. "She's coming round."

Daisy eyelids flutter. Her dry, chapped lips begin to move and she blinks.

I remove the oxygen mask then reach for her hand and squeeze it gently. "It's okay, Daisy, I'm here."

Daisy responds by slowly licking her lips.

The doctor smiles and pats me gently on the shoulder. "I'll leave you two alone. Ring the bell if you have any problems."

"What happened?" Daisy asks in a weak voice.

"You passed out on the tennis court but you're in hospital now."

Sister Lawson bustles through the curtains. "You'll be relieved, I'm sure, that she's not pregnant and her blood sugar is normal."

I frown. "Could you give us a moment."

Sister Lawson makes a tutting sound and hitches Daisy up to almost sitting. "In case you haven't noticed, we're phenomenally busy in here." She hands Daisy a glass of water with a straw.

"I can see that, but—"

"I want to go home." Daisy's voice is weak.

"We will as soon as they've finished running tests. They need to find out what's wrong with you." I spin round to face Sister Lawson. "I'm sure you're doing your best, but I'd like another nurse to attend to my daughter, someone a little more caring."

Sister Lawson's eyes widen. She brushes her hands down her tunic and thrusts back her shoulders as if she's just remembered the Patient's Charter.

"My pleasure," she says and stomps away.

A tear spills over Daisy's lids. "I wasn't drunk. I don't like alcohol. It's the truth. You have to believe me."

35

It's dark in Dylan's bedroom. Too dark. He rolls over and turns his bedside lamp to its dimmest setting. Not that his parents would care if his light is on or not. They're too busy fighting. He thought it didn't bother him anymore. But tonight it does because they're fighting about him.

"She's a bad influence. He's not doing any work," he overheard his mother say when he wandered down the landing after his bath.

He rolled his eyes but didn't hang around to listen to any more. No point. *She* was Daisy. But they were wrong. She wasn't a bad influence. How could she be? It was over. Daisy didn't want to see him anymore.

"And I mean never," she'd said before she ran away.

He lies on his back, hands behind his head, and stares at the ceiling. There's a crack in the white paint just above his head, a thin wiggly line that's escaped his mother's eagle eye. Incredible. She misses nothing, especially when it involves him. It drives him mad. But that's nothing compared with her temper. She never used to get angry, only now she's angry all the time. He wishes she were more like Megan. Daisy's lucky to have a mum like her. Shame she doesn't realise it.

Daisy. Why does everything always come back to her?

If only he hadn't screwed up. He thought she wanted him to touch her. She'd showed him how to do it, after all. But yesterday, in the shelter on the promenade when he'd shoved his hand under her jumper, she'd gone apeshit. Why? He thought she liked it.

"Well, I don't, okay?" she snapped.

"Okay! Okay! My bad. Hey. I've got a surprise for you. Ta-da!" He whipped out the bottle of whisky from his ruck-sack with a magician's flourish.

Her mouth dropped open. "Where d'you get that?"

He shrugged, unscrewed the top, and took a swig. The warm amber liquid burned his throat. He wanted to gag, but that would not be cool. He forced his lips into a grin and thrust it at Daisy.

She screwed up her nose.

"You're scared," he goaded.

"I'm not scared of anything."

"Prove it."

Daisy scowled but took the bottle. She held it to her lips but hesitated.

"Go on, scaredy-cat."

Daisy closed her eyes, drank a mouthful, and coughed, spraying whisky.

He laughed, took the bottle and patted her on the back. But Daisy, clutching her throat with both hands, slid down the bench away from him. He stared at her helplessly until her fit was over.

She leapt to her feet. "You idiot."

"I'm sorry, okay. I thought you'd find it funny."

"Funny?"

"Yeah. You know, like smoking?"

She shook her head then fixed him with a really mean stare, her eyes glinting scarily. "You don't know shit, Dylan."

That hurt. He wanted to tell her she was wrong, but she was running out of the hut. "Daisy, wait!"

She spun round, eyes flashing. "I don't want to see you again, Dylan. And I mean never."

And with those words she sprinted off down the seafront, leaving him alone.

Why? he wonders as he rolls over. Is it because of the rumours? She made out she thought it was cool everyone thought she'd been drunk.

"But were you?" he asked.

"Duh. No!"

And he believed her. No wonder she'd been pissed off about the whisky.

Bad job, Dylan. Really poor.

But then today, when he was in Brighton playing cricket, it happened again. He overheard Bruno's mum telling Josh about it on the boundary after they'd finished. She was in hospital but had regained consciousness and was going to be allowed home. He's relieved she was okay, but all the same, it didn't sound good. Dylan wanted to ask Bruno's mum if Dr Carter thought she was drunk, but he wasn't supposed to be listening. He isn't sure what to believe. She didn't like the whisky. She didn't want to drink it. Was that because she knew what it would do to her? But then why do it again?

He sighs. She didn't like it. Which means she wasn't drunk today.

His head hurts. He doesn't know what to do. He desperately wants to talk it through with someone. His dad perhaps. His mother was complaining of a headache earlier. Maybe she's gone to bed.

He gets up and tiptoes to the top of the stairs. His parents have stopped arguing. All he can hear is the steady murmur of the television. He's about to go down when he hears his father's voice.

"Have you seen my whisky, Jem?"

Dylan freezes. Damn. He left it in the shelter down by the beach. Shit. Shit. Shit. He strains his ears, but he can't hear his mother's reply.

"A couple of days ago," his father says. "You don't think … No. Stupid idea. He hasn't shown any interest in alcohol, has he?"

He tries, but he can't hear his mother's reply.

"And you definitely haven't used it for cooking? … Okay, okay. I'm not accusing anyone of anything."

Oh crap, he thinks, as he scuttles to his bedroom. How am I going to get out of this?

36

I'm drinking coffee in the kitchen after another sleepless night, when Josh appears in his pyjamas. Crumpled from sleep, his usually tidy hair is sticking out in all directions.

He yawns, stretching his arms, and pulls out a chair. "What's going on, Mum?"

They might drive me mad with their bickering but, when the going gets tough, the twins always turn to one other. After Guy's death, they were inseparable, sleeping in Josh's room, their single beds pushed together, holding hands. I grew jealous of their closeness. But then Daisy went spectacularly off the rails, and Josh and I sought comfort in each other. He's so much easier than his sister, more practical, more level-headed, more likeable. The only time he's ever grumpy is when he's hungry.

"I don't know," I say honestly.

He holds the back of his neck with his hands and folds his elbows inwards. "Do you think she was drunk?"

I lean over and pat his knee. "No, darling, I don't."

He sighs and lowers his hands. "She doesn't like alcohol."

My spirits lift. "Well, there you are then."

"So why did she collapse?"

I've been asking myself the same question all night and have reached the conclusion her water must have been spiked. But who would spike a child's drink? Another child perhaps? A jealous or an angry child? Do angry, jealous children do that? I recall the smug little smile on Georgia Young's face when Daisy collapsed the first time. Daisy had taken her place in the team. Maybe she was upset. Maybe tennis was her thing. Leo once remarked she wasn't bright, and her acting certainly wasn't going to set the world on fire. She had her art, although Anthony Swann implied her mother painted her pictures. Not that any of that should matter. She was only a child. There was plenty of time for her to shine. According to Robert, things weren't great at home. Her parents were obviously distracted, her father with the pneumatic blonde, her mother with Dickie. But spike another girl's drink? Was a thirteen-year-old capable of something that evil?

"She split up with Dylan, but don't worry. *She* dumped *him*," Josh says.

"Really? Why?"

Josh shrugs. "Dunno. She just said *he's a nerd.*"

"She doesn't mean that."

"Sounded like she did."

I frown. Maybe it's a good thing. If they're no longer hanging out, she won't be able to get him into any more trouble. Oh God, Megan. Really? "Was Dylan okay about it?"

"Nope. He actually cried on the bus to Brighton. He pretended he wasn't, but I saw him."

"Poor Dylan." I take a sip of coffee. But then it dawns on me, if Dylan's upset, it's likely he'll be angry with Daisy. Maybe it was Dylan who spiked Daisy's drink. Whoa,

Megan. You're getting way too ahead of yourself. You don't even know if her drink was spiked.

Josh leans on the table and rests his chin on his hands. "Easthaven is kinda weird. Strange things happen to people down here."

I smile ruefully. "Easthaven is not alone there."

He sits back with a jerk. "Okay, St Peter's then. First there was the body under the stage, then Ella Jones starts cutting herself, and now all this stuff with Daisy."

I put down my cup. "Just horrible coincidences. They're not related."

"Ella's being bullied, isn't she? That's why she hasn't come back to school."

"Yes, she is."

"Who by?"

"It's complicated."

"You mean you don't know."

I sigh. "Right!"

"Can I go and see Daisy yet?"

"Why don't I make her breakfast and you could take it to her on a tray."

"Nice one, Mum."

Any hope that Daisy has morphed back into adoring daughter, all sweetness and light, is obliterated by the ferocity of the scowl she levels at me when we enter the room. She seems pleased enough to see Josh, though, and manages a brief smile when he places the tray on her lap and sits next to her.

"How are you feeling this morning?" I ask.

Her scowl deepens. "Fine."

"That's good." I beam at her, but she doesn't meet my gaze.

Josh flexes his eyebrows, a look that says *don't push it*,

and turns back to his sister. He squeezes her foot, and I notice she doesn't pull it away. "I helped make the scrambled eggs."

Daisy nods her approval. "Sweet."

I feel a pang of envy at their easy intimacy. They're comfortable together in a way I've never managed to be with either of them. Why is that? I wonder, as I drag my weary body from the room.

I'm clearing up the kitchen, a couple of hours later, when the doorbell rings. My heart sinks on sight of Gabriel. His timing, as usual, is disastrous.

"Don't you ever use the phone?"

He flashes a smile. "Force of habit, I'm afraid. How's Daisy?"

"My, my, news does travel fast."

He laughs as only someone used to criticism can. "It's a small town."

Don't I know it.

He cocks his head. "So?"

I let out an exasperated sigh. "Tired but otherwise unscathed."

"Do you know what happened?"

"No," I reply but I don't elaborate.

"Is there anything I can do?"

"No, and please don't tell me you'll pray for me."

He shrugs. "Okay, I won't."

His impassiveness grates. "Won't pray or won't tell me you've prayed."

"Would it really matter if I did?"

I throw up my hands. "How can you have blind faith in something that can't be proved?"

"Or disproved."

"Darwin did a pretty good job of that," I retort. "God is all powerful, I can understand. But God is good? Pah. I mean, he goes around killing people without a thought for those left behind. And as for his need to be worshipped. It's a bit rich, don't you think? A bit Simon Cowell. So no, I don't see how praying to a homicidal, egotistical maniac could poss—"

"You're upset. I should go."

I clench my fists. "Ugh. Go use your Good Samaritan act on someone who actually needs it."

"It's okay. I understand," he says and walks away.

I head back to the kitchen muttering to myself. I'm cross for being rude and for flying off the handle. It wasn't as if Gabriel provoked me.

Josh wanders in, frowning. "Is he your boyfriend?"

"Gabriel? No. Whatever gave you that idea?"

"Because he always brings you flowers."

So they hadn't forgotten. "Not today, he didn't."

Josh narrows his eyes accusingly. "But you do like him?"

This time I think before I speak. Guy was keen that our children grew up to be tolerant and kind. I take a deep breath. "He drives me mad but, yes, I suppose he is a friend. But nothing more."

The doorbell rings a second time. Oh God, what now? I'm about to tell Josh to leave it but he's halfway across the hall already.

"Josh! Bruno and I bring you lunch."

At the sound of Madelena's cheery voice, I breathe a sigh of relief. I rush into the hall intending to hug her, but she's carrying a tray of terracotta dishes, and I lean over them and kiss her on the cheek instead. "This is unbelievably kind of you both. Come in, come in."

"She's made tortilla, patatas bravas, chorizo in red wine,

and pollo chilindron, which is basically chicken and red peppers," explains Bruno.

Josh rubs his tummy and whistles. "Wow, Madelena, a feast."

"A feast? No, no. Tapas." She winks then makes a more serious face. "How is Daisy?"

A different atmosphere settles over 17 Primrose Road, and my mood quickly improves. Daisy makes a brief appearance, but only after some gentle persuasion from Josh. She manages to smile at Madelena and thanks her for lunch, which is delicious, but otherwise she's sullen and withdrawn and picks at her food. She's been through a terrifying ordeal, I remind myself, when my patience slips. It's going to take time.

After lunch, Madelena suggests we take a stroll in the garden. The rabbits are grazing at the end of the strip of lawn. They look up as we approach, sit on their haunches, and wash their whiskers.

Madelena's eyes widen. "So tame."

"They're pets but they've broken out of their pen."

She laughs. "Oh, I see."

I steer her towards the bench on the paved area adjacent to the park, and we sit and zip up our coats.

"How's Gabriel?" she asks.

I groan.

"That does not sound good."

"He brings out the worst in me."

"Gabriel is a good man. He has a soft spot for you."

I shake my head. "Not my type."

"You have a type?"

I think about this for a moment. Before Guy, I had a series of flings: a safari guide I met in South Africa, a surfer in Brazil, a fixer in Khartoum, and two Englishmen – a *Times* journalist I met in China and an ITV reporter I fell in love with, well, almost – while living in Hong Kong in my early twenties. Like me, they were free spirits, but could I honestly say they had anything in common other than a love of danger?

"No, but I definitely don't date priests. I'm an atheist. Imagine the confrontations."

She touches her nose with her finger.

"What's that supposed to mean?"

"You have an open mind. You will see."

If you mean I'll repel my prejudices and fall in love with Gabriel, then you're wrong, I think.

One of the rabbits, Groucho perhaps, although I've never been able to tell them apart, wanders over and nibbles the end of Madelena's boot.

She prods it. "Cheeky rabbit."

The rabbit scampers off a short distance, sits on its haunches, and watches us. Apart from wondering where its next meal is coming from, it doesn't have a worry in the world.

"Do you think it's possible Daisy might have been drugged?"

Madelena tilts her head from side to side. "Did Mark say this?"

"Not in so many words, but he was keen to test the water bottle. How long will it take for the toxicology results?"

She shrugs. "Anything from five days to a week."

Midway through the afternoon, Samantha telephones to ask after Daisy. I'm surprised. It's been a long time since we spoke.

"As if you don't have enough on your plate," she says in

her quiet, overly polite voice. "Do you know why she passed out?"

I make an on-the-spot decision not to divulge any information that could be misconstrued. Samantha hasn't shown herself to be the gossiping type, but for some reason I don't feel able to confide in her. "I only know she wasn't drunk."

"Goodness. Do people honestly believe that?"

You tell me, I think irritably.

"Is there anything I can do?" she continues. "And I mean anything."

I have a sudden urge to ask her if she'll question her daughter about the incident, but I put myself in her position: *how would you feel if someone asked the same of you?*

"Did you find your staffroom swipe card?" I ask. "I gather you lost it."

There's a pause. "Who told you that?"

"I don't remember."

"It was stolen," she says tersely and puts down the phone.

37

Today I'm in such a nervous state of anticipation, I can't concentrate on anything. It's been six days since Daisy collapsed. I've spent the morning and the first part of the afternoon willing the telephone to ring. I'm convinced the toxicology tests will provide the key. Madelena has tried to persuade me otherwise, and Mark Carter, when he called in on Monday, was quick to point out he'd asked for the water to be tested because he was leaving no stone unturned. He also suggested Daisy shouldn't return to school. But Daisy was adamant she should, and I caved in. I don't want to put her under any more stress. Her Common Entrance exams are not far off and, unlike Josh, she's not a natural academic. Having changed school at the eleventh hour, she's had to learn a new syllabus in a very short time. It's been a struggle for her. Truth is, I'm proud she isn't scared to go back. Perhaps Guy was right about us being alike. She does seem to share my dogged determination. I only hope it's a good thing.

"I'm not happy about this," Mark said.

"But you've already told me it wasn't her heart."

"I meant her heart was still beating. The Echo might tell a different story."

On Tuesday evening, Anthony Swann called. I tensed at the sound of his voice. What now?

"I hadn't expected to see Daisy back at school so soon. In fact, I'd rather hoped she wouldn't return until you had the test results."

"She wasn't drunk."

"Believe me, Megan, it's her health I'm concerned about."

I apologised, and he assured me he'd keep an eye on her. He means well, I know, and I'm grateful, but I'm under no illusions. A busy man like him simply won't have time.

The telephone remains resolutely silent all morning. My mind running wild, I realise sitting around the house waiting for something that may never happen is doing me no good what-soever. Throughout the endless days of this rain-sodden week, I've managed to avoid all contact with the St Peters' mums. I've dragged myself around the lack-lustre Easthaven shops – which depressed me further; taken a trip to the Royal Pavilion in Brighton – which was heaving with children on a school outing; spent an afternoon huddled at the back of a cinema watching a film I didn't want to see. The rumour-mongering has isolated me to such an extent I'm in danger of withdrawing from society altogether. I haven't even returned Glen's many texts and answerphone messages. He has no idea what's going on, and I can't see the point in telling him. What could he do?

The only person I'm comfortable with is Madelena, but she's at work. I toy with the idea of calling Samantha or Jemma, but I've never felt entirely relaxed around them and decide against it. Samantha probably wouldn't answer my call after our last conversation, anyway. Leo could lift me out of my gloom but, as I'm convinced she instigated the rumour in the first place, I'm not inclined to phone her, either.

Or so you think, I remind myself. You don't actually have proof.

Margaret is an option, but I don't want to worry her, which just leaves Gabriel. But what with the kiss he planted on my cheek after Daisy's collapse and the conversations I've had with Madelena recently, the last thing I want is to encourage him. I've enough on my plate without having to fend off the advances of an amorous priest, never mind what effect it would have on Daisy and Josh.

This way depression lies, warns a cautionary voice inside my head.

I groan and reach for the now statutory, wet-weather gear, call out to the builders, and head off towards the cliffs. There's far less chance of bumping into someone I know up there than on the seafront. But it's cold and wet on the chalky hills, an icy wind whips my face, and I can barely see my hand in front of my face, let alone the fabulous views of the sea. Determined not to give in, I stride across the springy turf until my skin turns blue and my teeth ache from chattering.

Back home, I make a beeline for the telephone but, for once, the answerphone light isn't winking. Glen's finally given up, I think, and dial 1471 to check the hospital hasn't rung, but the last call to the house was yesterday evening. Madelena, I remind myself.

The house is unnaturally quiet. I find a note from Jasper on the kitchen table explaining that the builders are needed on an urgent job and won't be around for a fortnight.

But don't worry, darling, if they're not back then they'll

*get a tongue-lashing they'll never forget. And that, sweetie, is
a promise, not an idle threat.*

Peace at last and no more dust. Perfect. I'm about to
retreat upstairs for a warming shower before driving round to
St Peter's, when the doorbell rings. I'm wondering whether to
ignore it, when it occurs to me it might be Mark Carter, and I
rush over and open it.

Jemma Webster lowers the hood of her cream, fur-lined
waterproof jacket, and her fabulous hair spills over her shoulders. She looks in alarm at my dripping face and sodden
jeans.

I cringe. "I've been walking on the cliffs."

"You should have called. I'd have joined you. I go up
there myself most days. I love the view."

"The clouds were so low you couldn't see it today. Do
you want to come in?"

"No, no. I just wanted to check you're okay. Nobody has
seen you for ages."

I manage a brief smile. "I've been a bit worried, you
know, about Daisy."

"Of course you have. I gather she's back at school."

Dylan, I think, and take a deep breath. "I'm sorry they
broke up."

She retracts her chin. "Oh, really?"

I groan inwardly. She didn't know. "I should've called.
I've been so worried about Daisy. I don't seem to be able to
think straight."

"Goodness. You always seem so self-assured and
capable."

I squirm, even though what she says is partially true. I'm
the girl who can cope with anything. But times have changed.
My circumstances have changed. I've changed. I should have
talked to her. There's not a nasty bone in Jemma's body.

"Do you know why she collapsed?"

I shake my head. "Not yet, no. They ran lots of tests at the hospital. I'm just waiting for the results. Guy – my husband – died of heart failure brought on by viral myocarditis. It was a freak illness, but they need to rule it out." It's a partial lie, but I don't want to mention the toxicology tests for fear I might sound paranoid.

"It must be tough battling through this on your own, but I imagine Gabriel is being a huge support."

Thanks, Leo! I make a face. "I'm sure he would if I let him. But I'm an atheist so …" I pause, remembering her newfound faith. "I've nothing against religion…"

She holds up her hands. "I understand."

I smile sheepishly. "Sure you don't want to come in?"

"You'll catch your death if you don't change out of those wet things. But please let me know if there's anything I can do. I'd like to help if I can." She gives me another of her brief but unexpected hugs.

"Yes, I will. And thanks."

Jemma's visit gives me a lift, but not big enough to warrant a change in my new routine. I arrive at St Peter's about ten minutes late, pull up outside the gate to let the twins hop in, and drive straight off. It's an avoidance tactic I've used all week, and a good one. So far, I haven't encountered a single parent, or teacher either for that matter.

38

I't's a beautiful day, the sun beating down from a cloudless, forget-me-not sky, and not a breath of wind. Exhilarated by the prospect of a long walk, Gabriel eases his way through the mass of parents, pupils, and teachers, chatting animatedly as they wait for Anthony Swann to start proceedings. I'm a born-again positivist, he thinks, amused. Things are on the up. The future looks rosy. Anything is possible.

He steals a peek at his daughter, giggling with her best friend, Georgia Young. She's a different child from the self-harming shell of a girl she was at Christmas, thanks, in no small part, to Megan.

He'd been doubtful when she'd suggested he invite Georgia to tea to let the two of them work it out. If it went badly it would set Ella back. But Megan's advice to contact the police again about the cyberbullying had been spot on. He'd spoken to another officer, told them his daughter was self-harming, and insisted he took it seriously.

"I'm onto it," the officer had said. "Too many paedophiles are getting away with this kind of behaviour."

So, he'd invited Georgia over, and Ella had started back at school last week. Her idea, not his.

He feels different. More alive. More aware. Able to see things he hasn't noticed before, as though the veil he hadn't realised he was wearing has been lifted. He feels good about himself, too. Bolder. He's not even bothered that Jemma is standing six feet away from him. His confusion has cleared. He never meant to lead her on. He never meant to hurt her. It's up to her to deal with it. Judging by the way she's staring straight ahead, avoiding his gaze, it looks like she has.

Samantha Young catches his eye and waves at him with her clipboard before continuing her animated discussion with Anthony Swann. She's in charge of the day's events and has asked him to keep an eye on the girls, 'if he didn't mind'.

Mind? Not one jot. He's thrilled to be involved.

He watches Ella and Georgia skip over to where Josh, Bruno, and Oli Carter are standing, Daisy hovering awkwardly in the background, biting her nails. What happened to her? Why did she collapse like that?

After he'd carried Daisy home, and keen to gain more of an understanding of what Megan was dealing with, he'd asked Ella what she was like.

"Oh, you know. Thinks she's it. Why?"

"Be kind to her," he said. "She's been through a lot."

"I'll try but I don't think she likes me all that much."

Too cool for school? Is that it? Or a front, her way of coping with the death of her father, perhaps. Either way, I'll bet she's struggling as much as Ella.

He scans the crowd for Megan. He'd like to walk with her. The full ten miles, given the chance. The more he gets to know her, the more he likes her, even if she does keep giving him the full two barrels about his religious beliefs. It doesn't bother him. In fact, he respects her for saying it how she sees it. Strong but kind. That's why he wanted to tell her about Jemma that evening, but she'd had visitors, so he couldn't. Probably a good thing. Better to let it lie. He wonders how she'll react when he mentions he's thinking of leaving the church. It's not a decision he'll make lightly, but he doesn't see how he can stay. His heart isn't in it anymore. He doesn't believe the way he should. He hopes she'll be pleased. He desperately wants them to be friends. His intentions are honourable, for now at least. She's grieving for her husband, after all.

Out of the corner of his eye he sees Leo Carter, trying to control a sleek black Labrador straining on a lead while gesticulating angrily at Samantha. Samantha shakes her head vigorously and turns to go, but Leo grabs her arm, determined to ram home whatever point she's making. Oli darts through the crowd and joins them. His mother turns to him, annoyed, shrugs, and hands him the dog. Oli grins and runs off, and the women continue their argument.

He spots Megan, near the pavilion with Madelena and her husband, Ivan, and hurries over.

"Gabriel. Good to see you," Mark says, squeezing his way through the crush of people.

Pleased as ever to see the good doctor, Gabriel stops for a chat. They're still talking when the claxon sounds. The walkers move towards the gate at the far end of the field in a rolling wave, Megan somewhere amongst them. Lost her, he thinks. Bother.

It's nearing four when he and Mark, having walked together all afternoon, arrive back at school with Georgia and Ella. Melissa Gordon, the headmaster's secretary, ticks off the children's names and hands them a voucher for a drink and a hot dog.

"You'll have to hurry. They've almost run out," she says as a dark-haired boy dodges past them. "Hang on a minute, young man."

"Oi, Dylan," yells Mark, when the boy keeps going. "Hold up."

The boy tips back his head and reluctantly turns around, a hang-dog expression on his sunburned face.

"I need to sign you in," Melissa says.

Mark arches an eyebrow. "Not walking with Oli?"

Dylan shakes his head. "Nah. Hurt my ankle. Dylan Webster, Miss," he says and hurries off.

Mark laughs. "No sign of a limp. And judging by the colour of his face, it looks like he's spent the day at the beach."

"Girl trouble," Gabriel says.

"Ah, yes. I heard."

The smell of barbecued sausages lingers in the air, but only half a dozen walkers remain, hanging around the beer tent where Oli Carter is helping Grace Potter tidy away the bunting. On a blue inflatable castle, Coco and Sid turn somersaults, whooping with delight.

"Looks like Leo's not back yet," Mark says and heads off towards his children.

Gabriel scans the field. No sign of Megan, either. Or her children. Or Samantha, for that matter. Even Dylan's gone, whisked away by his worried mother, no doubt. Tough-talking Tom Swain is yelling orders at a group of helpers dismantling the marquee. A couple of teachers are folding up the trestle tables, while the headmaster, black bin liner and grabber in hand, picks rubbish off the field, aided by a few conscientious parents.

"See you soon," Mark shouts above the wail of an ambulance siren, shepherding his brood towards the gate.

Georgia tugs his sleeve. "Where's Mum?"

"She must have got held up. Better take you home with us."

She claps her hands. "Woo hoo!"

39

T he marquee has been stowed in the shed behind the pavilion, along with the tables, deck chairs, the barbecues, ladders, and the bunting. And the inflatable castle has been collected by Bounce-Mania, all in record time. Tom smiles. I may be old, but I haven't lost my touch.

He opens the boot of his estate, and Lady, who's been waiting for her walk all afternoon, leaps out. He grabs her collar before she dashes into the road and attaches the lead. Immediately, she strains to get going.

"Steady on, girl." He locks the car and heads along the cliff path to the beach. The tide is out, exposing a wide expanse of sand and rocks, strewn with fine green seaweed and rubbery brown kelp.

"There you go." He unhooks Lady and watches her charge across the pebbles, her auburn coat, sleek in the evening sunshine. "Worth the wait, eh, girl?"

He follows at a slower pace, to where the sea laps at the shore, leaving ripples in the sand as it ebbs further out. He stops at the water's edge and shields his eyes to admire the rocky reef. A couple of shags sit, sentry-like, facing the horizon, the light breeze occasionally ruffling their feathers. I love this place, he thinks, and smiles.

He swings his arms. His joints and muscles ache from all the lifting and carrying he's done today. He's not as young as he was. Perhaps it's time to finally hang up his tool belt. He's been thinking that a lot lately. Forty-five years at St Peter's, under six headmasters. He hadn't expected to be working at sixty-nine and probably wouldn't be if Mary was still alive. She's been gone three years, but he still isn't over the shock. Fine one minute, dead the next. Mary hadn't been aware of the tumour in her pancreas. No one had. A tenacious predator, it had crept up on her, killing her a mere three weeks after the cancer was diagnosed, leaving behind a gigantic hole in his life. He'd been thinking of retiring the Christmas before she'd died. But once she was gone, he couldn't bear the thought of rattling around alone at home. So he'd carried on working, with Anthony Swann's blessing, of course. A good man, Anthony Swann.

Sea spraying from her coat, Lady dashes across the sand, over the shingle to the foot of the sheer, chalk cliffs. She stops at a scrubby bush and sniffs. A rabbit most probably, he thinks, as she barks frantically.

"Here, Lady!"

But Lady ignores him and paws at the pebbles, whining.

"What is it, girl?" He scuttles over, slipping and sliding, but pulls up sharp. Sprawled on the samphire carpet, her scratched and bleeding limbs impossibly angled, lies the body of a woman.

He covers his mouth and steps back. He can't believe it. Not again? Lady stops whining and stares up at him, panting. When he doesn't move, she sidles over and nudges him with her cool, wet nose.

He blinks rapidly, frozen to the spot. Do something. Don't just stand here. Call an ambulance. The police.

He shakes himself, pats Lady's silken head and, with a trembling hand, whips out his mobile. "Hang on Tom. Better check she's dead first."

He swallows the bile that has risen in his throat and bends down to feel her neck. Impossible, surely? He keeps his fingers there, just to be sure. But, yes, there's a slow steady pulse. Somehow, the woman has survived the fall?

40

A year ago, I was in Afghanistan with Glen, dodging Taliban bullets in an opium field, praying we wouldn't be blown apart by a hidden IED. An adrenaline-fuelled sprint back and forth between two worlds with no time to get tangled up in life's minutiae, my life was more straightforward. Here in Easthaven, I'm dogged by self-doubt every step of the way.

"I've made a terrible mistake. I want out," I tell Madelena at the end of the walk.

She clasps my face and fixes me with her warm, chocolate eyes. "You need a job. That's all."

And then to put my woes into perspective, she telephones the following morning to fill me in on the awful news. Tom Swain, the school caretaker who, only weeks ago discovered the decomposed body of Natalia Topolska under the school stage, last night stumbled across the mangled body of Leo Carter at the foot of one of the south coast's most notorious suicide spots while taking his beloved Red Setter for a walk. Lying in the intensive care unit of the District General Hospital, Leo is in a coma, breathing with the help of a ventilator, her skull fractured, her pelvis, left arm, and both legs broken. Her devoted husband, Mark, sits by her bedside, desperately hoping the wife he adores will regain consciousness. The close-knit community is rocked. Why would a seemingly happy woman with a zest for life choose to abandon her three children by leaping to her death from a cliff during the school's sponsored walk?

"Geoff and Barbara Wild said she was drinking heavily in the halfway pub at lunchtime," Madelena says. "She is not the type to jump. But people saw her arguing with Samantha before the start of the walk and have drawn their own conclusions."

"I thought you didn't listen to gossip."

"I don't but Samantha was not at school at the end of the walk. Odd since she was in charge."

"Just when you thought it couldn't get any weirder," Josh says when I break the news to him and Daisy over lunch. "Still think it's a coincidence, Mum?"

"You've heard the saying, bad things happen in threes."

"Yes, but what if she was pushed?"

"Why on earth would someone try and murder Leo?"

"The same reason they killed a cleaner."

There's logic in what he says, however daft. "There were hundreds of people up on the cliffs yesterday. Someone would have seen if they had."

What other explanation could there possibly be?

It's Sunday, which means I won't hear from the hospital. In the hope of tempting Daisy into conversation, I try a different tack and offer to take her shopping in Topshop.

She frowns and shakes her head.

"What about a trip to the pier to play on the slot machines?" I suggest, something she knows I hate. "Or an afternoon go-karting?"

Josh's ears prick up. "Cool! Great idea, Mum."

Daisy, who has barely uttered a word all week, shakes her head again and slinks off to her room.

"I don't know what to say to her anymore," Josh says.

I sigh and shake my head. Welcome to my world.

"Can we go anyway? We could ask Bruno and Madelena."

The thought of an afternoon out of the house is appealing but impossible. "I can't leave Daisy alone."

Josh flexes his eyebrows. "You could ask Margaret to sit with her."

The afternoon is a huge success. Josh and I return home invigorated and reeking of petrol and sweat. We walk through the door and are greeted by the sumptuous smell of baking. My tense neck and shoulders, relax, and I smile and head off to the kitchen where Margaret, her face flushed, is squatting in front of the open oven. She stands up, holding two round cake tins in her oven-gloved hands, the perfect picture of domesticity.

"Mmm. Smells heavenly," I say.

Margaret places the tins on the granite surface and smiles. "Carrot cake. Daisy's favourite."

"How's she been?"

Margaret runs a knife around the sponges and tips them

onto a wire rack. "Fairly quiet. She's spent most of the afternoon in her room. I'm hoping the smell will flush her out."

I wriggle out of my jacket and hang it over the back of a chair. "I'll go and tell her we're home."

Daisy is sitting on her bed, cross-legged, flicking through *Heat* magazine. "How are you feeling?"

Her eyes remained fixed to the page. "Fine."

I force a smile. "Margaret's made a cake."

She frowns but doesn't look up.

"So you'll come down then?"

"Meh."

I've always assumed that sound means *yes, probably,* but an hour passes, and Daisy still hasn't appeared. I resist the urge to force her because I don't want to cause a scene.

Josh makes up for her absence by eating almost half the cake.

"He's a growing boy," I explain and apologise again for Daisy's rudeness.

Margaret dismisses this with a wave of her hand and reminds me she's always here if I need her.

The moment she's gone, I run upstairs to Daisy's room to have a quiet word with her, but the lights are off, and all I can make out of my daughter is her curled up form under the duvet. It's only just past seven, but I suppose a rest might be what she needs right now, so I head back to the kitchen to fix Josh's supper.

The fridge is almost bare. There's a half-full carton of milk, a bag of mixed lettuce leaves, a cucumber, a couple of wrinkled tomatoes, and some withered mushrooms. I rummage through the larder and find a packet of spaghetti and a jar of pesto. I chop the vegetables and dress the salad with olive oil and balsamic vinegar and convince myself the meal is now a healthy one. Even though he's recently consumed almost an entire cake, Josh devours his enormous portion in seconds flat, heads off to the freezer, pulls out the tub of caramel ice cream, and wolfs that down, too.

He clutches his forehead. "Ouch! Brain freeze."

The doorbell clangs, and I jump. Josh throws me a wary look. I shrug and glance at the clock on the wall. It's ten to eight. Who would visit so late on a Sunday night? I rise cautiously from my chair.

"Don't answer it, Mum."

I ponder this for a second then flop back in my chair. "Good idea."

Josh smirks. "I know." He holds the bowl up to his face and licks it clean.

I'm about to tell him to stop when the bell sounds again, accompanied this time with a loud knocking. No, that doesn't do it justice. It's a banging. A *thud-thud-thud* of fist on wood. I spring out of my seat.

"I thought you said—"

"They'll wake Daisy." I hurry to the door. "Who is it?" I call out, suddenly fearful, though of what I'm not sure.

"It's me."

The voice is deep, gravely, and instantly recognisable. "Glen?"

"No! Father fucking Christmas! Yes, of course Glen."

"What the hell are you doing here?"

"Jeez, Megs, I'll tell you if you'll open the bloody door."

I pause, recalling the effect his last visit had on the twins, when Josh taps me on the shoulder. "You should let him in."

I turn to face my son. "I'm sorry, I didn't know he was coming."

He shrugs. "It's cool."

Bearded, shaggy-haired, and bronzed, but otherwise relatively well-turned out in a red checked shirt and clean jeans,

Glen stands on the doorstep, hands on hips. "Are you sure about this? I mean, it only took me two flaming hours to get here, but I'm more than happy to drive straight back if that's what you want."

I tilt my head at Josh and hope Glen picks up on it. "I wasn't expecting you."

"I know. I didn't tell you I was coming."

I usher him in with an irritated wave of my hand.

"I'll be in my room," Josh says, heading upstairs.

I lead Glen roughly by the arm into the kitchen and glare at him. "What the hell do you think you're doing?"

He pulls a face. "Great welcome. Thanks, Megs. You haven't been answering your phone. I've left messages and sent you an embarrassing number of texts, which you haven't replied to. I was worried. I thought something had happened."

I bite my lip and lower my gaze, only to see Glen's scuffed leather boot tapping impatiently. I look up and manage a weak smile. "I'm sorry, I should have called. Things have been a little crazy recently."

As if on cue, Josh lets out an almighty scream. My heart skips a beat.

"Jeez!" says Glen.

We rush up the stairs, and almost collide into Josh on the way down. His face is pale, and his eyes are wide with shock.

"What is it? What's happened?" I ask.

He jerks a thumb down the landing.

"What? What?" My arms are on his shoulders, and I am trying desperately hard not to shake the answer out of him.

"Daisy! She's gone!"

"Gone. But I checked on her. She's asleep."

"No. It just looked that way. It was a pile of pillows."

I clutch my hands to my chest and tell myself not to worry. That this is something she does.

Josh stamps his foot. "She's run away. I knew she would."

"She'll come back," I say, although I'm not convinced because since waking up in hospital, she hasn't been herself – either self, for that matter – the mild or the wild version.

"But how did she get out without you noticing?" Glen asks.

"I don't know, okay," cries Josh. "Stop asking me all these questions. You're doing my head in."

"The back stairs," I reply in a quiet monotone. "It leads to the old scullery in the far end of the house that we never use. There's a door there. She must have gone out that way while we were having supper."

Josh unravels his hand to reveal a very creased scrap of paper. "I found this on the floor by her mobile."

My heart sinks. "She left her mobile?"

"Her charger broke."

Glen shakes his head and whistles.

"Why didn't she tell me? I'd have bought a new one."

Josh sighs. "That's what I told her."

A shiver runs down my spine. I take the paper from Josh and read the hastily scribbled address and telephone number. How on earth did Daisy find this? I look at Josh. His hands are behind his neck now, that familiar pose. "It's the name and telephone number of Eve's hotel in Easthaven."

Glen's eyes widen. "Eve? I thought she buggered off with an Italian gigolo."

"I thought she was dead," mutters Josh.

Glen is staring me with an *explain yourself* expression.

I shrug. "She paid us a visit three weeks ago."

"Crikey!"

Josh screws up his nose. "Do you think Daisy's gone to see her?"

I baulk at the thought, even if all the evidence points that way. But it seems unlikely. Eve's not the type to stick around. I call the hotel and ask the receptionist who tells me she left two and a half weeks ago.

"Maybe she went there anyway," Josh says.

I shake my head but then I recall the part-sympathetic, part-pitying look Daisy gave me the day she was late home a couple of days after Eve's visit. Had Daisy been to visit her? And did Eve have anything to do with her disappearance now?

Josh is pacing the hall, hands around his neck. He stops suddenly and turns to me, a haunted look in his eyes. "Leo didn't jump. I've read about suicides on the internet, and happy people don't jump off cliffs."

Glen's jaw drops. "Leo jumped off a cliff? Why?"

"See?" says Josh.

"Appearances can be deceptive." It certainly seems that way, although I can't quite believe it either. Leo's one of the most straightforward, happy people I've ever met – great marriage, well-adjusted kids.

"Yes, but what if I'm right and she didn't jump. What if the man who killed the cleaner, bullied Ella, and tried to kill Leo, has taken Daisy?"

Glen's eyes bulge. "Leo didn't die?"

Could the incidences be connected? No, it's impossible. Unless … What if she'd jumped out of guilt? What if Leo had spiked Daisy's drink? A doctor's wife would have access to every drug under the sun. And she had a motive. She'd been irritated Daisy was a better tennis player than Coco. And she'd been quick to accuse Daisy of being drunk. Perhaps she'd laced her water with vodka. No. Surely Daisy would've tasted it. Daisy ending up in hospital, though, wasn't part of the plan. Perhaps that's when the guilt had set in.

Yes, but why would Leo pose as a boy and email Ella? It doesn't make sense.

"Would somebody mind explaining what the hell is going on?" Glen asks.

"Daisy's hurt, Mum," says Josh.

"You don't know that."

He grabs his head. "I do. I can feel it, here."

"You're worried. It's given you a headache."

"No, Mum. You have to believe me. Daisy's in trouble."

Can they feel each other's pain? I wonder, trying to quash the rising panic.

Something twigs. A memory from way back. When Daisy had her tonsils out, Josh complained of a sore throat. Guy took him to a doctor who could find nothing wrong.

"Daisy's getting a lot of attention. He probably feels he's missing out," the doctor said.

But Guy didn't buy it. He was convinced all twins shared a special bond, a gene perhaps, that enabled them to intuit what was happening to the other.

I feel the blood drain from my face. Oh God, what if Josh is right? I wrap my arms around him. "She'll be back soon. And if she isn't, we'll find her."

"Nobody found Madeleine McCann."

"Yes, but she was four and she was abducted. She didn't run away."

But my heart freezes even as I say the words.

I call the police first, just in case. The kindly officer takes a description of Daisy, asks me to email a photograph, and adds her to the Missing Persons File. He tells me not to worry because hundreds of teenagers run away from home every day, as if I didn't know. He gives me the telephone number for the Runaway Helpline and suggests I ring her friends. I start with Jemma, but she's out and I speak to Dylan. But Daisy isn't there. Of course she isn't. They broke up.

Dylan, though, is worried. "Has something happened to her?"

I call Madelena who offers to come over. I explain Glen is here but beg her to call me if she hears anything. And then, because I have to do something, I phone Samantha and Gabriel, but neither of them picks up.

I wring my shaking hands. "I wish she'd taken her mobile."

"Call the service provider anyway," says Glen. "They'll have a list of numbers she's contacted recently."

It's a great idea. For the first time since he arrived, I'm glad he's here. I turn to Josh and ask him if he knows her Facebook password, which he does, and he hurries off to check her home page and her internet history. Glen trails me to the kitchen. I march across the room and open the drawer where I keep the most recent bills.

"Was she in any kind of trouble?" he asks.

I sigh. "What do you think?"

He clicks his fingers. "Right. So what's the latest?"

I explain the events of the last few weeks while I'm rummaging through the unfiled paperwork. I unearth the most recent Vodafone statement and hurry over to the handset on the table. "She just fell asleep."

"What, like drugged asleep, you mean?"

"Yeah, but the rumour-mongers are adamant she was drunk."

"But you don't believe that, do you?"

The evening Daisy came home smelling of alcohol, her speech and behaviour had been too controlled to be drunk. But she hadn't offered an explanation, and I felt let down and angry. In hospital, frightened and disoriented, she insisted she hadn't drunk alcohol, that she didn't like it. Did I believe her? Or did she just protest too much? Given the accusations levelled against her, it was odd she hadn't explained why she smelled of booze. Was she protecting someone? And if so, whom? Why, oh why hadn't I interrogated her?

I shake my head.

"Okay, so who do you think did it?"

"Christ, Glen, who would drug a child? Besides, we don't know she was for sure. The hospital still hasn't got back to me with the toxicology results."

He takes me by the arms. "But your gut instinct is she was. Right?"

I press my lips together and nod.

He shakes me slightly. "C'mon, Megs. When has your sixth sense ever let you down? And in answer to your question, there are plenty of psychos who'd drug a child. What does Daisy think happened?"

I shake my head miserably. Why hadn't I asked her? Was it because I was frightened of the truth? "I don't know."

"What do you mean you don't know?"

"We didn't discuss it."

Glen looks at me as if he's seeing me in a new light. A kind of *Christ sakes, you're her bloody mother* expression I've never seen before. He sighs before speaking. "But it's possible she could have figured it out? Or at least thinks she has. Maybe that's why she's gone. Maybe she's going to confront someone."

Yet again he's one step ahead of me. "Where would a child get the drugs?"

Glen raises his eyebrows. "Their parents' medicine cabinet!"

Of course.

The run through all the usual suspects gets us nowhere. I keep going back to the smug look on Georgia Young's face the first time Daisy collapsed. Was that relevant? Samantha was stressed about her missing staffroom swipe card. She told me it had been stolen. Was she telling the truth? Or was that just what she'd told the police to get them off her back? Madelena told me she'd been seen arguing with Leo before the sponsored walk. And, even though she was in charge, she hadn't been at school at the end. Was that because Leo had found something out about Natalia's murder? Did Samantha push Leo over the cliff to silence her? Did she spike Daisy's drink because Georgia's place in the tennis team was reliant on Daisy not playing? There's no love lost between the two girls. And I saw her at school that day, coming out of the gym. Neat theory, Megan, but where does Ella fit in? And why would Samantha kill Natalia? I shake my head. I'm losing it. Samantha and Leo are not murderers. It's a macabre set of coincidences. Natalia was killed by a loan shark. Ella was being groomed by a paedophile. Perhaps Leo was blown off the cliff. It's always windy up there. Perhaps she was standing too close to the edge. And Daisy was … What?

What *has* happened to Daisy?

Daisy's Vodafone statement throws up some numbers I don't recognise. We dial them all and the friends she's been chatting to on Facebook, but no one has seen her. With nothing else to do, I tell Glen I'm going to drive around East-haven to look for her.

"If she's on a mission, she'll hardly be sleeping rough," he says.

"Josh thinks she's hurt."

"Josh is scared."

I look around for my keys. "I have to do something. I can't just sit here.

"It'll be like searching for the proverbial needle. Why not wait till it's light? It'll be easier then."

He leads me into the living room where Josh is attempting to watch television. We huddle together on the sofa, each of us struggling with our thoughts as we wait for sunrise.

41

I 'm awake all night and rise before the dawn, eager to get going. Josh is asleep beside me, curled up on the couch under his Arsenal duvet cover. On a seat next to us, his limbs splayed like a starfish, head back, mouth open, Glen snores quietly. I scribble him a note, grab my puffa, my mobile and keys, and rush outside. A weak sun is shining in a china-blue sky, and the air is cool. A rash of goose bumps break out on my skin. I'm not cold, I realise, but frightened.

Pull yourself together. She hasn't been abducted, she's run away. Glen's right, she's tenacious. Sooner or later, she'll run out of whatever money she has, get hungry, and come home. She always does.

I climb into my car, start the engine, and drive into the centre of town. The murky streets deserted, I peer into every shop entrance, but there's no sign of Daisy. Mist crawls over the seawall, groping the wheels of my car with its spectral fingers as it feels its way through the town. I pass the pier and head into the unfashionable end of Easthaven, a strip of small hotels, grotty cafes, and B&Bs, hugging the kerb, praying that I'll find Daisy cold, tired, and dishevelled asleep on a bench perhaps, or trudging wearily down the pavement. I park the car to chase after a jogger and ask if he's seen a teenage girl sleeping rough, but he shakes his head awkwardly and hurries on his way.

If only I'd talked to her, she wouldn't have run away. I'd given up trying because it wasn't me she wanted to talk to, it was Guy. Exhausted, I peer up at the sky. And she's not the only one. I could do with some of your advice, too.

The energy that sustained me all night dips suddenly, and I drive round the mini roundabout at the end of the seafront and head back the way I came. By a rustic wooden café at the foot of the downs, a stone's throw from St Peter's, I stop the car and slam my palms on the steering wheel in frustration.

Why, Daisy? Why?

I groan, bury my face in my hands, and fight back tears. Urging myself to get a grip, I reach into my pocket for my mobile and dial the police, but no one matching Daisy's description has been found. I call Anthony Swann and explain what's happened. He's shocked by my news, sympathetic, and quick to lend his support.

"I'll make an announcement in assembly and get my secretary to email all the parents."

My spirits lift. Surely, she'll be found now. Somebody must know where she is.

I call Glen, just in case, but Daisy hasn't returned. "How's Josh?"

"Bearing up. Are you going to keep looking?"

"I have to. I can't sit around doing nothing."

I pass St Matthew's church and, catching sight of Jemma Webster's Panda, roll to a stop beside it. Perhaps she's heard something. The solid oak door ajar, I push it open and step into the narrow lobby. It's colder in here than outside. Clearly, God prefers his worshipers chilled.

I walk into the main body of the building but pull up with a start. "Oh my God!"

Gabriel and Jemma are locked in an embrace, her head nestled in the well of his shoulder, his nose nuzzling her hair.

"Megan!" Gabriel lets go of Jemma and rushes towards me.

I hold up my hands and hurry out of the church without a backward glance. My heart beating rapidly, the tips of my ears burning, I jump into my car, jam the gear into first, and stamp on the accelerator. The wheels screech in protest and spin on the gravel. I careen onto the road and have to brake suddenly to avoid a cyclist. He veers out of the way, wobbling precariously, and flicks two fingers at me, yelling obscenities. Letting out a frustrated roar, I take a sharp right past KFC and the Tesco on the corner to the Memorial round-about where I turn left onto the coast road. Only then do I process what I've seen.

A child is missing, for Christ's sake. How dare they? She's a married woman, and he calls himself a man of God. Lecherous bloody womaniser, more like.

Breathing heavily, I park my car at a forty-five-degree angle between two white lines. A trio of blue-rinsed pensioners sitting on a bench, wrapped up in warm winter coats, throw crumbs to a couple of huge seagulls with bright-yellow beaks and pink rubbery legs. I stare at them for a moment, marshalling my thoughts.

Where are you, Daisy? And what the hell is going on?

The house, on my return, feels electrically charged. I hear voices. Visitors? What do they want? I wonder, irritated. A door slams upstairs. Josh? Glen shoots out of the living room. He stops when he sees me and scratches his neck.

"How's Josh?"

"He's okay. A bit upset by the visitor." Glen nods towards the living room.

I raise my eyebrows questioningly.

"Bloke called Gabriel." He pulls a face.

Steaming with rage, I barge open the living room door. Gabriel opens his mouth to speak, but the telephone beats him to it.

Glen answers it. "The hospital." He passes me the handset and jerks his head at Gabriel. I nod, and he takes him by the arm, "C'mon, mate. Time to go home."

Gabriel shakes him off. "There's something I need to tell Megan."

"Later, sunshine," Glen says and shepherds him out of the room.

Josh darts in and sits beside me. I put my arm around him and take a deep breath. Somewhere along the line, I've forgotten all about the test results.

"The Echo and EEG were normal, but traces of diazepam were found in her blood and in the water bottle," the nurse explains. "You probably know the drug as Valium, a benzodiazepine used for its anxiety-relieving and muscle-relaxing effects."

My stomach lurches. So Daisy *was* drugged?

Josh nudges me. I turn to him and put a finger to my lips.

There's a commotion in the hall. The door opens, and Gabriel dashes in followed by a red-faced Glen. "Leave her alone. You're about as popular as a turd in a lunch box right now."

Josh covers his ears with his hands. I apologise to the nurse and put down the phone. "Honey, why don't you go and play on your Xbox."

Josh doesn't budge.

"I'll explain everything to you in a minute. I just need to talk to Gabriel."

Josh groans and trudges reluctantly from the room.

"Glen's explained, and I'm sorry. I had no idea Daisy was missing. Is that why you came to the church?"

Glen does a double-take. "Church?"

I shrug. "He's a priest."

"A God botherer? Bloody hell, Megs!"

Gabriel frowns. "Look, I know you mean well, but would you mind if I talked to Megan in private."

"Yes, actually, I would," Glen says, folding his arms.

Gabriel shifts uncomfortably and turns to me. I'm getting a weird satisfaction seeing him squirm and simply frown. He looks as though he's about to protest but seems to remember the awkward situation he's in and smiles sheepishly. "I was comforting Jemma, nothing more."

"I'm not interested."

He sighs. "Because the police got in touch to ask if I wanted to press charges."

"What's that got to do with Jemma?"

"Because it was Dylan sending Ella bullying emails. Dylan is Mickey Mouse."

Glen gives a short, sharp laugh and twirls his finger round his temple. "Okay, Vicar. That's enough now. Time to go."

He makes a move towards Gabriel, but I beat him to it and lodge myself between the two men. "Dylan? Are you sure?"

"Positive. The IP number was registered to the Webster's computer. I wanted to be the one to tell her. Jemma was upset and shocked, which is why I was comforting her."

Glen groans. "Will somebody please tell me what the fuck is going on?"

"Why would Dylan bully Ella?" I ask.

Gabriel shakes his head. "I've no idea, and neither does Jemma. But I'd hazard a guess it has something to do with his father's behaviour."

"Robert's all right," I say.

Gabriel frowns and purses his lips.

It doesn't make sense. Dylan doesn't seem the bullying type. Is there a type? Don't kids resort to bullying because they're jealous of their victim? But why would Dylan, a good-looking, clever child, be jealous of Ella? I'm about to point this out when I remember something Robert let slip about Jemma. *It would've been so much better if we'd been able to have another child. She devotes far too much time to Dylan. It's not healthy for either of them.* Hadn't Ella regained her place at the top of the class? Did Jemma's pushiness account for Dylan's behaviour? Was he jealous of Ella's academic success?

I scratch my head. It almost makes sense were it not for the fact that Dylan got caught smoking with Daisy. Why take the risk if he'd just got rid of Ella? Robert said he thought Daisy had done Dylan a favour. *He's been a mummy's boy far too long*, he'd said. And then he'd joked about Jemma finding religion. *Either that or she fancies the vicar.* But why hadn't Jemma risen to Gabriel's defence in The Singing Kettle the morning Leo poked fun at him? Was it because she didn't want to be found out?

Think, Megan, think.

Leo told me Jemma thought Robert was having an affair. Well, maybe he was. And maybe Jemma was using Gabriel to get back at him. Gabriel was uncomfortable when I introduced him to Robert that day in the church and again, at the play. Was that down to guilt?

My head throbbing with the strain of the past twenty-four

hours, I turn to Gabriel. "Are you having an affair with Jemma Webster? Because that would upset Dylan."

Gabriel flinches but shakes his head.

"Okay, I'll rephrase that. Have you ever had an affair with her?"

Gabriel scrubs at his face.

I can see I've touched a nerve and don't back off. "My daughter is missing, and there might be a connection. If I mean anything to you, you must tell me." It's a cheap shot fired to provoke a response.

Gabriel puffs out his cheeks. "I don't normally break confidences." He pauses for a second to collect himself and glances fretfully from me to Glen and back.

"Think of it as a one-off," I say.

"Okay, okay." He clears his throat. "People find it comforting to talk to a priest."

Glen raises his finger. "Ha!"

I wave him quiet.

"Jemma came into my church six months ago in a terrible state. I was sympathetic, I listened, and she told me about her unhappy marriage."

Glen narrows his eyes. "Bloody decent, mate, but was sympathy all you offered her?"

Puce in the face, Gabriel glowers at his shoes.

Glen walks over and slaps him on the back. "Aw, c'mon, Vicar, a good-looking, red-blooded man like you. I'll bet women fling themselves at you all the time."

"Most marriages are unhappy at one time or other," I say. "Maybe it was because she was desperate to have another child. Robert told me they couldn't."

Gabriel shakes his head. "She was unhappy because her husband abused her."

I exchange looks with Glen. "Abused her?"

"She had bruises on her arm where he held her when he punched her, a bruise on her cheek where she fell against the bedpost before he … before …" He stops, unable to continue.

The bruise she'd covered with sunglasses which she told me was caused by bumping into a wall, I recall.

Gabriel sighs and bows his head. "We kissed. Once. That's all."

Glen snorts. "You've got yourself in a bit of a tizz over one lousy kiss."

"It was awkward and embarrassing. Jemma was upset. She wanted more but …"

Suddenly it all makes sense: his reaction to Robert, his embarrassment, his disappearing act at the play when Jemma showed up. Dylan must have known what was going on and decided to take it out on Ella.

"I wanted to tell you when I came around with the flowers."

"Time to go home, mate. You've caused enough trouble." Glen takes Gabriel by the arm and leads him to the door.

Gabriel shrugs him off and looks at me bleakly. "I'm sure you have, given it's what you advised me to do, but have you been through Daisy's things?"

I stomp upstairs into Daisy's bedroom, followed by Glen. Unlike Josh's, Daisy's room is a mess – magazines, sweet wrappers, and CDs strewn over the floor, clothes heaped in piles, the bed unmade. Under her pillow I find an old Rolling Stones T-shirt and gasp. Guy's favourite shirt. A memento from the Stones' gig at Wembley Stadium, June 1982. *One of the best moments of my life before I met you,* he'd said. The huge red tongue and the dark-grey cotton is faded, the seams frayed, but it's still very much the shirt Guy used to lounge around the house in.

The one I thought I'd given to Oxfam.

Why did you give everything of his away? Daisy screamed when she discovered his empty wardrobe the day I took his clothes to the charity shop. She must have wagged school to buy it back. I bury my face in it and breathe in Guy's scent. Incredible it still smells of him. He's been dead almost a year.

Welling up, I sink to the floor, lean against the bed, and try to compose myself. Glen stops picking through some clothes and eyes me curiously, so I roll onto my hands and knees and make a play of peering under the bed. A can of men's deodorant is lying on its side. Strange. I pull it out and see it's the brand Guy used. Well, that explains the T-shirt's smell. A surge of affection for my daughter washing over me, I run my hand along the carpet. My fingers connect with something flat. A diary?

But it isn't a diary, I realise, as I retrieve it. It's a ring-bound notebook, the pages covered in Daisy's untidy scrawl. I read the first entry:

- ***GOD.***
- *Did God make us the way we are, either good or bad? Or does goodness come from us, our thoughts and actions?*

Existentialism in its most basic form, I think, surprised.

- *Can you only be good if you believe in God?*
- *Dad did not believe in God, but he was good.*
- *If God did not make us good (or bad) who did? Are parents? Or areselves?*
- *Dad said God didn't make us as some people*

beleived. And he also said are character, the
colour of are hair, are eyes actually come from are
jeans!
- ***MR PLATT***
- *My PE teacher is a total perv and a sadist and*
  needs to be taught a lesson.

I'm shocked Daisy feels this strongly about her PE teacher, but with no reason noted, I move onto the next page, a list that includes learning lines, doing maths prep, downloading an Alt J album.

I flip the page and read the next entry.

- ***EVE***
- *Why was Eve bad? Did somthing happen to her to*
  make her that way? Or was she just selfish?

- ***MEGAN***
- *When Dad was alive we were invisible. When Dad*
  died I became visible but all I did was make her
  angry. Better to be invisible.
- *Megan thinks I'm a bad person, unlike Josh who*
  is good. Am I bad because my mother doesn't love
  me or because I don't love her or both these
  things? Is it enough that Dad loved me?

Utterly wretched, I turn another page.

This entry surprises me. ***GABRIEL.*** No one, it seems, is immune.

- *If God dosn't exist (which I beleive is true) does*
  that make Gabriel plane stupid? Josh told me
  there's something wrong with his daughter, wich

he cant see. Stupid I think. Dad said people who prayed were lazy. They should try to help themselves insted of asking some metafizzycal being to solve their problems. Dad would be surprised Megan likes Gabriel. Josh is. I asked him about Jeans too. G-E-N-E-S! he said. God Daisy your such a retard. But I'm not. And I don't drink and I'll proove it. I'll take Dad's advice and go and proove who did this to me on my own. If I can proove I wasn't drunk will Megan ... love is crossed out ... *like me more?*

My heart pounding, I turn the page.

- ***SUSPECTS***
- *1. That cow Georgia Young.*
- *2. Dylan*
- *3. Platt the perv.*
- A couple of names crossed out.
- *4. Tilly Styne's father. He killed one person, why stop there?*

"Find anything interesting?" Glen asks.

"Oh, Glen, I've really let her down."

"Don't be daft."

I stagger to my feet and thrust the book at him. "She hasn't run away, she's gone to find out what happened to her. She has a list of suspects." I pace the room. Diazepam was found in Daisy's blood sample and her water bottle. Who has access to a drug like that?

"I agree with this bit about Gabriel. What the fuck was a vicar doing pissing around with a married woman?"

I stop pacing and look at him. "Wait a minute. Gabriel

implied Jemma was anxious when he first met her, didn't he?"

"Yeah, but—"

"Anxious enough to be taking Valium perhaps?"

"Go on."

"It's not inconceivable Dylan knew his mother was anxious. The smoking incident can't have helped, and the time he came to supper without telling her."

"What?"

I close my eyes to think it through. Maybe he knew his father was hitting his mother. Maybe he knew about the pills. And then after everything he'd gone through, Daisy dumped him. Maybe he was unhappy enough to seek revenge. "Shit! I think Dylan drugged Daisy."

"You're kidding, right?" says Glen. "He's just a kid. What about this pervert, Platt? He sounds like a real schmuck."

"If Dylan is capable of sending vicious emails to Ella Jones, he's capable of drugging my daughter. The nurse just told me traces of diazepam were found in her blood and her water bottle. My guess is, Dylan wanted to get back at Daisy for the smoking incident. What better way than to make it look like she was drunk? Daisy must have figured it out. That's why she dumped him."

"Okay, I get where you're coming from, Megs. Jealousy and revenge. But why do it a second time?"

"To get her expelled!"

Glen stares at me as if I've lost the plot. "Strewth! And there I was thinking Easthaven was a quiet town full of wrinklies."

"It all makes sense. The alcohol on Daisy's breath when she went missing the day I was in London, having lunch with you and Eric. Dylan gave her the whisky. She didn't tell me because she wanted to protect him. And I guess he forced it on her because when she came to in the hospital, she was desperate for me to believe she hadn't been drinking."

Josh storms in, a thunderous expression on his face. "You said you'd come and see me in a minute an hour ago." His mouth is a thin quivering line. The bags under his eyes are sooty from lack of sleep.

I rush over to him and give him a hug. "Darling, I'm so sorry."

"How are you bearing up, mate?" Glen asks.

"I bet you're hungry. Let me fix you some food."

Josh flops onto Daisy's bed and stares at the ceiling. "I'm not hungry. My head is killing me. I feel sick."

I sit beside him and hold his hand.

"Daisy's hurt, Mum. I know she is."

I look pleadingly at Glen who shrugs. "I'm going to drive over and speak to Jemma. I have to."

"Why?" Josh asks.

I look at my son's expectant face. I have to tell him the truth or at least what I believe it to be. "I think there's a chance Dylan knows where Daisy is."

42

It's gone nine-thirty, but Dylan isn't at school. His mother dropped him at the gate this morning. It's crazy. He lives around the corner, a fifteen-minute walk tops, but his control-freak Mum won't let him walk. Why? What could possibly happen? I mean, really? He's a thirteen-year-old boy, not some ditzy girl who'd accept a lift from a paedophile. Duh!

"I have my reasons," she says.

Sure you do. But what are they? You never explain. Scared I might be abducted by aliens? Run away, maybe?

Now there's an idea.

He waved goodbye, even managed a smile as she drove off. But instead of going inside, he walked down the asphalt, past the tennis courts, up the bank, out the back gate to the seafront, just as he had the day of the sponsored walk. His mother had been waiting for him at home that evening, in a right state, worried as well as angry. He'd been pleased. She shouldn't be allowed to have it her own way all the time.

A seagull scavenges for food on the pebble beach. He leans against a groyne and watches it attack a Tesco bag. He's thinking about Daisy, wondering where she is. Her mother was worried, he could hear the strain in her voice when she rang last night. Daisy was always running away. It's what she did when things got bad. What was different about this time? She'd come back, wouldn't she?

She blames me. Because of the whisky.

He clutches his head, willing the thoughts buzzing around in it to stop.

Why give a fuck? She dumped me.

His heart aches. How is that possible?

She's wounded me, he thinks.

The plastic bag torn to shreds, the seagull casts his beady eye over Dylan, waddles across the shingle, and jumps onto the promenade, pecking about for food.

Dylan's shoulders droop. He's tired. He spent the night tossing and turning, too scared of the nightmares he might have if he closed his eyes. Has she run away to frighten me? He feels about as miserable as he's ever done. It's bad enough that they've broken up, but it's way, way worse she's not talking to him. He wants to be friends.

I need to make it up with her. But how?

He mulls this over. It's not a problem he's had before. He's never fallen out with anyone. Perhaps Josh will know what to do. He'll ask him.

No. One hundred percent, no. He'll tell Daisy. She'll either laugh at me or go crazy. Bad idea. Very, very bad.

He'd seen her at the sponsored walk from his hiding place behind the pavilion. She'd been standing slightly apart from Bruno, Josh, and Oli, eyes fixed on the ground.

She's not happy either.

But the thought doesn't cheer him.

He wishes his dad were home. But he's away on business,

a-*gain*. At least that's what his mother told him after his dad walked out on the back of another argument.

"I've put in all the hard work, nursed him, babysat him, ferried him around, disciplined him," his mother screamed. "I'm the bad guy, and then in you waltz, Mr Fun Guy. It's not fair. Of course I'm resentful."

"I've tried, God knows I've tried, but I'll never be enough for you," Dad said as he slammed the door.

He's scared he might have left home, left Mum. Left him. When he called last night from a hotel in Barcelona, Dylan told him Daisy had run away.

"I'm worried," he said.

"Don't worry, son. She'll be all right. She's a firecracker, that one."

He wanted to tell his father about the whisky. But what was the point? Dad would get angry, demand to speak to Mum, and all hell would break loose. The pills were meant to calm her down. They helped, but she still got mad. With him. With Dad.

"I'm disappointed," she said. "I try so hard. I feel let down. And it hurts. I've had enough."

Really? Was it really so bad he hadn't got straight As in his report card? That he wasn't top of the class anymore? That he couldn't speak fluent Spanish? That he wasn't head boy? Surely there was more to life? Daisy thought so. She knew how to have fun. He hadn't liked being caught smoking. He hated Swanny making an example of him. But he got over it. Daisy was funny. She made him laugh. She made him happy. She was all he thought about every minute of every day.

I miss your strawberry kisses, Daisy. But most of all I miss you.

Mucus dribbles from his nose to his chin where it mingles

with his tears. Annoyed, he swipes his face with the back of his hand. He can't believe he's crying over a girl. A mean, stupid girl who doesn't give a toss about him, can't even be bothered to reply to his texts.

The sun goes behind a cloud. He shivers, lifts the collar of his blazer, and looks at the fluffy white balls sweeping across the washed-out sky. Seagulls glide on the strengthening wind. Now and again, one swoops and dives into the grey-blue sea.

I'm going to be reminded she led me on then dumped me every sodding day for the next five years. It sucks. She's always saying she'll fail Common Entrance. But she won't. No one from St Peter's ever does. If only we were going to different schools. If only I'd never met her. If only she didn't exist.

He thumps the pebbles until his palms are red and bruised.

I hate her.

His mobile bleeps. A text. From her?

He stuffs his hand into his blazer pocket, pulls it out, and stares at the screen. Dad. His disappointment overwhelms him. He draws back his arm to throw the phone into the sea but stops himself. One second's satisfaction will not be worth the shit he'll get when his mum freaks out.

He reads the message.

Guess what? I'm on my way home. Love you. Dad xx

His spirits lift a little. He taps in his reply.

Cool.

He slips his mobile away, stands, and tramps across the shingle onto the promenade, ignoring the puzzled looks from three old women sitting on a bench. He knows they're wondering why he isn't at school.

He scowls. Mind your own.

A woman jogs past him towards the pier, her ponytail swishing from side to side. An overweight man runs by in the other direction, red-faced and wheezing. There are runners everywhere, and men and women walking dogs. Hundreds of them.

A group of shrieking girls on rollerblades whiz by.

Why aren't they at school? he wonders, and climbs the steps to the road.

43

———————

I t's just past ten-thirty when I arrive in Holbrook Gardens. The Monday morning shoppers are out in force, and the road is stacked with cars. I find a space big enough for my Golf, just around the corner in Magnolia Avenue.

Jemma answers the door, smiling brightly. She invites me into her pristine kitchen and offers me coffee. Odd behaviour for someone who's just been told her son's a cyberbully.

Has Gabriel told her? I wonder. Or was he lying to me?

"Our relationship must have come as a terrible shock to you," she purrs.

I stare at her, baffled.

She smiles and strokes her glossy hair, her head inclined to one side. "We're in love. I'm sorry you had to find out like this. I should have told you. I just didn't know how."

I slap the table. "I don't give a stuff about Gabriel."

She jumps but quickly recovers her composure. "I'm sorry. I knew you'd be devastated."

I lean my elbows on the table and hold my head in my hands, trying to keep a lid on my temper. "Listen, Jemma, what you and Gabriel get up to is no business of mine but, I have to admit, I'm surprised, given Gabriel knows what Dylan's been doing."

Her expression hardens. "I don't know what you're talking about."

I don't hold back. I explain about the emails from Mikey, the self-harm, Gabriel's concern. "I know all about it. Everything."

Jemma's mouth twists. "That wasn't Dylan."

"The emails were sent from his computer."

She shakes her head. "That's what he wanted everyone to think."

"Gabriel?"

"No, of course not Gabriel. Robert." Jemma leans forward until her forehead rests on the table, and starts to sob.

I stare at her folded form, nonplussed. Why would Robert be sending emails to a thirteen-year-old girl? Unless... unless Robert was grooming Ella. Gabriel found out but, being the kind-hearted sort, decides to protect him. Why? Because the police come down hard on paedophiles, the press and public, too. It wouldn't just be Robert's life that was ruined but Dylan's and Jemma's, as well. They had to lie to me. And, for a split second, I understand.

But what about Daisy?

Sounds like a real firecracker, your daughter.

My heart flips. I clutch Jemma's arm and force her to look at me. Her beautiful face is stained with tears, her mascara smudged. "Where is Robert?"

"In Barcelona. Why?"

"Daisy is missing."

Jemma stares at me, not comprehending. I'm on the verge of yelling when a light goes on and her expression changes. "Oh no! You don't think he's taken—"

"She was drugged, Jemma. Twice. And now she's disappeared. And you've as good as told me your husband is a paedophile."

"Drugged?" Jemma gasps and covers her mouth with her hand. "I thought she'd been drinking."

I squeeze her arm. "What do you mean?"

She wriggles free, plucks a tissue from the box on the table, and dabs at her face. "A bottle of whisky went missing. Robert must have plied her with it."

I twig, recalling the comment in Daisy's notebook. "Ha! That'll be the whisky your precious son gave my daughter. But like I said, Daisy wasn't drunk, she was drugged."

She sighs and shakes her head.

Oh God, it's true. What has he done to her? Where is she? I stand up. "I'm going to the police."

I've barely uttered the words when the doorbell sounds. Jemma freezes.

"You should answer that," I say.

Dropping the tissue into the bin, she hurries into the hall with me on her heels.

Her mouth drops open in surprise. "Gabriel! What are you doing here?"

Gabriel ignores her and looks at me, concern clouding his dark-brown eyes.

I barge past him, down the steps to the pavement, where I swivel around. "My daughter is missing. You might have had the decency to tell me the truth. I thought that's what priests did. But oh no, silly me. It's the liars, adulterers, paedophiles, and murderers who will inherit the earth, just as long as they confess." My heart is racing. My cheeks, I sense, are blistering red.

Gabriel turns on Jemma. "What have you said to her?"

She shrugs. "The truth, of course."

I groan and turn to leave.

"Megan, wait," says Gabriel.

"No! I haven't got time for this. My daughter has been kidnapped. I'm going to the police."

Inside the house, the telephone rings. I hurry around the corner, Gabriel calling my name. But I ignore him. Will he pray for my daughter after he's fucked Jemma Webster's brains out, I wonder, as, shaking violently, I climb into my car.

44

D ylan walks the short length of Arundel Terrace and turns right into Holbrook Road. The Panda is parked outside, which means his mum is home. Crap.

His attention is grabbed by an angry woman, rushing in the opposite direction. Reaching her car, she gets in and slams the door.

Megan? Shit. Why is she here? Is she looking for me?

He glances at the bathroom window he left open this morning, his alternative method of entry. He's never attempted it in broad daylight, though. Someone might see. He sneaks through the garden gate, ducks down, and crawls across the decking beneath the open kitchen window. His mother is talking to someone. He stops to listen.

"What do you mean he's not at school? I dropped him there this morning."

He holds his breath.

"I'll check his room."

'Jemma, wait."

A man's voice, but not his dad's. He sprints around the

side of the house and presses his body against the wall. His breathing quickens. His chest tightens. He waits. One minute. Two minutes. Three.

The man's voice again. "We need to talk."

"I can't, Gabriel. Dylan's missing."

Ella's dad? What's he doing here? Curious, he crawls back and peers over the windowsill. Ella's dad has his arm around his mother. Dylan gags before he can stop himself and squats back down. Scared he's going to be sick, he clutches his throat, springs to his feet, scampers up the spiral fire escape, and prises open the window. He clambers into the bathroom and out onto the landing.

"Do you think he's with Daisy?" Ella's dad asks.

"I don't know."

Dylan clenches his hands.

"Perhaps it's time to call the police."

"No, Gabriel, please leave," she says sharply.

The front door opens and closes. Dylan tiptoes into his room and shuts the door, silently. He slips off his blazer, drops it on the floor, and flings himself on his bed.

What is going on?

He wants to cry, he really does. It's all too much.

I should tell Mum I'm home, he reasons. Otherwise, she might take the vicar's advice and call the police.

The sound of breaking glass has him sitting up. He strains his ears, but all he can hear is the steady rumble of traffic and the mewling cries of the gulls. No. Better to wait until Dad gets back. Dad will calm her down. He lies down, reaches for his iPod on the bedside table, and plugs in an earphone. An ear-piercing scream makes him jump.

Somebody shouts. A girl?

Another scream, not so loud but worryingly close. He scampers to the window, draws back the curtain, and peers at the immaculate strip of lawn, bordered by flowerbeds. He sighs and is about to move away when another scream sets his nerves on edge. It's coming from the garden.

His mother?

He sprints along the landing, down the stairs, along the narrow hallway, into the kitchen, flings open a drawer, and takes out the rolling pin. Brandishing it, he runs out the back door on to the patio but pulls up abruptly. His mother is dragging Daisy across the lawn by the hair.

His eyes bulge. What the …?

Daisy twists her head awkwardly under his mother's arm. Her clothes and face are dirty, and her head is bleeding. "Dylan! Dylan! You've got to help me. She's crazy!"

Dylan doesn't know what to think. His mother wouldn't hurt a fly. Would she?

Daisy claws at his mother's face, spitting as she's hauled towards the garden gate.

"Let go of her," he says. "You're hurting her."

"Please, Dylan, help me."

He drops the rolling pin and tries to prise his mother's fingers off Daisy.

"I found the stupid girl in the shed."

"I've been in there all night. She wants to hurt me. Can't you see she already has? Call the police."

"Let go of her, Mum."

"For God's sake, Dylan, shut up and help me get her in the car."

He can't understand what's going on. Why was Daisy in the shed all night? Why is she bleeding? Why is his mother so angry with her?

His mother bundles Daisy into the back of the car and shuts the door. Daisy tries to open it, but the child lock is on, so she hammers on the window, yelling. A couple of pedestrians on the other side of the road glance fleetingly in their direction but continue walking.

"I've had about as much of this as I can take." His mother climbs into the driver's seat and slams her door.

Dylan is scared. He doesn't like the look in his mother's eyes. It's like she's totally flipped or something. He reaches for the driver's handle. The lock clicks shut. He bangs on the window. Daisy's hands are pressed against the glass. Tears are streaming down her cheeks. And as the car kicks into life, Daisy opens her mouth and screams.

45

I sit in the car, mobile in hand, finger poised over the nine. Have I missed something? Where was Robert the day of the tennis match? To drug Daisy's water bottle, he would've had to go into the girl's changing rooms in full view of the CCTV cameras. Somebody would have seen.

I slam the steering wheel with the heel of my hand. Dammit! Jemma's lying. She must be. But why? Gabriel insists the Websters are unhappy, that Robert abuses his wife. But what if Robert thought Jemma was having an affair with Gabriel? Could he have sought his revenge by sending emails to Gabriel's daughter?

Would he stoop that low?

Yes, if he abused his wife. But was that true? Had Gabriel lied about that to protect his reputation? And had Jemma lied in the first place to get close to Gabriel? Robert's a shameless flirt. Does he really prefer young girls?

I shiver. Who, if anyone, is telling the truth? Gabriel disappeared at the play. It's possible he was embarrassed and wanted to avoid Jemma. It's also possible that, if I'd listened to what Gabriel had to say just now, I might have answers to some of these questions.

The phone in my hand rings and vibrates, and I almost drop it. Hand shaking, I hold it to my ear.

"Megan, it's Anthony Swann."

"Have you found her?"

"I'm sorry, we haven't, but I thought you should know Dylan Webster is also missing. It could be a coincidence. Dylan hasn't been his usual sunny self recently, but he and Daisy were close, and there's a chance it might be connected."

The news comes as a shock. "Does Jemma know?"

"Yes, of course. I've just put down the phone to her. Why?"

Why indeed? "I'm sorry. I'm not thinking straight. I was just about to phone the police."

I cut the connection, convinced that either Gabriel or Jemma is lying. Despite everything that's happened, I'm pretty sure Gabriel is an honest man. And as for Jemma, if she's lying, it's to protect Dylan, or Robert, or herself, or all three of them.

Only one thing to do. I'll go back and confront them.

I lock the car and walk back. About thirty metres down the road, an elderly man and woman are staring open-mouthed at a dark-haired boy, running after a Panda, screaming at the driver to stop. And a man, sprinting towards the moving vehicle, waving his arms.

"Jemma! Stop the car!"

My pulse quickens. Robert and Dylan.

The car swerves, missing Robert by centimetres.

Dylan runs towards his father. "Dad! You have to stop her."

339

My eyes are now glued on Jemma, negotiating a three-point turn. She revs the engine and accelerates back down the middle of the road where Robert and Dylan are standing.

The elderly couple gasp.

The car hurtles towards them. Dylan darts out of the way. But Robert, hands on hips, doesn't budge. The bumper connects with his shins with a loud crack and throws him into the air. He lands on the bonnet with a thud, rolls up the windscreen onto the roof, and topples off the speeding car, landing on the road in a crumpled heap.

I break into a run. By the time I reach Robert, Dylan is standing over his father. His face is deathly pale. Mucus dangles from his chin, and his whole body is shaking uncontrollably. I glance at Robert. His eyes are closed, his face puffy and blue. Blood trickles from his nose.

"I … thought he'd be able … to … calm her … down," stutters Dylan. "Is he … dead?"

I crouch and feel for a pulse. I find one in his wrist, but it's faint. "He's alive."

"I'll call an ambulance and the police," says Gabriel, appearing out of nowhere.

"What the hell has happened here?" I ask.

But Gabriel is talking on the phone and doesn't reply.

Dylan mumbles something and reaches for my hand. I squeeze it.

Gabriel squats down beside me. "The ambulance and police are on the way."

My pulse is racing. "What's going on?"

"I don't know. I left shortly after you but came back because something didn't seem right."

I stare at him, but he returns my gaze. He's telling the truth. But then it dawns on me. Daisy is still missing. "It wasn't Dylan who sent Ella the emails, it was Robert. He's a paedophile and he's hidden Daisy somewhere."

Gabriel's shocked face pales. "The bastard!"

Dylan tugs at the sleeve of my shirt. I turn to him. His eyes are red, and he's trembling with shock. "Mum went crazy. Dad was trying to stop her."

I shiver and look at Robert's broken body. Did Jemma hate him so much she wanted to kill him?

Dylan tugs at his hair and stamps his foot in frustration. "Why won't you listen to me? Mum found Daisy in the shed. She's taken her in the car."

I frown. "Daisy's in the car?"

He nods furiously. "In the back."

My heart thumps. "What was she doing in your shed? Did your dad put her there?"

"No. Dad was away. He's been away all week. Daisy was hurt, and Mum was angry, and I think it might have been Mum who hurt her. Daisy said she spent the night in there. I don't know why, and I'm scared. Mum has never been this bad before, and Dad said the pills would help."

It's like I've collided head-on with a brick wall. "Pills?"

"I make her anxious, so she takes pills."

I clasp his face. "Are the pills diazepam?"

"I don't know."

"Jesus Christ. Did *you* put the pills in Daisy's water? Is that why your mother is angry?" My voice isn't far off a shout. Dylan shrinks away from me. "Diazepam, an anti-anxiety drug, was found in Daisy's blood and in her water. That's why she collapsed on the tennis court," I explain, quieter now.

"No, but I did take the whisky. I thought it would impress Daisy, but it didn't. She hated it and then she dumped me."

"Have you been sending bullying emails to Ella?" Gabriel asks gently.

"No," Dylan whimpers.

My throat constricts. "Where's your mother taking Daisy?"

"That's just it. I don't know."

46

My hair is plastered to my scalp, my shirt clinging to my back. I flick away the sweat trickling into my eyes and grip the steering wheel until my knuckles turn white.

This is my fault. I should never have left London. I shouldn't have been so damned impulsive. I should have stayed and worked things out.

I unwind the window, and a blast of sea air hits me. Why did Daisy spend the night in the shed? Was she hiding there? Had Jemma found her and locked her in to teach her a lesson?

No. She couldn't have. Not if Daisy was hurt. Not sweet, kind Jemma. Dylan must have been confused.

Ah, but Jemma's not that sweet and not that kind, is she? She just tried to kill her husband. Would she have run down Dylan, too, if he hadn't got out the way?

I shiver. No, of course not. She loves her son.

Ah, but why did she let Gabriel think Dylan was sending Ella those emails and then tell me it was Robert? What if she wrote them, posing as a boy to distract Ella from her work because Dylan was behind her in class?

No. Impossible. She'd fallen in love with Gabriel. To hurt his daughter would be crazy.

Yes, but he didn't know about the emails. And she had no idea Ella was cutting herself. But when Gabriel turned down her advances, the emails became a vicious vendetta. Only now Dylan was being distracted by Daisy. He wasn't head boy, and his grades were falling. Her perfect son wasn't so perfect anymore. Daisy had to be punished, so she drugged her.

I thump my head. I'm going mad. It isn't possible. Not Jemma.

My mobile rings. I glance at the dial, taking my eyes off the road for a split second. I veer across the central line. A horn blares. Tensing, I steer back, but the oncoming car brakes and skids. The driver, a young woman, seeing my mobile pressed to my ear, taps her temple with her finger and glares at me.

"Megs, where are you?" asks Glen.

"I'm driving. Is Daisy there?"

"Listen, I want you to pull over. I need to tell you something, but you must try and stay calm."

There's something in his tone that sends shivers down my spine. "Okay," I say, pulling up alongside the pavement.

Glen takes an audible intake of breath. "Mark Carter's been on the phone. Leo's regained consciousness."

"That's great …"

"Hold up, Megs. Leo didn't jump. Jemma pushed her."

My heart leaps into my mouth. "What? Why?"

"A couple of weeks back, Leo found a swipe card stuffed under the cushions of Jemma's couch."

"Oh my God, Samantha's," I say breathlessly. "Jemma stole it."

"Spot on. When Natalia went to clean the staffroom that

Saturday night, she apparently disturbed Jemma photo-copying the mock scholarship papers, amongst other things. Terrified she'd be found out, Jemma picked up a chair and hit Natalia over the head with it, knocking her unconscious before throttling her with Natalia's own necklace. To cover up the crime, she shoved Natalia's body in the X-cart, pushed it to the theatre, dragged it onto the stage and, after wrapping the body in an old rug she found backstage, dumped it down the trapdoor."

The bruises Gabriel saw on Jemma's arms were made by Natalia's fingers as she fought for her life. No wonder Jemma was anxious. Her son might have been top of the class, but she'd had to commit murder to get him there. "And she told Leo she'd stolen it?"

"No, she lied about the swipe card. But Leo was concerned. Jemma had been acting strangely for a while, so she rifled through her medicine cabinet and found diazepam. She tried to talk to Samantha about her discoveries the day of the sponsored walk, but Samantha was busy and told Leo she was being paranoid. Leo was furious and, after a couple of glasses of wine at lunch, found the courage to confront Jemma on her own. Trouble was, they were on the cliff, although apparently, Leo didn't imagine for one minute her life was in danger. Jemma confessed everything and shoved her friend over the edge. They were the last of the walkers. Nobody saw."

"Oh my God. Jemma's got Daisy in her car. Why didn't Leo talk it through with me or Mark? Why didn't she go to the police?"

"The police are out looking for Jemma now."

An image flashes before my eyes. I'm sitting at the foot of the stairs cradling Guy's body. I can't let this happen. I have to find her.

A moment of clarity. My mind stops spinning. I'm driving again. Accelerating quickly, I take a sharp left, and the car swings on its axle. "I'm going to the cliffs. Jemma likes to walk there. And it was where she pushed ..." My throat tightens, and I can't say the words.

"Good. That's good. I'll tell the police. But, Megs, if you find her, don't scream at her. She'll respond better if you're sympathetic."

"You're not a fucking psychologist, Glen!"

"She needs to think *she's* the victim, not Daisy."

He's right. She's a needy woman feeding off the sympathy and kindness of others. I fell for it. Gabriel and Leo, too. They tried to protect her, that's why neither of them went to the police.

The road steepens. I take the hairpin bends as fast as I dare and turn onto the cliff road, a rolling patchwork of ploughed and green fields to my right and an undulating strip of downland to my left. I scan the lay-bys for a pale-blue Panda. What if I'm wrong and they're not here? I wonder miserably.

I shake my head and remind myself that Daisy's strong, like me. Guy said so. She's a tiger, not a sheep.

But Daisy's just a child. I saw what Jemma did to Robert, have just heard what she did to Natalia and Leo, never mind poor Ella. What if she is up here on the cliffs? She's capable of anything. What chance has Daisy got? This would never have happened if it had been me who'd died and not Guy. If only I'd been around more when they were young. I should have given up my job and been a full-time mother.

"You'll be frustrated and unfulfilled," Guy said whenever my guilt reared its ugly head. "Why shouldn't you pursue the career you love? You'll be a better mother for it."

Wrong again, Guy. I'm a crap mother. I always was.

And then I see it. A blue Panda with a broken bumper, dented bonnet and roof, roughly parked in a lay-by at the foot of a grassy incline. I pull up behind it, leap out, and peer inside, face pressed to the glass, hands cupped around my eyes.

The car is empty.

A twig snaps behind me. My heart pounding painfully against my ribs, I whirl round. A rabbit scurries up the hill, its white tail bobbing up and down.

Something moves on the edge of my vision. I spin back. A curtain of long grass shimmers as it bends in a gust of wind.

A cry. Short, sharp, human.

Daisy?

Fighting the urge to call out, my pulse in overdrive, I scamper up the slope to where the downland flattens out to form the headland and, beyond, the muddy-blue sea stretches to the horizon.

And then I see them. Jemma is standing perilously close to the cliff edge, her arms locked around my precious daughter's neck. Daisy's terrified face is grimy and streaked with blood oozing from a wound to her head. Her hair is tangled, her baby-pink T-shirt filthy and torn. My instinct is to run to her, but I can't. To try to wrestle her from Jemma would be madness. My tongue is sticking to the roof of my dry mouth. Blood hammers my ears. There is nothing I can do. I am helpless.

No, you're not, I hear Guy say. *Your entire life has equipped you with the strength to act under duress. Think, Megan. Think.*

Jemma has seen me and is viewing me cautiously with her cornflower eyes, her pretty rosebud mouth contorted and ugly, her glossy chestnut hair blowing in the breeze. A perilous beauty pockmarked with evil.

Glen's right. Negotiation. Key when a life is at stake. I just need to convince Jemma I'm on her side. I keep my eyes fixed on her. "Hello, Jemma. Are you okay?"

"Of course I'm not, and it's all her fault." Her voice is shrill, discordant.

I shudder. No matter what lies she spouts, say nothing just listen.

"Dylan was doing so well until this nymphet with her big breasts and her sluttish ways turned up and corrupted him. She's evil. Twisted. I have to stop her while Dylan still has a chance."

Nymphet? Sluttish ways? Coming from the mouth of a thieving, psychotic murderer, her words are ridiculous. I want to grab her by the throat. Squeeze the life out of her. I inhale deeply, count to ten. "I know."

"You do?"

I keep my voice flat and expressionless. "I'm her mother. She's an impossible child. A nightmare."

Daisy's terrified eyes bulge in her white face, and she whimpers. I flash her a look that says *please, trust me*. Tears streak through the dirt and blood on her face, spilling off her chin. My heart lurches painfully. But still I resist the urge to run and save her.

"She's ruined everything," Jemma says.

I dare to inch closer. "I know she has. She knows it, too, and she's promised me she won't ever do such naughty things again."

Every step I take is cautious. I can't afford to frighten Jemma. She's a foot from the edge, maybe less. My progress is slow, agonisingly so. But mercifully, Jemma remains anchored to the spot, and Daisy stays quiet.

When I am close enough to touch them, I hold out my hand.

Jemma tightens her grasp. "IT'S TOO LATE. She has to be punished, don't you see?"

Daisy cries out.

My body jolts, but I keep my arm outstretched. An option. It's shaking. Has Jemma noticed? "Yes, she does. But by me, don't you think?"

I'm close enough to see Jemma's face twitch involuntarily, and to see that she is squeezing the breath out of Daisy.

"You're hurting her," I say as impassively as I'm able.

Jemma blinks rapidly but slackens her grip on Daisy's throat. "I've got no choice."

My upper lip is sticking to my teeth. I swallow with difficulty and try to maintain a sympathetic smile. "Yes, you have. I'm her mother. I'm the one who should punish her. If Dylan was naughty, you'd punish him."

"Dylan is never naughty!"

I suck air through my teeth, willing myself to remain calm. "I know. But if he was."

Jemma looks up as though pondering the alternative. A hundred metres below, waves break over the rocks and pebbles with barely a murmur. Birds on the wing, no bigger than insects, circle the lighthouse. It is a long, long way to fall. I'm giddy and light-headed. My knees buckle.

A shadow passes across Jemma's face. She refocuses on me. "Why should I believe you? You're a liar and a thief!"

"Help me!" Daisy's voice is tiny and scared. A little girl's voice.

I try not to panic, but fear is sucking the air out of me, and I'm not smiling anymore. "I'm not a liar and I'm not a thief."

Jemma's eyes blaze. "Liar! You stole Gabriel from me!"

Of course. Gabriel. The one line of bargaining I have left.

I force my cracked lips into another smile. "Gabriel loves you. He's besotted with you. He talks about you all the time. Nothing ever happened between the two of us."

I hold my breath. Jemma inclines her head and loosens her grasp. "Really?"

I exhale with relief. I have her attention again. "Really."

Her smile transforms her face, and for a moment she is truly beautiful. She opens her mouth to speak but stops, distracted by a thudding sound to the right. She snaps her head round. A blackbird with a yellow beak rises from a gorse bush, flapping its wings.

I seize my chance, lunge at Daisy and pull her towards me. Caught off balance, Jemma loses her footing and staggers forward, away from the cliff edge, still gripping Daisy. She stumbles, trying to regain her balance but can't and falls on top of Daisy, on top of me. Winded, I gulp for air, my arms wrapped around Daisy's waist. Jemma clambers to her feet, grabs Daisy by the ankles, and tugs. I hang on. I'm bigger and stronger than Jemma, but madness seems to have trebled her strength, and she manages to drag us a little way back towards the edge.

Daisy cries out. My blood runs cold, but I cling to her. If I let go now, the pair of them will topple over the cliff.

"Help!" cries Daisy.

"It's okay. I won't let go, Daisy. No matter what." It's fighting talk, but all it does is fan the flames of Jemma's denial.

"You think you're better than the rest of us with your brilliant career, your famous husband, your clever son, your sassy daughter. But you're not. You're irresponsible. Selfish. And you have absolutely no idea what it takes to be a mother. You're nothing. Do you hear me? Nothing." Her voice is an ugly shriek.

The dying embers of my negotiation go up in smoke. "You're sick. You need help."

"Don't you dare lecture me!"

I take a deep breath, roll myself on top of Daisy, and kick my legs like a mule. My feet strike Jemma hard in the chest. She lets out a puff of air, loses her hold, and hits the ground.

Footsteps thunder over the springy turf behind me, but I dare not look because Jemma is on her feet again. Eyes glinting, hands like claws, she hovers over us.

But then she's gone. Tackled to the ground by a blur of a man. He lands a centimetre from the cliff edge, but the force of his thrust has sent Jemma's torso over the edge, and she is screaming.

"It's okay. I've got her, Megs."

I want to laugh at the sound of his voice, at the sight of the familiar boots, inches from my face. But Jemma is dangling over a cliff, Glen holding her legs, and I am certain someone is going to die. I hold my trembling daughter close, not daring to let go.

A siren sounds in the distance.

Glen drags Jemma to safety, flips her over, straddles her, and tugs her arm behind her back. His freckled face is red, and his unkempt sandy hair is littered with strands of dry grass.

Daisy clings tighter. "I thought I was going to die."

I breathe in her candy-sweet scent, loving every bit of her body that I know so well. "It's okay. Everything is going to be all right."

"I wanted to talk … to Dylan. I thought he drugged me to get back at me for dumping him. I was … hiding in the shed … waiting for his mother to go out, but she found me and hit … me with a spade and knocked me out."

I gasp, my nerves shot. "Darling girl, you should have told me. I'd have helped."

"I'm sorry, Mummy," whispers Daisy, between sobs.

It's the first time she's called me that since Guy died. I bury my face in my daughter's hair, the child I thought I'd lost forever. Silent tears spill from my eyes. "You've nothing to be sorry for."

"I miss him. I miss Daddy so much. And it hurts. It really hurts. That's why …"

I feel her pain, embedded in my heart also, twisting and turning like a shard of glass. "I know, Daisy. We all miss him terribly. But you know what? You, me, Josh, we're going to take care of one another, and together we're going to get through this. I promise."

"It's my fault, isn't it? Dad died because of me, because I'm bad."

I sigh and clutch her to me. "Daisy you are not bad."

"I am. That's why Dylan's mum tried to kill me."

I flinch. "No. Jemma Webster did all this because she's crazy."

But Daisy isn't listening. "I don't blame you if you hate me. I'm a failure. Not like Josh. He's good at everything, like you."

There's a lump in my throat the size of a pebble. I kiss my daughter on the top of her bloodied head. "You have more talent in your little finger than the rest of us put together, Daisy Truman. You're beautiful, and I love you, more than you will ever know."

In my arms, Daisy's body judders. I'm crying too now, heaving. It's the relief, I know, that I've found Daisy and that she's alive. But it's also the hurt I've bottled up this last year. The grief I bear for Guy.

A strong hand touches my shoulder. I look into Glen's

smiling, weathered face. Over his shoulder I see a uniformed policeman leading Jemma Webster, in handcuffs, towards a waiting police car, it's blue light flashing. A tall man in a crumpled navy jacket and fawn chinos approaches us. I wipe my tears away with the sleeve of my puffa.

"DCI Marshall." He flashes his ID and runs his hand through his light-brown hair. "We're taking Jemma Webster to the station where we'll be questioning her about the murder of Natalia Topolska and the attempted murder of Leo Carter, Robert Webster, and your daughter."

I shake my head in disbelief. "She seemed so ... so ..."

"Harmless? I know, but people aren't always what they seem. Take your daughter to hospital, get some food and sleep, and we'll call on you tomorrow, all being well, to take a statement."

"Okay," I say. "And thanks."

"What for? You did all the hard work." He smiles, hands me a clean white handkerchief, and hurries off to his car.

"Come on," says Glen. "Josh is waiting for you at home with Margaret. We'll stop by on our way to the hospital."

I dab Daisy's head wound with the handkerchief, drape my arm around her, and follow him to his Land Rover, parked alongside my Golf.

"How did you know where to find us?" I ask.

"You told me where you were going, and Josh explained how to get here." He lifts Daisy onto the front seat.

A moment later and ... I shake my head. What might have happened next doesn't bear thinking about. "I couldn't believe it when that bird ..."

Glen's face creases into a smile.

I give him a gentle shove. "Spit it out. I can see you're dying to."

"I was hiding below the hillock, wondering how the hell I

was going to help you when I had the idea that if I chucked a stone in the bush, the noise might distract her. You did the rest."

"I owe you one," I say and climb into the car next to Daisy.

As she leans against me, I think of all the ways a mother can make a mess of things, as Eve did, and me, and many others either living or dead, and all those who haven't yet, but will. And I tell myself it doesn't matter whether you work or not. Being a mother is about the love, trust, support, and honesty you provide for your children. It's tough, but it's also a joy. It's never a burden, and it is most definitely not a competition. And I close my eyes and make a silent wish that, although at times I know I'll get it wrong, with a bit more practice, more often than not, I will get it right, or something like it.

Beside me, Glen exhales long and loud.

"What's up?" I ask.

"Well, see, I kinda got used to all these life-and-death situations with you, Megs. And by the way, Daisy, I'm not kidding. I've got the scars to prove it, but I hadn't bargained for a mini-Megs turning up in my life. Double trouble! Life is one hell of a ride with the Truman family."

I glance at Daisy, who is smiling.

"You better believe it, Glen," I say.

The sun peeks out from behind a cloud that's spitting rain and a rainbow, rising from the sea, arcs inland against the pale-blue sky.

ACKNOWLEDGEMENTS

I'm indebted to the memories of Adam Mynott who, for many years, worked as a BBC Foreign Affairs Correspondent. Thank you for sharing them with me. The Reverend Chris Macdonald and Neil and Jane Green, thank you for giving up your valuable time to answer my questions about God and the church, no matter how infuriating you found them. Thanks also to Ali Wicks and David Haggis for providing an insight into life on the other side of the gate; to Adam de Belder for explaining the workings of the heart; to Dr Javier Gonzalez-Polledo for explaining hospital procedures, self-harm and the effects of drugs; to Inspector Adam Hayes for his advice on police procedurals; to Rachel Angel for detailing the work of an Interior Designer; to Holly and Sam for their laidback teenage years and for a translation of the fascinating language they spoke while gliding through them; and to my beta readers - Fran Kazamia, Susie Horner, Lesley Frame, Cath Prendergast and Simon Bottomley, thank you for your time, your loyalty and your endless support.

Thanks also to my editor, Emmy Ellis, a hawk-eyed master of the English language, working with you has been a pleasure and a privilege. And to Adrian Newton for yet another brilliant cover. Where would I be without you, Ade?

In researching this novel, I read the following books: *Desperate Glory* by Sam Kiley, *Small Wars Permitting* by Christina Lamb, *Cupcakes and Kalashnikovs, 100 Years of the Best Journalism by Women*, edited by Eleanor Mills with

Kira Cochrane, *On the Front Line*, the collected journalism of Marie Colvin, *The Kindness of Strangers* by Kate Adie, *Killing My Own Snakes* by Ann Leslie and *Twenty Tales from the War Zone* by John Simpson.

But most importantly, the biggest thank you, and a big hug, must go to Holly, Sam and Simon for understanding this great love I have for writing and for being there for me, every step of the long and winding way.

ABOUT THE AUTHOR

Born and educated in Sussex, Fiona graduated from Exeter University with a degree in Philosophy. She worked in London in film and entertainment PR, before moving back to Sussex where she divided her time between coaching tennis and writing books. To date, she has published three mysteries – A *Push too Far, A Song Unsung,* and *Killing Fame* – the psychological thriller – *When the Dove Cried* – and the critically acclaimed literary thriller, *The Other Side of the Mountain.*

Thank you for reading *A Push too Far.* If you enjoyed it, please post a review and help others readers discover the story.

Fiona Cane at Amazon
www.fionacane.com

ALSO BY FIONA CANE